AS SEEN ON TV

Sarah Mlynowski

RED DRESS INK
™

First edition October 2003

AS SEEN ON TV

A Red Dress Ink novel

ISBN 0-373-25036-3

Visit Red Dress Ink at www.reddressink.com

Printed in U.S.A.

ACKNOWLEDGMENTS

Loads and loads of thanks to:

The ever-reliable and always-encouraging
publishing people: my editor, Sam Bell;
my agent, Laura Dail; and the RDI team
(Laura, Tara, Margie, Margaret, Pam and Tania).

My truly incredible mom, Elissa Ambrose,
and friends Robin Glube, Bonnie Altro,
Jessica Braun, Lynda Curnyn and Ronit Avni,
who edited, plotted and listened to my whining.

My dad, for being wonderful
and nothing like the dad in this book;
my sister, Aviva, for making me laugh;
and my soon-to-be in-laws,
the Swidlers, for continuing to pretend that
they're not embarrassed by my subject matter.

Daniel Laikind and Jessica Davidman,
for sharing their reality TV insights and experiences.

Corinne Gelman, for her
please-tell-me-he-doesn't-do-that Bilerman stories;
Mark Boidman, for his "expert" legalese;
and Jay Takefman, so he'll stop bugging me
to put his name in a book.

Pripstein's Camp, for my sweetest summer
memories, and for appointing me color captain,
not once but twice.

For Todd

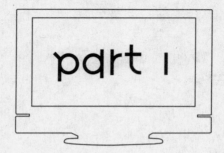

part 1

Job Listing

NYC—Assistant Manager, New Business Development

Soda Star, America's leading beverage company, seeks candidates for its growing New Business Development department.

Candidates should have bubbly personality, positive outlook on life (glass is always half-full!), free-flowing ideas, excellent contacts. Sparkling written, communication and organizational skills. A drop of administrative work required. An all-you-can-drink opportunity!

If you have Star potential, please e-mail your resume as a Word document ONLY to hr@workforcheap&beourbitch.com.

I

Moonlighting

"**W**hy are you calling?" the HR woman asks me, panic-stricken, as if recess is over and she hasn't finished her Fruit Roll-up. "Didn't the ad say not to phone?"

"Yes, I understand that, thank you, but I'll only be in New York for a few days. I would really like to set up an interview." I need a new job. I attempt to shield myself behind the pay phone's plastic divider, since this is the only nicotine-friendly cafeteria on the block and anyone from the office could easily sneak in for a smoke.

The smell of this stale smoke combined with the plates of shepherd's pie lined up on the counter make me wish long-distance calls from my cell phone didn't make me sound as though I'm calling from Zimbabwe. I also wish I knew how to make a calling-card call from my office without getting the IT department.

"Once the hundreds of resumes we've received for the Assistant Manager, New Business Development position are reviewed," the HR woman says, "the managing director will choose the candidates to be interviewed. If you're one of the fortunate ones selected, I assure you, you'll be called."

Obviously the first thing this woman does when she gets home is kick her dog. "Thank you very much for your time," I say.

I redial Soda Star's number.

"Florida Telephone Systems." *Brrring.*

I dial my calling-card number.

"Soda Star, the shining light in beverages," the receptionist sings. "How may I help you?"

"May I please speak to the managing director?"

"Which managing director is that, miss?"

Which managing director? Shouldn't there only be one director who manages? Or maybe one manager who directs? "The new business managing director, please." Please let that be right.

"Whom should I say is calling?"

A person he's never heard of before? "Sunny Langstein."

"One moment, please. I'll transfer your call."

Foiled again, HR.

I'm probably going to get his voice mail. Why would he be at his desk at 10:30 a.m.? He's probably out managing. Or directing. Or managing directors when it gets really crazy. I hunt through my recently started job-search notebook where I wrote possible messages to leave on prospective employers' machines.

Ring, ring. Heart beating erratically.

"Ronald Newman speaking."

Good. Damn. He's there. It's a he. Concentrate on exuding confident, sexy, sweet voice. I flip back to the page of possible things to say to prospective employers. "Hi, Mr. Newman? This is Sunny Langstein calling. I'm presently the assistant manager of new business development for Panda in Fort Lauderdale, but I will be relocating to New York for personal reasons. I'm very impressed with your company's work and would like to continue my professional growth in the beverage industry. I'll be in New York next week, and I was wondering if you'd consider meeting with me to discuss any potential job openings in your department."

"How did you get this number? Aren't you supposed to go through HR?"

Sounds cranky. Must accent the sweet voice. "I'm *so* sorry to *bother* you, sir." Now confident. "I just assumed calling you would be more efficient."

He laughs. I picture him reclining in a brown leather reading chair, a pipe dangling from his lips. "Well, Sunny, you're probably right. Do you think you could handle working in the big leagues?"

Oooh. The big leagues.

"I'm quite confident I can, sir. I have excellent—" this is where I exploit the many hackneyed and meaningless qualifications employers salivate over "—communication and organizational skills. I multitask, prioritize, problem-solve and self-start. I pay strong attention to detail and work effectively with both creative and production staff. I have a proactive approach toward current products and new business, and I have a personable, team-player personality. Will you be able to meet with me for an informational interview?"

Pause. "Are you aware that I'm looking for an assistant manager right now? To report directly to me?"

No kidding. "Really? I'd love to come and talk to you about it. I'll be in New York next Monday. Do you have a free half hour?"

He laughs again. "You're a go-getter. I like that. Hmm. Let me check."

He's clicking on his keyboard. Clicking…clicking…more clicking.

"Did I mention I'm proficient in most computer programs including Windows, Macintosh, Microsoft Office and Photoshop?" I ask.

He whistles his approval. "How about right before my golf game? Four o'clock?"

Liza, my boss, strolls through the doors. Damn. Now why am I using a pay phone in the cafeteria across the street from my office in the middle of the morning? She knows I don't smoke. I ram my notepad and pen back into my bag. "Perfect. I'll see you then. 'Bye."

"Okay. Great…um…" Come on, Newman, spit it out. "Will you fax me your resume?"

Liza doesn't see me yet. She's ordering something. Is she sneaking a cup of coffee? Since she announced her pregnancy, she's been strutting her water bottle all Mormon-like around the office, boasting how effortlessly she gave up caffeine, smokes and Chardonnay.

"No problem," I say. "Thanks. 'Bye."

"Do you know where our offices are?"

"On Forty-third Street, right? It's on your Web site?"

"Yes and yes. I'm on the sixth floor. Just tell Heidi you're here to see me."

I assume Heidi is his receptionist. "Great. 'Bye."

"Don't you want my fax number?"

"Isn't it the one on the Web site?"

"No, I have a personal fax number. Do you want it?"

Of course I want it! Just tell it to me already! I crouch against the wall and a ketchup-stained table eclipses my face. "Yes. Yes, I do. What is it?"

"Hmm. Good question. Let me check. Hold on, it should be on my business card, right?" Clunk. Did he just knock over his chair? Is he completely incompetent?

Liza pulls out her wallet.

"Okay, got it. Two-one-two-five-five-five-nine-four-three-six." Uh-oh, nothing to write on or with. Two-one-two-five-five-five-nine-four-three-six. Two-one-two-five-five-five-nine-four-three-six. I'll remember it. No problem. I can remember one stupid fax number. Especially this one. Nine times four equals thirty-six. How can I forget? Two-one-two-five-five-five-nine-four-three-six. Or is it four-nine-three-six? This is a terrible plan.

"It was a pleasure talking to you. I look forward to meeting you." Two-one-two-five-five-five-four-nine-six-three? I should take out my pen and notebook. Who cares? I could be writing something besides a fax number for a future employer down. Like the lunch special.

"I'm looking forward to meeting you, too," he says.

As quietly and quickly as possible—two-one-two-five-five-five-three-six-nine-four—I hang up the phone. One interview scheduled. A good start.

"Sunny?" Liza asks. Her hands leap to her rounded stomach. She does this often, as though she's checking to ensure she's still pregnant.

Maybe she thinks I'm getting coffee. Not a ridiculous assumption. Office coffee is like the hot dog of the java industry. They get the leftover beans that don't quite make the cut at Starbucks. Two-one-two-five-five-five-six-three-nine-four.

Liza isn't a horrible boss. Besides the fact that I do all her work and she takes all the credit. And that on staff birthdays she refuses to order "terribly fattening" chocolate cake and instead insists on serving celery sticks and low-fat tzatziki. And since she's gotten pregnant, she's become a walking bitch machine.

But the workload isn't atrocious and she always writes me nice reviews and pays me fat bonuses.

She glares at my cupless hands. "Is there a reason you snuck out of the office to use the phone here?"

A first-rate question. "My grandmother is sick, Liza. I needed to talk to her in private." It's a good thing both my grandmothers are already dead.

She looks doubtful.

"What did you get, Liza?" I ask, motioning to her small plastic cup. There was an article in the *Miami Herald* that said that people respond more positively to you if you frequently use their names in conversation. It hasn't worked for me yet.

Her face flushes a shit-you-caught-me red. "Hot chocolate."

Funny, it doesn't smell like hot chocolate. Smells like good old will-deform-your-baby caffeine. That's terrible. Doesn't she know that she's risking her baby's health?

She slides into a metal chair. "I'm going to stay here for a while and look over some notes."

Should I insist on sitting with her to make sure she doesn't try to sneak a smoke, too? Maybe I should get a better sniff of what's in that water bottle. Or maybe I've got to get somewhere and write down this number. "See you later, Liza."

Two-one-two-five-five-five-three…three times twelve… twelve? Damn.

During my leftover pineapple pizza lunch, I respond to the first of two of my friend Millie's e-mails:

To: Millie

Subject: Re: Where The Hell Are You?

I just got back last night. He asked me to move in with him. I'm going. It's insane.

Her second e-mail, tagged with *Fw: Purity Tampons Cause Cancer,* is one of those health forwards. Millie, one of my closest friends, knows that I love spreading these millions-of-women-die-needlessly warnings. You never know, one day one of these e-mails could save someone's life.

I received this from a friend—please read and pass along. Have you heard that Purity includes asbestos in their tampons? Why? Because asbestos makes you bleed more, and if you bleed more, you are going to use more…

I tried a Purity tampon once, but it felt as if I was trying to shove a cement brick up my vagina. I forward the e-mail to Liza because she loves chain letters, especially those feel-good chain letters that promise you instant death if you don't forward immediately. I forward the Purity Tampons Cause Cancer e-mail to my older sister Dana, too. This way she knows that the reason I didn't call her when I got home late night was not because my plane crashed, or was hijacked by terrorists, but because I am an extremely busy career woman who is also very concerned with women's health. And who knows? Maybe she'll get a story idea out of it. Dana does the nine o'clock news for the radio station WCMG Miami. She's desperately trying to move to TV. She also sells feature articles to newspapers all over the country in an attempt to build up her portfolio.

Six seconds after I hit Send, my extension rings.

As always, I contemplate answering the phone with, "What?" But I don't. "Sunny Langstein speaking."

"Why didn't you call me when you got in? You know I worry about you."

"Sorry, Dana. I got in late and I didn't want to wake you."

My sister snorts. "I told you to wake me. Did I not tell you to wake me? Did you have a good trip?"

"Very nice trip, thanks." Do I tell her? I have to tell her. "Hold on one sec," I say. I put the phone on the desk and close my office door. I sit down in my swivel chair and take a deep breath. Liza hates when her staff's doors are closed, always asks us to please leave them open so that the other departments don't get the impression we're unfriendly.

Her door has been closed for about six months now.

"He asked me to move in with him."

Silence.

"Hello? You still there?"

"I'm here," she says. "He wants you to move to New York?"

"Yes. What do you think?"

"Do you care what I think?"

"Maybe."

"Are you going to go?"

"Yes."

"You're just going to quit your job and leave everything behind? Isn't that a bit irrational?"

And the guilt begins. Maybe I shouldn't have told her. Maybe I should have moved and called her from New York. "What's new?" I could have asked. She would have rambled on for hours, and when she finally stopped for breath, I could have interjected, "Call me at this new number, 'kay?" And that would have been it. I should have banked on Dana's tunnel vision— her ability to only see and hear what she wants to see and hear. It would have taken her months, maybe even years, before she realized that 212 wasn't Fort Lauderdale's area code.

Case in point: after I graduated from college, she admitted she didn't know that I had studied business at University of Florida.

"What did you think I was studying?"

She shrugged, straightening the neck of my gown. "Communications."

I laughed. "Why? Because you studied communications?"

"No," she answered, sounding insulted. "I thought that's what you said. That you wanted to study communications."

I did. When I was eleven. When Dana wanted to be a star reporter like Barbara Walters and decided to major in communications, I said I wanted to be Barbara Walters and study communications. What do they teach you in communications anyway? How to talk? But then I decided that business was a little more practical. That's what my father told me.

And journalism isn't the only way to make a difference in this world. I'm going to change the structure from within.

One day, armed with all types of theorems, my business degree and women's studies minor, I would break through the corporate glass ceiling.

One day.

Coming up with the next Snapple wasn't exactly what I had in mind. The problem is, I haven't found a ceiling really worth breaking. Panda recruited on campus and I dropped off my resume, mostly because I didn't know what I wanted to do and then they called me in for an interview and then they offered me a job. I am quite talented at convincing people to do what I want, even when I'm not sure I want it.

But I'm only twenty-four, still building the resume. One day I'll do something *real*. Change the world. And in the meantime, unlike Dana, since the day I started college, my father hasn't had to lend me a dime.

A piece of pineapple is trapped behind my bottom teeth, in the wire that my orthodontist glued on after I got my braces off. "It's not irrational," I say, while digging for the stray piece of fruit.

"I can't understand you. You're mumbling. Are you going to quit your job?"

Spit or swallow? I spit the de-wedged pineapple into a tissue. "I thought of flying in every morning, but it'll be difficult."

"Don't be a smart-ass."

Dana breathes heavily in my ear, waiting. I don't breathe that loudly, do I? Now that Steve and I will be permanently sleeping in the same bed, I'll have to train myself to inhale and exhale through my nose so that I don't kill him with my morning breath.

I see Liza huff by through the two window panels by my door. They don't let us lowly assistant managers have blinds for fear we'll spend all day playing Tetris, downloading porn or write to the higher-ups that we're secretly doing their jobs.

"I'll find a new job."

"Isn't Panda considered one of the top five companies to work for in Florida? Aren't you on the fast track over there?" Of course, that she remembers.

"I won't be promoted for another year."

"Why? Don't you do all of your boss's work?"

True. "But I'm not ready to be a manager. I still need to have someone look over my stuff. And I'm only twenty-four. They don't let twenty-four-year-olds be managers."

"You're a mature twenty-four. You should have asked for a promotion by now. Don't be such a pushover."

I bite my tongue to keep from telling her to take her own

advice. First she was a freelance journalist. And now she's been a radio reporter for over a year. When is she going to go after the job she wants?

She takes a breath. "Have you even started looking for work?"

"I already have one interview," I say. Not that I expect to get a job right away. I know it takes time. But hopefully not too much time. I don't want to quit my job until I have a new one. But I have to give my landlord at least thirty days' notice before I want to move out, and I can only move out on the last day of a month. Which means that if I want to move out by October thirty-first I have to tell her by the end of September, next Tuesday. Otherwise I have to wait an entire month and Steve will end up paying for his entire apartment for all of November, since his roommate is moving out at the end of October.

This is all way too complicated.

"Don't you think you're a little young to move in with your boyfriend?" She sighs for effect.

"I thought I was a mature twenty-four?"

"Not that mature."

"Dana, by the time Mom was twenty-four, she had you."

"I can't believe you're going to quit your job, give up your apartment, sell your car—you can't bring a car, never mind a convertible to Manhattan, you know—to follow some guy across the country. Are you going to get married next? Take his name? Become a stay-at-home mom? Buy a bread-maker?"

I wish I'd been offered a fabulous job in New York first and then met Steve while buying a hot pretzel from a street vendor. "I've always wanted a bread-maker."

"I worry about you."

"Don't."

"What if you can't find a job?"

"Then I won't move."

Dana snorts. "Don't think you can bullshit me the way you do everyone else. I know you. Do what you want. But don't come crying to me when you're forty, have five kids, no life of your own and need help filling the two-car garage with carbon monoxide. You should live a little. Experience life."

Instead of finding a job after college, Dana did a one-year women's studies master's (that's why I did the women's studies minor—she kept bugging me to do it). Then, she decided she needed a master's degree in journalism. Dana never believed in settling down. Especially for a man. Last year she slept with twelve. A bona fide member of the Man-a-Month Club, she quantifies life experiences as men's boxers over her bedpost. "You're too inexperienced to make such an important decision," she continues. "And you've been dating him less than a year. You don't know him long enough to know he's not a complete asshole. You haven't done enough research. You're making a mistake."

I hang up the phone and turn back to my e-mails.

Millie has already written me back.

My phone rings. I'm not going to talk to her if she's going to be annoying.

It rings again.

Still ringing.

I pick up. "Uh-huh."

"I'm sorry. I'm going to miss you, okay? I like having you an hour drive away. If you're sure, I mean absolutely one hundred and ten percent sure it's the right decision, I'll stop protesting."

I imagine an army of stoned, ponytailed picketers waving felt-tipped marker-written signs and chanting at the airport, "No, no, don't let her go!" "She's too young, have more fun!" "She's delirious for getting serious!"

"It's the right decision," I say.

Of course it's the right decision. I'm in love. He's in love. If it's going to work, we can't live in different cities forever, and he can't leave New York. Saturday night was the ten-month anniversary of our first date, and after an hour of wine and sweaty sex he placed a little blue box on top of his pillow and whispered, "Happy anniversary." My heart stopped, as if its plug had been ripped out of the wall. Holy shit, I thought.

Is it a ring? Is he proposing? Am I going to get married? Do
I love this man? I'm too young to get married. How can I
marry him when we're never in the same city for more than
forty-eight hours? He loves me. I'm going to get married.
We're going to have a home. And then I opened the box. And
it was a silver key chain. Smooth and silver, the inscription
said, *Move in with me? I love you, S.* My heart turned over
again, and still not sure if I was relieved or disappointed I
kissed him, kissed him again.

Yes, yes, yes.

It'll work. It'll be perfect. I'm in love. Aren't you supposed
to take risks when you're in love?

But if—and it's a big fat unlikely if—I'm wrong about this
(and I really doubt that I'm wrong about this) and he turns out
to be a complete asshole like Dana warned, it's not like my life
will be over. I can find somewhere to live in New York if I absolutely had to. The *Village Voice* lists tons of people looking
for roommates in Manhattan. Or if I discover I hate New York,
I can always move back to Florida. I can stay with Dana until
I find a place. Maybe Liza will give me back my job. Or I can
teach English in Japan. I know someone who did it and loved
it. She claimed it was the most incredible learning experience
and that all she needed was a bachelor's degree and that she
made a shitload of cash. I could use the money to travel through
Asia and even to Australia or New Zealand and I love miso
soup and at least five Japanese schools have positions available immediately.

I checked.

The message from Millie:

Oh my God! You are so lucky! NYC! Very jealous. When
am I going to see you? Save Friday—we're having a
major girls night! Lucy, Laura and some of her friends
from work. Cocktails here, dinner and clubbing on South
Beach. You'd better come. You haven't been out in years.

You missed a crazy night on Saturday! We all ended up skinny-dipping with a bunch of Italians in Lucy's pool! lol. Want to go for sushi tonight?

Ding! A message from Dana:

Love you. Worried about you that's all. You don't use Purity tampons, do you? Do you think I should write a story about this? Of course you do, you crazy hypochondriac. I just sold a feature about American teenage prostitutes. Prada purse here I come!

The dichotomy that is my sister: She refuses to write about fashion, but is secretly obsessed with it. Before she got her news radio gig, she was offered a fashion column and she turned it down. She believes that publicly writing about clothing will brand her a frivolous journalist, a lightweight. I tell her that obsessing about fashion, spending all her money on fashion makes her a frivolous person. But that doesn't seem to bother her.

Ding! Message from my boss Liza:

In case you've forgotten, I'm pregnant. What do I need tampons for? I'd appreciate if you don't send chain letters during company time. Thanks, L

If I weren't planning to quit, her e-mail would have annoyed me. Maybe she didn't have her morning nicotine fix, after all. I respond to Millie's many exclamations:

I'm going back to NY this weekend for interviews. I have to keep looking for jobs this week. When I get back?

As soon as the message goes out, I delete it from the Sent folder. Then I delete it from the Deleted folder. I've got this Big Brother technology down pat.

I set out down the block in search of a less visited pay phone.

"No pay phone here," a bald man says. "There's one up the street."

Pay phones are like men. Never a decent one around (by decent I mean in good working order) when or where you're looking.

Take my Europe trip for example. Who doesn't want a summer fling? I wasn't still a virgin—it wasn't as if I had my heart set on losing it in a hostel bunk bed or anything like that—but I believed that having a wild affair was part of the backpack experience. Isn't that why college students go to Europe? I called dibs on the Scots and Brits, and Millie reserved the Italians, so of course we mostly met frat boys from Miami. I met one overly freckled, broad-shouldered, seemingly interested Scot on the overnight ferry from Brindisi to Corfu, but by the time we got to Greece, he had dropped two tablets of E and found his way into a sleeping bag that boasted a brunette and a foot-long Canadian flag.

Now, as I continue my hike up Flamingo Road, in search of a pay phone, the sun follows me like the evil eyes of a mysterious painting in a *Scooby-Doo* episode. It's a good thing I have my sneakers on today. As I do every day. Dana tried to convince me to buy two-inch heeled pumps for the office. "But I'm allowed to wear sneakers," I said.

"It's about image," she said. "Your ten-year-old sneakers don't scream sophisticated, now do they?"

"At least they don't scream pain." I don't get why anyone would choose to be uncomfortable.

Dana and I have very different understandings of the purpose of clothes. I see it as something you wear so you're not walking around naked. Dana sees it as something worth going into debt for. Or at least worth borrowing money from my father, the person she can't stand the most.

The sweater and jeans I'm wearing (which Dana has already vocally disapproved of—"they're too straight leg and too light. You've had those jeans since eighth grade. You've got to think darker, boot cut."), were chosen with an air-conditioned office in mind, not the Florida marathon.

Did I put deodorant on this morning? Last time Steve came to visit me he forgot his deodorant and had to use mine. He smelled like summer tulips all weekend.

Sweet Stevie. How we met is an example of how great men appear when you're not looking. It was one week after I moved into my new one-bedroom ocean-view Fort Lauderdale apartment, when Steve spilled his mocha latte down my shirt.

I was at Pam's, one of my favorite coffee shops in Miami, a small, homey, southwestern decorated café on Washington Avenue. I was on my way to meet with a research firm for a new chocolate soda we were developing, when the spilling took place. I wanted to maim the idiot but he kept apologizing and throwing coffee holders at me, thinking they were napkins. I kept telling him to stop, that it was fine even though it was *not* fine.

"You look like a Gestalt test," he said staring at my shirt, and I laughed. He wanted to buy me a coffee, but I said no. When he told me he was visiting from New York, and was on his way to spend the afternoon at the retirement community, Century Village, where his *Bubbe* lived, I almost relented. That was pretty sweet. His parents lived in Miami, too. And he was Jewish. Not that I cared, but I knew it would make my father happy.

"I understand. But if you're ever in New York, come to my family's restaurant. I run it now that my dad moved here. It's kosher but still nice," he said, and wrote down *Manna* and an address on a preferred customer card, right above a bunny-shaped hole punch, and told me if I ever came to the restaurant, to ask for him and he would make it up to me. He had a nice smile. I told him my father worked in Manhattan and that I just might.

A month later, I went to visit my dad in New York. I hadn't seen him since the January before, he'd been really busy, but I decided that if he didn't have time to visit me, then I would make the trip. As usual, Dana wanted nothing to do with him. She prefers his checks as direct deposits, rather than through person-to-person contact. On the second night of my visit, when my dad told me he'd be stuck at the office again and would miss our dinner plans, I thought of the boy with the nice smile.

It wasn't until I told the cabbie to take me to the restaurant and he said he'd never heard of it, did it occur to me that maybe Steven wasn't the owner of Manna. Maybe Manna didn't exist. Maybe Steven wasn't his name. Maybe he didn't have a *Bubbe*. Maybe the guy I met ran around Florida, using his fictitious Jewish grandmother the way a single father uses his kids as bait to attract women who feel the need to be maternal.

"Here it is, West Ninety-first Street," the cabbie said, pointing ahead of him.

After I was seated in a small table by the window, I asked the waitress if I could speak to Steven.

"I can't believe you came," he said, a carafe of wine and two plates of kosher ravioli later.

Like a water cooler in the desert, a pay phone glistens through an upcoming window. There's even a—gasp!—nearby bench to sit on.

"Florida Telephone Systems." *Brrring.*

I dial my calling-card number. "Hi, can I please speak to Jen Tore, please?"

"One moment."

"Jen speaking."

"Hi, Ms. Tore? My name is Sunny Langstein. I'm presently the assistant manager for new business development for Panda, but I will be relocating to New York for personal reasons. I'm very impressed with Fruitsy Corporation's work. I'll be in New York next week, and I was wondering if you'd consider meeting with me to discuss any potential job openings in your department."

"You're the one who e-mailed me her resume last night, right? Panda, huh? I know you guys. You did that strawberry-flavored water I liked. You know, we don't run a huge operation here at Fruitsy. We're not as fancy as Panda."

"I appreciate that, Ms. Tore."

"Call me Jen."

"I appreciate that, Jen. I've worked at a large operation and am looking forward to exploring my professional growth options in a smaller work environment." I'm amazed at the crap I come up with.

"Well, I'd love to meet with you. How's Monday at nine?"

But not as amazed as I am that they buy it. "Perfect. Where are you located again?"

"On the southeast corner of Twenty-first and Ninth." She coughs. "I'd like to see the stuff you've worked on, too, if you could bring a portfolio." Three-percent chance she's interested in hiring me, ninety-seven-percent chance she wants to rip off Panda's ideas. "My office is on the fourth floor."

Nine o'clock, fourth floor. Nine times four. Two-one-two-five-five-five-nine-four-three-six. Aha.

2

Sex and the City

I spit into the airport sink. Then I reapply the baking soda, super whitening, plaque/cavity/tartar/gingivitis-prevention gel to my toothbrush, repeat, and wonder if all these extra-strength ingredients will give my mouth superpowers.

In the mirror, my hair looks flat from leaning against the airplane pillow.

Dana constantly nags me that I should get some highlights and layers. "You're naturally pretty, fine, but you'd be gorgeous if you made a tiny effort. A little blond never hurt anyone."

I'm not really the blond type. I prefer my shoulder-length brown hair, off my face and in a ponytail.

I rummage through my purse for my lipstick, the only makeup I wear regularly. Due to a lifetime of (ew) cold sores, my lip color is a bit irregular. I like to make my lips look smoother, a bit more even.

Is that red mark on my lip the beginning of a cold sore?

I wipe the red blot away.

Phew. Just tomato sauce gone awry.

I hate cold sores.

My father gets them, supposedly my grandmother got them, and way back somewhere in Europe my great-grandmother probably got them. When I was four, I tripped on a pair of Dana's discarded fluorescent-pink Cindy Lauper-esque leggings and ripped the left side of my top lip on her carpet. Since then, about once a year, I suffer from a cold sore in that exact spot on my lip. It could be worse, though. My father told me my grandmother got them in her nose.

Steve has never seen my reoccurring deformity. One major advantage of living in different cities. Last time I had one, about four months ago, I claimed I had the flu, couldn't fly and had to postpone my weekend trip. By the next weekend I was able to camouflage the tiny scar with a cover-up stick Dana helped me pick out to match my skin tone and my lipstick.

I wheel my first fits-under-your-seat suitcase, purchased at the beginning of the Steve relationship as a time-saver investment, out of the bathroom and into the miraculously short line of cabs.

"He's not picking you up at the airport?" Dana asked, which sounded suspiciously similar to her "he's not taking off work on Saturday night for you?"

"Should he pick me up on his flying carpet?" I said. He couldn't take off work on Saturday night, anyway. This time of year Saturday is his busiest night. Since Steve's grandfather opened Manna in 1957, it's always been closed on Friday evening and Saturday, reopening after the sun goes down on Saturday. According to Jewish law you can't run a restaurant on Shabbat, because you can't work. In the spring and summer the restaurant stays closed all day Saturday because the sun sets so late, but in the fall and winter it opens one hour after Shabbat ends.

There's a calendar of this year's Shabbat's starting and ending times taped to his fridge. When I first saw it there, after pouring myself a glass of post-sex water during my first weekend sleepover, I did a little cringing. I had no intention of dating anyone religious, Jewish, Christian, Buddhist, whatever. Any type of complete devotion to any deity was too much commitment for me. And besides, it was eleven-thirty and I wanted to watch Letterman and turning on the TV is somehow considered work to religious Jews. Thank God, I thought when Steve explained that the calendar was for work purposes only. When he took over the restaurant, he decided to keep it kosher. He's actually quasi-kosher in private—no bacon or shellfish at home but anything is game when we leave the apartment.

I position my luggage in the trunk and slam the door shut. "Sullivan and Houston please," I tell the cabbie. He grunts his response.

"Hi! I'm Jennifer Aniston," a recorded voice in the taxicab says. "I tell all my friends to buckle up!"

I fasten my seat belt. As a kid, I used to mentally leapfrog over the streetlamps when we took the highway. As we approach the city, I do my imaginary exercise with the building-size billboards on my left.

I'm not sure if the funny feeling in my stomach is because of excitement, nervousness or because of the meatball sandwich they served me on the plane.

I give the cabbie twenty-six dollars, which covers the fare, the toll, the additional nighttime charge—what's a nighttime charge?—and exactly a fifteen-percent tip.

"Can I help you?" the doorman asks, his head bobbing up from his small television set.

"Apartment 7D," I say to the man who works every Friday night and never remembers me.

He dials upstairs, waits a minute, then scratches his goatee. "No one's there. I think I saw Steve leave about an hour ago."

I pull my suitcase toward the elevator. "I'm Steve's girlfriend? Remember me? I have a key." I have a key. A key. A key, a key. Sounds like *yucky* if you say it too fast.

"Right. Go ahead," he says.

In the elevator the poster tacked below the emergency phone advertises, "Dog walker available! I live in the building and am very responsible!" If I can't find a job, I can always become a dog walker. I've always wanted a dog. My father wouldn't let me have one in the house because he didn't want anything scratching his wood floors, or discoloring his white furniture. My college dorm didn't allow pets. When I took the job at Panda and moved to Fort Lauderdale, I felt too bad leaving a poor pet locked in a one-bedroom apartment all day by himself.

When the elevator stops, I wheel the bag toward Steve's door. Here it is. The momentous occasion. I pull the key, my key, out of my purse and insert it into the lock.

And insert it into the lock. Still trying to insert it into the lock. It's not inserting. Why isn't it inserting? What floor am I on? The sticker beside the peephole says 7D. Maybe someone changed the label as a practical joke? Did I press the right floor?

I wheel the luggage toward the apartment beside his. It says 7E.

He gave me the wrong key. I ring the doorbell in case he's home, after all. No answer.

He's a riot, I think as I wheel my bag back toward the elevator. This is by far one of the top five Steve-isms, as I've coined them, on the Steve-ism list. The Steve-ism list includes his leaving a bag of Gap purchases on the subway after an afternoon of shopping. Then there was the time he forgot his cell phone at my apartment post a weekend visit. When I answered the ringing under my bed he was laughing hysterically from the airport. Silly, Stevie.

My sentimentality lasts until the elevator doors open at the lobby level. I'm moving in with a man who might one day accidentally leave our child at a baseball game.

"Key's not working," I tell the doorman.

He looks at me suspiciously. Yes, I'm a crazy woman who

gets off by riding elevators with luggage. "Can I use your phone?" I ask. Despite its supposed roaming capabilities, my cell phone never works in New York.

Steve says that while most of New York has gone back to normal post 9/11, cell phone service hasn't been the same.

Sometimes when I see a stranger on the subway, I wonder if anyone she knew or cared about was killed. No one Steve knew was in the towers. He had friends of friends of friends that were killed, but no one whom he knew personally.

He was asleep when the planes hit, heard the commotion outside and watched the burning from his roof. For the next two weeks, he needed to show identification every time he came home from work because his apartment is below Fourteenth Street, where the lockdown was. He told me that for the following two months, he kept a pair of sneakers beside his bed in case he needed to make a run for it.

My father was on a project in Montreal when it happened, which I didn't know. I called his office, his cell phone, his home number but I couldn't get through. I knew he worked in midtown, but I still wanted to hear his voice to hear he was okay.

He called me on September fifteenth.

The doorman nods reluctantly and waves me toward a rotary behind his desk. Who still uses rotaries? Thankfully, the other amenities in this building aren't also from the 1950s.

The message on his cell phone clicks on right away, so I know he's left it off. He always leaves it off. What exactly is the point in having a cell if it's never on?

Why can I remember this seemingly innocuous idiosyncrasy and he can't even remember to give me the right key?

I call the apartment in case Steve decides to call in from whatever nook of the city he's hiding in.

"Hey, this is Steve and Greg. Leave a message." Beep.

"Hello, Steven, it's me. I'm standing in the lobby of your building. You gave me the wrong key. If you're checking your messages, please come home. I'm going to wait at the Starbucks on the corner."

When do I get to leave the announcement on the machine? Hi, you've reached the happy residence of Steve and Sunny. We're very much in love and are too busy expressing our love (wink, wink) to come to the phone right now. Please leave your name and number, time you called, and maybe when we're taking a break from all this exhausting loving (wink, wink) we'll call you back.

Why hasn't Steve taken Greg's name off the machine? I guess he's still paying the rent, but he's never there. He's not moving in with his fiancée until the first of November (that's when he officially starts splitting her rent) but he's been practically living there for the past four months. His room at Steve's is empty except for his double futon. Steve also has a double futon. What is it with bachelors and their double futons? What is it with bachelors maintaining college-esque décor?

Not that I'm an interior designer, but their place looks like an abandoned warehouse. The living room could use a comfy, fluffy, non-cigarette burned couch, a TV stand, a coffee table, lots of throw pillows, some blankets, picture frames, candles, a plant or two and some funky posters. (The current décor consists of: *Reservoir Dogs* poster, a beer bottle collection, a Dennis Rodman–signed basketball on the television and a few sports magazines on the kitchen table and in the bathroom.) The kitchen could use some cutlery (due to no dishwasher, they prefer plastic disposables). The bedroom could use a queen-sized bed, inviting duvet, a dresser (belongings are supposed to go in piles on the floor?), a night table (alarm clock is often found under bed) and some candles and picture frames. And every wall in the apartment is thirsty for some color.

After years of living in my father's sterile white-walled, minimalist decorated house, I prefer my living environments to be homey.

Greg deciding to move in with Elana, his fiancée, was the impetus for Steve asking me to move in with him. Steve said he'd lived with enough roommates. He had always figured that when Greg moved out he'd find his own place—he couldn't afford to keep a two-bedroom on his own. But then it occurred to him that maybe I could move in and split the rent.

I give him the benefit of the doubt that his desire to move in with me is based on wanting our relationship to proceed to the next level and not because he's cheap or too lazy to move.

I hang up the phone and turn back to the doorman. "Can you tell Steve to come get me next door when he's back?" I consider leaving my suitcase behind the desk while I go for coffee, but what if he's a pervert who wants to smell my underwear?

My suitcase bumps down the concrete stairs outside the building. My jacket is in my bag and I contemplate pulling it out, because the crisp wind is blowing straight through the light sweater I'm wearing. It's only the end of September and it's already freezing. Why couldn't Steve have asked me to move in during the summer? What if I turn into an ice sculpture when the snow starts? I think I'm going to miss the ocean even more than I'm going to miss the perma-warmth. I've been a swimmer forever. I was the only girl in my bunk at Abina, the Adirondacks summer camp my father shipped me off to every July (he had gone there as a kid—he was from New York originally) who didn't pretend I had my period every time we had swim instruction. I was also the only one who didn't cry every time a nail broke. I still loved camp though. I got a job there as a junior lifeguard, and then eventually as a senior lifeguard, and then eventually as assistant head of swimming.

I should have been the head of swimming: I was a better lifeguard than the guy who was above me, but for some reason I hadn't applied for the top position. The idea of being ultimately responsible for children's lives was a little too scary for me. I liked knowing there was someone looking over my shoulder. In case I screwed up.

Where am I going to swim here? In the Hudson?

I'll have to spend half of my first paycheck on winter appropriate clothes. After living with minor variations of one season, hot, I'm going to need a coat, scarf, hat, boots. Tomorrow

might have to be a mall day. I hate malls. Today is an I-have-
to-drag-my-suitcase-to-a-coffee-shop-because-I'm-locked-
out-of-my-apartment day. I pull my suitcase down the last
step and get mad about the key-thing all over again.

Do they even have malls here?

"Changed your mind already?"

Steve is standing on the sidewalk in front of the apartment
building carrying a bag of groceries, a bottle of wine popping
out the top. A lock of light brown hair has fallen over his right
eye and into his wide smile, and he's trying to shrug it away.
He has a bit of a bowl cut, the kind that all the boys I went to
grade school with had. When Dana met him, she told me he
needed to see a stylist. I think it's sweet. He has a dimple in
each cheek. How can I be mad at a face like that?

"Had the locks changed already?" I ask. "I couldn't get in."

He pulls me into a hug, squishing my chest into the groceries. Then he starts humming "New York, New York" as he's
done on my voice mail every day since I agreed to move here.
He waltzes me back up the stairs toward the entranceway. The
top of my head reaches the bottom of his chin.

I laugh and try to get him to stay still. "What are you doing?"

"Celebrating."

A woman trying to open the front door, which my suitcase
happens to be blocking, glares at me. "Can we celebrate inside?" I ask him.

"Hey, Frank," Steve says to the doorman in passing. After
the elevator door closes, he pushes the grocery bag between
us and kisses me gently on the lips. Then the kiss becomes
harder and his tongue slips in and out of my mouth. I love the
way he kisses me. His face is smooth and soft and freshly
shaven. A trickle of dried blood is on his neck, from where he
must have cut himself. It seems he can never use a razor without leaving a nick.

"Hey look," he says pointing to the poster on the wall. "Let's
be dog walkers. Or let's get a dog."

"I'd love to get a dog, but I have a bad feeling about who's going to have to remember to do all the feeding and all the walking."

"No, Sun, I'd be great with a dog, I swear."

"You can't even remember to give me the right key. Go," I say when we're at seven.

"What's wrong with the key I gave you?"

"Maybe someone gave me the wrong key?"

He seems to be mulling something over and then laughs. His green eyes turn to little moon slices and his mouth opens. He has great big white teeth. His laugh is loud and deep and waves through his body.

Another Steve-ism is coming, I bet. "Yes?"

"Guess who has a key to the restaurant?" he sings to the tune of "New York, New York." He pulls me close for another hug.

"You gave me the extra key to the restaurant instead of the key to the apartment?"

He continues his made-up song, unlocks the door and tries to waltz me down the hallway and past Greg's empty room.

I put on my mock-concerned face. "Does one of your waiters now have the key to our apartment?"

"Is that bad?" He cracks up and then says, "Our apartment, huh? Say that again."

I'm concerned that I'm not more concerned. I kiss his neck. "Our apartment. Our room. Our fridge. Our phone. Our answering machine. When do I get to change the announcement on the machine? I want to leave the new message, okay?"

He puts the groceries on the kitchen table and tugs me the short distance to his bedroom.

I still can't get over how small New York apartments are. My place was bigger than his, and his is a two-bedroom. His is also older. The appliances have a gray sheen. Or maybe that's just dirt.

I hope he's not thinking of touching me before he cleans his hands. "I want to wash up," I say.

He follows me into the bathroom. "Yes, my little sex-pot."

I pick up the half-dissolved bar of deodorant soap he uses for his hands, body, face and hair, which is wedged to the side of the bathtub. "We're taking a trip to the pharmacy tomorrow to buy some supplies." Like a non-corrosive facial soap. And shampoo and conditioner. I used to bring my own whenever I came to visit, but moving here entitles me to invest. As Steve lifts my hair and kisses the back of my neck, I notice that the soap scum around the sink has fermented into miniature statuettes. "We're also going to invest in some sponges," I add. "Do you have Comet?"

He bites my shoulder. "Let's go into the bedroom and I'll show you my comet."

Tingles spread from my neck, to my stomach, down my legs. Mmm. "Bedtime already? And it's not even eight o'clock."

I follow him into the bedroom and onto the bed. His faded gray sheets, which I assume were once black, are crumpled in a ball with a long tail draping the floor. You'd think he'd make his bed for me, wouldn't you? How long could it possibly take to straighten the sheets and throw on the comforter? Half a minute? I'm not talking hospital corners here. I don't like immaculate, but I like tidy. He moves what I'm assuming are yesterday's jeans, straddles my thighs, then pulls off his sweatshirt and T-shirt. I love touching his chest. The hairs feel soft and ticklish like blades of grass.

I push him down on the bed and undo his pants. I trace my way down his body with baby kisses. At his waist I add a little tongue for effect.

"Mmm," he groans.

The woman across the street is loading her dishwasher. "I'm just closing the blinds," I say. "Do you want to listen to music?" I press Play on the CD player. James Brown "I Got You" comes on.

"Let's sixty-nine," he says, pushing his pants off and onto the floor.

The thing is, I hate sixty-nine-ing. It's not something I'd ever admit to Steve. What guy wants to hear that the girl who is about to move in with him *hates* a sexual position? That's like a man telling a woman he never wants to get married. It's not the oral sex part I don't like. It's the two-in-one action that bothers me. First, I can't concentrate on what I'm doing. I've always prided myself on giving good head and I absolutely cannot concentrate on two things at once. Television and conversation, driving and cell phones, salad and pasta. I like my salad first, my pasta second. Why have them both on the plate at the same time? You end up with tomato sauce on your lettuce and noodles in your Thousand Island. It's a mess. So I end up focusing on what he's doing until he's limp in my mouth or I concentrate on what I'm supposed to be doing, unable to compute what's going on down there. It's a waste, I tell you. A complete waste.

"I'm in the mood to do you," I say. Is it possible for a woman to be in the mood for a blow job? Except, of course, for porn stars who crave them anytime, anywhere, pool, library or den.

Steve has the Hot 'n Sexy Channel, and I've become a porn connoisseur. A porn critic, actually. For instance, the shrieking woman is something else I find absurd. Why does the woman sound like her partner is yanking out her nails, while the man can't even get out a simple grunt? I guess the lone male viewer prefers his action stars silent. This way he can pretend that the Brazilian-waxed blonde's "Oh God!" and "Oh baby!" or my personal porn favorite, "Fuck me, big cock man, fuck me!" refers to him.

Since no guy in the history of mankind has ever turned down a blow job, Steve lies back.

"Your turn," he says a song later, just in time, too, because my lips are starting to numb. He turns me over on my back and kisses his way down my body. Mmm.

Two songs later I'm moaning and wet and he looks at me. "Tell me what you want," he says.

Steve always wants me to tell him what I want. I want him to stop asking.

"Sex?" I ask.

He thrusts himself inside me, sending waves of heat through my body. I squeeze his shoulders.

He pulls out of me and tries to make me orgasm with his hand. The song changes. The song changes again. His fingers must have lost feeling by now. "Does it feel good?" he asks.

"Yes, almost there," I say. Why aren't I orgasming? I hate when I can't orgasm. I'm not sure what the problem is. He's doing all the right moves. I'm certainly aroused—there's a wet patch under me to prove it. But it's as if I'm in a hurry and waiting for the subway—obviously when you have somewhere important to go, it's not going to come. There's some sort of jam at the last station, sorry, take the bus.

The look of concentration on Steve's face is intense. Is this how he looked when he wrote his college exams? Maybe if I distract myself with thoughts of him studying, I can trick myself into forgetting that I want to orgasm and then I'll orgasm. As soon as you climb upstairs to hail a cab, the subway speeds underground into your station.

Steve's penis droops to the left.

"I'm coming!" I lie. I'll come tomorrow.

The first time a guy put his hand down my pants, I came the instant his finger touched my clitoris. Since I thought this was abnormal, as no one had ever mentioned it in *Seventeen,* I didn't shriek out one "Oh God" or "Oh baby" or even one "Fuck me, big cock man, fuck me!" and he kept at it until I was sore, and the whole time I was worried that the girl on the camp bunk bed above me could feel the frame shaking.

Unfortunately that party trick only worked once, my being able to come with just one touch. Now I have about a forty-percent success rate, which isn't a bad rate. As long as it's not your oncologist who's doing the quoting.

"I love you," he says and slides back inside me.

* * *

"How much do you love me?" I ask him later, tracing the letters I L-O-V-E Y-O-U on his back. He doesn't know what I'm spelling, because I'm using the cryptic Palm Pilot alphabet, Graffiti. I even draw the underscore it makes you use to create a space between words. Sometimes I give the letters extra swirls at the end to confuse him in case he's catching on. Not that he's ever used a Palm Pilot. L-O-V-E M-E, I write next.

"Who said I love you?" he asks.

"Fuck you."

"Again? Can't we eat first?" He pushes his groin into my thigh.

"You're not going to change your mind, right?"

"I can change my mind?"

I slap him on the back. "Once I move here, it's over. You're going to have to love me forever."

He bites my earlobe. "Forever?"

"I'm serious, Steve."

"You're always serious."

"It's a serious thing. I'm about to quit my job and move to a strange city to be with you."

"You think New York is strange?" He pulls himself up. Our skins make a slurping sound as we separate. "Let me tell you about strange. Did I tell you that someone asked me for a French fry yesterday? I was in Washington Square Park minding my own business, eating some fries, reading my book—" he points to *The Tommyknockers,* the Stephen King novel lying on his floor "—when some guy comes up to me and asks if he can have one."

"We were being serious here, Steve."

"He was being serious."

I picture him waltzing me down a hospital corridor an hour after I have a miscarriage, offering fries to the orderlies. At least he'd make me laugh. "So what did you do?"

"I gave him a fry. And some ketchup." He moves to the edge

of the bed and tugs his boxers back on. "I'm going to make my chicken stir-fry, okay?"

I love his chicken stir-fry. He tosses random ingredients in the wok and it somehow ends up tasting gourmet. "What should I do?"

"You come tell me about your day." He takes my clothes from my hands. "But you have to stay naked."

"All weekend?"

"Buck naked."

"Should I go to my interviews naked?"

"Definitely. Isn't it a man who's interviewing you?"

"One man, one woman. At nine and four. I'm not sure if they'd get the joke."

"Okay, you can wear a sweater. You might get cold on the subway."

I might get lost in the subway. I open my suitcase and take out a clean pair of panties. I can walk around topless, but his plastic chairs are cold. I take out my laundry bag and put my pants and sweater inside. "Is the place I'm meeting my dad for dinner tomorrow subwayable or walkable?"

I open my purse and take out my birth control. I pop the blue Friday pill into my mouth and swallow. I can even do it without water. Every night at ten o'clock. I've never forgotten. It's kind of impressive, if you think about it.

"Eden's is in the West Village. Walkable."

Tomorrow night is dinner with my dad and his new lady friend. His new thirty-one-year-old lady friend who years ago was in Dana's bunk at camp. Needless to say, Dana refuses to acknowledge the relationship. "Carrie was a slut, and still is," she reminded me. "When we were Butterflies, she had the top bunk beside me. She used to give Michael Slotkin head under the covers. It was disgusting. How does she even know the jackass anyway?" It doesn't matter anyway—he never keeps a girlfriend around longer than three months. And every three months they get younger and blonder.

Carrie was my counselor for two summers in a row, when

she was eighteen and nineteen. Unfortunately, she always had more time for her blow-dryer and male staff than for us. She was somewhat apathetic about me. She seemed to like me more than the nerdy girls who stared into space while writing letters home and listening to the Backstreet Boys on their Walkmans, but less than my twelve-year-old bunkmates who had blond highlights and early onset eating disorders. As a teenager, she was tall, blond, tanned, busty, talked with her hands and brought her nail file along to every activity. Until two months ago when my father started dating her, I hadn't heard her name since I stopped going to Camp Abina.

Steve moves his sweatshirt and T-shirt combo off the floor and back over his head. "Is she hot?" he asks, his voice muffled.

"Yes. I'm not sure what the advantage would be of dating an ugly thirty-one-year-old."

"Tighter ass and firmer breasts?"

"Honestly, Steve, if you ever trade me in for some chickee twenty years younger than me, I'll post the picture of you in the plaid skirt all over the Net."

"I don't normally date four-year-olds. I like my women with a little more flesh." He licks my breast, as if to make his point. "It was a kilt, by the way. And I only wore it to that costume party because you have a thing for Scottish men."

He does aim to please.

The sun is finally seeping through the blinds. Steve has a full-length blackout shade on the window and the pitch-blackness freaks me out. I hate darkness. It makes me think about dying, and why would I want to worry about dying when I'm only twenty-four and in the arms of the man I love?

I'm going to need a night-light or something.

When I was sixteen and alone in my house I would jump at every noise, convinced a murderer was breaking in. Once I locked myself in the bathroom for over two hours, clutching a carving knife, curled up in the fetal position in the dry bathtub.

My father fully alarmed the house, knowing how jumpy I was, and twice I pressed the panic button in my closet, bringing the police over.

A car horn blasts for the tenth time in the last twenty minutes. How does anyone sleep in this city? It's so loud. The alarm clock says seven-twelve. I duck under Steve's arm and shimmy down the bed.

We normally wake up late on Saturdays, around one. I tiptoe into the bathroom and gently close the door. I like to brush my teeth before he wakes up. This way, when he wakes up and rolls on top of me, I can have a discussion with him without worrying what I smell like. I realize that I won't be able to do this every morning for the rest of my life, which would be insane, but I've managed to do it every morning so far and he's never awakened. I brush, spit, rinse, spit, repeat, then climb back into bed and pretend to be asleep.

3

Wonder Woman

Should you be concerned if your boyfriend lies about you?

We're lying on the grass at Union Square Park. My head is on his stomach and every time I move, I scrape my ear against his belt buckle. I shift so that the ants don't crawl up my skirt while Steve tells me about when he was a junior in college and his mother found a crushed cigarette in his jean pocket.

"Why was your mother still doing your laundry?" I ask. "You were twenty-one, right?"

"Not everyone has her own house when she's sixteen."

A cloud covers the sun and the sky looks like one of its lightbulbs has burst. "My father flew in once a month for a weekend," I answer.

"If I were your father, I never would have let you live by yourself," he says, puffing up his chest.

"He asked me to come with him. I said no." Even though I am looking down at Steve's feet, I can tell that he is shaking

his head. Is he wearing two different socks? Yes, he is wearing two different socks.

"I wouldn't have given you a choice. There's no way I'd
leave my sixteen-year-old daughter by herself. Especially after
what you've been through."

He says "been through" with dread and awe, like a nine-
year-old girl asking her older sister what getting her period
feels like. Dana called it the Double D effect. Divorce and
Death. "First that, and now *this,*" mothers of friends would
whisper, not wanting to look us in the eye for fear the bad luck
would spread through the room like cancer. Snapping the
shoulder straps of our bras would be our secret signal, our
"they're feeling sorry for us" or "they don't know what we
know" sign.

Sometimes Dana makes fun of these people, behind their
backs or to their faces. "It must be so hard for your father," one
of her co-counselors said, a co-counselor who was new to
camp. Dana couldn't stand her, thought she was an airhead.
"Not so hard," Dana replied. "He left her three years before
she died, and he'd been fooling around since the day he married her. At least he doesn't have to pay alimony anymore."

When my friend Millie's parents separated in high school
and she lost ten pounds from "not being hungry," I tried to pa-
tiently coax her to have a slice of pizza, to get over it, but eventually I snapped. "For God's sake, at least they're not dead," I
yelled at her and then felt cruel and horrible and spent the next
week apologizing.

Any kind of loss is painful. But after your mother dies, divorce
seems like a sprained wrist, compared to an amputated hand.

Dana and I divide people into those who know what we
know and those who don't. A secret club with loss as our badge.

Steve doesn't know. He looks into the murky and bottom-
less future and sees something sparkling and blue. I love it that
he doesn't know, but constantly worry about the day he will.
Sooner or later everyone does.

His grandmother died last June. It was sad for him, she was

his last remaining grandparent, but it didn't exactly rock his world. He still laughed at the Letterman's Top Ten list that night.

I think the funeral was harder for me than it was for him. I hate funerals. I don't breathe well and the walls start to contract.

I met his grandmother a few times before she died. Steve brought me to see her whenever he came to visit me. We sat politely with her at her retirement home while she fed us stale chocolate and tea. She liked me right away, I don't know why, but she kept grabbing on tight to my wrist. "I want to dance at your wedding," she said and we blushed. "You have to do it soon, I don't have that much time," she'd say.

We'd wave her comment away ("don't be silly, you have lots of time") but what are you supposed to say to an eighty-seven-year-old?

"You can have this," she said and pointed to the engagement ring she still wore. It was beautiful, platinum band, a large round diamond, two baguettes. We kept blushing and she kept insisting.

I wonder what happened to the ring.

Back to my validation.

"Dana was doing her master's, the first one, so she was only an hour away from my dad's house," I say. "She made the drive at least once a week to keep an eye out for me." Dana had reveled in the pop-by—she'd claim to be drowning at the library and then sneak into the house to make sure tattooed men and acid tablets weren't decorating the furniture.

My dad had invited me to move with him to New York. What was he supposed to do, not take the promotion? I told him there was no chance I was going. No way. Have a good time. Enjoy. I'd visit. Tobias, the guy I had been in love with since the first day of my freshman year in high school had finally realized what I had been telepathically telling him for twelve months—that we were meant to hold hands and laugh and sneak kisses between classes. There was no way, *no way,* I was moving now that we were finally a couple.

The idea of senior year, of trips to the shopping center's food court where we'd hog tables and not buy anything, of destination-less drives of where-should-we-go-I-don't-know-where-do-you-want-to-go taking place in my absence made me feel claustrophobic and abandoned, as if I'd been waiting in the back of the storage cupboard between the winter coats, not knowing that hide-and-seek was long over.

I told my dad that after all I'd "been through" it would be too traumatizing to have to leave behind the final memories of my mother.

When I was eleven at summer camp, I found out a boy I liked didn't want to go to the social with me. Humiliated, I locked myself in the wooden bathroom stall at the back of my cabin and sobbed and sobbed until Carrie, my father's now girl-friend, and my then-counselor, knocked on the door and begged me to tell her what was wrong. I told her I missed my mother.

Unlike Carrie, my father should have known that excuse was full of crap.

Before my parents separated, we all lived in Fort Lauderdale. When I was three, my mother started receiving a plethora of silent, heavy-breathing phone calls (Dana was ten so she remembers these things), which led to the discovery that my father was sleeping with his secretary. Very original, Dad. Anyway, when confronted, instead of begging for forgiveness, buying jewelry and taking large amounts of Depo-Provera, or whatever today's chemical castration drug of choice is, my father decided that marriage, like last winter's coat, no longer suited him. We stayed in the house we had grown up in and my dad bought a condo in Palm Beach. When we'd visit for a weekend, we'd transform the living room couch into our bed ("Sunny, doll, be careful with Daddy's things please."). "Fa-ther," Dana would say, she always said his name like that, in two syllables, until she was older and started referring to him as The Jackass, "we're here for two days, do you think you could make a little room for us?"

"It's okay," I'd say quickly hoping to placate them both.

Once every few months he would take us to Walt Disney World. "Sunny," he'd say. "Do you want to go on 'It's a Small World' again?" He tended to address questions to me, or to "You Kids" instead of directly to Dana. She was always watching him with her best Andy Rooney I-Know-What-You're-Up-To look, full of mistrust and loathing. I'd walk between them holding their hands, trying to bridge the gap.

When I was six and my mother died, my dad bought a bigger house in Palm Beach. We got our own rooms. Mine was upstairs and Dana's was in the basement.

My father viewed us as goldfish. Feed three times a day, or at least make sure housekeeper prepares meals. Drop three hundred dollars into jacket pockets weekly to cover transportation, entertainment and clothing costs. Occasionally, press face against glass bowl to make sure children are still swimming.

As a strategy consultant he spent most weekdays in other cities and most weekends in the company of various women we were only occasionally allowed to meet. Growing up we had various housekeepers/baby-sitters who lived with us until Dana was eighteen and I was twelve. After that they came Monday to Friday during the day only. Dana decided to stay in Palm Beach with me for college instead of going away to school, so I was never on my own. She only moved out when she was twenty-two and got into her first master's program in Miami.

When she told me the news, we were eating chicken wings from our favorite Florida restaurant chain, Clucks, while lying on the white couch. I knew we wouldn't drop anything, we'd been eating like this since we'd moved in whenever no one was around to tell us not to.

"Forget it, I won't go," she said.

"Yes, you will," I told her. "It's an hour away. I'll be fine. It's not like I'm living *alone*—I live with my father. I'll only be alone for a few nights at a time, tops."

Two months later, he took the job in New York.

When I went to visit Dana in Miami for the day, and told

her that our father was moving, she was furious. "That Jack-ass wants to play bachelor in the city. What kind of a father leaves a sixteen-year-old to live in a house by herself?" I begged her not to complain, not to ruin it. I was mature, I could do it.

"Sunny," Steve says, mercifully interrupting my train of thought. I love listening to him say my name.

I roll over so I can see his beautiful face. "Yes, Steven?"

"I have to tell you something." He sounds so serious, like a college recruiter asking me about my plans for the future.

Uh-oh. He's changed his mind. Now? He changed his mind now? A week after he asks me to move in? Why did he change his mind? Bastard.

Maybe it's worse. You don't say, "I have to tell you some-thing," unless you're unleashing appalling news. He cheated on me. He's already married. He's a woman.

"I…" He plucks a blade of grass from the ground instead of continuing.

Hello? I prefer the quick-motion Band-Aid removal rather than the taunting millimeter-by-cruel-millimeter torture. "Yeeeees?" I say, attempting to stretch the word into a multi-syllable confession prompter.

"You're so going to think I'm lame when I tell you this."

He's getting lamer by the second by not coming out with it already. "I won't."

"It's just that…" His voice trails off again.

"What? I will not get mad, I promise, just tell me." You have to act like you won't get mad, otherwise they'll never tell.

He sighs. "I can't put your name on the answering machine. I don't want to tell my parents that we live together. They'll freak out."

Is that all? I almost laugh out loud. Why should I care what he tells or doesn't tell his parents? I put on my best I'm-the-most-even-tempered-girlfriend-in-the-universe smile. "Tell your parents whatever you want," I say, my voice full of pep-pered reassurance.

"Really?" he asks, and his chest droops back to its deflated state. "I thought you'd be insulted."

Insulted? Why would I be insulted? Unless what he said was intended to be a snub. Was it a snub? Was he cunningly letting me know that his parents don't approve of me and will never accept me in their family? Because my mom converted to Judaism and wasn't born Jewish? Am I not good enough? I met them a few times and they smiled and joked with me and invited us for dinner every time Steve was in town. The first few times he stayed with them, but eventually he told them he was staying at my place. Is Steve embarrassed of me? Is he never planning on telling them? Ever? Is he keeping me in the closet? I storm into a sitting position, jutting his stomach with my elbow. "Are you going to lie to your friends, too? Am I some dirty little secret that you think will parade around the bedroom in slinky lingerie but whom you'll never take out in public?" Who does this guy think he is?

He turns the color of smoked salmon. "Of course, my friends know you're moving in. What kind of person do you think I am? I've never been more excited about anything in my life. It's just that you know my parents are religious. My mom would freak out if she knew we were living together without being married. It's not like I'll have to hide any of your stuff ever, they live in Miami. It's not forever."

"What do you mean it's not forever?" I turn to glare at him. "So you think I move in with all the guys I date? That we're living together until you find something better?"

He wraps his arms around my shoulders, pulls me back to his stomach and pinches my nose with his fingers. Normally, when he pinches, he says, "Honk," which is one of his favorite and most embarrassing games to play in public places. "What I meant, Psycho, is that eventually we'll get engaged."

Oops. "I see," I say, for lack of coming up with anything more clever.

"If it bothers you, I'll tell them. Be truthful. Do you care?"

How can I be mad at him after an "eventually we'll get engaged" comment? Is he planning on proposing? How long are we supposed to live together before we get engaged? Are we pre-engaged? Do his parents not approve of me? "I don't care. Honest."

Eden's is loud, busy and green. The walls are covered in leaves. Pots of sunflowers stem up beside various tables. The waitresses are wearing skirts made of petals and sunflower-patterned bikini tops. My dad and Carrie are waiting at the bar. I can't believe he made it. Hah! I told Dana he'd show.

As I approach, Carrie waves her Fendi bag at me with one hand and a martini glass with the other. I know it's a Fendi bag because it has the FF logo trampled all over it, as if one medium-sized FF isn't obnoxious enough.

My father's arm is wrapped around her tanned, bare shoulders. "Hi," I say, approaching them.

"Sunny!" she shrieks, and covers her mouth with both her hands. "Look at you! You are so gorgeous. Look how gorgeous you are! You got so big!"

She hasn't seen me since I was twelve and she was my counselor, so I won't be insulted. "Thanks," I say. "I think."

"Last time I saw you, you had braces and hair down to your waist! Adam, isn't she gorgeous?" She waves her hands at the word *gorgeous* as if she's Moses thanking God for the Ten Commandments.

My father nods. "Gorgeous, doll, gorgeous." Am I the doll or is Carrie the doll? I haven't seen him in about six months, since I met him for dinner at China Grill on South Beach when he was in Miami meeting a client. He only had the night free because he was meeting "a friend" in the Keys. It's strange that I hadn't seen him in so long, considering that lately I'd been coming to New York every few weeks. The last few times I was here, he wasn't, which was fine with me, because it's not like I came to New York to see him.

"Stop making excuses for The Jackass," Dana says inside my head.

Two months ago he was supposed to meet Steve and me at Manna, but he didn't show. "You surprised?" Dana asked later.

My sister hasn't spoken to my father in three years. "He's like tobacco," my sister once told me. "Toxic. You'll feel better about yourself if you cut him out of your life."

Dana sees us as two orphans against the world. She's either been reading too much Dave Eggers or watching too many reruns of *Party of Five*.

Tomorrow, I'll definitely call.

You know how when you see someone daily, you don't notice him getting older, but when you don't see him for a few months, you're shocked by the change? Like when you pick up *People* once a year and see a picture of Harrison Ford and you can't believe how gray Han Solo got? Well, that doesn't happen with my father. His looks never seem to change—he's six feet, wide-shouldered, with a full head of chocolate-brown hair, wide blue eyes framed by dark spidery lashes, and a Tom Cruise smile that takes up half his face. Whenever he decided to show up on Parents' Day at camp, all the female counselors would flock to him as if he were a free chocolate sampler at the supermarket. "Oh, Mr. Langstein. How are you? It's *wonderful* to see you, Mr. Langstein."

"Call me Adam," he'd say, resting his hands on their seventeen-year-old shoulders.

I guess that's when he first noticed Carrie.

My ex-counselor continues to review my outfit. "I love that dress. Did you get it here?"

I'm wearing Dana's white V-neck cashmere sweater dress, one of the many items she bought but still had the tag attached when she handed it down to me. "Get good use of it, it's Nicole Miller and cost three hundred dollars," she told me. As if that would impress me. Tell me something, can anyone tell the difference between a three-hundred-dollar dress and a thirty-dollar dress? And would anyone who could tell the difference think less of me if I were wearing the thirty-dollar dress instead of the three-hundred-dollar dress? And if anyone would think less of me, is she really the type of person whose opinion of me matters?

The dress is really soft. I thought my dad would like it. It's so girly.

"And your hair looks gorgeous." All right, she's made her point. I put it back in a low bun, because my father has always nagged me to "pull your hair back and show off that pretty face. Why are you hiding it with all that hair?"

Okay, Carrie, that's enough sucking up for today. The occasional batting-eyed hopefuls I was allowed to meet have always held the mistaken idea that a nod from Dana or me would high-speed them from "we hang out on Saturday nights" to "look at the Harry Winston rock on my finger" status. As a teenager I was bombarded with tickets to see Michael Jackson ("Let's do the moonwalk together, Sunny!"), Cabbage Patch Kid dolls ("Let's change her diaper! Maybe one day we'll have a real baby to change!") and subscriptions to *Teen Beat* ("Isn't your father as handsome as Tom Cruise, and by the way, do other women come over to the house, Sunny?").

Sometimes I actually liked these women. Of course, as soon as my father moved on, I was expected to move on, too.

On my twelfth birthday, one of his ex-girlfriends sent me a card, wishing me a good year and telling me to call her if I ever needed anything.

"Throw that out," my father said. "She's only using you to get to me. Besides, it's not appropriate for you to still see her socially."

I threw it out.

Carrie always looked very—*Vogue*. Now her hair has that three-hundred-dollar blond highlighted, blow-dried straight then attacked with a curling iron look. She's wearing black boot-cut pants, a tight silver strapless shirt and a black cashmere pashmina draped behind her back and over her arms. She looks shorter than she used to, despite her three-inch stiletto boots—ouch—but I think that's because the last time I saw her

I was only four feet tall. Now she looks about my height, five foot six. My brown patent leather pumps only add an inch. I don't normally wear shoes like these out, they're my suit shoes, my interview shoes. According to Dana, they're called Mary Janes, meaning they're pumps with a strap. They're the only shoes I have that match with this dress. I'm not a fashion connoisseur, but I didn't think my sneakers would go.

The hostess shows us to our table while batting her eyes, swooshing her petal skirt and thrusting her sunflower bikinied breasts at my dad. Carrie notices and wraps her fingers around his wrist like a jaywalking mother clinging to her daughter. Thankfully the waiter in our section is male. For some reason only the female staff members are dressed in garden-appropriate costumes. Maybe no one wants waiters clothed in fig leaves handling their shrimps. Carrie and my dad claim the seats in the corner, facing outward, and I slide into the art deco highly uncomfortable metal chair across from my father and an ivy-covered wall.

Carrie passes me her drink. "Their apple martinis are to die for," she says. "Try mine."

I take a careful sip, not wanting to touch her red lipstick marks. "Pretty good."

"Do you want one?" my dad asks me. He looks at Carrie. "You want another one, doll?" That answers my previous unanswered question. She's Doll tonight.

Alcohol will surely increase this evening's enjoyment factor. "Why not?" I answer before Doll has a chance to speak.

Carrie raises her hand and waves over our waiter. "She would like an apple martini, please. Can I have another one, too? Thanks."

We order appetizers and the main course after listening to Carrie's endorsements. ("The crab cakes are heavenly, trust me. Do you like ostrich? It's fabulous here. Try it. The shrimps in black bean sauce are also to die for.") Eating ostrich sounds mildly grotesque, so I decide on the shrimp. Once we've ordered, my dad asks me about my job search.

"I have interviews set up all day on Monday," I say. "Hopefully some sort of job offer will come out of it."

"All you need is one, right?" Carrie asks. "Just like a man." She smiles at my dad. I want to tell her she shouldn't get her hopes up.

I wonder what she does for a living. What's the etiquette for asking? People always strike me as crass when they inquire about my work. It's as if they're trying to sneak a peek at my paycheck. And what if she doesn't work? She might be one of those Manhattan socialites. Maybe she's never set a pedicured toe into a job since summer camp.

Oh, hell. "So what do you do, Carrie?"

She finishes the rest of the martini and swishes it around her mouth like mouthwash. "I'm an associate at Character Casting. It's a talent agency."

"Cool. You find actors for movies and commercials?"

"Basically. Lately we've been doing a lot of reality TV."

"I thought reality TV used real people."

"They do use real people," she declares. "The reality shows all have open casting, but they also rely on agencies to find people with unique abilities and diverse backgrounds. We cast most of the singles for *DreamDates*. Have you ever seen it?"

"You watch those reality TV shows?" my father asks me.

"Not really," I say. "I'm not a huge TV watcher. I watch the news, and Letterman. I used to watch a ton of TV when I was in high school."

When I lived on my own, there wasn't much else to do when all my friends were having dinner with their families.

"Honestly, I haven't gotten into the reality TV trend thing. I watched a *DreamDates* episode once, and it was kind of funny." If you consider witnessing someone else's complete humiliation funny. Ex-boyfriends were there, background music was blasting, people were crying. I was surprised when I read an article reporting the show was incredibly popular.

"They're everywhere," Carrie whispers, leaning in like a conspirator. "The networks are premiering dozens more this season. They love them—they don't have to pay the writers or the actors. Even stodgy cable networks like TRS are launching them. These days it's the only surefire way to get into the eighteen- to thirty-four market. In the past year we've casted for *Freshman Year, The Model's Life, Party Girls,* and get this one—*Call Girls.* Yup. It's a reality show about a Vegas whorehouse. Unreal, huh?"

I shake my head, incredulous. Don't individuals have enough problems without wanting to burden themselves with other people's exaggerated ones? "How did you cast for that? Answer the *Village Voice* ads?"

"You don't want to know." Our drinks and appetizers arrive and Carrie continues between bites of crab cake. "We're swamped these days. You know what—if none of your interviews work out, we could definitely use a temp at Character." She looks over at my father, as though seeking approval in the form of a nod or pat on the knee.

My dad says, "That's a great idea."

If Carrie were a Labrador, her tail would wag.

Flipping through pictures of anorexic wanna-be actresses all day? Thanks, but no thanks.

A tall brown-haired man wearing a Hawaiian-patterned shirt, black pants, shiny leather loafers, a square goatee and tiny John Lennon glasses approaches our table and lays his hands palms down on our table. "Carrie! What's up?" he says, his glance glossing over my father and me.

Carrie straightens up in her chair. "Howard, hello. You know my boyfriend, Adam." He shakes my dad's hand. "And this is his daughter, Sunny. Sunny, Howard Brown."

"It's a pleasure," he says to me. I lift my hand to shake his, and he kisses the back of it. His lips feel oily and he reminds me of a counselor I knew at Abina, Mark Ryman, who had thought he was the camp's Danny Zukoe. He would buy the fifteen-year-old counselors-in-training shots of tequila to get them drunk enough to sit on his lap.

Carrie looks around the room. "Who are you here with?"

He rubs his hands together as if he's trying to warm them up. "My wife. She's getting us another table. I don't like where they sat us." He motions across the room at a blonde in a fur-collared white sweater.

Carrie waves but the wife doesn't wave back. "Tell her I say hello," Carrie says.

As soon as he walks away, Carrie hunches toward me and whispers, "That was the executive producer for the show *Party Girls* I was telling you about. His wife is a complete bitch. A jealous freak. She's convinced he's screwing half the women in New York."

"Why?"

"Because he's screwing half the women in New York."

"He has the slime vibe," I say.

"Yeah, but he's a genius. He created the show, too. He's even the one who sold the idea to TRS, which is miraculous, considering that the network is so conservative. Since I cast two of the girls for his show, he's considering hiring me as a liaison. You know, to make sure they stay gorgeous and do their job."

"So what are these brilliant producers going to do next? Tape people going to the bathroom?" my dad asks, nipping back into the conversation at the word *gorgeous*. Maybe Carrie should start peppering her everyday conversation with sexy adjectives. *Sizzling* weather. *Spicy* clients.

"You're so funny, honey." Carrie giggles a little-girl laugh.

"What does a producer do exactly?" I ask. I've never understood what that job title entails.

"Not much," my father says.

"Very funny, Adam, that's not true. They plan everything, hire everyone, manage the money, make sure everything is on schedule, premiere the show."

Sounds like what I do, but with TV shows instead of carbonated fruit juices.

"This concept is very original. It follows four girls at different bars on Saturday nights."

Aren't there a million shows like that? "Very original," I say.

Carrie nods, either missing or ignoring my sarcasm. "The camera only follows the girls on Saturday nights. The unique part is that the show airs the next night. We call it ALR taping, Almost Live Reality. An incredibly quick taping-to-broadcasting turnaround." Her voice switches into sell-mode. I imagine her shaking hands with prospective *spicy* clients, nodding profusely. "No one knows what's going to happen next week, not even Howard. Also, this show is going to be far more accurate in terms of the scene than other Real TV shows. Usually these shows are taped in their entirety, then edited, then broadcasted. But even though a club is sizzling hot during the summer, it could easily be out by winter. With ALR, *Party Girls* will be a lot more immediate. Much more *now.* Much more *real.*"

Much more ridiculous? How could anyone be real when she's being stalked by a camera? I can't even be natural taking a passport photo. "So how do you pick the girls who are on the show?" I ask.

She rolls her eyes. "You would not believe the process. Applicants had to fill out forms and send in sample tapes, then we did a round of interviews, then we finally chose four girls." Carrie looks over at my father to make sure he's listening, but realizes that he's busy watching the waitresses in their garden outfits. I can tell she's contemplating what she can say to break him out of his two-timing reverie. Doesn't she know it's never going to happen? "Why four?" I ask.

She seems to be searching her stock answers for an appropriate response. "Women are normally friends in groups of four."

I laugh. "And has that happened since *Sex and the City* became a huge success?" I don't have HBO, but both Millie and Dana do and they've made me watch enough episodes. Not my life (the Mr. Bigs, the Cosmopolitans, the Manolo Blahnik obsession), but I still laughed. Is that show even on anymore? I take another sip of my martini.

She searches for a stock answer for that, too, but appears to come up blank. She nods. "I suppose so. I need another drink," she says, motioning to the waiter.

Two martinis later, there's a commotion behind me.

Carrie strains her neck to see what's going on. "Yikes, something is going down over there." She points multiple fingers over my head. I turn to take a look.

A blond woman in a tweed Newsboy cap is standing in front of her chair, clutching her neck. A flushed man beside her is frantically trying to convince her to drink a glass of water. "Take it! Karen? Kar? Are you choking?"

I doubt the bluish tint to her face means no. She's fine, thank you very much, and why don't you sit down and finish your black beans and shrimp?

Apparently, Carrie was right. The dish is to die for.

Is it too late to change my order?

Silence creeps through Eden's like frost. Karen, the choking woman, motions to her neck and throws the water on the floor. The glass splinters around her.

The man spears his eyes around the restaurant. "I need a doctor!" he yells. Our waiter howls. The hostess starts to cry.

No one stands up.

"Oh my. Oh my," Carrie says. "She's choking. She's choking." She giggles and her hands respond by waving. "Oh my. What do we do? Adam? What do we do?"

Karen heaves silently, without emitting a single sound. Is she going to pass out? Is she going to die? Are we about to witness a woman die over a plate of shrimp?

Way back when, in the days before Hotmail, DVDs and Britney Spears, to get my lifeguard certification I had to practice doing a stomach thrust. Unfortunately I've never actually performed this activity on anything except a mannequin.

There must be a doctor somewhere in this restaurant. I look for someone exploding into action with a stethoscope around his neck, or a prescription pad in hand. Someone must be more qualified than a has-been summer-camp lifeguard. I don't even think my certification is still valid. I'm barely qualified to throw her a lifejacket.

I coached children on the front crawl. I blew a whistle during free swim. Once every summer we'd pretend a kid had lost his buddy and we'd hold hands, sweep the water. Since we knew the kid was hiding in the flutter-board shed reading an *Archie* comic, that's not saying much for my emergency skills.

The woman is the same color as the curaçao in her martini glass. "Can't anyone help?" the man begs.

Shit.

My head feels light and I wish I hadn't had that second cocktail, but I jump to my feet and sprint toward the air-challenged woman. "I'm going to do the Heimlich on you, okay?" Are you supposed to ask permission? Or does that scare them? Too late.

I stand behind her, make a fist with my right hand and place it, thumb toward the woman, between her rib cage and waist. Her stomach feels squishy and hot. I put my other hand on top of the fist. Okay. So far, so good. I'm already congratulating myself and I haven't done anything yet. All right, it's outward and inward. No, inward and upward. That's it. I thrust my hand inward and upward. Nothing. Inward and upward. Again. Inward and upward. Fuck. How many times am I supposed to do this? She can't die while I'm touching her, can she? There should be some kind of rule—someone can't die in a stranger's arms.

A chunk of shrimp soars out of the woman's mouth, landing in her glass and splashing blue liquid onto the white tablecloth. She coughs. She breathes. She turns around. She throws up.

The restaurant claps.

"Are you okay, Kar?" her husband/date/male friend asks her.

She inhales again and nods. I hand her the cloth napkin that was on the floor. I assume it's hers.

Dazed, she sits down and says, "Thank you."

You're welcome! Everyone is looking at me, pointing. Wow. I can't believe I just did that. Pretty impressive. I'd love to see what that looked like. Any chance anyone got that on videotape? "How do you feel?" I ask.

"Light-headed," she says, "but all right." A waiter hands her a glass of water and she downs it.

People are still clapping. I look at my table in the corner—Carrie is honoring me with a standing ovation, her hands gesturing all over the place. My father has his glass raised to me in a toast. A toast. My father is toasting me!

I do one of those shy I-do-what-I-can smiles. I might be a superhero. I saved a person's *life*. Aren't there customs where she's supposed to become my slave?

The maitre d' comes over and thanks me. Maxwell the chef tells me I'm a star. Karen and her husband start to cry and tell me they can't thank me enough. Karen then hands me her business card and a hundred-dollar bill. I decline the bill but take the business card. Why not? It says Karen Dansk, VP Programming, Women's Network. Who knows? Maybe I can get Dana a job as a Manhattan reporter.

Ten minutes and thousands of accolades later I head back to my table. My father motions to his mouth and then to his chest.

"What?" I ask. He's so proud he's speechless? I've touched his heart? I've rekindled his hope in the human spirit?

"Wipe your sweater," he says.

I look down. Dana's three-hundred-dollar cashmere dress is covered in shrimp and black bean remnants.

I wonder if I can ask Maxwell to make me the ostrich instead.

4

Six Feet Under

Sixth Avenue. Uh-oh. Wrong way. It's three fifty-four. I have six minutes to find the right office. Time to sprint. Ow. Feet hurt. Can't look sweaty. Click, click, click. Need this job. Not that I expected to get a job right away, but how many Mondays can I get away with calling in sick?

I have spent the last fifteen minutes being dragged by the commuter undertow, not having a clue that I was going the wrong way.

Sometimes I'm so off, yet sometimes I'm so on.

I still can't believe I saved a woman's *life* the other night. My lifeguard skills certainly came in handy.

I fell in love with the water when I was six, the summer my mother died. Whenever I felt lost and alone at camp, I would take solace in being immersed in the water.

I loved listening to the ping of the bubbles, flowing around me.

When I couldn't stand the sadness, when I felt utterly over-whelmed, I would sink to the sandy bottom, feet of water above me and open my mouth and scream. I would scream and scream and scream, until I felt empty and calm.

I'm going to need to find a place to swim in this city.

I keep walking. Next to the soaring buildings I'm a speck of dust on a crowded Monopoly board. One of these buildings is my dad's. I know his office is near Grand Central (not that he'd ever go slumming in the subway). With each step the cor-rosion of the soles of my brown Mary Janes intensifies. These pumps are made for walking, as the song kind of goes, except walking ONLY to and from boardrooms, in and out of eleva-tors, not journeying along miles of jagged concrete. My feet have swollen to bee-sting proportions and each step pinches. Where are my sneakers when I need them?

Finally, at exactly five past four I arrive on the sixth floor of Soda Star.

"Hi, Heidi," I say to the receptionist, feeling remarkably clever for remembering her name. "I'm here to see Ronald Newman."

"You're late." A balding man wearing a lime-green golf shirt, beige shorts and golf shoes stomps across the waiting room.

How come he gets to wear sneakers and I don't?

"Excuse me?" I say.

"I'm Ronald." He sticks out a pudgy hand. "Sunny, right? Lis-ten, Sunny," he says before I finish nodding. "I have to get to a golf game. I'm running a little late, so let's walk and talk?"

I nod and follow him back into the elevator. Fabulous. More walking.

"I'm hungry," he says. "And you could probably use some coffee. Let's do this down the road at my favorite diner. The cafeteria in this building is appalling."

Fabulous. More coffee. I've already had two cups trying to wake up for my 9:00 a.m. interview. My 9:00 a.m. useless in-terview that began with my pal Jen at Fruitsy telling me, "It's unfortunate we have no positions open. Your stuff is very impressive. Let me see it again."

I can't believe she duped me into waking up at seven—*at seven*—just so she could drool all over my portfolio. She knew she wasn't hiring, but vulturelike, wanted to see what ideas and clients she could embezzle from me.

Then I had another two cups trying to stay conscious all day after waking up so early.

I hope there's a bathroom at this diner.

Ten minutes later we're in a seedy diner down the street, and I'm wondering exactly what his idea of appalling is. "They make the best sweet potato fries," he promised as I sat on something sticky in a booth near the back.

My feet feel like they've been driven over by a bus. How unprofessional would it be if I took off my shoes? I accidentally on purpose drop my spoon and lean down. I can't take them off, obviously, but what harm could there be if I unbutton the strap the tiniest bit?

Yes. Oh, yes. Much better.

"So if you worked for me, that's what you'd learn," Ronald says and takes another bite of his cheeseburger. After thirty-five minutes of lengthy descriptions of his swot analysis, his hatred of bottled water and his theories of advertising, all of which I couldn't care less about, I congratulate myself on my skilled ability to stare someone in the eye, appear as though I'm hanging on his every word, while ignoring him completely. It's all about the nod. "Between digital TV and integrated marketing services—we're about to experience the modernization of the marketing of the soda industry as we know it—" Nod, nod. Between nods, I treat myself to sips of my coffee, while still maintaining eye contact.

I wonder if he conducts an interview a day just to hear himself talk.

"I can tell you're highly intelligent," he tells me.

And he can tell this by my continual nodding? He's good.

"Thank you, Ronald. I think you're very intelligent, too, and

I am quite confident I would learn an immeasurable amount from you."

He nods. Not quite *my* nod, but not bad, I grudgingly admit. "That you could." His gaze drifts to the ceiling. Probably thanking the heavens for his virtuosity. "When we did the launch for our mandarin-and-vanilla-flavored caffeine-free soda…"

I have to use the bathroom.

Now.

"…you should have seen their faces when we won the ADDY award for the…"

Can I interrupt him to use the bathroom? People don't like being interrupted. I have to wait for a natural pause in the conversation.

How is he not taking a breath? How has he not toppled over for lack of oxygen?

When he takes another bite of his burger, I make a jump for it. "Excuse me, I have to use the rest room. I'll be right back." I slide away from the table while he's still chewing.

Ronald is staring at me strangely. Once I'm standing, I realize that a) the stall is only a foot away from the table, and b) he is staring at my unstrapped Mary Janes. Can't do anything about the shoes, so I just smile as if nothing's wrong.

If I ever design a restaurant, I'm putting the bathrooms all the way in the back.

The door handle rattles in my hand.

"I'm in here!" Someone screams from the other side.

Now what? Do I sit back down? Can I just stand here ignoring him? What's she doing in there? Washing her hair? Why do women take so long in the bathroom? Don't they consider that other people need to use it? She has rudely barricaded herself in there for over five minutes. I slink back into our booth and cross my legs. No more coffee.

Ronald is perusing my resume with one of his short stocky fingers. "What are your salary requirements?"

I hate that question. Do I say more than I want so he can

offer me less, or less than I want to undercut the competition? "What range are you offering?"

"Forty to fifty." Fifty's not bad. I'll take fifty. "Depending on experience."

"I'm looking for fifty. I have the experience."

"You don't have Manhattan experience, but I think you'll work out fine. Forty-five." He smiles, showcasing gold fillings. "When can you start?"

Is that a job offer? Or a casual question? I take another sip of coffee to try to appear calm and normal and not as though his every word has the power to alter the course of my life. "I...um...I'd have to give two weeks notice. And then I'd like a week to move and organize myself. So if I give notice immediately I could start in three weeks."

"Good. Then I'll see you in three weeks."

That was an offer. I just got an offer. I squeeze the metal rim of the ketchup-stained table in excitement. "Really?"

"Really. I'll have all the paperwork drawn up and at your office by Wednesday morning."

"Thank you," I say, overwhelmed with gratitude. Ronald pays the bill, shakes my hand and then makes a run for his golf game. "We'll be in touch," he says, and disappears outside.

The bathroom door flies open and the toilet hog sashays through the restaurant. I notice that a woman in a beige suit is slowly rising from her seat, eyeing the open door, about to make a run for it.

I hurl myself to the empty stall before the suit-clad woman beats me to it. Since I'm far closer, I get there first and lock the door behind me. In my hurry, I almost trip on my de-strapped shoes, but in midfall I catch myself on the sink.

I might be a direct offspring of the goddess of agility.

Two minutes later, while still cramped in the stall, I decide that I'm going to surprise Steve and drop by Manna to say goodbye. I still have some time before I have to catch my flight. I undo the bun in my hair—wet and scrunch it because

Steve likes it down and sexy, and then rummage in my purse for my lipstick to smooth out my lips.

There's a knock on the bathroom door.

"I'm in here!" I scream while doing up my shoes.

Funny, there's never a rush when you're on the inside, is there?

"I did it," I tell Steve.

"That was quick. It's only nine-ten." His morning voice is raspy and sexy and I wish I were lying next to him instead of back in my office with the door closed.

"I wanted to give Liza the full two weeks notice."

"How'd she take it?"

"She was pissed. Told me I screwed her or something. But she would have said that no matter how much notice I gave. I want some time off to move. I don't want my last day here to be a Tuesday, the trucks come Tuesday night, and I start at Soda Star 9:00 a.m. Wednesday." I kick my feet up on the desk and swivel in my chair, executive style. I love my chair. I hope Soda Star has good chairs. Really, a proper, comfortable turbo chair makes all the difference in one's performance.

"Congrats on your unemployment. I still can't believe you got a job on your first try. Have you heard anything more from Ronald McDonald?"

After Ronald Newman's cheeseburger appreciation, Steve has named my future boss after his favorite so-not-kosher hamburger joint. "Not yet. He said tomorrow, I think. Okay, gotta go. I have to give my thirty days notice at my apartment." I estimate the discussion with Jocelyn, the superintendent, will take at least a half hour. She's a talker.

By later Tuesday morning I've given Jocelyn notice ("New York! How exciting! Good for you! Can we show your place tonight? The rental market is fantastic these days. Do you know—"), e-mailed all my friends and acquaintances about the furniture I'm trying to sell, with digital pictures included, and placed an ad for my car in the weekend classifieds.

I am a goddess of efficiency.

"But you didn't hear from Ronald McDonald?" Steve asks me on the phone that night as I turn my lights out, crawl into bed, and recount my excellent organizational skills, the portable phone balanced on my shoulder.

"I'm sure he'll send me something tomorrow."

By Wednesday at five-thirty, I'm starting to get a wee bit edgy. After biting my nails until my fingers are raw and red, something I haven't done since I was twelve, I call Soda Star.

"Thank you for calling Soda Star. Our office hours are nine to five, Monday through Friday. If you know your party's extension, please dial now. Otherwise, press one to leave a message for marketing, two for operations, three for sales…"

Ten minutes later: "If you do not know the department you wish to speak to, please dial the first four letters of the person's last name you wish to reach. Have a nice day."

"N" is six. "E" is three. "W" is…where's "W"?

"I'm sorry, you lazy moron, you've run out of time." The phone disconnects.

Bitch. I hang up and plan my attack. First, I write the numbers on a Post-it note, and then I redial.

"Thank you for calling Soda Star. Our office hours are nine to five, Monday through—"

Why does she tell me every possible number combination except for the one that means fast forward? Do all Soda Star employees get off on hearing themselves talk?

Finally I reach Ronald Newman's voice mail.

In my frantic attempt to come across as utterly cheerful and imperturbable, I end up sounding pathetically desperate. "This is Sunny Langstein calling? I just wanted to catch up and make sure all the papers are in order? I gave notice here so I'm all set to start in two and a half weeks? Looking forward to hearing from you?" And then I repeat my home number, office number and cell number. Twice.

When I arrive at my office on Thursday morning, Liza is sitting cross-legged on my desk. "Guess what!" she says, patting her stomach. I'm not sure if she's talking to me or to the baby.

"What?"

"I found your replacement. She's fabulous. She has no work experience, but just finished her MBA. An MBA! I've always wanted someone with an MBA to work for me. Isn't that exciting?"

"Exciting," I say, and flip the power button on my computer.

"And she can start on Monday, giving you five days overlap to train her. Isn't that fabulous?"

"Fabulous," I say somewhat warily. A small pang tweaks through my body, like I swallowed water too fast and it went down the wrong pipe. How did she find someone so quickly?

Am I that replaceable?

I call in for my home messages. The message on my machine from Jocelyn tells me that she has great news:

"My niece just got evicted from her apartment last week—well, that's not the great part of course, no one likes getting evicted—but she wants to move in by October fifteenth! So you're off the hook for half of October's rent, which I know will please you. But you have to move out by the fourteenth, okay? Isn't that perfect timing!"

I call Ronald again. I don't want to leave a message, again, so I hang up on his voice mail. And then I call my home answering service, again, and my cell answering service, in case Ronald is too dim-witted to realize that during working hours I am at the office.

"You have no new messages you big, fat, pathetic, jobless loser."

I repeat this process at eleven. And at two. And at 2:30. At 3:30. At 4:00. At 4:15. At 4:21 my heart is beating louder than call waiting and I can't take it anymore. I leave another message.

What's his problem? I've always gotten anything I applied for. I had a full scholarship to the University of Florida. I was assistant head of swimming at camp. The youngest assistant manager at Panda. I was voted treasurer of my high school student body. My boyfriend wants me to move in with him, dammit.

"Sunny," Liza points her pointy, pregnant head into my office. "Tomorrow, can you start writing up descriptions for everything you do?"

"What?"

"For the new MBA. It would help if she had To-Do lists. If you could write out everything you do and how you do it, that would be fabulous. Thanks."

Great. Like I have nothing else to worry about. I'm going home.

That night I dream about sitting at the diner and Ronald picking hamburger meat with fat fingers out of the space between his two front teeth. He's telling me that he's decided to hire Liza's unborn child instead of me.

I wake up hot and cold and sweaty, tangled in my clean cotton sheets. It's 4:00 a.m. I can't fall back asleep, so instead I shower and go to work.

I compose the list of things the MBA should do, and then at eight close my door and begin my morning ritual of calling Ronald.

"Ronald Newman speaking."

My mouth is immediately zapped of all moisture. He's alive! He's alive!

Why didn't he call me if he wasn't dead?

"Hi, Ronald," I say, wishing I had a glass of water nearby. What's wrong with my mouth? "Sorry to bother you? It's Sunny Langstein calling? How are you?" Must stop talking in question format.

Silence. Why is there silence?

"Sunny," he says slowly. "I've been meaning to (ahem) call you—" Why the ahem? No one likes an ahem. "I have some bad news I'm afraid."

Bad news? No one likes bad news.

"It's very unfortunate, but we found a candidate with more New York experience."

"More what?"

"More New York experience. Someone more familiar with the bars, the concert venues, the retail stores, the arenas. Television contacts. You don't have any contacts here, Sunny. We need someone with a higher profile. What would you be bringing to the table?"

My new business experience in the soda industry? "I...um...didn't you already offer me the job?"

"Like I said, the news is unfortunate. My secretary was supposed to call you and send you a fruit basket. Should I assume you never received it?"

What stupid fruit basket? "Why were you interviewing other candidates after you offered me the job?"

"You can never give up on finding the perfect candidate," he says. I wish I'd received the fruit basket. I wish he was in the same room as me. Then I'd hurl an apple at him.

"I hope this hasn't caused any inconveniences," he says.

I have no job and no place to live, but what inconvenience? "Oh, oh, none at all," I say in a singsong tone.

He doesn't sense my sarcasm. "You never know, we could have another opening any day. Why don't you give me a call once you've settled in the city?"

I am not going to cry. "Uh-huh," I say, then add "'Bye." I hang up. Rage and frustration and disappointment and what-a-fucking-asshole overwhelm me, and I sink into my fabulous swivel chair that now belongs to the fabulous MBA. I stand up and stand directly behind the closed door because it's the blind spot, the one corner of personal space in the entire office where no one can see in. No job. No apartment. What am I going to do? I lean against my *in-case* umbrella and tears spill down my cheeks like rain.

5

The Wonder Years

This is the history of my parents: Father is in business school. Mother is a nurse. Father is Jewish. Mother is Catholic. Father meets Mother in Brooklyn. Father and Mother fall in love. Mother gets pregnant. Father proposes marriage but insists Mother convert, otherwise Father's children will not be Jewish. Being Jewish is very important to Father because it's important to Father's parents. Father's father, Daniel, died five years ago and Father promised he would marry Jewish woman. Mother cares more about Father than she does about religion so she agrees. Mother's parents do not agree. Mother's parents are horrified that daughter is pregnant and converting and tells Mother to never return home again. Mother converts. Process is far more strenuous than Mother imagined. Mother marries Father anyway. Father gets offered high-paying consultant job in Fort Lauderdale. Mother and Father move to Florida. Mother has baby girl, names her Dana, after Father's father. Mother wants to return to work but has difficulty finding new nursing job with baby at home. Father becomes increasingly distant. Father's job requires much traveling. Mother tries to have another child. Gets pregnant. Miscarries. Gets pregnant again. Miscarries again. Gets depressed. Gets pregnant again. Carries to term. Mother sees baby as shining light in marriage and names baby Sunny. Sings "You Light Up My Life" to rock baby to sleep. Father leaves Mother for secretary. Mother's older daughter doesn't understand where Daddy is and sits on the porch stairs waiting for him to come home. Mother puts three-year-old back to bed and explains to ten-year-old again. Mother gets sick. Mother doesn't tell children that she is sick, but instead calls her own parents who she hasn't spoken to in ten years and begs them to come take care of them. Parents come. Grandmother and Grandfather move into Mother's house until summer when Mother dies and children move into Father's new house in Palm Beach.

"It's not the end of the world," Steve tells me.

My office door is still closed. "Whatever you say, Judy Blume."

"What?"

"Nothing." One at a time, I pull unused thumbtacks out of the corkboard walls, and then group them on my desk by color. Red, yellow, green, white.

"So you'll look for a job here. It'll be easy to find something once you're in the city."

I attempt to keep my voice at a consistent pitch, above the sinking level. "Everything is all screwed up. I didn't want to move until I had a job. I don't want to be the jobless girlfriend who has no life and sponges off her boyfriend, all right? How do you know I'm ever going to find a job?" I turn the thumbtacks around and stab them into the wooden desk.

"First of all, you'll find a job. Second of all, you're not sponging off me. I'm happy to cover the full rent until you find something. And second of all—"

"You already said second of all. You're on third of all."

"Third of all, you never thought you'd get the first job you applied for, anyway. And you only applied to jobs in the beverage industry. Can't you apply for any new business job? And can't you apply for manager positions, too? Not just assistant managers?"

"I wanted a job in an industry I'm familiar with. I don't like not knowing what I'm doing. And I'm not ready to be a manager yet."

"If you need to make some money, you can wait tables at the restaurant."

I can't get sucked up by his world. I need to have my own job, my own life. I can't depend on him for everything. Is he not listening? "But I wasn't planning on quitting until I had a job. You don't understand."

"What don't I understand?" He sighs into the phone. "Sunny, I know you're afraid you'll end up like your mother. But you're not her, okay?"

My head hurts. I close my eyes. "How did you know that was bugging me?"

"What do you mean how do I know? I know."

"Carrie? Hi, it's Sunny."

"Sunny?"

"Sunny, Adam's daughter?"

"Sunny! Hey! How are you? I am so busy here today. We're having a major crisis. Major. Can I call you back? Why are you calling?"

Why am I calling? I rub the palms of my hands against my temples. "Sorry, I didn't mean to bother you. The job that I thought I had fell through and I was wondering if you still had some temp work for me? You seem like you're in a rush, though, so call me whenever you have a second."

"Sure, Sunny, no problem. Let me ask around and I'll get back to you as soon as I can, okay? Gotta run! Crisis! 'Bye!" She hangs up.

She's not calling back. Maybe my father has already

dumped her and she's going to make me wait by the phone as payback.

The bulletin board walls in the room start to contract, like the trash compactor scene in *Star Wars*. My breathing feels shallower, faster, harder.

When we moved in with my father, this happened to me whenever my dad tried to take us on vacation. On a flight to the Florida Keys, I pretended to be asleep on Dana's lap, imagining air leaking from my mouth as if from the rim of a balloon. Leaving me shriveled and empty.

When I was seven, on a trip to Epcot Center, on the Spaceship Earth ride, as Dana, my dad, his new girlfriend and her twelve-year-old son journeyed "to the dawn of recorded time…" I began to slowly hyperventilate. When our seats rotated to reveal a vast star-filled night sky, I felt as if I was being buried alive. Rambling, I told my father I had to find a bathroom, now, and Dana took my hand and led me through the blackness, toward the red exit sign. As soon as we entered the lit corridor, I started crying. She pulled me into her and smoothed my hair until I felt calm.

When Dana was seventeen, on the morning of Rosh Hashanah, the Jewish New Year, she knocked on my father's door, still in her pajamas, and told my father she was not going to synagogue. She'd had enough. She didn't believe in God, and what was the point in pretending she did? Moronic, she said. Religion was moronic, so why should she be a hypocrite?

Sitting in the kitchen, eating my cereal and milk, dressed in my new striped gray Rosh Hashanah suit and black pumps, I thought about how after my mother died, Dana used to tell me that she was watching us from above, making sure we were all right. But as I heard Dana stomp toward her room and slam her door, I realized that it had been something she had to say, because what else do you tell a six-year-old girl?

Headhunter. Why don't I e-mail a headhunter? I'll write up a polite cover letter, using Steve's New York address.

By noon Liza has passed by my closed door, scowling, at least twenty times. I'm about to send off my cover letter to Great Jobs NY when my phone rings, annoying me.

"What?" Did I just say that?

"Sunny. It's me. Omigod."

Will Omigod one day make it into the *Oxford English Dictionary* as an expression of disbelief or amazement among generation Y women?

"Oh, hi, Carrie." Maybe she found something? Be calm.

"Omigod. Guess what? You're not going to believe this. Are you ready? Are you ready for this? Are you sitting down?"

No, I'm lined up vertically against the wall in a headstand. "Yes, I'm sitting."

"Okay. Okay. One of the girls—not one of the two girls I found, but one of the girls my assistant Lauren discovered, my ex-assistant I should add—was arrested last night. Arrested! By the cops! I fired Lauren, of course. A bad judge of character has no future at Character. No future in this business at all. I can't believe I hired her in the first place."

"What girls?" I ask. What is she talking about? She's sounding a bit pimpish. I change the screen of my computer to my To Do list in case Liza peeks in. No need to antagonize her for no reason.

"For *Party Girls*. The reality TV show. I told you about it, didn't I? The camera follows four women on Saturday nights. And the unique part is that the show airs the next night because it's ALR taping which is—"

"Right, Almost Live Reality. You told me."

"Yes, Almost Live Reality and taping starts in eight days. Eight days! Eight days!"

Wow, I have good timing. I might be a timing goddess as well as deity of efficiency. Lauren got fired *today*. I need a job *today*. I am good. I can demean myself for a few months, while I make contacts and earn some cash. If it looks that bad on my resume, I don't even have to put it on. I swivel my chair three hundred and sixty degrees, and smile. "I'll take it," I say.

Carrie squeals. "You will? You're awesome! You're going to be amazing. You're going to be a TV star."

What did she just say? Me? A what? "You mean a Character star, right?"

"Whatever you want to call it, honey. I'm going to make you famous."

Famous? "Carrie, are you offering me a job at Character?"

She laughs a high-pitched, girly laugh. "I'm offering you a role on *Party Girls.*"

I drop the phone and then pick it up again. "Excuse me?"

"You'll be great."

"On TV. What do I know about TV?"

"You don't need to know anything. That's the point. It's a reality show."

I can't be on TV. What would I do on television? "I don't understand."

Carrie is beginning to get impatient. "Sheena was arrested for shoplifting two thousand dollars' worth of merchandise from Bloomingdale's. She'll be tied up in court for the next year. And we can't have the show's reputation tarnished before it even starts. And she was supposed to be the Miranda."

"The what?"

"The responsible one. Remember my client Howard? At Eden's? He had the Hawaiian shirt and the jealous wife. He called me at 3:00 a.m. last night and told me that Sheena was in jail and that I had to find a new girl, pronto. We need to have four girls. Four girls, Sunny, four girls. I've been frantically trying to find a replacement all morning. Howard nixed the runner-ups. All of them. He said, 'If I didn't hire them the first time I saw them, why should I hire them now?' But isn't that the point of runner-ups? Anyway, he said to find someone new. So I've been searching for a lawyer or an investment banker, someone sexy yet serious, but no one wants to take a sabbatical from work, and even if someone could, her management probably won't allow her to moonlight in case the show's material reflects negatively on the firm. But we need someone capable. And then *you* called. Didn't you always want to be on television? Be like Barbara Walters?"

How did she remember that? "I don't know—"

"Do you believe in fate? I believe in fate. I called Howard, after remembering that he already met you. I told him you were a career woman, moving to the city and wouldn't you be perfect and do you know what he said? Bring her in for a screen test."

"Really? Me?" Well, I never. He must have been impressed with my life-saving show at the restaurant. "He saw me do the Heimlich and thinks my life-saving skills will make me a good character?"

"Um...no. He left before that happened. He decided he didn't like their table and they went to Nobu instead. But he thought you were cute."

I'm oddly flattered. I catch my smiling reflection in the computer screen and attempt to make my smile TV appropriate. Am I showing too much teeth? How much teeth is too much teeth?

"Are you in?"

"I...um..." This is a bit psychotic. How can I be on TV? Who am I? Everyone has his or her own show, and who are they? But on *Party Girls?* The bubble gum of television?

Why not? It's a job in New York. "I do need a job. I could certainly use the money."

"Exactly. Although, I should tell you the show doesn't pay much. But—"

"What's the salary?" Isn't that the whole point in being a star? That you get to be rich?

"There's no salary *per se.* But there is a stipend of a thousand dollars. And there are a million perks. You'll get a complete makeover. We'll fix up that hair and the uneven skin. And we'll definitely do something about those eyebrows."

Those eyebrows?

"Plus," Carrie continues, "because *Party Girls* is on TRS and TRS is owned by Metro United, you get tons of free stuff from everything Metro United owns. Including a thousand dollars a month clothing allowance at Stark's, so twenty-five hundred in total for two and a half months. Isn't that amazing? It's amazing. And you'll get fifty percent off any additional Stark's purchases. They have everything there, Sunny. Everything. You can get a new couch. A sheepskin coat. Prada shoes. And since they pick up shipments around the country, I'm sure we can find a way for them to deliver your Florida furniture to your new Manhattan apartment. And Metro United, MU, also owns Gourmet Market. You haven't tasted smoked turkey until you've bought some from their deli. You get a four-hundred-dollar expense account per month at any of their locations. And a free membership to Hardbody gym. There's like one on every corner. They have spinning rooms, boxing rings and Pilates studios. They even have fantastic pools. Incredible, I know. Oh, and Metro United also owns Rooster Cosmetics. They make those fantastic facial-cleaning strips. And Purity tampons. You'll get free Purity tampons. As many as you need. Sanitary products get expensive."

My pubic region clenches at the very mention of a Purity tampon.

Free move? Clothing allowance? I could use that winter jacket. And Steve's place could certainly use some new furniture. A lot of new furniture. A nice comfy bed, some lamps, blankets, candles…and a thousand dollars would pay for at least the first month of my rent…

What's wrong with my eyebrows?

"It's only ten weeks," she continues. "Ten weeks. That's it. Two and a half months of your time. And it only films once a week."

That's great. All that for only one night a week? I'll have tons of time for a real job. "So I'm free the rest of the time?"

"Exactly. But Howard would prefer that his girls concentrate on the show and not work anywhere else. You'll need to be free for press purposes. But you can certainly set up a job for after the show."

No work? "But how will I pay my share of the rent?"

"Sunny, honey, big picture, big picture. *Party Girls* will make you high profile. You'll meet everyone in the city. In ten weeks, companies will be begging you to work for them because of your contacts. You'll know everyone in the bar and television industry. I couldn't come up with a better career move for you if I tried. I'm kind of in human resources, remember? I know these things. You can put the stipend toward one month of rent. So you don't pay December rent. You'll cover food. And furniture. Can't you borrow money from your dad?"

I don't borrow money from my dad. My mom had to beg my father for alimony. He made her defend every purchase she made for us for two years. My sister owes my father about thirty thousand dollars, and hates him and herself for it.

I don't ever want to depend on anyone else for money. For anything.

But this is only ten weeks. I can depend on Steve for ten weeks, can't I?

"Your father thinks it's a terrific idea," she says.

"He does?" Why do I have a feeling my father couldn't care one way or the other?

"Of course. Why not? He called it an incredible introduction to the city. And he's happy we'll get the chance to know each other all over again. Sunny, it'll be a blast. What's not to like? And I'll be there with you every step of the way. Howard hired me full-time to help with the girls."

She's absolutely right. Why not? "Okay," I say, suddenly giddy. "Let me just call Steve and make sure it's okay with him. He will be covering my rent."

"Really? Awesome. Okay, I'm sorry to rush you, but I have to know now. I'll call you back in five. Okay? You'd really be saving my ass." She hangs up the phone.

I call Steve at the restaurant.

"Hi, it's me. Carrie offered me a job on a reality TV show in New York. It only pays a thousand dollars, but I'll make amazing contacts. All I'd have to do is go to a bar once a week for a few hours and they'll give us free food and free furniture and they'll pay for my move. And it's only ten weeks. But I have to tell them in five minutes. I'd be crazy not to, right?"

I hear the clatter of clanking pots in the background. He must be in the kitchen. "They're going to give you free stuff just to be on television?"

"Yeah."

"Cool."

"But, Steve, I'll need you to cover December's rent."

"I told you I could cover a few months."

"You're sure? You think I should do it?"

"Why not? Sounds like a blast."

I pick up the ringing phone.

"And?" Carrie says.

"Why not." Why not? It's just one night a week for ten weeks. Not that a big a deal. Does anyone even watch TRS? It'll be something funny to show my grandkids one day.

"Great. Great! Filming starts in eight days. Next Saturday."

"Perfect. My last day of work is on Friday." See, I am the goddess of timing.

"We'll need you here a bit earlier than that," she says. "To ensure you'll be screen compatible. To buy you the right hair, clothes, publicity."

Buy hair? Buy publicity? "When do you need me?"

She takes a deep breath. "Tomorrow morning at nine."

Yikes.

I shake my head. "Tomorrow morning at nine?"

"It'll be fab. TRS will pay for your flight out tonight. Let me e-mail the travel agent. There's a seven-fifteen flight with American Airlines. Perfect. Pick up your ticket at Fort Lauderdale airport. Go to sleep as soon as you arrive tonight so you won't have bags under your eyes in the morning. I'll send a car to pick you up at 8:00 a.m. Wear something sexy and sophisticated. I'll brief you in the car."

I scan the many multicolored files on my desk and around my office. It's like a paper rainbow in here. I was supposed to sort through them before I left to make sure everything is in order. And what about my e-mails? And my personal documents? "All right," I say, and begin sifting. I'll do what I can. The poor, poor MBA. "Do you know where Steve's place is?"

"Who's Steve?"

"My boyfriend, remember? He runs the restaurant? The reason I'm moving to New York?"

"Oh shit. Right. Steve. That's where we dropped you off the other night after that woman choked, right? Listen, Sunny, I wouldn't mention anything about Steve to the TRS people. You're a wild, sexy, single girl, okay?"

"But—"

"There's not much public interest in boring-pass-the-remote relationship types."

Boring? I can barely keep up. "But when will I pack up my apartment? I have to be out by the fourteenth."

"Don't worry, everything will work out. All settled? See you tomorrow." She hangs up.

I definitely need to take my phone contacts with me. Will anyone notice if I plunk the entire Rolodex in my purse? I write my new number and e-mail address on my pad of paper along with a note for the MBA: "I'm so sorry I didn't get to train you. If you have any questions or concerns, please call me anytime. Good luck! Sunny."

Liza throws open the door. "You know I don't like when you keep your door closed for so long."

"I…I just got the most horrible phone call," I say, and try to appear misty-eyed and bewildered. "My grandmother…is sick again, very, very sick this time and I have to go to New York to take care of her." Good thing I don't believe in hell.

"That's terrible," she says, showing surprising compassion. "Is she going to die?"

What kind of question is that? You don't ask if someone's going to die. "She might," I say, casting my eyes downward.

"But you'll be back on Monday, right?"

"I don't know if I can, unfortunately. She's very sick."

"Can't someone else look after her?" Liza is beginning to look panicked. I hope she doesn't go into labor. "I *need* you here next week."

I widen my eyes, all innocent-girl like. "Well, since my mother is dead, there isn't really anyone else. And if she does die, how horrible would it be if she was all alone without anyone to comfort her?" Yikes.

Liza still looks miffed. "When are you leaving?"

"I have to go home and pack a bag and attempt to make the seven o'clock flight. It's all terribly sudden," I say. At least that part is true.

"So that's it? You're leaving? This is your last day?"

I need to be at the airport for 5:30, which means I need to leave for the airport at 4:45, which means I need to be home by 3:30, at the latest—no, make that 2:30—to get organized. I'll need to leave here at 2:00.

I look at my watch. "I'm going to have to say my goodbyes now, unfortunately."

Liza turns white. She better not go into labor. I don't have the time to take her to the hospital.

In the taxi on the way to the airport I call the *Miami Herald* to cancel my subscription ("Are you sure you don't want to transfer it?") and then quickly call my sister to tell her the news.

"Do you really want to be associated with the pimple on the ass of the history of media?" she asks.

"What?"

"Don't you think being on a reality TV show is horrendously cheesy?"

"Don't you think spending five hundred dollars on a new purse is horrendously cheesy?"

She ignores the dig. "What if you end up villainized like

Geri from *Survivor* or that Simon guy? You're not going to pose for *Playboy,* are you? And look at the Real World people now. They're always whining. I think they even had to start a twelve-step program or something."

"It's so not a big deal, Dana, it's just for a few weeks."

"How can you be part of something that encourages people to aspire to the lowest common denominator? That promotes 20-somethings as asinine, shallow and incompetent? That's so not *you.*"

Asinine? Shallow? Incompetent? "The shows aren't that bad," I say, apprehension fermenting in my stomach like bad yogurt.

"Have you ever even watched one?"

"Of course." Once or twice. I haven't watched a lot of TV since I moved out of my father's house.

"What about your privacy?"

"I'm only taped on Saturday nights. I can make nice to the cameras for five hours a week. It's a job. And there are so many of these shows, the characters are swapped faster than coffee filters. No one will remember my name two weeks after the show."

"You don't know what you're getting into."

"Dana, you're making a big deal out of nothing. I'll meet people. I'll make a life for myself in New York and not have to rely on Steve for a social life. I'll get a ton of free stuff. I'll make contacts. I thought you'd see this as a good thing."

"Don't complain to me when you become a public mockery and they're doing skits about you on *Saturday Night Live.*"

"Thanks for the support." I turn my phone off.

Is she right? Is this actually a big deal?

Oh. Right. She's jealous. Of course she's jealous. She's been trying to make her mark in television for the past five years. And I get this offered to me on a silver platter. She would kill for an opportunity like this, and I'm not even taking it seriously. Maybe I should call her back and apologize.

Forget it. She didn't have to be so rude.

We get stuck in traffic, of course we do, and the driver attempts to engage me in a discussion about a new sales tax, but I'm too worried about missing my flight and therefore my new job, to partake in conversation. I grumble and close my eyes.

Finally I'm fastened in my middle seat on the plane—you'd think they could have sprung for business class—and there's no room overhead for my carry-on so I have to cram my suitcase under my feet.

Not the best start to my new adventure.

When I get to LaGuardia Airport, I wait thirty minutes for a taxi and then fall asleep on the drive to the apartment. Finally, finally, I'm here! Here I am! I'm going to see my Stevie, I think smiling. The doorman doesn't remember me, of course not, so I have to remind him who I am, and once he nods, I drag my bags into the elevator, and then to Steve's door.

He doesn't know I'm coming. In the past year I've never surprised him with a visit. What better opportunity than this to be spontaneous? At least he finally had the right key made for me last weekend, if he's not home.

As I unlock the door I have a terrible thought: What if he is home, but he's with another woman? What if they're having sex on the couch, clothes dripping all over the floor? I just left my job for him, bastard. What would I do? His loss, I decide. I'm going to be on TV. I'm going to be a TV star. I'm staying in New York. I'm taking this job even if he is a cheating bastard and I have to stay with my father until I can find my own place. Maybe I should have knocked so they have a chance to get dressed. But then I won't be able to catch them in the act, and they could always deny it. Say she's a friend or a waitress from the restaurant or something.

I swiftly push open the door and storm into the living room.

Sprawled on the couch is Steve, alone, his right hand resting down his jogging pants, like it always is when he forgets I'm there. The TV is blaring (why does he need it so loud?) and a bowl of popcorn is overflowing onto the coffee table.

"I was wondering where you were," he says. He smiles and

I love him and he removes his hand from his pants and bear-hugs me.

"Surprise," I say, feeling foolish. I press him back toward the couch and recount the events of the day.

part 2

Party Girls!™

APPLICATION FORM
Please use pen
(YOU WILL BE DISQUALIFIED FOR USING PENCIL)
and mail (DO NOT, WE REPEAT, *DO NOT* E-MAIL).
ABSOLUTELY NO PHONE CALLS PLEASE.

NAME:_____

PROPOSED PSEUDONYM: _____
(For credibility purposes, we would appreciate if you did not use your pet's name, your middle name or the street you live on. You are not a porn star. Thanks.)

AGE: _____
(21 to 25 only please. We cannot have underage drinkers or biological clock watchers. Thanks.)

CELL PHONE: _____
(It is mandatory that you have one.)

To be considered for this show, please fill out the answers TRUTHFULLY, CANDIDLY and SERIOUSLY in an un-superfluous manner.

If you are chosen to be on *Party Girls!™* are there any persons you would prefer not be mentioned on camera? Examples: an ex-boyfriend who is itching for revenge or an ex-roommate whose boyfriend you slept with. Please share.

_____
_____
_____
_____
_____

Please tell us the biggest lie you ever told a boyfriend and got away with.

_____
_____
_____
_____
_____

Do you have one-night stands? If so, please write the name and phone number of your latest.

_____
_____

Please describe the six most traumatizing events of your childhood.

1 _____
2 _____
3 _____
4 _____
5 _____
6 _____

How old were you when you lost your virginity? Describe experience in one sentence.

_____

_____

Have you ever had a lesbian experience? Describe in one sentence.

_____

_____

A threesome? Describe in one sentence.

_____

_____

Please describe two additional episodes of sexual experimentation (no animals, please).

1 _____

_____

2 _____

_____

What is your breast size (pre- and post-surgeries, if applicable)? _____

Please answer True or False (T or F is fine).
I will be able to take a three-month hiatus from my job to film **Party Girls!™** ____

I am currently NOT married, engaged, living with a significant other or involved in a monogamous sexual relationship._____

If a stranger saw me on the street, he would consider me "hot." _____

Please complete the following sentences with the most appropriate answer (a/b/c).

My drink of choice is _____.
a) water
b) Cosmopolitan
c) beer

My favorite television show is _____.
a) *60 Minutes*
b) *Sex and the City*
c) *Beavis and Butt-head*

I buy my clothes in/through _____.
a) flea markets
b) boutiques
c) catalogs

Are you fat?
Please circle Yes or No.

Please sign and date the following TRANSFER OF RIGHTS.

By signing this application, you hereby consent to the use and reuse, ad infinitum, by the program **Party Girls!™** (hereby known as "The Show"), the network Television Radio Systems, the multinational Empire Consolidator and any of their licenses, assignees, subsidiaries, parents, affiliates, officers, neighbors and pets (hereby known as "The Conglomerate") of your voice, actions, likeness, name, biological information, application answers, footage from the sassy, sexy video, sexual perversions and any other information you used on this application (hereby known as "The You") for the production, promotion, marketing, advertisement of The Show in any and all possible media outlets regardless of whether or not you are chosen to appear on The Show. You agree that The Conglomerate can use The You and may modify or alter The You however The Conglomerate desires, including showing The You out of context and making you look like an asshole. You agree to never make a claim against The Conglomerate as a result of The Conglomerate using The You even if you become a national laughingstock and social leper.

You have signed the release on the _____ day of _____, 20 _____.

Signature _____

Name (please print or type) _____

Thank you for your TRUTHFUL, CANDID and SINCERE answers.
Please remember to mail with your sexy sassy videotape.
Do not forget to attach your 8" x 10" front and rear glossy photographs.
Good luck!

6

My So-Called Life

I have never been a morning person. While most of my friends were up watching *Spider-Man and His Amazing Friends* and other Saturday morning cartoons, I was fast asleep and cozy under the covers until at least eleven. At my dorm in college, whenever I didn't have a morning class and occasionally when I did, I was out cold until at least one.

My father predicted that once I started working and I had to wake up consistently at seven, my internal clock would readjust and I would spring Pop-Tart-like from bed on Saturday mornings before nine.

Wrong. When I'm alone, I still don't wake up naturally before one on weekends. Luckily Steve shares my nocturnal sleeping pattern. On Saturday afternoons, after I've brushed my teeth and climbed back into bed, I fall asleep again and Steve and I slowly blink open our eyes around one. Sometimes I'll wake him with a special morning surprise, and other times

I'll wake up with his morning friend unintentionally stabbing me in the thigh. Then we'll roll on top of each other and later we'll flip on the television and watch the news. By the time we've showered and dressed it's after three. Our biggest annoyance is finding a restaurant that still serves brunch.

When the alarm starts screaming at seven on Saturday morning, about four minutes after I finally managed to doze off, I furiously hit the snooze button. I spent all night trying to fall asleep. At first I was nervous about what I would wear, what I would say, how I would smile, and then I looked at the clock and began freaking out. I know what I look like after a night of no sleep, and this caused me even more stress, preventing me from falling back into la-la land. Then I began the ritual of glancing at the clock every few seconds, then I tried to force myself not to look at the clock every few seconds, then I tried not to think about looking at the clock every few seconds, and then, hallelujah, I must have finally fallen asleep, because the alarm was suddenly screaming.

Great. I've had seven minutes of sleep. Seven minutes in heaven? Isn't that the name of that kissing game we used to play when we were kids?

I'm going to look like hell.

I drag myself out of bed, shower, pat my hair dry, put on some lipstick to even out my lips, and then squeeze into my black pants and black shirt. Sexy. Black. With my black shoes, I think I look like quite the sophisticate. I know they're running shoes, but they're my black Diesel running shoes. Carrie will like the label, right?

There is a stain on my black pants. You'd think that was impossible. How can a stain be visible on black pants? Nonetheless a mutated patch of black blares from my knee. I run to the kitchen and start scrubbing with a paper towel and dish soap. I took only one pair of pants with me to New York. My wardrobe consists of jeans, tops and two suits.

I think it worked. The stain appears to have disappeared. I wish I owned a blow-dryer. Will they fit in the microwave?

Steve opens the bedroom door and joins me in the kitchen.

I must look ridiculous. I'm wearing a shirt, socks and a thong, and my pants are in the microwave. "'Morning," I say and smile.

He gives me his best what-you-talking-about-Willis look. "Sexy," he says.

"Just getting ready," I say.

He kisses me on the cheek. "Good luck," he says and heads back to bed.

Ten minutes later I'm in the back seat of a black sedan beside a clipboard and coffee-bearing Carrie. I can't see the driver's face, only the back of a bald head.

"You can't wear that," she says, shaking her head.

"Why?"

"You can't wear all black on camera unless you're tanned, thin and blond. You'll look washed-out and puffy." She reaches into a leather bag and pulls out a blue V-neck. "Wear this. It's Marc Jacobs."

Who? Does she expect me to change in the car? She expects me to change in the car.

"Are you wearing sneakers?"

I look down at my feet. "No."

"Take them off."

"They're my only black shoes."

Carrie sighs. She pulls a pair of stiletto black pointy-toe boots out of her bag. "Here."

I kick off my shoes and put on her boots. Ouch. My toes are squished. "These are too small. What size are they, five? I'm a seven."

"So am I. Didn't you ever hear the expression, 'You have to suffer to be beautiful'?" She pulls out her makeup bag. "Why don't you wear foundation?"

"Why do you wear it?"

She applies the beige liquid to my face. Then she covers me

with powder, then eyeliner, then three shades of eye shadow, then blush, then another coat of mascara. "Better," she says, analyzing my face with more scrutiny than the school nurse sifting through a first grader's hair for lice. "I'll put your lipstick on after you have your coffee. Remember this. Listening?"

I nod and sip. I hold the coffee cup carefully over the middle hump. There is no time for additional spillage.

"If they give you water, do not drink it unless your mouth is absolute sandpaper. If you do, you will have to go to the bathroom and you will look fidgety on camera. Maintain eye contact with the host, or with that magic spot right above the camera lens. Do not look at the ceiling and do not look at the floor. Pretend the camera is a new man who you are desperately trying to get to fall in love with you. Do not blink excessively. Keep your posture. Don't slouch. Imagine a hanger holding up your shoulders. Do whatever it takes to make yourself look animated. Facial expressions, hand gestures. If you do not animate yourself, you are not going to look interesting on television. You want to look in control, though, so remember, no fidgeting. No scratching, no twirling your hair, no twisting your rings around your fingers or earrings—" She sits up abruptly and gawks at my ears. "Why aren't you wearing earrings?"

"I don't have any."

"You don't have pierced ears?"

"I do, I just don't wear jewelry."

"Why do you have pierced ears, then? You need to wear earrings. The holes are going to close up if you don't." Her hands fly to her earlobes and she removes dangling silver drops from her own ears. "Put these on."

Nasty. I'm feeling way too close to my father's liquids right now. I put them on. My fingers smell like ear.

"Voice. Modulate. Don't sound like an Arthur character, don't sound like the professor on Ferris Bueller. Mo-du-late," she articulates, flashing her hands for emphasis. "And don't sound like you're full of shit. You can lie if you want but sound sincere. Don't mumble. Don't swallow the ends of your sentence. Don't be too loud. Don't speak too softly either. E-nun-ci-ate. Let me hear you enunciate."

"E-nun-ci-ate." I say. In camp, Carrie was a color war captain. She forced us to sing a song about the merits of the yellow team, which she had written to the tune of Chicago's "You're the Inspiration."

"Don't let your mind wander," she concludes.

"Got it. Go team."

Carrie madly flips through the pages on her clipboard. "Are you taking this seriously? You have to take this seriously. It's going to be a serious interview."

How serious can this be? It's a TV show about bars. I doubt there's an IQ prerequisite. "They're not going to ask me my opinions on global warfare."

Carrie looks me in the eye, apparently staggered at my naivety. "Do you have any idea how many women want to be in your shoes?"

Instinctively, I glance down at my newly squashed toes.

"Do you?" she presses on. "Thousands. I waded through hundreds of resumes myself. You are lucky, darling, lucky." She casts her head downward and sighs loudly, obviously saddened by my lack of reverence. "If you don't respect the genre, it's not going to respect you."

I'm not even sure that means anything. This whole job is a joke. If they like me, they like me, if they don't, who cares?

"They're going to ask you a lot of questions. They'll ask about your relationships, tidbits about your childhood, tiffs with your sister and your roommates—"

"I've never had a roommate."

"They'll want to know what you do for fun, how crazy of a party girl you are, if you drink too much. They'll try to ferret out, very subtly, if you have any prejudices."

"So I shouldn't tell them about all my bisexual experiences?"

She points a manicured finger at me. "No, definitely tell them those."

Um…I was kidding?

By the time we pull up in front of the TRS building, I feel as if I'm perched on the top of a ski hill, ready to go. Equipment—check. Attitude—check. Skills—check. I can do this. I've always been a comfortable public speaker; I won the annual public speaking contest in high school with my magic formula:

1. Pick one serious issue (divorce, abortion, suicide, anorexia).
2. Begin with confessional-style story. (When Marsha was thirteen her father told her he wouldn't be living at the house anymore.)
3. Throw in statistics. (One in every two couples gets divorced.)
4. Add lighthearted jokes. (Marsha gets twice as many Christmas presents.)
5. Boomerang the speech back to the confessional-like story. (Marsha realized that her parents would lead happier, more fulfilled lives apart.)
6. Add a reconciliatory ending. (Marsha's family wasn't broken. It was just different.)

Voila! First place.

Inside the steel elevator Carrie pinches my cheeks. "You need more color. But you look great."

You know that ski hill I mentioned? When I was ten, my father brought us to Vale and I broke my leg when I met up with a tree.

With each ascending floor my breathing becomes faster and shallower. I can do this. They want me. They asked for me. I certainly didn't ask for them.

The elevator door opens into a plush white room. White walls, white couch, white furry carpet. I feel as if I'm in a cream cheese commercial. Pictures of their Emmy-award-winning TV shows, including *NYChase,* and *American Sunrise* line the walls.

I follow Carrie to the reception desk. "Sunny Lang and I are here for her *Party Girls* interview."

Lang?

The receptionist nods toward the couch. "Victoria's interview is running a bit late. Do you have her application pack?"

Victoria? Who is Victoria? Why do I have to wait for Victoria? Someone else is interviewing for the role? Who is this "Victoria"? I imagine her with red-cropped hair and a collared shirt, realizing that she is after my part. My part. Does she think she can out-Miranda me?

This will not do. This is my job, and no whiny little suck-up is going to steal it. I try to catch Carrie's gaze.

Carrie doesn't look up. Instead, she reaches to the back of her clipboard and pulls out a stack of files. "Sunny will bring her application in with her," she says, and motions her chin toward the couch. "Let's wait over there."

Did she know other women were after my role? I sit down beside her. "How many people are auditioning?" I ask through a clenched jaw.

"I sent one yesterday," she whispers back. "And other associates in my firm sent two this morning."

I go into cardiac arrest. I'm competing for this job. I have slashed all ties with Panda for a measly *audition*. I am a wanna-be. Is Dana right? There could be dozens, hundreds even, of sexy, serious women lurking around this building, preparing to be asked about their siblings and non-homophobic tendencies, hoping for their big break in cheese-town, and I am just as pathetic as they are.

Carrie hands me a stack of papers and a pen. "Sign the last page."

I'm certainly not signing something I haven't even read. I flip through the pages. "What is this?"

"Your application, your references, your background check, proof that you were never arrested, names of family members, interesting things about you…"

A hundred pages, all about me. "Where did you get this stuff?"

"Some from your dad. And you'd be surprised what's available on the Net," she says. "Don't worry," she adds in a whisper. "No one cares about the background check. As your agent I'm the one responsible for making sure you're clear. Once I approve you, you're golden. I got your dad and Marcus to write two of your references."

Marcus? The owner of Abina, my childhood sleep-away camp? "How did you get in touch with Marcus? And who are these other people?"

"I called him, and made up the others. No worries." She pats my knee.

No worries. I need some Pepto-Bismol. "Anything I should know about myself before I go in?"

"Just be yourself. Your sexy, wild, single self. You're articulate, you're ambitious, you're soulful, you don't take shit from men, you practically raised yourself. I played up the dead mother thing. They loved that—every show needs a sob story. You'll be wonderful, trust me. They'll want you. I know what they need. I endorsed you over the girls I sent yesterday."

The girls? As in plural? What happened to "I sent *one* yesterday"?

Twenty minutes later Victoria prances from the closed doors in a tight Chanel suit, high heels and cropped blond hair. I give her the evil eye. The receptionist lifts her head. "Ms. Lang?"

Carrie pokes me. "That's your pseudonym. Langstein was too ethnic."

"Everyone in New York is ethnic."

"Trust me."

"I sound like a stripper."

"Good luck," she says. "Remember, show them soul. And no drinking."

I'm ushered down a stark, low-ceilinged white hallway, into a square, white-walled room. A man is half hidden by a large studio camera. Two other men and a woman are sitting on one side of a boardroom table. I recognize Howard. The door slams shut behind me. I feel as if I'm in the final scene in *Flashdance* when Jennifer Beals arrives at the academy in leg warmers and comes face-to-face with judges in suits.

She got them clapping and singing, didn't she?

"Hi!" I say. My heels click-clack as I walk across the room. These things could take out someone's balls with one swift kick. I place my application on the table.

Silence.

"Hello," the man who is not Howard finally says. He rubs what remains of his gray hair and scans my application.

A polar bear-shaped man steers a large camera in my direction. The red light is on. I blink at the blazing flash and look away.

The gray-haired man moves his chair, and the squeak echoes through the room. He points to a pitcher of water in the center of the table. "Would you like something to drink?"

No water, no water. "No thank you," I say.

I assume I am supposed to sit in the one empty chair facing the judges. As I sit, the camera follows me downward. Am I supposed to look into the camera or at the men? What were Carrie's instructions again?

The room is quieter than a funeral. Howard is directly across from me, wearing a funky silver shirt, too far unbuttoned, revealing ghastly white skin and coarse black chest hair. The older, gray gentleman is sitting to his right, in front of the cameraman. A woman who looks like an older version of Kelly Osborne, same body size, same first season red-orange hair, same Cindy Lauper clothing, is grimacing on Howard's left. Why the long face? She doesn't like what she's doing? She should try switching places with me. I like her hair. I like her outfit. I look down at my own Marc Jacobs cleavage-enhancing shirt.

Does she think I like this outfit?

Howard smiles and starts rubbing his hands together. "Nice to see you again, Sunny."

"Nice to see you, too."

"I hear I missed quite a spectacle at Eden's the other night." He turns to the older Kelly. "A woman was choking and little Sunny here saved her life with the Heimlich."

The Kelly's scowl melts from her face and she appears almost interested. "Really? How'd you know what to do?"

"I was a lifeguard."

The Kelly nods. "I'm Tania, the show's story producer. I work with Howard to create character development and story arcs. That's Pete," she points to the cameraman. "You already met Howard, and beside him is Stan. He's VP of programming at TRS. Story editors, sound editors, production assistants and interns will also be working on the show, but you don't have to worry about them. Ready to start, sexy, wild, skinny thing? Let's go."

Sexy, wild, skinny thing? Are those the adjectives I want to be known as? Maybe I should tell them, sorry, pick Victoria, then bend into a four-legged crawling position and slither out the door and back out through the hallway.

Unless I want this. Do I want this? Am I no better than the *Girls Gone Wild* girls who flash their breasts so they can get a free T-shirt?

I need a job in New York. This is a job in New York.

I am so full of it.

I stop and breathe and smile. Why don't I get the job first and analyze it to death afterward?

Stan pours himself a glass of water. My mouth feels like the Sahara Desert.

They'll start with easy questions, right? Name? Sunny Langstein. I mean, Lang. Birthplace? Florida. Siblings? One. Parents? Dead mother. No problem.

"Tell us, Sunny," Tania says, reading a question off a paper in front of her. "About the most unusual way you've ever met a guy?"

Sunny Lang, I'm about to answer. No. That is not the right question.

I have a flashback to a business school case. The professor was prepping us for interviews with consulting firms. "How many gallons of ice cream are sold in the U.S. each year?" he asked.

At first the entire class panicked and screamed out politer versions of "How the Fuck Are We Supposed to Know?" The professor's answer was that we weren't expected to come up with the right answer—firms were more interested in seeing how we think.

You can assume that eighty percent of Americans eat ice cream. And there are about three hundred million people in the United States. That makes three hundred million consumers. But then are ice cream sales seasonal? Gender specific? Do southern states sell more ice cream than northern ones? Do—

"Sunny? Interesting way of meeting a guy?" Howard twirls a pen like a baton between his fingers.

I realize with horror that I have been twirling my hair. Automatically my hands drop into my lap. How come he gets to twirl and I don't?

They don't care about my answer, I remind myself. They care about my personality.

"I was rappelling in a South American rain forest. Suddenly, the rope that attached me to safety became unhitched from the treetop and I plummeted to the ground. Thank God, the man rappelling just beneath me held open his arms and caught me. When I looked into his wide green eyes, I knew that this man and I would have an exciting future. We dated for two years."

Tania looks up, amazed. "That really happened?"

I snort. "I wish. No, of course not." I am the sexy, obnoxious cynic. "No one meets someone like that in real life, unless your name is Jane and you're stranded in a jungle. I met my previous boyfriend at a café. I've met all my boyfriends at cafés. If I wasn't a caffeine addict I'd never get laid."

Tania spits out the water in her mouth and laughs. I am the wild, sexy, witty, obnoxious cynic.

"How old were you when you lost your virginity?" Howard asks.

"Which time?" This emits another chuckle and I say, "I was seventeen. I got drunk and seduced my best friend's younger brother. No morning-after regrets. Until I saw the pictures on the Internet, of course."

"You're kidding, right?" Stan says. More laughs.

"No." I keep a straight face. "Yes. I don't think anyone knew how to use the Internet for humiliation purposes back then."

"What was the worst thing you ever did that you hid from your parents?" Tania asks.

"My mom died when I was six. When I was sixteen my dad moved back to New York and I lived in the house by myself. His only rules were no drugs or alcohol. There were stories all over the paper about parents suing other parents when their children died of alcohol poisoning at a guardianless house party. My father was terrified of getting sued. I had wild parties at my house every weekend. Lots of booze—"

All four of them lean toward me, wanting to know what I'm going to say next. They like me. They like me!

"—and everyone slept over. One Sunday morning I counted twelve crashers all over the house. Four on the living room couch, three in my sister Dana's room, one in the bathroom—he passed out after drinking too much beer—and four in my room, including me, crammed in my single bed, two on each side, our legs and sheets tangled. No massive orgy or anything, we just stayed up, laughing. A week later, about ten minutes before my dad arrived for his monthly visit, I had an urge to check the DustBuster that was in his bedroom. It was one of those clear, see-all-the-dirt-inside ones, and when I picked it up, I realized that there was a hunk of hash in it. I don't remember vacuuming it up, I don't know why I suddenly had the urge to check it, I don't even smoke hash, but there it was. I never got caught."

Stan shakes his head, worried. "You lived on your own since you were sixteen?"

"Yes." I wave away his concern. "It wasn't as lonely as it sounds. I like my space."

Howard scans over my application. "I see you have a business degree. Why was school so important to you?"

"Because I want to be successful. I've always had a job."

"What kind of jobs did you do?"

"I lifeguarded in the summer. During high school I wait-ressed on weekends and after school. At college I worked at the student services center. I worked behind the counter the first year and then managed it for the next three."

"But why did you need to work? Your father couldn't sup-port you?"

"I like my independence."

"Why are you moving to New York?" Tania asks.

I hesitate and then answer, "Fresh start. I ended a relation-ship and I need a change. Rumor has it this is the city where anything is possible." This is the truth. I ended a relationship. I ended many relationships before Steve. And it's true I need a change, or I wouldn't be here, right?

Tania looks down at her notes. "What was your best life experience?"

I guess saying that it was Steve asking me to move in with him would be counterproductive. I need something that spells excitement, spells adventurous, spells single... "Backpacking through Europe. I went with my best friend and we had the time of our lives."

"What did you do?"

"What didn't we do? We lived in London, swam naked in Nice, flirted in Florence." I am the goddess of alliteration. "Drank ouzo in Corfuzo."

Okay, so I'm no poet, but they laugh anyway. I have them in the palm of my hand.

"What was your worst life experience?" Howard asks and then sighs. "Your mom dying?"

No, slimeball, it was when *My So-Called Life* got canceled.

"Of course," I say, and drop my voice a few notches for ef-fect. "I was young, only six. I didn't understand what was going on."

My audience leans closer.

"Can you tell us about it?" Tania asks.

I don't even need leg warmers to pull this off. "My mother spent so much time at the hospital that my grandparents had to come stay with us. My parents were already divorced at this point."

Tania puts her hand to her lips. It's all about the Double D.

"My sister and I used to crawl under the covers with my mom at the hospital, and we'd tickle her back. She loved having her back tickled. We used to spell out words and see if she could guess them."

"Was it cancer?" Stan asks, clenching his coffee mug in his hand, but not taking a drink.

I nod. "Ovarian."

"My wife's girlfriend had that," Howard says, and shakes his head. "It was terribly sad."

"Did you know she was going to die?" Tania asks.

At first I think that Tania is addressing Howard, but then I remember that I'm the one being interviewed. I'm the one whose life is being laid out like a documentary. Opening up to strangers like this is a bit weird. It's like kissing someone you just met.

"No," I say slowly. "My father took me house shopping and kept asking me if I liked this, if I liked that, for my new room. I told him I already had a room at my mother's house, so why do I need another one?"

Tania's sob sounds like an elongated hiccup.

I'm a hit, all right. Lose my virginity or lose my mother— it doesn't matter, does it? It's all the same to them. They don't want *me,* they want a soap opera star. Fine. I can do sob story.

"My mom's condition was worsening," I continue. "And my father decided it wasn't appropriate for my sister and me to watch her die. So in June he shipped us off to the sleep-away camp in the Adirondacks he'd gone to as a kid, Camp Abina. I was six. The youngest kid in the Junior section, the youngest kid in the whole camp. I got a ton of attention, and I was asked to be the newcomball team's mascot."

Tania and Stan look perplexed, and in less than two seconds I come to my second grand realization: only Jewish girls at North American summer camps play newcomball.

"Newcomball is like volleyball, except you catch the ball and then throw it over the net. Anyway, the fourteen-and-over team, The Abina Bears, asked me to be their mascot when they played against Camp Walden. Obviously I was the envy of all the other Junior girls. The girls on the team had made me a little bear costume with furry ears and a tail. All I had to do was a little dance whenever the team scored a point."

Their eyes are glossing over, I'm losing them, I can't lose them. Time for the kill. "The morning of the game—I hadn't slept the entire night, I was so excited—the camp owner came over to our bunk's table in the dining hall and whispered something to my counselor and then she asked me if I could come outside. My sister was waiting for me on the balcony. She told me that my mom was really sick and that she wanted to say goodbye. And that our father was coming to get us. We went back to our cabins to pack up some of our stuff. Dana was crying and then I started crying, a little bit because Dana was crying—I hate when she cries—but mostly because I'd been waiting for the big game, the day when I got to be the star, and who would wear my costume?"

Suddenly I can't stop myself. I want to tell them everything. These people care. These people love me and I love them.

"My father drove into camp, right up to our bunks in a rental truck. This was vaguely exciting since only the head staff was allowed cars in camp, and all the kids ran to their porches to see what was going on. We drove to the airport in complete silence and then the three of us flew home, and when the stewardess asked my dad if he wanted pretzels or raisin cookies, tears started streaming down his cheeks and he tried to cover them because he didn't want us to see. We got to the hospital and my mom's parents and her older brother were all there. She looked horrifically frightening, white and bloated. We held her hands and then she said goodbye. My dad took us out of the room and then she died. My sister and I sat shiva. That's Jewish mourning. You have to sit on these horribly uncomfortable chairs for a week. We sat at my father's new house. Over the summer all my things had been moved into my new room, at my father's new house. After the seven days were up, my father decided to send my sister and I back to camp. My sister didn't want to go. She didn't want to do anything but lie face-down on her relocated bed. My father put me in charge of convincing her that I needed her to come with me.

"Everyone was really nice to us when we went back. I had a few sleeping problems. In the middle of the night, I would put my sneakers back on and sneak across the baseball field to Dana's cabin and climb up to her top bunk, into her sleeping bag. At first my counselor told me I wasn't allowed, but I kept doing it, anyway. Then she told me she didn't want me wandering across the camp at night by myself, so she promised that every night, if I wasn't asleep by the time she got back to the cabin—counselors' curfew was at one-thirty—she would walk me over. Every night I was still awake. She would walk me over, and even if my sister was already asleep, I would climb into bed beside her."

I stopped talking. How's that for soul?

No one moves. Tania's cheeks are stained with tears.

Now can I have a glass of water?

7

Friends

Thirty minutes later I walk out of the room in a mild state of euphoria.

I think I'm a natural.

"How'd it go?" Carrie says, jumping off the couch.

"I'll tell you about it outside." She deserves to be kept waiting as punishment for not telling me about my competition.

When we reach the concrete stairs outside the TRS building, I decide to put her out of her misery. "It went great," I say, and do the little hooray jump I usually reserve for when I'm alone. The hooray jump is not as easy to do in stilettos. "I think they liked me."

Carrie does a jump, too. "They did? I knew they would. What did they ask? What did you say? Tell me everything."

"Can we get something to eat? I'm starving." Stardom has made me hungry.

We go to Salad Time, a restaurant down the street. We're the only ones in line. It's too early for the lunch crowd.

"I want to hear every detail," Carrie says. "Romaine lettuce, Asian chicken, mandarin oranges, a few Chinese noodles, carrots and a dash of low-fat sesame dressing, please."

"That sounds good," I say to the woman in the hairnet across the counter. "But I'll have a Caesar salad instead." She mixes the ingredients in a metal bowl and switches the concoction into a plastic container. "They asked me a million questions. Worst experience. Best experience. How old I was when I lost my virginity."

Carrie opens the refrigerator and takes out a purple Vitamin water. Those drinks are everywhere in this city. I wish I had come up with the idea. "How old did you tell them?"

"Seventeen."

"You were seventeen when you lost your virginity?"

"No, I was eighteen. But I lost it to my best guy friend on prom night so I had to come up with something a little less clichéd." The woman across the counter hands me my salad. I take a Coke from the fridge and we carry our trays to the cash register.

"I was fifteen," Carrie says, pulling out her wallet. "Both," she tells the cashier.

"You don't have to pay for mine," I say. "What? Fifteen? That's young. Thank you."

Salad Time's round, barlike tables are mostly empty. We pick one by the window and put down our trays. "Not that young," she says.

I take the top off my salad and dig my fork in. "You don't even have pubic hair at fifteen."

"I had everything at fifteen."

Yum. I love Caesar salads. "I remember. Every day you'd ask us to tie up the strings to your porn-star bikini tops."

"Great role model, huh? You should have seen what I was doing after daylight. Or who I was doing."

"Did you lose your virginity at camp?" I lost a sweatshirt and a couple pairs of socks there, but that's it.

"On the beach in the sailboat shack."

"But that place had nails sprinkled all over the floor. You could have picked up tetanus."

"I could have picked up gonorrhea. Not an experience I want to relive."

I don't want to know from my dad's girlfriend and gonorrhea, but I can't help myself, and I ask, "Who was it?"

She smirks. "You don't remember the story?"

"No, should I?"

"There was a whole scene about it in *Staff Laugh.*"

Every summer two male counselors wrote *Staff Laugh,* a play that makes fun of and often makes cry as many counselors as possible. Usually the female counselors. The oldest campers in camp perform it for the entire staff. "I don't remember," I say.

"It was Mark Ryman. We were in the sailboat shack and he asked me to masturbate for him. And then we had sex. And then he told the whole camp."

Mark Ryman was three years older than Carrie. He would have been eighteen. I had just been thinking about him recently. Why was I thinking of him? Oh, yeah. "Howard reminds me of him."

Carrie spears a slice of mandarin with her fork, lifts it and then puts it back down. "I was in love with him. Thought he was so hot. That gorgeous, thick hair and that yummy body. You really don't remember the play? They had one of the fourteen-year-old girls play me. She stuffed her bikini top with melons, and randomly appeared on the stage with her hands down her pants pretending to masturbate."

If that had been me, I would have anchored a brick to my leg and jumped in the lake. "But you were only a CIT at fifteen. I thought CITs weren't allowed to be made fun of in *Staff Laugh.*"

"A special exception for me, I suppose." Carrie shrugs, brushing off the memory. "So now we wait. With our fingers crossed."

"But that's it? One interview?"

"Not everyone only had one interview. The other three girls

filled out a written application, sent in a demo tape, had two interviews and a thorough character evaluation," she says.

"Thorough enough that they missed at least one penchant for shoplifting." I take another bite of my salad and then put the lid back on. I'll save the rest for dinner. Steve will probably eat at the restaurant, and I'm too tired to even think of joining him there.

"I hope you get this. Did I tell you Howard hired me as a consultant for the show? He wants me to help the girls find the right look and hang around at the tapings, making sure everything runs smoothly. Won't your father be thrilled that we'll be able to get to know each other all over again?"

Thrilled. Especially once he's over you and on to the next girl. I nod and try to change the subject. "I wonder what happened to Mark Ryman."

"He got married. Lives in Connecticut. Cheats on his wife."

"Men don't change."

"Sometimes they do." Carrie stands up and puts on a pair of Jackie O sunglasses. "He went bald and gained a hundred pounds."

When I get home I have to go to the bathroom. Badly. And I mean number two. As I unlock the door I'm praying Steve is still sleeping.

Nope. He's picking up a long-sleeved shirt from the floor. He pulls it over his head. "So how'd it go?"

Why can't he hang up his shirt? You take it off, you hang it up. You finish the tissue box, you throw it in the garbage. Why not take the next logical step?

"Good, I think. Who knows?"

He kisses me on the cheek. "I'm sure you were outstanding."

I shrug. I might have been. It's not hard to tell people what they want to hear. Instead of saying this out loud, I take off my pants and set them on a hanger.

"What do you want to do today?" he asks.

I want him to go back to sleep so I can use the bathroom.

I know it sounds stupid, but what if he can hear? What if I make noise? Won't listening impair his sexy image of me? The bathroom door is really thin. I normally hold it when I'm at his place and wait for him to go to work. I know it's weird and that eventually I'll be able to go to the bathroom when he's in the apartment. But I can't yet. I just can't. I can hold it.

"What time do you have to go to work?" I ask.

"Not till six. What time is it now?"

Not till six?

Steve doesn't wear a watch. He claims not to like watches. Can you have negative feelings toward something that tells the time?

"My watch says two," I say.

"I know, let's go to Roller Dee's. They have bowling and minigolf and laser tag. It's awesome."

I'm a little too tired for that. "But it's so nice out. We shouldn't waste the day."

"Let's go to Central Park. We'll throw a Frisbee."

There's no way they have decent public bathrooms in Central Park. "We don't have a Frisbee."

"No? We'll stop at Toys 'R' Us."

Steve reminds me of a windup toy that shoots across the table until it dies or falls off the edge.

I smile, trying to create that I'm-the-perfect-girlfriend-who's-up-for-anything glow.

I have a plan.

When we're in the lobby I say, "You know what, Steve? I heard it might rain. I'm going to run up and get the umbrella. You wait here."

He peers outside.

I jump into the elevator and hit Close Doors before he can comment that the sky is bright blue.

Ten minutes later, I return to the lobby. "Sorry," I say. "Couldn't find it."

* * *

After the afternoon of Frisbee, Steven walks me through the park, showing me his favorite places. We stop at The Great Lawn, the Angel of the Waters Fountain at Bethesda Terrace and Bow Bridge. Bow Bridge is a stunning cast-iron bridge spanning sixty feet across a serene lake. Green, red and orange trees frame the lake and look like they've been finger-painted. Office buildings tower in the distance, and I'm reminded of the feeling of being at peace in a canoe in the middle of the Camp Abina's lake, the sun warming my face. I wrap my arm through Steve's and say, "I think this is the most beautiful spot I've ever been."

Steve suggests I spend the evening with him at his restaurant, and gets so excited by this idea that I can't say no. "What else are you going to do?" he asks.

"Sleep?" I'm tired. Frisbee is hard work. "Okay, okay."

"You always want to sleep."

It's true. "Maybe I'm sick." I've been thinking there might be something wrong with me. Some disease that attacks your immune system, sucking energy. Mono, maybe? Cancer? HIV? Wouldn't that be my luck. I get a part on a TV show and then can't take it because I have to be admitted to the hospital. My health insurance lasts another three months, and right now I can't afford a new policy. If I got a disease now, no one would ever insure me and then I would never be cured and I'd die broke and alone.

I don't share my thoughts with Steve as I don't want him to realize how crazy I am.

Except for the help, the restaurant is still empty when we get there. We sit on the cushioned stools by the bar and open a bottle of overly sweet Manashevitz wine.

I'm reintroduced to Jerry, the assistant manager, then the cooks and the waitresses as they begin to trickle in. Thank God for his incredible staff, especially Martin. If it wasn't for them, Steve would never have been able to take off time to visit me in Florida.

It's been a while since I've spent an evening here.

The restaurant is small, with only fifteen tables and a bar next to the kitchen. Eight-by-ten black-and-white photographs of Italian synagogues line the wall. Behind each picture is a light, and the effect makes the photographs look golden, almost holy.

I should just work here. It would be so easy.

And then I'll never bother finding my own job, my own life, will I?

I decide to play hostess instead of offering to work as one. I watch Steve move and schmooze and take control around the restaurant. He's amazing here, everyone loves him, everyone wants to talk to him as he walks by. He shakes hands, waves, smiles and makes this place run. And he's all mine. He introduces me to all the regulars.

"We've heard so much about you!" Mr. Weinberg announces, patting me on the head. "What a face! Such a *shayna punim.* We've been friends with Joy and Abe forever, and they absolutely love you, honey, love you."

They do? Good to know. Joy and Abe are Steve's parents.

"So when are you two going to have some news?" Mrs. Weinberg asks, wagging her eyebrows.

Maybe I should tell them that I'm pregnant. "Guess what, Mr. and Mrs. Weinberg? We're having a baby!" What would they do? Would Mrs. Weinberg have a heart attack? Instead I play dumb. "What type of news?" I ask.

"Sunny is moving to New York this week," Steve says.

"Really," Mrs. Weinberg says. "Where are you going to live?"

"With—" Right. Not with Steve. Oops. Almost blew that one. Good thing *Party Girls* isn't a sitcom. I'd never be able to remember my lines. "I found someone nice in the Village who was looking for a roommate."

"Jewish?"

I consider answering Palestinian, to see what she'll do. "Jewish."

"How wonderful. Tell me, have you found work here yet?"

"Not yet." I'm not sure what Steve's plan is regarding the

show. His parents probably wouldn't approve of their potential future daughter-in-law parading around the city, drunk and slutty. "Still looking," I add.

"Talk to the kids. They all have terrific jobs," Mrs. Weinberg says. "They'll be here soon."

I nod, but have no idea what she's talking about. Kids? What kids have jobs? What kids are coming here? And why would these kids want to talk to me about my job?

At ten-thirty I'm exhausted and thinking about taking off. Take your girlfriend to work day is about over.

By ten-forty the place is packed, the "Central Perk" of the twenty-something religious scene. These must be the so-called kids Mrs. Weinberg was referring to. Steve pats them on the back when they pass him. Except some of the women, who apparently aren't allowed to be touched by men other than their husbands. Not that all of them are that religious. One particular curly brunette (every woman in here is a curly brunette) seems happy to run her palm up and down Steve's arm.

I decide to find Steve to say goodbye. He's in the kitchen, pulling bags of noodles out of a cupboard. "Who's the girl who keeps touching you?" I ask him. In a boxing match, jealousy would beat the crap out of exhaustion.

"Keeps touching me?" he repeats, blushing.

"The brunette. In the skirt."

"Oh, in the skirt," he says. All the girls are wearing skirts.

"The one whose skirt has a slit halfway up her thigh? Don't they wear skirts to be modest?"

"Ruthie?" he says.

"That's Ruthie?" I say, surprised. "*Ruthie* Ruthie? Your ex-girlfriend Ruthie?"

He shrugs. "That's her."

Steve pointed out Ruthie in his Carmel High School yearbook. I asked to see it, wanting to patch together the seasons before me in his life. If only you could rent the earlier episodes from Blockbuster. Season One: childhood. Season Two:

Carmel High School. Season Three: NYU. Season Four: working for Dad. Season Five: taking over for Dad and meeting me. Season Six: …tbd.

His yearbook picture looked like a caricature of today's Steve. His nose and chin were exaggerated, too large for his skinnier face. The caption had included all the regular cheesiness ("What a long strange trip it's been" and the note to the person he then believed was the love of his life: "Ruthie, 1 day we'l gt marEd, IluvU.")

I thought it was cuter when she was an old profile photo with too-thick eyebrows. Now she had exploded into an ex-girlfriend Andie MacDowell look-alike who had attacked my Stevie in plain sight.

"Relax, her boyfriend's here, too," he says.

The boyfriend doesn't mind her mauling my boyfriend? Maybe I'll stay a bit longer.

I anchor myself at a small table in the corner of the restaurant and pull out the *Newsweek* magazine I purchased on my way home from the audition and planned on reading in bed. Ruthie and company are sitting at the table next to mine, close enough for me to secretly study her from above the magazine. I feel like Cybil Shepherd in *Moonlighting*.

She's eating pizza. Cutting square pieces with a fork and knife and then carefully depositing them into her mouth. Her mouth that kissed my Stevie. Didn't sleep with my Stevie, though. Steve's first lover was another freshman in college. Until he went to NYU, he had followed his parents' wishes and been somewhat religious. Only after moving into a dorm and meeting new people did he decide that for the moment, he wasn't sure if he wanted to follow all the Jewish laws.

Ruthie is tall, has wide eyes, a thin nose, and wears her curly hair half up. Her dinner group consists of two other couples and the man I assume is her boyfriend (he's short and dark-haired. Steve is a million times better looking—no wonder she's still touching his arm). Everyone but the two of them are wearing wedding rings.

Ruthie leans toward one of the women. "I can't believe you're already on your third. Maybe a boy this time?"

Third? How old is she? Twenty-four? I wish Millie or Dana were here so we could all roll our eyes.

One of the husbands looks up at me and waves.

He caught me staring.

"Sunny?" he says. "How are you?"

Suddenly he looks familiar. A friend of Steve's? I met him once, bumped into him on Broadway and Houston. Jake? Jon? Jason. Yes, Jason. A high school buddy.

"Jason, hey," I say. Damn. I was enjoying my anonymity. I see the girls whispering to one another. I put down the magazine and walk over to their table, and stand across from Ruthie, who looks me over. I'm sure there are grass stains all over my clothes from playing in the park. Lovely. Thanks, Steve, for letting me know what a scene this was. I'm wearing jeans, a zip-up orange sweatshirt and sneakers. I wish I still had on Carrie's boots.

Steve is watching me through the window to the kitchen and I wave him over. He joins us and ruffles Jason's hair. "Hey, man, how's the food?"

Jason punches him in the arm. "What's going on?"

"The usual," Steve answers and takes my hand. "Do you guys know Sunny?"

"No," everyone but Jason says. Steve introduces me around and I try very hard not to look at Ruthie.

Steve returns to the kitchen and I'm forced to sit with these people. And chat. How can I be impressive when I'm practically falling asleep? My eyes keep drooping. I definitely have a disease. And I'm making it worse by staying up so late. Is Steve going to be embarrassed of me? I must look smashed. They're going to think I'm a lush. The word around Jewish New York will be that Steve's new girlfriend is a drunk.

At one in the morning, the friends take off. Now it's just Steve, me and the staff.

"Do you mind waiting another twenty minutes?" he asks and kisses my forehead. "We're almost done."

"No problem," I say, and try to appear awake. As soon as he walks away, I put my head down on the table. Rest my eyes for a sec.

I wake up to Steve playing with my hair. "Honey, wake up. I'm done." The restaurant is dark and we're the only ones left. The photographs glow, dreamlike.

"I'm not asleep," I say. I hope I wasn't snoring.

He takes my hand again as we walk toward the street. "Guess who gets to sleep in tomorrow…"

"Us? Promise?"

"Promise." He raises his arm to hail a cab. "We'll sleep till our stomachs wake us."

I climb into the taxi next to him and rest my head against his shoulder.

"Wake up," he says when we're in front of our apartment.

"Wasn't sleeping," I murmur.

While Steve checks the messages, I quickly make the bed. I've never been a terribly anal bed-maker (when I had time in the morning, great, if I was running late who cared?) but I feel that it's somehow part of my duty. Not that Steve expects me to make it. Or maybe he does. No, he doesn't. But won't he grow to love having a made bed with crisp cool sheets to sleep on at the end of the day? It'll be one of the little things he'll start to depend on, to need, to love. To not be able to live without. A made bed. Me.

As soon as the sheets are tucked in, I climb into them and close my eyes.

"Six new messages," Steve says from the other room. His voice is starting to sound hazy, far away. "Wow. This phone is much more popular since you've moved in. It's Carrie. Do you want to hear?"

I shake my head no, even though I know he's in the other room.

"She says call her back right away…. It's Carrie again. She

says she has news.... It's Carrie again. She says why haven't you called her back.... It's Carrie again. She says you got the job. You got it!"

I'm going to be on a reality TV show. Am I ruining my life? His religious friends will think I'm a slut. I'm too tired to worry about the ramifications. Tomorrow.

I smile. They picked me. I'm going to be on TV. I turn on my back and laugh.

Religious people don't watch slutty shows, do they?

"She says to call her back immediately.... It's her again. She says she's going to sleep, she can't wait up any longer but you have an emergency spa appointment."

Sounds fine. Sounds fun. That rhymes. Does it? Did I say that out loud? Am I asleep?

"And she's picking you up tomorrow morning at eight-thirty."

But he promised.

8

Transformers

I love *Star Wars*. Growing up, I collected the action figures in my Darth Vader carrying kit: Princess Leia, Han Solo, Darth Vader, C-3P0, R2-D2, Boba Fett, Yoda and two Luke Sky-walkers. One was Luke Skywalker the X-Wing Pilot, the other Luke Skywalker the Jedi Knight. The ultimate movie makeover moment of all time is watching Luke, all serious and dressed in black, coolly stroll into Jabba the Hutt's cave, kill everyone and save his friends. You barely remember the farm boy he was in Episode IV.

I've always wanted a makeover. True, I was hoping for one that would make me capable of mind manipulation and transcendental object-lifting. But I suppose a spa makeover will do.

I have been told I have a colorist appointment, a stylist appointment, a facial appointment, a body facial appoint-ment (I'm not sure what a body facial is. Apparently it involves something called an alpha-beta peel and cleansing mint mud?), a manicure appointment, a pedicure appointment, an eyebrow-wax appointment and a bikini-wax appointment, all at Bella, a Soho spa, all compliments of *Party Girls*.

Not sure why a bikini wax is necessary. Do Manhattan bars have hot tubs?

My Jedi training begins in the skin room, on a foamy lawn chair covered in a white paper towel motif. The walls are mirrored and windowless. A magnifying glass the size of a satellite dish is suspended above me. The room smells like pineapple. Beside me, Carrie sits on a stool, reading *Elle*. She will be accompanying me through all levels of preparation. I think she's concerned that if left alone, I might bolt.

Post-alpha-beta peel (I still don't know what that is), a cold and heavy mud mask hardens my face and limbs. I'm annoyed that the rims of my cotton panties and bra are mud-stained. Washing bras is such a pain.

Carrie looks up from her magazine. "Have you ever been to Pompeii?"

"Is that another salon?"

"It's the city in Italy where the volcano went off and covered the whole town in lava. Quite remarkable. I was there last summer."

"No. Did you see dead people?"

"You don't actually see the dead people. More like the papier-mâché moldings of dead people. It was cool."

"Is there an article about Pompeii in *Elle?*"

"No." She looks back at her magazine. "Something reminded me of it."

"What?"

"You."

Next, I'm transported to the eyebrow room, which is essentially another cushioned lawn chair, with mirrored walls and a massive magnifying glass. "All the rooms are exactly alike. Why can't I stay put and have the estheticians come to me?"

Carrie sits down on her new chair, which looks exactly like her old chair, and opens her magazine. "Look who's already a princess."

A shorthaired Brazilian woman in a white smock opens the door to the room. "Hel-lo, hel-lo," she says. Her voice has a Mr. Rogers singsong quality. "I'm Ja-zelle, are you ready?"

I don't think so. I've never waxed anything before. I shave my legs and bikini line when necessary and occasionally pluck my brows. Why spend hundreds of dollars on hair removal when I can do it for free?

Dana makes a trip to the waxer once a month for full hair removal. She raves about it but can never wear shorts or a bathing suit for two weeks a month because the hair has to "grow out." What's the point of all that pain and money if you can only show it off for half the month?

Jazelle lowers her face until she is just an inch above mine. I wish I had a breath mint. "Eyebrows and lip?" she asks.

My lip?

"Um...only my eyebrows."

She nods.

"What's wrong with my lip?"

She runs her finger over my upper lip. "You have lots of dark hair. If I were you, I'd remove it."

Lots of dark hair? I have a mustache? Why hasn't anyone mentioned this? Isn't that something that your best friends are supposed to tell you? "Okay. Take it off." Do it! Do it!

She spreads the wax over my lip. That doesn't feel too bad. Kind of nice, actually. Soothing, even. It's—

"Fuck!" I scream as she rips the skin off my body. The sting slowly subsides.

"Lie back down, lie back down. I have to do the sides."

After the sides, she moves on to my brows, which aren't as excruciating.

When I'm escorted to the body-waxing station, I catch a glimpse of myself in one of the seven thousand mirrors and am pleased to see my brows looking fantastic. My lip makes me look like I'm part of the *Got Strawberry Milk?* campaign, but Jazelle promised that the red marks would disappear in an hour.

A Korean woman is standing, arms crossed, beside her room's lawn chair. "Take off your pants and panties," she tells me.

Carrie freezes. "I think I'll go get a coffee."

"Don't leave me," I plead in Carrie's direction, but faster than the Roadrunner, she's outta there.

I enter the room. The esthetician slams the door behind me.

I take off my jeans, fold them and place them on what should be Carrie's chair.

The woman sticks her finger at my crotch. "Panties off."

Why do I have to take off my panties? Can't she just move them to the side?

I place my mud-caked panties on top of my jeans and lie back on the paper-covered chair. This is ridiculous. A Kleenex box is on the counter, so I pull a tissue out and cover the area between my legs.

The woman smells like antiseptic. She dips a Popsicle stick in hot wax and then spreads it on my right lower leg. This won't hurt this won't hurt this won't hurt this won't hurt.

Ouch.

It's not as bad as my upper lip. I can handle it. And again.

Ouch.

She climbs her way up my right leg. And then over to my left leg.

Thank God I don't have a lot of hair on my upper legs. It hurts a bit, but I can handle it. I'm a waxing pro.

She picks the tissue off of my privates. "Spread your legs."

What? Does she double as a gynecologist?

"You don't trim?" she asks.

Is this a lecture? "Sometimes," I answer.

"What shape you want?"

"What are my options? I've never done this before." As if she hasn't figured that out.

"Take it all off first time. It grow back thinner."

All off, huh. Sexy. Steve'll love it. I'll be just like the girls on the porn channel he loves, Hot 'n Sexy. What a fantastic surprise. I won't even tell him, I'll just wear a skirt and tell him I'm going commando and then...it'll be fantastic. I'm the best girlfriend ever.

She spreads the wax over the outer edge of the left side of my pubic region. That feels nice. Hot. Oooh. Is it gross to get aroused at a bikini wax? And then—

OH. MY. GOD. I've never known such pain.

She pushes my legs apart. "Keep them open!" she orders Gestapo-style.

This is worse than the gynecologist.

She spreads the wax over the right side of my pubic region and then—

OH. MY. GOD. This is the most horrific pain I have ever felt in my entire life. Worse than when I spilled hot water all over my hands. Worse than slamming the car door on my fingernail. Worse than a visit to the dentist.

I try to see what she's doing, but I feel dizzy. She's spreading the slimy material over the top inch of my pubic region. This is going to hurt. I know this is going to hurt. Here it comes. She's going for it—

"Owwwwwwwwww!"

She looks up at me and shakes her head. "If you open your legs properly it won't hurt so much."

Why would it make a difference how wide my legs are? It would make no difference. Absolutely no difference. This woman is a psychotic sadist.

"How much longer is this going to take?"

"I'm doing the lips now, and then the anus. Ten minutes. Spread wider."

Anus? She thinks she's waxing my butt? Ten more minutes of this torture? I don't think I can do it. My body wasn't made for this type of pain. She coats the left vaginal lip in wax. I take a deep breath.

Here it comes. And there it...

…goes. I think I passed out. I open my eyes and push her hand away as she's about to coat me in more torture. "No, I can't take it."

"I'm not stopping now. Only half of you is done. You look stupid."

I close my legs and jump off the table. "I don't care. No more. I'm done."

The woman huffs and stands back from the table as I hastily step into my muddy underwear. "It would have been easier if you kept your legs open," she snarls.

Now I know why Dana made me get both my ears pierced at the same time.

The colorist and stylist loom behind me, one on each shoulder, like the angel and devil who personify TV characters' consciences. Carrie sits at the unused hair station next to me, to coordinate.

"So what are going to do? A trim? A few highlights?"

"I could," says the colorist. She's about sixty-five and looks like a grandmother. Her shoulder-length hair is layered, blow-dried and colored adult-lady blond. When I first saw her from the back and didn't see the wrinkles around her eyes and lips, I thought she was in her forties.

"No," Carrie says. She's filing her nails. "Not enough. Think glamorous starlet at the Oscars, not girl next door."

I see the bags under my eyes in the mirror. "So what do you want to do? I'm too tired to care."

The colorist picks up a strand of hair from above my ear and carefully studies it. The bags are really awful. I need to buy some more of that concealer stuff. Where did I put the one I bought once? Do I get free makeup with this show? This whole day has been full of mirrors. Who wants to stare at herself for that long? Are you supposed to look into your own eyes? Are you supposed to pretend you don't see yourself?

"Love it. Love it!" Carrie says.

Sorry, too busy staring at myself, can you repeat that? "Love what?"

The colorist picks up another strand, this one from the top of my head. "I said let's do something really different. Let's make you beautiful."

There's an insult in that, I'm sure.

The colorist drops my hair. "Let's make you blond."

Blond?

"You'll look gorgeous," she says. "Like a beach babe."

Blond? No way. "I'm not blond material."

The stylist is nodding. She has short choppy purple hair. Why can't I do that? "I'm thinking shorter," she says. "Much shorter."

Why do hairdressers always want to cut it all off? You'd think they hate hair or something. Shouldn't they be picketing to protect the hair?

"Not too short," I say. "Shoulder length? And no blond."

Carrie pulls out a bottle of clear polish. "We have one redhead, one brunette and one blonde. Two blondes would work," she says. "We live in a blonde-loving world." When she talks, she watches herself talk in the mirror.

"No," I say, louder.

"Lightbulb, lightbulb," the colorist says, tapping her forehead.

"Anything but blond," I say.

"Black," she offers.

"Black?"

"Jet, wet black."

The stylist nods. "Chin length."

Carrie sighs. "You'll be striking."

I hesitate, then nod. "It's better than blond."

The colorist disappears into a secret room, and twenty minutes later applies a purple concoction to my head.

Carrie is blowing her nails dry. "It'll be perfect. We'll have a blonde, a brunette, a redhead and a black-haired…what's a black-haired person?"

"A dominatrix?" I suggest.

While the color is setting, I'm sent to the manicurist and then to the pedicurist. I've only had one manicure before, for prom, and never a pedicure, so I let Carrie choose the color. She picks red, to "contrast my hair," whatever that means.

Then I'm back to the sink and the color is rinsed. Ah. Scalp massage. With a towel on my head like a turban, I'm whisked to the stylist's station. Carrie follows and sits down beside me. She attempts to engage me in conversation so that I don't pass out at the sight of my hair accumulating on the wooden floor.

The stylist spins my chair around when she's blow-drying. "No peeking. You'll see when it's done."

I love the paper flip-flops the pedicurist gave me. I could really use these in my apartment. Will they be in my loot bag when I leave?

"Sexy," Carrie shouts over the blow-dryer, pointing to my toes. "I love red." She should see my inflamed vagina. I caught a glimpse of it in the bathroom and it didn't look good.

"Flip your head back up," the stylist says. "But don't look."

She blows and brushes and sprays and plumps.

"Your hair is gorgeous!" Carrie shouts. "Stunning!"

"You swear?"

"I swear. Why would I lie? I need you to look gorgeous. If it didn't look gorgeous, I would make Dina do it again. You were right about the blond. It wouldn't have been you."

The blow-dryer is turned off.

"Are you ready?" the stylist asks. Suddenly she spins me around.

Lara Flynn Boyle stares back at me.

Kind of. Not as gorgeous, obviously. Or as skinny. But not bad. I think. But I look so pale. Washed out, even.

"I look like I'm on *The Addams Family*," I say.

Carrie is smiling. "No, you don't. You look so gorgeous, you could be a model."

I smile. You could be a brain surgeon, just wouldn't have the same effect.

"I need a tan." Why didn't I tan when I lived in Florida? I've seen the pasty color of the snowbirds when they come down for the holidays. It ain't pretty.

It's black. Black, black, black. I just have to get used to it. I want my hair back.

I can't cry at the salon. I think I'm going to cry at the salon. I can be a grown-up. It's just hair. Why do I care so much about hair? I've never given it a second thought before. I swallow the tears. There. No one noticed.

The stylist looks at Carrie and shakes her head. "Honey, if she still hates it tomorrow, we'll change the color, okay? It'll be fine. But tell her to stop crying, already."

After I have calmed down, Carrie takes me for lunch and then to my clothing makeover at Stark's Department Store. Every time I see my reflection, I startle myself.

My personal shopper covers her eyes with her hands, in an attempt to give herself some vision. "You're wearing the clothes on television. To nightclubs. You want trampy or you want sophisticated? There's a difference between trampy sexy and classy sexy," she adds with authority.

I wonder where she gets her definition of trampy, with her short, tight skirt and plunging neckline.

"Sophisticated and sexy," Carrie says as we enter a private dressing room decorated with bowls of potpourri, a lush velvet couch and more mirrored walls.

My skin looks flawless. I also look about six feet tall and size two. "These are definitely good mirrors," I say.

"Fabulous, huh? It's a fun house in here."

"And I get a thousand dollars of free clothes."

"Yes, a thousand dollars a month. But don't use that up today. Fashion evolves. Buy two fabulous outfits for the opening credits and promo ads tonight and something else for the first show on Saturday."

"But the show airs a week from today. Why do I need something for promo ads? Haven't you already been advertising?"

"Yeah, occasionally." Carrie rolls her eyes. "I should warn you that not everyone at TRS is as gung ho about *Party Girls* as Stan, the VP you met, is. Some of the more traditional execs aren't exactly rolling out the red carpet. But yeah, they made a commercial, and Sheena, the girl who was arrested for shoplifting, is in all of them. We need to reshoot with you. I'm sure there are elements of the first commercial they'll use, so tonight shouldn't take too long."

"Tonight?" No one mentioned a shoot tonight. I'm beginning to understand how this works. Reality happens on Saturday night, but the *real* reality—the preparations for reality—takes place all week long. And I only find out about them about four and a half minutes before the event. "I'll get to meet the other girls?"

"Obviously."

The personal shopper returns with a metal trolley filled with sweaters, tops, blouses, dresses, skirts, pants, stilettos and jackets—all, including the footwear, in a size seven. I read the labels: Kenneth Cole, Anna Sui, Betsey Johnson, Nicole Miller, Calvin Klein, Helmut Lang, Marc Jacobs, DKNY and BCBG.

I bet Dana would appreciate this a lot more than I do.

I'm the first Party Girl at Night, the bar where we're filming. It's a narrow and low-ceilinged rectangular space that is already crowded with Howard, Tania and various other crew members who are in the process of setting up. At the far end of the room a diamond-shaped window looks out onto the West Village.

Howard whistles when he sees me. "Is that our Sunny? Love the new do. Great outfit."

I'm wearing my new Helmut Lang tight black pants and red scoop-neck top, red jeweled dangling earrings and black, stiletto, way-too-high, pointy boots.

Obviously I allowed Carrie to outfit me. I think I might have heard her call me Barbie by mistake.

Tania pops her head up. "Very *Vogue*," she says, and disappears behind the bar. "Martin is waiting for you in the back room. Makeup."

I hold on to passing tables and chairs for balance as I head around the bar. The back room is as small as a coat closet and is cramped with bar stools and one small desk. Martin steers me onto a stool. He brushes his bleached-blond hair back with his hand and then immediately smothers me in foundation.

"Can you make it natural looking?" I ask.

"It's not supposed to be natural looking. It's for television." Martin has an emerald stud nose ring. Why do people want to draw attention to their noses? Is anyone's nose that exquisite? What if he has a cold?

"Am I next?" A short, curvy girl in a black skirt that just about covers her crotch, a fuchsia tank top, black stiletto heels and a wide, black beaded belt. Chin-length chunky-platinum locks frame her face. "You must be Sunny," she adds. "I'm Erin. The slut."

"Sorry?"

She laughs. "The slut. I'm supposed to be the slut on the show. You know? You're the anal one and I'm the slut."

"Good to know. Nice to meet you."

She drags over a stool and sits down. She crosses her legs, rotates her top ankle. "You don't wear a lot of makeup regularly? You one of those natural types?" she asks, accusatorily.

Is that bad? "Yeah, I guess."

"I don't understand why someone wouldn't wear makeup. Don't you want to look your best?"

Um… Who is this girl again? The slut or the bitch? "I don't care that much, I guess."

"Look up," the makeup artist says. I tilt my head toward the ceiling and he lines the bottom rim of my eye. "Stop blinking."

"Sorry."

Erin rummages through the guy's makeup bag. "This whole free clothes, free makeover thing is out of fucking control."

"I guess," I say. I'm not sure what to say to this person. Why would they put someone so rude on television?

"I love makeup. I get off on changing my look. My hair used to be your color. Black. Have you considered going blond? It might suit you better."

I shrug. Is she trying to intimidate me? That must be it. She's trying to make me feel ugly.

Erin continues: "I've dyed it red, blond, black, pink, everything. The best part about being a woman is our ability to reinvent ourselves. I'm speaking from two nose jobs and a boob job's worth of experience."

Information overload. I'd look at her breasts but makeup man still has me looking at the ceiling. "Two nose jobs? What was wrong with the first one?"

"Not perfect," she says, shrugging. "Have you ever thought of a boob job? You could probably use an extra cup size. Have you had any work done?" she asks.

Makeup man reaches into his bag to find something and I take the opportunity to get a better look at Erin. Her nose is small and slightly turned up. I don't know if I'd have noticed if she hadn't told me. The breasts on the other hand are too big and too perky to be anything but silicone-based.

"Me? No." I had braces. But I don't think that quite counts. The makeup artist interrupts me to brush my lips with red.

"So how did you get to be on the show? I heard you had it easy," Erin says.

Excuse me? I don't think that's any of her business. I decide to ignore the attitude. "I worked in business development in Florida. I wanted a change of scenery so I moved here and then I heard about this. You?"

"I wanna be a dancer. Like in music videos. I'm hoping this is my way in. Get noticed. You know. But back to you having it easy. You only had one interview, right? I had to produce a whole video—my friend taped me flashing bouncers to let me into red-roped bars."

What a freak. "Intense," I say.

"All done," the makeup man says.

"My turn. How old are you? I'm twenty-four."

We switch places. "Me, too."

"Yeah? We're the oldest. Have you met the other girls?"

"Not yet. Are they here?"

"You can't hear them? I can hear Michelle's nasal screech from here." Erin snorts. "Michelle's a total bitch. The whole city thinks she's a bitch but everyone's too chicken shit to say anything bad about Little Miss Page Six. She sits on her golden throne on the Upper East Side and fucks over anyone who isn't paying attention."

"So do you like her?" What's Page Six?

Erin laughs and the light glares off her face. She has acne scars on her forehead and around her nose and when she sees me noticing, she turns away.

Back in the bar Carrie is leaning against the diamond-shaped window, talking to two women. One of the girls has Carrie laughing. I don't think I've ever seen anyone as spec-tacular-looking as this girl who is making Carrie laugh. She's like a lightbulb in a room full of mosquitoes: You can't take your eyes off her. She looks like a real-life Ariel from *The Lit-tle Mermaid,* with red, first-season Felicity-style curls, fas-tened haphazardly on top of her head with a long tortoise hair claw.

Carrie air kisses me on the cheek. "Sunny, these are your costars, Brittany and Michelle. Brittany and Michelle, this is Sunny." Michelle is the stunning one.

"It's so wonderful to meet you!" Brittany says and leans over to hug me. She towers over me by about three inches and her wavy brown hair falls in front of her face.

She tries to put her arms around me, but they can't make it across. Her massive breasts are in the way. They're huge. They're bigger than Erin's and they hang down twice as long. I've never seen breasts this large. Bigger than Dolly Parton's, I'm not kidding. A quadruple D, maybe.

"It's nice to meet you, too." They must be real. They're too outrageous not to be.

Michelle is rolling her eyes. Is that at me or at Brittany's cheesy friendliness? Michelle's skin is smooth and freckled, the perfect showcase for her wide green eyes.

Brittany looks down and then starts to laugh. "They're always getting in the way."

"As long as they're getting," Carrie says and puts her arm around me. "Now you've met everyone. Hopefully you'll hang around a little longer than your predecessor."

Michelle twirls a curl around her thumb and looks me over. "You're not going to pull a Winona on us, are you?"

What if these girls never like me? What if I can't fit in?

"I don't know," I say. I motion to her purse. "I'd hold on tighter to that Louis Vuitton bag if I were you."

Michelle tilts back her head and laughs, her long red hair cascading over her shoulders.

Carrie pats me on the back. "I can't believe you knew it was Louis Vuitton."

"The ad nauseum logo gave it away," I say. "Or maybe I'm learning."

Howard kisses each of us on the cheek. He lingers a little bit longer than necessary on Michelle. "The bar is ours until ten," he says.

"We look like a Clairol hair color commercial," Michelle says. "Red, black, brown and blond."

"Charlie's Angels," I say. "Four of them."

Howard laughs. A trickle of spit lands on his bottom lip and he licks it off, lizard-like. "We need some replacement footage. Sunny, I'm sure you've seen the commercial—"

"How could she have seen it when it's never on?" Erin interrupts. Post-makeup, her skin is looking flawless. Martin must have applied a thick layer of foundation.

"It begins with a panoramic shot of the Manhattan nighttime skyline," Howard continues, ignoring her. "Then a montage of images of the outside of clubs. Bouncers, long lines, secret entrances. Then, and this is what we need to replace tonight, we'll get you girls drinking and dancing together. And we need an individual profile shot of Sunny. We already have the rest of you, from last time. We'll shoot here and then move onto the street and then do a costume change and head over to Princess to get some interaction shots. First, let's loosen you up a bit. Sound good? Mike?" he calls out across the room to the bartender. "Put anything the girls want on my tab. Sunny? Order your cocktail and then we'll start with your profile shot right here. Nice makeup."

As I sip my apple martini, Howard positions me in front of the window. "Gorgeous. Pete's going to video, and Dirk's going to snap some stills. Ready?"

I have no idea what to do with myself. Do I drink? Do I pose? Do I drink and pose?

"I want to see you smile, babe, okay?" Dirk says.

I smile.

"A real smile. A sexy smile."

I try to smile sexy.

Dirk removes his head from behind his camera and flashes Howard a "she's hopeless" look.

I'm horrible. I have no idea how to smile sexy. They're going to cut me out of the show.

The three girls are whispering in front of the bar. What are they saying? They must be talking about me. They think I'm awful.

Fuck 'em. I can do this. Pretend I'm a Hot 'n Sexy woman. Stick my chest out. Sexy smile. If Steve could only see me now he'd have a hard-on in a millisecond.

I take a big sip of my cocktail and smile sexy for the camera. I laugh at myself and Dirk clicks away.

"Fantastic!" Dirk says. "Now turn sideways, give me a profile shot, perfect, now smile again, sexy, pretend you're a Party Girl now, fantastic, now take another sip of your drink, there we go, you're a natural, stick your chest out a bit, perfect, let's see those sparkling teeth, rub your glass against your lips, angle your head to the right a bit, gorgeous the money shot, now take a sip, shit, be careful, can someone get Sunny a napkin? I think that's a wrap."

Erin, Michelle, Brittany and I are on the bar. Yes, on the bar. Short, tall, tall, short; huge-breasted, small-breasted, big-breasted, medium-breasted. Skirt, jeans, dress, pants. Blond, redheaded, brunette, black-haired. We're like a rainbow of Caucasian diversity. A red strobe light is blasting and Howard has told us to dance.

"But there's no music," Erin protests.

"We're going to superimpose music for the clip," Howard says.

"We can't dance without music," Erin says. "We're all going to be on different beats. Can't you turn something on?"

"Fine. Tania, can you put on something the girls can dance to?"

Tania puts on a remixed dance version of Britney Spears's "Oops!...I Did it Again."

Our own Brittany adjusts her breasts. I'm not sure how she remains upright with those things. "I hate when they destroy good songs with a dance beat," she says.

Michelle rolls her eyes again. Aha! She's rolling them at Brittany, not at me.

I pinch her shoulder.

"She considers this a good song?" I mouth. "What's a bad song then?"

Michelle smiles.

"Now dance," Howard tells us. We dance. We go low. We go high. We wiggle our behinds. We dance carefully to avoid falling off the bar and cracking our heads open. When the song ends, we stop.

"Keep going," Howard says. A new Britney dance mix begins.

We keep wiggling. This song seems to be the extended version. We wiggle some more. Don't they only need about

two seconds of this? Stiletto boots are not made for bar
dancing.

"Sunny, dance with Brittany. Erin, dance with Miche,"
Howard says.

Miche? *Meesh?* That's the strangest sounding nickname
I've ever heard. Why does he have a nickname for her? I want
to call her Miche.

We couple off and continue dancing.

"I meant dirty dance," he says. "You've got to work it, girls.
Hollywood ain't all glitz and glamour."

Hollywood?

The last time I dirty danced was in 1987 when I had a *Teen
Beat* poster of Patrick Swayze taped to my bedroom wall.

And I was alone. Not with another member of my own sex.

Erin shakes her behind the ground around Michelle.
Michelle's hands are up in the air. They really do look like porn
stars.

I don't think we're as sexy as the other team. Brittany's
breasts accidentally hit my thigh. I lose my balance but then
steady myself before I topple headfirst into the bottles of vodka.

At one-thirty I creak open the front door. Two women are
making out on the television. Steve is lying on the couch.

"Hi," he says. "You look gorgeous. Very sexy hair. So how's
my favorite TV star?"

"You're sure I'm your favorite?" I nudge my head toward
the TV. I attempt to yank off my boots, but they're too tight and
finally they're off and I slump on top of Steve. "My feet are in
serious pain. I'll give you a thousand dollars to rub them."

The women on TV moan as Steve rubs little circles into the
soles of my feet. "Packages from Stark's were delivered."

"Oh, good. I got a ton of new clothes for the show."

He runs his hand down my tight baby-blue dress and then
up my leg. "What you're wearing now is hot."

"Thanks. I am so tired, you have no idea. They made us
dance for hours on top of a bar and I thought I was going

to fall off. Then they made us do a hundred shots of tequila."

"What? Did you pass out? I've never seen you do more than two shots without slurring your words."

"The first one was real. Lick the salt off your hand, do the shot and then suck a lime. But then Howard thought it was too boring, so he made us lick the salt off each other's necks and then down the tequila. Michelle, one of the other girls on the show, almost puked, so Tania suggested we shoot apple juice instead, but make a tequila face at the end. Then they filmed us hailing cabs on the street. They wouldn't let us get into the cab, they just filmed us hailing them, which really pissed off the cab drivers when they stopped. And then we had to change outfits and redo our makeup and our hair and we went to a dance club, as if we hadn't done enough dancing for one night. Princess, the club's called. Have you ever been there? Everyone in the bar had to sign a waiver in case they end up on the show. They made us dance for another half hour. And then they made us do more shots. Then they got one of the guys to give us all body shots. Basically, he licked the salt off our—"

Steve's eyebrows gather together. Abort discussion! Abort discussion! Perhaps the story regarding the male model licking salt off our necks, biting a shot glass from our cleavage and then sucking a lime out of our lips is not a good story to share. Since they're only going to use one of those shots in the final commercial, what's the chance that my inferior cleavage is chosen?

"Yes? Off where?" Steve says.

"—off Erin's neck. One of the other girls. She might be a bit psycho. She had two nose jobs. Two."

"Who is she, Michael Jackson?"

"Possibly. And she made a big deal about warning me about Michelle, saying she's a bitch, but I actually like Michelle the best." I start laughing. "She couldn't hold up the shot glass because she's so flat-chested and the apple juice spilled down her shirt."

"Erin or Michelle?"

"It was, it was, it was just…" A thought occurs to me. He's not concerned about the four of us girls all gyrating against one another and licking the salt off each other's skin, but he practically blows a circuit when he thinks other guys are involved. Why do men not seem to think of their girlfriends engaging in a lesbian experience as cheating?

I'm too tired for this. "Why don't we go to bed?"

"Bed. Yes, bed." His face brightens. Is it me who put the hopeful look in his eyes, or what he's been watching on the Hot 'n Sexy channel?

I follow him into the bedroom. I'm being silly. Of course it's me he wants. He loves me, doesn't he? I lift the blue dress over my head. My new Betsey Johnson dress. As I start removing my thong I feel a minor problem. Half of my pubic region has been waxed and the other half remains nicely carpeted. Crap.

Can I tell him it's the new style? The Jekyll and Hyde?

He's naked and changing the CD. "How about Barry White?"

"I just want to jump in the shower," I say. I'll be fast. I'll shave it off. He won't be able to tell. "I'm all grungy from the bars. Two minutes. Not even. Start thinking nasty thoughts and when I get back I have a surprise for you."

Before he can react, I scurry into the bathroom, close the door and turn on the shower. I quickly wash my hair—where is my hair? There's no hair left to shampoo. Then I soap myself, cover my bikini area in shaving cream and timidly bring the razor down south.

This is worse than brain surgery. One wrong move and it's a clitorectomy.

I slowly and carefully shave off as much of the offending strands as I can. All clean.

I pose in my most provocative lean in front of the light switch. "What do you think?"

Steve recoils. "What happened to your pussy?"

Excuse me? "It's a Brazilian." I stomp over to the bed and hide my head under the covers. "I thought you'd like it. Excuse me for trying."

"I do like it, let me see." He tugs the covers off me and lightly touches. "It looks like a hairless cat."

I yank the covers back up. "A Sphinx? You think I look like a Sphinx? That's the last time I endure excruciating pain for your viewing pleasure."

"I like hairless cats," he says. "Let me see it again."

I pull down the covers. "Wo-ow," he says. "Very hot. Very sexy." He continues stroking me and I feel myself getting turned on. After a few minutes of fooling around I climb on top of him and we start having sex.

I'm not sure if it's because of the lack of hair barrier, but I'm much wetter than usual and I feel an orgasm coming on.

"You are so juicy," he tells me. "Your pussy is so juicy like this."

I wish he would stop saying *pussy*. And *juicy*. I was already having a hard time getting rid of the image of the Sphinx. Now I'm picturing a slobbering Sphinx.

"I'm going to come," I tell him and continue thrusting on top of him. He's holding me by the waist and helping me move.

"Me, too," he says. "Tell me when."

"Any second," I say. Almost there…almost there…Steve is a wonderful lover. A considerate lover. He never allows himself to come until he's sure I already did. Or I at least tell him I did.

I orgasm and then he orgasms and then I stop and lie on the soft brown hairs of his chest and fall asleep.

Later I wake up and remind myself that if I don't pee right after sex I'll get a bladder infection.

Hey there, I think to my vagina while I'm peeing. I haven't seen it bald since I was eleven. I've forgotten what it looked like. I pat it and the sensation feels both smooth and bizarre. I flush, wash my hands, brush my teeth, then go back to bed.

9

A Different World

He cocks his trigger.

In spite of my fascination with Detective Derrick's trigger, I feel an immediate affinity with the villain. The gap-toothed killer, who looks like a geriatric (wrinkled, hunched) twelve-year-old (blond, skinny, short), grins at Derrick, revealing a space between his bottom front teeth, as wide as an empty mall parking lot.

I had similar smile issues before my braces. I tried to close the gap by binding the wayward teeth with a twist tie, which I unintentionally swallowed when it broke. Now a wire is glued to the inside of my bottom teeth, holding them together. I remember it's there only when it traps nuggets of food.

Derrick is still pointing his gun. His chiseled chin and coifed black hair make him look magnificent and stoic, like the statue of Michelangelo's David with gelled Ken-doll hair. Before he was Derrick, Matt Rowler played the sexy teenage son on the family sitcom *Close-Knit,* for about six years. I fell in love with Matt (our relationship was, of course, on a first-name basis) after reading in *Teen Beat* that he was a major *Star Wars* fan. He said if he could choose any role to play, it would be Luke Skywalker. Way, way, way before I met Steve, when I should have been too young to know of these things, Matt had played the star role in my sneak-in-through-the-window, stroke-my-body, make-me-orgasm-with-his-tongue fantasy.

"Tell me where Mary and Jane are," he demands, his jawbone tensing.

The gap-toothed killer runs his fingers through his mullet-shaped blond hair. "Do you want to know why I did it?"

Enter background sinister organ music. The sun glints off Derrick's gun and black rimless sunglasses. "Why?" he asks.

"Every time a woman gets into her car, she checks the back seat, wondering if I'm waiting to slit her throat. I'm not the kind of guy who doesn't live up to a woman's expectations."

"You're insane."

"I'm infamous." The killer lisps his S, the way I used to before my dad sent me to speech therapy.

"You're under arrest. You have the right to remain silent. You have the right…"

The image switches to a joyful man in plaid as he places a TV dinner into the microwave. "I can make chicken Alfredo when my wife is stuck late at work," he says with pride. "And it's so easy!"

I now know the TRS morning lineup by heart. At nine there's *American Sunrise,* starring fluffy-haired Betty and serious-looking John. I think I love Betty. She reminds me of what I always wanted my grandmother to be like. She's extremely articulate, always fair and even brings banana bread in for the crew (I read that somewhere, I don't actually see the banana bread).

The scheduled show after *American Sunrise* is the cooking show *Mature Palate,* and then the soap opera, *To Love and To Hold;* the news; the soap opera, *Long Days, Lonely Nights;*

some kind of *The Price is Right* knockoff except the prizes are food baskets; then reruns of TRS's cops and robbers show, *NYChase.*

I never used to watch *NYChase,* but seeing Matt Rowler as Detective Derrick is like discovering a twenty-dollar bill in a forgotten purse. I'd forgotten about him.

Why am I up so early today? I am hunting for the *Party Girls* commercial.

On Tuesday Carrie called to tell me that she just saw the fifteen-second promo and I looked fantastic. Of course, I was in the bathroom and missed the message and the commercial and now I have no idea when it will be on again.

By Wednesday Steve is losing patience. "Can't you call someone and ask them when it's going to be on?" he says when I refuse to change the channel for the sixth consecutive hour. He puts his feet up on the couch and lays his head on my lap.

They make recording machines that can be programmed not to tape the commercials, don't they? Why don't they make recorders that zap through the shows and tape only the commercials? "I don't know who's in charge of the show's marketing," I tell Steve. But mainly, I don't want to be *that* girl. The pain-in-the-ass who calls up producers at all hours, asking ridiculous questions. I'm mature. And patient. And I'll just watch hours of television. What else do I have to do?

Steve points to the television. "Is that it?"

There I am.

On TV.

I'm dancing. My hair looks fantastic. I will always wear red. I will never buy clothing in any other color. Erin, Michelle and Brittany are also dancing. We are all dancing on the bar. A faster dance version of "Girls Just Want To Have Fun" pumps through our living room. A panoramic shot of nighttime Manhattan is superimposed behind us and then there's Erin. She's smiling seductively at the camera. Her name is spelled at the bottom of the screen in a white font that I vaguely recognize as Comic Sans from Microsoft Word. Her breasts perk towards the camera. I never want to look that slutty. There's Michelle. That hair is incredible. Her name flashes under her face. She blows a kiss at the camera and then laughs. Now me?

No. Brittany. Brittany from a side view, a profile, her massive breasts peeking out the side. Never mind peek. Those things are climaxing out. She flicks her hair with her hand and I'm next, I'm next, I'm next!

And there I am, smiling.

"Hey, that's you!" Steve says.

My hair looks gorgeous, my eyebrows sophisticated, my upper lip mustache-less. I love Carrie.

Erin giving a body shot to some guy. Thankfully that wasn't me.

And there's me giving a body shot.

Oh-oh. Through the corner of my eye I watch as Steve's face drains of color.

I was just totally busted.

"They're sexy, they're single, they're wild," a sultry voice announces.

Another panoramic shot of a lit-up Manhattan. "And they party in the city that never sleeps."

Shot of us dancing at Princess. "This Sunday at 9:30 p.m., watch what these PARTY GIRLS were up to the night before…"

Erin and Michelle dirty dancing.

"And move to the music with TRS's new reality series…*Party Girls*."

Party Girls!™, TRS, SUNDAY 9:30 flashes across the screen and *To Love and To Hold* resumes.

A twinkly-eyed woman in a full-length ball gown sobs on screen. "Oh, what will I do? Arnold Mackenzie III is the secret father of my child!"

I sit shell-shocked on the couch.

"I was on TV," I say.

"You looked um…very sexy," Steve says. "You didn't tell me that…um…" His voice trails off. He better not ruin my moment with male jealousy. I think he senses my eyes narrowing and instead says, "You're a star."

Yes, I am. I was on TV. And it wasn't a home video. I was on cable. Oh, my. Anyone could have seen that. TV stars. Movie people. Tom Cruise. Julia Roberts. These people watch TV, don't they? They could easily have turned it on a few minutes ago and seen me. I'm sure someone I know saw it. Maybe someone I went to high school with. Maybe someone saw it and is going to call right now.

I stare at the phone. It doesn't ring.

Steve takes my hand and kisses it. The red polish is all chipped. I definitely have to schedule myself a manicure before Saturday. Can't looked chipped, can I?

It's Saturday. Saturday. Saturday!

At two-thirty, I leave Zodiac Nails with a French manicure. Thought I'd try something a little different. Michelle had one and it looked cool, natural but better. I'm wearing my boots again tonight, so there's no need for a pedicure. I stop at a Duane Reade pharmacy and buy a pair of tweezers. Unwanted hairs are starting to sprout around my eyebrows and I think my own pair is too blunt. On one side of the aisle are tweezers for two dollars apiece. On the other side they're ten.

I opt for the ten. What if the cheap ones screw my face up?

I am trying to occupy my thoughts with superficialities so I don't hyperventilate. All I've had to eat all day is half a bagel with margarine. I'm afraid anything else will come back up. I stop at an Au Bon Pain and pick up a cheese sandwich. I have to force myself to eat something, otherwise my drinks tonight will definitely come back up.

At three, when I get home and check my messages, there's one from Carrie. "Hi, hon! Hope you're excited! Car service is picking you up at three-thirty to take you to Tribeca's Bolton Hotel. Bring whatever you're planning to wear tonight and whatever you'll need to get ready."

I'm supposed to be ready in thirty minutes? Why does no

one mention these things? I call Carrie, panicked. "In a half an hour? I just got home! What if I wasn't home yet? They're shooting us getting ready?" At a hotel? "I thought you said someone's doing my hair and makeup?" I will not panic. I will not panic. I am panicking.

"They will, but they want it to look like you're doing it yourself. You're supposed to be everyday party girls. You can't have people doing your makeup. Don't worry, just bring your stuff and you'll be filmed putting it on and we'll turn off the camera and the makeup artist will fix it up. Same with your hair. How do you want to wear it?"

"I don't know. Straight with the layers curled around my face? So I shouldn't shower here? I don't have a ton of makeup."

"No, I told you, you're getting ready at the hotel. Don't freak."

Thirty minutes later I'm plucked and packed and waiting downstairs, my heart exploding in my chest. A black sedan pulls up to my building. The back window opens and Erin's face pops out.

"Sit in the front, you're the last one to be picked up."

I hate sitting shotgun in a hired car. I always feel compelled to make small talk with the driver. I climb into the front seat and smile at the other girls.

They ignore me and continue their conversation.

"I'm surprised they even sent us a car," Erin says. "I was expecting them to tell us to find our way over there. When they're not filming, they don't care if we're dressed in garbage bags."

They could have managed a hello.

Brittany nods. "They're so cheap. We're the stars, but do they treat us like stars? No."

Michelle seems to be ignoring them as well, so I don't take her snub personally. She's filing her nails.

"We're already prima donnas before we film our first show?" I say. The problem with sitting in the front is that by the end of the drive, my neck will be in severe pain from constant twisting. I turn to the driver. "How are you?" I ask.

He grunts.

"You're new to all this, you'll see," Erin says to me. "They couldn't give a shit about us. We're completely replaceable."

"One of us was already replaced," Brittany says. "I think you'd better realize right here and now who your real friends are. You never know what can happen."

Real friends? I've known her for one week. "Excuse me for breaking up the team," I say and spend the rest of the cab ride staring at the bumper of the taxi in front of us. I'm not straining my neck for them if they consider me a scab.

When we pull up to the hotel, a porter comes to take our bags and we follow him through the brass door onto the lobby's marble floor.

Carrie scurries toward us, arms flying. "Hi, girls! All ready?" she asks and kisses us each on the cheek. "Here's the plan. We've got four rooms. Are you excited?"

We squish into the already crowded elevator. "Can you press twelve?" Carrie asks Brittany, since she's closest to the number pad.

Brittany's hands are full, with bags she didn't trust with the porter, but she bends down and tries to press it with her chin.

Instead she hits eleven and twelve. "Oops. My chin is worse than Jay Leno's."

"You don't have a big chin," Carrie says.

"Yes, I do," she answers. "There's nothing I can do about it, so I've accepted it. What am I going to do, get chin liposuction?"

"Erin would," Michelle says, raising an eyebrow.

Brittany squishes her massive chest. "Do you think I should get a breast reduction?"

Erin smirks. "I think Michelle could take your leftovers."

"I'm told that after you've breast-fed they go down in size by themselves," I offer.

Brittany and Erin look at me as though I've just told a joke but omitted the punch line. I feel my cheeks grow hot. Was that a stupid thing to say?

I suddenly feel uncomfortable in my own skin, like I'm too pale, and trying on too-tight bikinis that cause protruding stomach and hip flab. Who are these people? How did I end up in this claustrophobic elevator?

The doors open at the eleventh floor and everyone giggles. I contemplate making a run for it. I think I'm going to be sick.

The doors close.

"Can someone explain to me why we're at a hotel and not in our own apartments?" Michelle asks. "Aren't we supposed to live in New York?"

Carrie pats me on the shoulder again. "It's because the budget only allows for two cameramen. They couldn't be at all four of your apartments at once. This way they can film all of you getting ready at the same time, and they can hire one beautician and one hair stylist who works on you all. And I think M.U. owns the hotel."

The doors open again on the twelfth floor. We shuffle out. The hallway is a madhouse. Pete, Dirk, Tania, Howard and other people I don't know are running back and forth between four rooms, two on each side of the hall, with cameras and clipboards.

It looks like a scene in a movie about people making a movie.

"Brittany and Erin," Howard says, waving. "Your connecting rooms are here." He points to the doors on his right. "Sunny and Miche have the connecting rooms on the other side. Good luck."

Carrie's cell phone rings and she reaches in her purse to answer it.

Howard is deep in discussion with Dirk.

The four of us don't move. What are we supposed to be *doing?*

"Howard," Michelle says. "This setup is adorable. But do you mind telling us what we should do?"

Howard looks up, his face registering surprise that we're all still standing there. "We're starting with Erin in the shower—"

Erin raises an eyebrow.

"Don't worry," Howard says, smiling brightly. "It'll be classy naked. Artsy. I want a shot of you peeking out behind the curtain and saying hello to the camera."

I'd prefer not to have anyone anywhere near my shower, thanks. I don't even like sharing my shower with Steve. Bathroom time is alone time. No matter how long we live together, I'm never going to be a pee-with-the-door-open type of girl.

A cloud of confusion crosses Brittany's face. "But, Howard, aren't we supposed to pretend the camera isn't there?"

"Good point, sweetheart. Tell you what, just wave at the camera. Anyway, after Erin we'll pop over to Miche, Sunny and finally to Brittany's shower."

Sunny's shower. My shower. IN THE SHOWER? All of America will get to shower with me before Steve does. I don't think he's going to like that. I don't think I'm going to like it. Distressed, I ask, "What, uh, are the chances of that clip ending up in the final cut?"

He looks at me like I'm an idiot. "I have no idea what ends up in the show until we're editing the show. We're filming about nine hours of footage. We're using twenty-two minutes, and the first five minutes has to be about you prepping, then chatting. If the viewer doesn't get to know you, she won't care." The cheese ball places a hand on his heart. "If she doesn't care, she won't watch."

I give it another shot. "It's just that I, uh, don't think we should treat the audience like idiots. We're supposed to be alone. This is a reality show. How are the viewers supposed to buy into the show's authenticity if we're waving at the camera? Is it supposed to be a postmodern interpretation?"

He rolls his eyes. "Don't worry your pretty little head about the technicalities, sweetheart." He narrows his eyes. "But I get your point. No waving. Just smile sweetly when you poke your head out. Remember, at the beginning it's important to make them *care*."

Brittany shoots me a dirty look, then slings her arms around Erin. "Of course, they'll care about us, Howard. We're awesome."

He shakes his head. "Sure, you're awesome, babe, but remember that the viewers also care about scandal. About humiliation. They want to see you squirm. They want you to talk crap about each other. They want to see alliances and betrayals and backstabbers. Don't be too nice."

We all laugh. Hah, hah.

What bad things will they say about me? What am I going to say about them? Is it better if they say fake bad things, or real bad things?

Howard continues. "Then we'll have about ten seconds of you getting to the bar, in the cab, and then a few seconds of you entering the bar, and then of course the next fourteen minutes will be of you girls at the club. And we want to see you strutting your single selves. Flirt, pick up, dance, get phone numbers. You're on the prowl."

"I don't even know what club we're going to," Erin says.

"Stirred," Howard says.

Groaning, Michelle takes a seat on the faded mint-green carpet, her back pressed up against the door. "One of my exes hangs out there. Can we not let him in?"

"Sounds like good TV," Erin says.

Howard scowls. Why is he scowling? Won't that make good TV? "The last few minutes," he says, "will be of you girls on your way home, separately, commenting on the night. Of course, if any of you want to use the hotel rooms to entertain any new friends from the club, we've installed cameras beside the smoke detectors." He winks at us. "And the rooms are all yours for the night. If you stay, don't turn off the cameras."

Michelle starts laughing. "Hilarious. Reality porn?"

Yeah, Steve would love that. Me bringing back a guy. Unless, of course, he's the guy. He's always hinting about wanting to film us in the act. I suppose we could "accidentally" meet at the bar and I could bring him to the hotel. I quickly dismiss the idea. Steve might have a few particular quirks, but I don't think he's ready to share them with the world.

And neither am I. I can just imagine his mother Joy saying to me, "Oy vey, Sunny! You let him put it in your *mouth? Is* that even kosher?"

No. Not going to happen.

"I'm not asking you to have sex," Howard says. "I'm only mentioning that sex makes great television. Remember. Hollywood ain't all glitz and glamour."

Then it's prostitution?

"Why don't you put cameras in our apartments?" Erin says, posing with her hand on her hip. "Then you could watch us twenty-four seven."

"Forget it," Michelle says. "There's no way you're installing anything in my apartment. I didn't sign up for full-time surveillance."

"I second the motion," Brittany says.

"That seems fair," I say in my best aw-shucks-I-could-go-either-way voice intonation.

"The budget on this show isn't paying me to sift through hundreds of hours of footage of you guys flossing your teeth," Howard says. "Saturday nights will be sufficient. Also, each of you will be wearing mikes the entire time while you're out and they can't be turned off."

"Even when we're in the bathroom?" Brittany asks.

"Even then," Howard answers.

"Nine hours of footage," Michelle says. "For twenty-two minutes of film?"

Howard nods. "Exactly."

"Hilarious," she says.

"And you're going to mix and match the images with our comments and conversations?" I ask.

"Yup," Howard answers.

Carrie closes her phone and returns to our huddle. "That was your father. He has to work late again."

Nice of him to wish me good luck.

We open the doors to our rooms. Wow. Make that our suites.

In my room a king-sized bed faces a television the size of a wall. Beyond the bed is a sitting room with a beige couch, a wooden table and two wooden chairs. Beyond that are French doors which look out onto a balcony. I bet there's even a Jacuzzi. I love Jacuzzi baths. I open the bathroom door, and just as I suspected—a Jacuzzi. There is nothing I love more than sitting in a Jacuzzi with a book and a glass of wine. Those jets hit the spot. I wonder if I can sneak one in now.

Forget it. They'd probably want to film it.

Steve loves Jacuzzis, too. On the sixth-month anniversary of our first date, he rented us a room in a luxury hotel in South Beach. The room with a Jacuzzi cost an extra hundred dollars, but let's just say we got our money's worth. By the time we emerged from the water, our skin was so soft you could peel it off.

This is the nicest hotel room I've ever been in and I can't even share it with Steve.

But I get to share it with the rest of the world.

I move my bag from near the door where the porter left it, to on the bed. Will they want to film me taking my clothes out of the bag or out of the closet? Am I supposed to be dressing in the hotel or making it appear as though I'm staying in the hotel?

Why doesn't anyone tell me anything?

I decide to unpack my second pair of new black pants and my new purple shirt—I wanted to wear the red one again but Carrie wouldn't let me.

Maybe my boots will be more comfortable tonight now that I've worn them in?

Am I supposed to get in the shower and wait for them to

come and film me? But I have the key. How will they get in?
Unless they have duplicate keys.

I guess I'll wait.

I sit on the edge of the bed. I click on the television. I can
order a movie. Why are half of the movies porn?

A half hour later I'm lying across the white sheet—I don't
care how nice the hotel is, I'm not sitting on a germ-infested
comforter—and am halfway into an episode of *Friends* when
there's a knock on my door.

"One sec!" I yell and then remake the bed.

I guess they don't have keys. I open the door.

Howard, Carrie and Pete crowd in.

Carrie claps her hands. "Let's get you naked!"

My lungs seem to arrest at the word *naked.* And having my
father's girlfriend being the one to tell me doesn't help matters. Naked. Naked. TV. Naked.

I can't just take off my clothes. I barely even know these
people. "Um…how about I get undressed in the bathroom and
then let you know when I'm ready?"

Howard glares at his watch. "Hurry up."

After painfully removing my clothes as if I was peeling an
onion, I fold them and put them in a pile in the corner. A few
minutes later I'm in the shower, wetting my hair. "I'm ready,"
I say. The shower curtain is beige and opaque, so no one will
be able to see behind it. I hope. Unless they bring the camera
into the shower, which they won't. This isn't porn. Are cameras even waterproof?

Good thing it's not a porn. My pubic hair is completely uneven. The non-waxed side keeps growing back. I hope the
rumor that waxing makes your hair thinner isn't true. Otherwise my pubic hair will be forever off-kilter.

"Sunny? We're coming in," Howard says.

Oh my. I take a deep breath in an attempt to calm the building hysteria, and the desire to rip the shower curtain off the pole
and wrap it numerous times around my exposed body.

Two shadows become visible through the curtain. I peek

out. Pete's leg is up on the toilet and he's fiddling with the camera lens.

"What should I do?" I ask, panic creeping into my voice.

"Why don't you soap up your hair and then stick your head out?" Pete says. "An action shot."

Who wants her first image on television to have soapy hair and no makeup? "I had more of a wet-haired sexy look in mind," I suggest. One move and I flash the entire country and I'm worried about soapy hair?

"We'll do that, too," Howard says. "If we end up using any of this at all, it will be only the most intriguing image. The best one."

The best for who? Me? I don't even let Steve see me like this. I unscrew the lid to the hotel shampoo. It smells like strawberry pudding. Can they see me in here? They're not looking, right?

Soapy, I pop my head back out and force a smile at the camera. Got to make them *care*. Then I try to look like I'm not looking at the camera, but happen to be standing in the shower with my head peeping out from behind the curtain, while gripping the edge of the curtain for dear life. What am I doing here? Why aren't I sitting behind a desk working on a PowerPoint presentation?

The bathroom door is open and I can see their shadows entering and exiting the room.

There's no conditioner. I hate when hotels don't provide conditioner. If I don't use conditioner my hair will look like a big bird's nest.

"Um...can someone get me a conditioner?" I ask. "I didn't bring and the shower doesn't have."

"I have enough film," Pete says. "I'm done."

I exhale the large breath that couldn't have been helping my silhouette.

"I'll get you some," Howard says.

They leave the bathroom and a few minutes later, I see the outline of a shadow behind the curtain.

"Hello?"

"Hi, Sunny," Howard's voice says.

That was so creepy. I didn't even hear him sneak in.

"I borrowed Michelle's conditioner for you. Where do you want me to put it?"

"On the counter is perfect, thanks."

Where else would he put it? In the shower with me?

Oh. Gross. Is he coming on to me? He's stationed way too close to the curtain. "I'll be out in five, thanks," I say.

He slithers back out the door.

When I'm done, I hop out of the stall and quickly lock the bathroom door. I wrap myself in a towel and tie the top over my chest in a funky knot. When my mother used to dry me off after a bath, she always designed my shower towel on me in what she called my Oscar dress. Pink, fluffy, regal.

I'm a pro. My towel dress looks quite sophisticated, if I do say so myself.

I open the door. Pete is filming me.

Tania looks up from her clipboard. "We're going to film you blow-drying your hair. Then the stylist will come and do it for you. Then we'll get you putting on your makeup and I'll ask you a few questions, okay?"

I nod and remove the blow-dryer from the wall. I whisk it over my head while looking in the mirror. I feel the camera filming me.

I flip my head over and blow-dry the underneath. A motion shot. I'm fun. I'm frivolous.

I hope the towel doesn't fall.

"That looks great!" Pete yells over the sound of the dryer. "You can stop now!"

I turn it off and flip back up. Pete and Tania are already gone, presumably to film one of the other girls in their state of preparation. I drop my towel and then…damn, damn, damn. The camera next to the smoke detector. Turn my back to the evil eye and attempt to cover my privates with my hands, while lunging for the terry-cloth bathrobe I spotted earlier in the cupboard.

"Ready?" a voice from nowhere says. I look up to see a

woman surrounded by numerous hair-styling tools and products standing in the sitting room.

I just walked through the room naked, without even seeing her. "Sorry, I…uh…didn't mean to change in front of you." Or in front of the entire world, I think, looking up again at the smoke detector. I sit down in the empty chair.

Thirty minutes later, my hair is styled and glossy and has that I-could-never-do-this-by-myself look.

I open the door that connects my room to Michelle's and hit a second door instead of her room. I bet all the girls are sitting around relaxing. I wonder if they're talking about me. I knock. I hear giggles.

"One sec," she says. She opens the door, also in her bathrobe. Her hair is wild with red curls. "Come sit with us."

Her room is the same as mine, just reversed. A flushed-faced Howard is sitting on the couch.

Does he sleaze up everyone? Something naughty going on here?

He stands up. "Why don't I get Pete and film you girls gossiping and having a drink?"

"Sure," says Michelle.

Howard picks up the phone. "Room service? Girls, you want Cosmos?"

Pete clips our lavaliere microphones to our collars, and hides the small, black, body-pack transmitters in our pockets.

"Remember, girls," Howard says. "I am a ghost. Nothing I say is going to make the cut. So repeat my questions into your answers. And speak in the present tense. We'll use some of your comments with other images."

Pete starts filming Michelle and me in bathrobes, sipping martinis. Here we go. I better not say anything dumb. I bet I say something dumb.

We silently sip our drinks.

So.

"I liked your boots the other day," Michelle says. "I mean, I like your boots."

"Thanks." That sounded squeaky. "Yours, too." Not that she's wearing any boots at the moment. But she was in the past.

"Were they Kenneth Cole?" she asks. "Are they Kenneth Cole?"

I carefully nod. Don't look at the camera. Don't look at the camera. "I think so."

"I'm *obsessed* with Kenneth Cole."

Halfway through the drinks and the useless small talk, Howard says, "So what do you think about breast implants?"

I almost choke on my drink. We don't answer.

"Would either of you get them?" Howard asks, pressing for information.

"I wouldn't get breast implants," I say, carefully incorporating his question into my answer. Did that work? Did my voice sound steady? My bathrobe won't stay closed. Can they see inside? I can see inside. Great, I'm flashing America.

"What would you implant?" Michelle says to me, laughing and almost spilling her drink. "You have perfect boobs."

I cross my legs and attempt to sit up straight so that the top of my robe stays flat. Steve loves my breasts, even if I do catch him once in a while ogling the even more endowed.

"Would you ever do it?" I ask Michelle.

She shakes her head vehemently. "Never. Ouch. I'm not cutting my chest open. Besides, I'm happy with my body. Some women are never happy with the way they look. It's sad. I think that anyone who has cosmetic surgery has some serious self-esteem issues. And it's a turnoff for guys. Men sense desperation when a woman starts cutting herself up or adding silicone."

I'm impressed with her on-air self-confidence. No worries. She just goes.

I'm not sure I agree with her. Is a woman's self-esteem even something a guy thinks about? I mean, picture a bombshell walking around in a low-cut blouse, her boobs a mile ahead of her chin. I sincerely doubt that the men who gape at her are thinking, I wonder how the poor dear is feeling.

Ooh. That was good. I should say that. It sounded quite clever. I think. It did. I open my mouth to speak—

"Besides," Michelle continues, and my opportunity is missed. "They wouldn't be *real*. Guys know these things."

And her point is…?

We chat a bit longer and then Pete motions to me. "Time to do your makeup."

Having a drink was a good idea. I'm far more relaxed. Wheee! This is almost fun. Pete and Tania follow me back to my room and into my bathroom. Good thing the fogged mirrors have cleared up. I pose behind the sink and counter, peering at my reflection.

The camera's light is hot. Pete has returned to his station on the toilet. Tania stands outside the bathroom, by the open door. "Now, Sunny, answer as much as you want," she says as I pat a dab of foundation on my cheek. "Talk and relax. Why did you move to New York?"

An easy one.

"I moved to New York because I wanted to experience a different atmosphere. I wanted to meet different people. New York is a cool city. I thought, why not?"

I sound fun.

"Do you date a lot?"

"I date a bit. I broke up with someone before I moved. Now I'm looking for a few good men."

"Do you let men pick you up or do you pick them up?"

Another easy one. "If I'm interested in a man, I'm not afraid to talk to him."

"Give us an example of when you tried to pick up a guy."

Oh-oh. Pick up a guy, pick up a guy. Think adventure, fun, flirty. Ooh. I have a good one. "I was backpacking through Europe and we were in Nice. The friend that I was traveling with was shopping, and I was tanning—and trying to avoid being stabbed by one of the jagged rocks under my beach towel. Actually, it was also my shower towel—some jerk had swiped my beach towel along with my Hard Rock Café Amsterdam T-shirt from my balcony in Brouge."

No one cares about my towel. What had Carrie warned about rambling?

"Anyway, I spotted a buff blonde close to the shore, so I packed my bag, strolled ever-so-casually to where he was reading a magazine and he looked up and said hi. I was like wohoo!—he speaks English! I planted my towel beside him. As a conversation initiator, I asked him for the time while applying sunscreen as if I had just gotten to the beach. Two hours later we made plans to meet for dinner. Voila."

Isn't that a great pickup story?

"So what happened on the date?" Tania asks.

More? Um… "He met me in front of my hostel and we walked to Vieux Nice for a perfect, picturesque romantic dinner. We sat in the courtyard. First came the wine. We toasted, we drank, we refilled, we laughed. We had mussels. And then…"

Shit. I forgot where this story goes. Damn. Can I change my story? Is it funny?

"And then?"

What the hell. "During dinner I noticed he had a red mark on the upper corner of his lip. I figured he would just lick it off, but it lingered, ruining the entire fantasy. Like the way an anchovy spoils a Caesar salad. I hate anchovies. I tried to be, you know, seductive, and I dabbed at the spot with my napkin, but like a permanent marker it wouldn't budge." I can't believe I'm telling this story. Why am I telling this story? It's a gross story. Who tells gross stories on TV? If it's stupid, they won't put it in, right?

"What was it?"

"It wasn't a tomato remnant. It was a cold sore."

"Gross," Tania says.

I am a horrible person for telling this story. How can I make fun of someone who gets cold sores, when I get them myself? I'm definitely throwing a stone from my glass house.

"I felt bad for him. It happens. But I felt less bad when during the walk back to the hostel, he dove in for a kiss. How nasty is that? Doesn't he know they're contagious? Isn't that rude? I told him I didn't kiss on the first date."

"What did he do?" Tania asks.

"He pouted. Obviously not his best move since it emphasized his predicament." I raise my eyebrows for effect.

Pete bursts out laughing and gives me a thumbs-up.

Go figure. I guess cold sores make good copy.

The four of us are standing outside the hotel. We are dressed, we are glam, we are made up, we are smiling, we are tipsy and we are fabulous.

The two cameras film us from across the street. Our lavalieres are clipped to our collars and concealed under our hair, and the transmitter is clipped and hidden in our pants, near the tag.

"Now pile into the back seat of the taxi," Howard says.

We pile into the taxi. Michelle is kind of sitting on Brittany's lap. Why would four people sit in the back seat of a taxi? Is this reality? Is this legal? The taxi drives a few feet and then stops.

Tania opens the taxi door. "Can we do that again? I want to get two of you climbing into the taxi from each door."

We pile out.

"Filming," Dirk says.

We pile back in.

"Let's try it one more time," Tania says. "A bit sexier."

This is ridiculous. One clip of supposed real life takes thirty minutes of dry runs.

Pile out, pile in.

This time we are successful and the taxi speeds off. At the end of the block the cabbie slams on his brakes. Brittany, Michelle and I slam into the dividing wall. Erin slams into Michelle.

"Will you be careful," Michelle says.

"What, you think I did that on purpose?" Erin says.

The taxi driver reverses back toward the crew. Pete opens

the front door and sticks his head in. "Girls, I need you to get back in one more time. I want Pete to film the drive from the inside."

We groan and pile out again. Michelle says that she's not sitting in the middle this time. Tania tells us we have to keep the same spots. "For continuity," she explains. "Last time, I promise. Straight to the club now, I swear."

Pete attaches a light to inside the cab's roof and adjusts his camera.

"Filming," he says.

We climb back in, close the doors and take off. At the light the taxi driver slams on his brakes again. Michelle jabs her elbow into Erin's stomach.

"Sorry," she says and shrugs. "Continuity."

part 3

9:30(TRS) *Party Girls!™* (CC) Reality show 30 min 432781 TV14

Y ou just got home. Yes, *you.*

You drop your plastic bag of take-out Japanese food, along with the mail (bills, bills and more bills) you've neglected to pick up all week onto the kitchen table. You shed your boots under the table, your jean jacket onto the carpet. What are the chances you remember to put those away later?

"Hello?" you say. "Anyone home?"

"I'm on the phone!" your roommate yells.

You change into your ripped-in-the-knee sweatpants and your high school ex-boyfriend's frayed football T-shirt (so soft and worn-out, an essential element in your pajama roster), grab one of your roommate's Diet Cokes (this time you'll remember to buy her a new one, you swear) and plop yourself on the couch.

You had a date last night. It was a blind date, which normally isn't your favorite but actually wasn't as car-running-over-your-foot excruciating as you anticipated.

He was tall, on-time, asked questions about your job and paid for the meal. Four out of four ain't bad.

Dinner for a blind date is always risky.

On your last dinner blind date the evil man left his cell phone on the table and then *took his calls.*

Anyway, last night's date was sweet and cute, and after a long dinner of too much wine you kissed him and then kissed him some more and then went back to his apartment and then...

...slept with him.

Yeah, yeah, yeah, you know you're not supposed to sleep with a guy on the first date, but this time it's different. Really. You swear, you've never done it before. He liked you, really liked you, you could tell. He looked deep into your eyes and laughed at all your jokes and asked questions, thoughtful questions about your ideas and opinions and philosophies...

He said he'd call this week and he will. You just know.

Smiling, you slouch on the couch. Something good had better be on.

You bite into your California roll. You wonder why it's called a California roll. What do they call them in Japan? A Tokyo roll?

It's 9:40. You press Power on the remote.

News. You've heard enough about death and destruction for one day. You flip the remote. A commercial. Flip. More news. Flip.

Your television is filming a club. The windowless walls are covered in ceiling-to-floor murals of martini glasses. Each wall has its own bar. About a hundred twenty-something men and women in tight black outfits are either dancing in the center, relaxing in one of the sunken, black velvet couches or ordering drinks. Techno music is playing in the background.

"Let's do some shots," a platinum blonde says. Under her face, in white writing it says Erin. Four girls head over to one of the bars. The bartender is blond and muscular and is wearing a tight black short-sleeved shirt and what you assume to be his best sexy smile.

You can't remember the last time you walked into a club, walked straight to a bar and got served right away.

"Four shots of tequila!" yells a chest-heavy brunette. The sign post says Brittany.

She doesn't have to yell. She knows she's wearing a mike, right?

"Make that eight," Erin says.

The girls chitchat. Mr. Suave Bartender brings their shots.

Erin raises her glass. "Here's to you, here's to me, best of friends we'll always be, and if by chance we disagree, well, BEEEEEEP you and here's to me!"

They lick the salt, do the shots, suck the lime.

"Wohoo!" Brittany screams, raising her empty glass into the air. She's really tall, towering over the other girls.

A black-haired girl, Sunny, begs for a glass of water. "My mouth feels like it just swallowed burning lava," she gasps after downing the entire shot.

"Next one," Erin says, handing out the remaining four.

"Another one? I'm going to be sick," a gorgeous redhead, Michelle, says.

They lick the salt, down the shot, slam the glass on the bar and suck the lime. Three of the girls, anyway. Michelle stops halfway. "I can't," she whines. "It's too vile."

Two hot guys join them. One looks like Ethan Hawke and the other, next to Brittany, like a shrunken Michael Jordan.

Ethan leans against the bar and squeezes Erin's shoulder. "You girls must be tired."

"Why?" Erin asks.

"Because you've been running through my mind all night."

Erin giggles and slithers up closer to him.

You can't believe she just fell for that. That has to be the worst pickup line you've ever heard. Even you wouldn't have fallen for that.

The image switches.

Ethan is pressed up against Erin, near a black painting of an olive. Her superimposed voice says: "I have problems meeting good guys. Most of them are just out for sex. Nothing feels worse than realizing you've just been used." Ethan's hand is on her waist, slowly moving its way up, and they appear to be whispering sweet nothings into each other's ears.

Silly, silly Erin. Picking up a guy at a bar is never going to work.

Michelle and Sunny are perched on bar stools, watching. Michelle's hand is covering her mouth in gleeful shock. "I can't believe what's going on there. Omigod. His hand is on her behind. Look! Look!"

Sunny shakes her head and laughs. She sips from her martini. She doesn't talk much.

Switch.

Ethan and Erin grope each other on the dance floor. Ew. Is that tongue? His tongue is in her mouth. He's licking her mouth. Pull the camera away! There's saliva everywhere.

Switch.

Thank you.

Brittany and little Michael are dirty dancing, but there's no tongue. Boring.

Switch.

"Let's dance," Sunny says to Michelle. They slide off their bar stools and the camera follows them to the dance floor. Two creepy-looking men attempt to squirm their way into dancing with them, but Sunny and Michelle ignore them and box them out.

Sunny is doing a little hand-up-in-the-air, butt-grooving thing, but Michelle is really good. You wish you could gyrate like that. Sometimes, when you're too drunk you think you can.

Switch.

You don't believe it. Ethan's hand is up Erin's shirt. He is fully feeling her breast. And she's letting him! Slut bag. He is feeling her breast on television. Does she have no shame? She's not even that drunk. Romeo over here is never going to call her tomorrow. He's only hooking up with her so all his friends will think he's Mr. Stud.

You are so embarrassed for her.

Oh, God. Your blind date. He's not like Romeo here, right? He will call. He will. Will he?

Gross. He's sticking his hand down her pants. She has no shame. You would never go this far at a bar. You can't watch. You close one eye. Why isn't Brittany stopping her? Where is Brittany?

Switch.

Michael is buying her a shot. Make that two shots. Three. Slow down, Brittany! Yoohoo, Brittany! What is she doing? She just downed five shots. Does she think her stomach is made of steel?

She's draped on Michael. "I...you...I'm on TV." She starts laughing uncontrollably. She's way too tall for this type of behavior. Tall girls shouldn't drink so much. The fall to the floor will be so much longer.

She's starting to teeter. She can't even stand up properly. Michael tries to kiss her. What is he doing? Doesn't he see how drunk she is? Gross.

Switch.

Sunny and Michelle are dancing but Sunny freezes and says to Michelle, "Brit just made a mad dash to the bathroom. I'm going to make sure she's all right. Why don't you go check on Erin before she gets herself pregnant?"

The television follows Sunny into the bathroom. Can they do that? Can they just follow her into the bathroom? What if there are other people in there? Shouldn't they knock? You see the back of Brittany's shoes peeping out from a stall.

Sunny knocks on the door. "Brit? You okay?"

The sound of puking reverberates through your speakers. Gross. Thanks for sharing, Brit! Do you really need to hear that? Good thing you already finished your sushi.

Sunny tries to open the door, but it's locked. Silence. Then: "Do you want me to get you some water?"

Silence.

"Brit, you okay? Answer me or I'm breaking down the door."

"Fine. Don't feel too well. Water would be great. But not tap water. Too many pollutants."

Now that's interesting, you think. A lush who's monitoring her chemical intake.

"I'll be right back."

Switch.

Michelle searches for Erin on the dance floor. She spots Sunny coming out of the bathroom and shrugs her shoulders. "Erin has pulled a Houdini," Michelle says. "She disappeared."

"She couldn't have. You can't disappear when the cameras are following you and you're miked."

"I don't see her."

"Let me get some water to Brit and then I'll help you find Erin."

Sunny's awesome. Why don't you have a friend like Sunny?

Michelle follows Sunny back into the bathroom. Sunny knocks on the stall. "I'm slipping a bottle of water under the door, 'kay?"

Switch.

Screen flips to a couch in the corner of the bar. Ethan is lying on top of Erin. Her shirt is hiked up around her neck and he's dry-humping her. A crowd is gathered around them, observing.

Why do you get the feeling you're at a sports match? The score: Erin, two oh, babys. Ethan, one small grunt. Erin's definitely ahead. "Go, Erin, go!" Who said that? Disgusting.

What kind of perverts watch this stuff?

Is that the bartender taking bets?

Through a small crack in the crowd, Michelle and Sunny spot them. Michelle covers her mouth with her hand, as if in midyawn. Sunny's mouth just drops.

Michelle says, "What a ho."

"Maybe she's drunk and doesn't even realize what she's doing?" Sunny asks. "We should stop her."

"She hasn't had that much to drink," Michelle says, and starts laughing. "She is so dirty."

"I want to make sure she realizes the consequences of her

actions," Sunny says. "I don't want her to be embarrassed tomorrow." She tentatively pushes her way through the masses of people, toward the dueling duo. "Erin?" They ignore her. "Erin?" she says again, her voice a wee bit louder.

Erin's eyes flutter open and she stops moving. Ethan stops on top of her. He turns to glare at the intruder who seems intent on ruining his porn debut.

"What?" Erin asks, rolling her eyes.

Commercial break.

"You have to come watch this!" you scream to your roommate. Her door is closed and she doesn't answer. "Come here!" you scream again.

"What?" she asks, opening her door and sticking out her head out, the phone against her ear.

"The most ridiculous show is on. People are having sex and puking all over the place. It's about single girls in New York!"

"I heard about that. What's it called?"

You flip through the TV guide. "I think it's called *Party Girls.*"

10

Night Calls

(Steve, Carrie, my father and I are sitting in the living room of my dad's sprawling Park Avenue apartment watching the show. Carrie has ruled that there is to be no talking until after the show.)

On television, I'm squatting beside the humping duo. (Those are really great black pants I'm wearing.) "Um…want to come dance?" I ask Erin on the screen.

"I'm kind of busy right now," Erin says, pulling Ethan tighter to her naked chest.

I cross my arms under my chest. "Are you sure you want to do this now?" I say.

"BEEEEP, Sunny, I'm fine," Erin says, running her blood-red fingernails down Ethan's back.

("She said *fuck* in case anyone's wondering," I tell Steve, Carrie and my father.)

I look back at Michelle. Michelle rolls her eyes and beckons me to follow her. We head back to the bar and order Cosmos.

On screen, I lean against a bar stool. "I feel bad leaving her like that," I say. "She doesn't even know him."

"She's a big girl," Michelle answers. She twirls her long, curly hair around her fingers, her face draining of color. "Uh-oh. My ex at six o'clock. That BEEEEP loser—"

I turn to look, but Michelle lays a hand on my shoulder. "Don't look. I don't want him to know I'm here."

I take a sip of my drink, doing a damned good job of appearing nonchalant. "You've been spotted. He's on his way."

Switch.

The camera shows a dark-haired, thirty-something hottie in pressed slacks and a gray shirt, maneuvering his way through the crowd toward them.

Michelle starts giggling. "Is it too late to run?"

("I don't know what her problem is," Carrie says. "He's not that bad. A little old for her, though." I don't comment, but I'm not sure if she realizes how ridiculous that sounds, coming from her.)

The guy taps Michelle on the shoulder. "Miche?"

She turns around and feigns surprise. "Daniel! So nice to see you." She kisses the air at the side of his cheek and smiles.

("She's a bit of a liar, huh?" Steve comments.)

"You look amazing," Daniel says.

"Thanks. You, too. What are you up to?"

"Same old, same old. I'm still at Goldman. I just bought a place in the Hamptons."

"Good for you." Behind her back she yanks my hand. "Listen, we're being called over to that side of the bar. Great running into you." She kisses the air next to his other cheek, and still holding my hand pulls me to the dance floor.

"What was that all about?" I ask.

"Hilarious," Michelle says. And dances to the music. "Just an ex."

"What happened?"

"Didn't work out. He became, like, my stalker."

("Stalker?" Steve laughs. "The guy looked normal. He's even wearing pants, not jeans. And he's clean-shaven." I shush him.)

Michelle and I continue dancing. Suddenly Michelle points to the door. "Erin's leaving."

"What?" I ask. "She can't just take off without us."

"She just did."

The screen fills with Erin's hand in Ethan's back pocket, as both climb the staircase that leads out of the bar. "I'm going to BEEEEEEP your brains out," she whispers.

("Did she not realize the mike picks up whispers?" I say, cracking up.)

"Do you think she's taking him back to the room?" the televised-me asks.

Switch.

Erin undressing, Ethan sprawled on a double bed.

Erin is wearing nothing but a black thong and blurred nipples.

Switch.

Still at the bar, I say, "Michelle, I'm going to check on Brittany."

"Don't leave me. I don't want to get stuck with Daniel."

Michelle and I, holding hands, search for Brittany and find her on one of the sunken couches, mouth open, drooling slightly.

("Brittany wasn't that drunk," I say magnanimously. "I swear she looks worse on TV!")

Michelle starts laughing. "Has she passed out?"

"I think so," I say. "I think we should take her home."

"It's only one-thirty," Michelle says.

"I'm tired. You can stay. I'll take her home." I bend over and try to gently nudge her awake. "Brit? Wake up."

Michelle prods her other shoulder. "I'll go with you."

Brittany groans.

Switch.

Brittany, practically comatose, has her arms around Michelle and me, and the three of us climb into a cab. ("You have no idea how much those breasts weigh," I say to Steve. "Honestly, they're like a thousand pounds each.")

Switch.

Same position, me and Michelle dragging Brittany out of the hotel elevator, down the hallway.

"Check her purse for her room key," I say.

Michelle opens Brittany's purse and pulls out a room card. I lean Brittany into a wall.

Michelle slides the key card into the slot on the lock. A red light flashes. She tries to open the door but it doesn't budge.

Brittany groans. "I don't feel well."

"Are you going to be sick again?" Michelle says. "Turn your head. These are Dolce & Gabbana." She gestures to her pants, then sticks the card in the slot a second time. It turns red again.

"You have to wait for the light to turn green," I say.

Michelle tries again, but it's still red.

"You hold her." I dip the card into the slot and it turns green. The door opens easily.

"My head hurts," Brittany wails.

We drop her facedown onto the mattress. I get a glass of water and the garbage pail from the bathroom and place them both beside the bed.

Michelle's ear is pressed against the wall. "I hear moaning," she says. "That's Erin's room."

I leave Brittany's side and lean against the wall, too.

Switch.

Erin's room. Two human-sized lumps appear to be rolling under the covers. "What do you think they're doing?" My superimposed voice (tee-hee, my voice is superimposed!) breaks into the moaning.

"What do you think they're doing?" Michelle's voice answers. "Playing Trivial Pursuit? Brit? You okay? I think she's going to puke again. Turn your head, Brit! Oh, God, she missed. She better pay for dry cleaning."

Switch.

Brittany's room again. "It's going to be a long night," I say, looking up as if I'm addressing the ceiling.

The "Girls Just Want To Have Fun" dance version starts playing and the credits run on the left side of the screen.

I am the nicest girl on television. I am helpful, I am considerate, I am responsible. I love myself.

Steve squeezes my arm and kisses me on the cheek. We're sitting on my father's black suede couch, directly facing the TV. The apartment is about five times the size of mine and Steve's, and the ceilings are twice as high. There might be an echo when I speak.

Even though my father's been living here for years, the place reminds me of an unused expensive hotel room. Obviously pricey furniture, yet sparse and aloof. There are no blankets, no photos, no personal touches. No scrapes on the furniture either. My father's entire body tensed up when Steve poured himself a glass a water (from the tap!) and then set it down on the glass table without a coaster.

"You were awesome," Carrie says from the love seat beside us. My father's arm is draped casually around her shoulder.

"You think?" I *was* awesome. I saved Brittany from dehydration. I attempted to save Erin from gonorrhea.

Did people watching think I was awesome? Or did they think the whole show was ridiculous? It was kind of ridiculous. Who cares about watching me and three other nobodies drink and dance? Who cares what we think, say or do?

I can't decide if I'm providing entertainment or filling people's minds with crap.

"Incredible," Steve says, and kisses me again, this time on the lips. "You were hot. And you're all mine."

Getting a little possessive, are we? When those creepy guys tried to dance with us, his hand got a little tight on my knee.

"I wouldn't want to be Erin's father," my dad says.

What, he so badly wants to be *my* father? "She must be pretty upset," I say.

Carrie wags her finger at us and then picks up her glass for my father to refill. "She knew what she was doing."

"I know, but they showed us making fun of her the entire time," I say.

Leaning back, Steve is watching my father carefully. Whenever my father's in the room, Steve always gets this intense look on his face, scrunching his eyebrows together as though my father is a puzzle he's trying to crack.

Carrie gets up and dances around the living room. "It was fantastic. Incredible. Sex, booze, betrayal, friendship. I won't be able to sleep tonight until the ratings come out."

Ratings? Already? "But don't shows like this take some time to build up a following?" I ask. "I mean, we can't be expected to have good ratings from the get-go."

Carrie shrugs. "If ratings suck, they'll cancel the show."

What? Cancel? Who said anything about canceling? They can cancel? After one episode? Okay, if it gets canceled, it's not the end of the world. I got a bunch of free stuff out of it. I already received the thousand dollars. The whole thing was still a funny experience. I have the first episode on tape, so I can show it to my grandkids. Being the wanna-be reality TV starlet whose show was so awful no one could bear watching it more than once is a little embarrassing, but people who know me will think it's funny. Of course the downside is that I'll be in a bigger rush to find a job. But last week I sent out at least thirty resumes, and I already have an interview set up for next week, at a furniture company. Maybe something will pan out. "When do we know?"

"The first ratings come out tomorrow," Carrie says. "Don't freak. Nothing you can do now."

I'm not freaking. But how can the ratings *not* be good? I was great. I was awesome. Howard could have screwed me during editing, by using my inane remarks about my fictitious ex-boyfriend—somewhere between the Cosmos and the taxi, I gave him details about my fake ex, who had supposedly propelled my move to New York. Howard could have also screwed me by including my absurdly awkward cold sore saga. Why did I think it important to blab on and on about cold sores? No one wants to hear about cold sores. What was I thinking?

I was great. I was awesome.

I was lucky.

I yawn and lay my head on Steve's shoulder. "Do you want to go home soon?" he asks. "You must be exhausted."

I nod. Last night, Howard wrapped up filming a little after three, finally unclipping our mikes from our shirts and turning off the cameras. My stomach started growling, because of the full night of activity and because I had barely eaten anything all day. Michelle laughed when she heard it and said I was lucky the mikes were off. She said she was starving, too, and we went downstairs and ordered food at the bar. I sneaked into the lobby to call Steve from a pay phone and tell him I'd be home in about an hour. I need to get a New York cell phone. Who uses a pay phone? I'm surprised they haven't dismantled them already.

Steve was awake and picked up on the first ring. "How'd it go?"

"Good, I think. I'm not sure. It depends what they use."

"It's over?"

"I couldn't call you otherwise. Imagine if one of the cameras taped it? I'd get booted off the show."

"Come home soon. I miss you."

Miss me? How can he miss me? I see him *all* the time. We spend all morning together, and then every night together whenever he's not working.

After the quick phone call, I returned to the bar just as my cheese and pepperoni pizza and Michelle's fruit salad arrived. As I took my first bite, I saw Erin's sketchy Ethan Hawke guy get out of the elevator and exit the building. It didn't take a brain surgeon to figure out he wouldn't be hanging around for breakfast.

After our snack, we debated waking Brittany up to send her home, but we figured there was no point. "Next time we should just crash at the hotel," Michelle said.

Steve would love that. "I can't. My roommate would be worried about me," I answered. "And I don't think I would be able to sleep, knowing a camera was watching."

"Like if you drooled in your sleep or something?"

When I finally got home, it was almost five. Steve was reading in bed. "Welcome home, Party Girl," he said as I stripped—not in a turn-on manner but in an I'm-about-to-fall-asleep-on-my-face way—and fell into bed beside him. As he ran his fingers through my smoke-stained hair, I described the evening. He laughed and groaned at all the right parts until I must have fallen asleep, because the next thing I knew it was morning.

"Ready to leave?" Steve asks now, a hopeful look in his eyes. I take his hand, and we go.

"I don't want you worrying if my dad likes you," I say, later that night, when we're in bed. I'm lying on my side, covers pulled up to my ear, arm pressed against Steve's warm waist, fingers on his back.

His face is two inches from mine, and I can feel his breath on my forehead. He has a small scar on his chin, a half inch of a stubble-less white patch from a boyhood game of street hockey. Or was it when he slipped and hit himself on the kitchen counter? I don't remember.

"I don't worry," he says.

"No? So why do you always have a funny look on your face when he's with us?"

He's lying on his left side, left arm bent under his head, right hand playing with my hair. "Just trying to figure it out."

"Figure what out?"

"How a man could leave his wife and two kids without feeling like a complete asshole for the rest of his life."

My chest feels tight, like an iced-over lake about to crack. I'm allowed to call my father an asshole, but I haven't decided yet if Steve is.

I decide to make a joke out of it. "What, you're planning on leaving me with a bunch of kids and you want to come up with the best plan to remain guilt-free?"

"You know that's not what I mean."

Close up, his eyes look less green and more like an Impressionist painting with distinct speckles of yellow and blue.

"I know," I say, and roll over.

I pick up the phone on the first ring. It's nine o'clock in the morning. I groan.

"Guess who has a hit show?" Carrie says.

"Good." Less pressure to find a new job right away.

"It ranked ninth in its time slot, and fourth among eighteen-to twenty-five-year-old women. It's a go."

Ninth and fourth. That doesn't sound like a hit.

"Howard is thrilled. Just thrilled. Everyone is talking about it. Everyone loved it. And you—you were the show's soul. You were the heart. You're going to be America's sweetheart."

Steve rolls over, his eyes still closed. "Who is it?"

"Carrie. We got good ratings."

He nods and rolls back to his side of the bed.

"Hi, it's me. It's Tuesday night, ten o'clock. I'm home and I wanted to catch up, I'm sorry I haven't called earlier—"

There's a loud squeaking sound as Dana picks up the phone. "I am totally going to kill you."

"I've been really busy, I swear."

"Why didn't you tell me your show was starting already? I didn't even see it. I came home to a million messages on my answering machine from people asking me when you had become a TV star, Miz *Lang*."

I knew the name change was going to get me into trouble. "They said our name is too ethnic." I turn to Steve, who's sitting next to me on the couch, watching the news. "Do you want some blanket?" I whisper to him.

"Thanks." He puts his head on my lap and wraps the blanket around the two of us.

"You're sitting with Steve?" Dana asks.

"Yeah."

She sighs. "Can't you go somewhere private?"

What's her problem? I can't just go in another room when I'm on the phone, can I? I think that would be weird. Like I'm keeping secrets or something. "So who phoned?" I ask, deliberately changing the subject. "A million people? Really?"

"Two old friends from high school. Why didn't you call me?"

"I'm sorry, Dana. Everything's been so crazy. And the truth is I wasn't sure if I wanted you to see it in case I came across as completely moronic."

"Never mind, it's all right. Someone taped it for me."

And? She's going to make me drag it out of her. "So, what did you think?"

Pause. "Your hair looked amazing."

"Thank you."

"And you waxed your eyebrows. They're so thin."

Is thin good or bad?

"It's a bit freaky, actually. You looked completely different. Nothing like me anymore at all."

Dana's the same height as me, but her hair is lightened with blond highlights. These days it serves to mask her premature gray as well as to brighten her face.

Two years ago she called me with the news of her first gray hair. "It started," she said.

"What?"

"The curse." Our mother was fully gray by thirty-two.

"Don't worry about it, just dye it."

She didn't answer.

"Dana? Dana?"

I heard a sob.

"Dana, are you crying?"

"No," she said.

"Don't cry, it's just hair."

"Stupid, huh?"

Dana has my father's nose, straight and turned up at the end, and my mother's eyes, wide, brown, long lashes. I have the reverse, my father's blue eyes, light, more like ice with a hint of sky, and my mother's nose, so small it's barely there.

But looking at Dana used to be like looking in a mirror. Because of the mouth. We both have small, thin lips and a big smile.

"Who dressed you for the show?" she asks. "You looked fantastic. Those boots are amazing. Where did you get them?"

"Kenneth Cole."

"They're even nicer than mine. Are you allowed to have nicer clothes than me? That might screw up the balance in our relationship."

I laugh. "You're psycho. But seriously, what did you think about the show?"

Pause. "Well…it was a little silly, don't you think?"

Silly? Suddenly I don't want to talk about this with Steve right next to me. I don't want him to also start thinking the show is silly.

I lift his head up. "Sorry, honey. My conversation is bothering you, isn't it? I'll just go into the bedroom."

"You're not bothering me," he says sleepily.

I kiss him on the forehead and close the bedroom door behind me.

"It's supposed to be silly," I say, plopping down on the bed.

"You're not embarrassed?"

"No. It's just for fun." Embarrassed? Should I be embarrassed?

She sighs. "Aren't you at all concerned about what appearing in pop trash will do to your professional persona?"

"Isn't it possible that maybe you're a little bit jealous that I get to be on television and you don't?" I ask, a little bitchily.

She laughs. "I would never want to be on *Party Girls*."

My head hurts. "I have to go."

"Don't be a baby, Sunny. We can talk about something else. So. Are you going to get married on me?"

The walls are way too thin in this apartment for me to be talking about marriage. What if Steve hears? I'm holding one of my recently purchased multicolored candleholders up to the light. It looks like a kaleidoscope. "We haven't talked about it much."

"I bet he proposes. I can't believe my baby sister is going to get married before me. It seems anachronistic."

"We haven't even officially moved in together. That's one of the reasons I called, actually."

She snorts. "I knew there was something."

"The movers are coming on Friday at nine and I don't think I can make it back in time. I can't find a flight. Any chance I can bribe you with Stark's purchases in return for packing up for me?"

"Have you sold your car yet?"

"No." I don't know what to do with my car. I've been secretly looking for a cheap parking spot in Manhattan. No such luck.

"Can I drive it until you get very poor and need to sell it in return for packing up? Mine is on its last legs."

"Deal." Putting off the inevitable. Fantastic. "My stuff won't actually get here until Tuesday. It's like the movers walk my furniture on their backs."

"Do you want me to send everything?"

"Um…furniture, dishes, clothes…."

"Even the ugly ones?"

What ugly ones? "Use your judgment. We don't need the sheets. Or the towels. Maybe we do need the towels. Men never have enough towels. And they don't understand the concept that after a shower a woman needs one for her body and one for her hair. And maybe—"

"You know what I keep thinking of?" she interrupts.

"What?" The candleholder slips from my hands and it comes a half an inch from smashing me in the forehead. Yikes. I could have had a massive, horrendous, audience-repulsive welt.

"I keep thinking of that Jewish story," she says. I hear her inhale and then exhale. "What was it, Leah and Rachel? How Jacob was in love with Rachel but then Leah's father tricked him into marrying Leah because he couldn't marry off the younger daughter before marrying off the older one?"

My father sent my sister to Sunday school until she was eleven. I never had to go.

"Vaguely," I say. "But—"

Steve opens the door and wanders through the room.

"Hold on a sec," I say. I don't want him to hear me talking about marriage. Even if I'm not talking about me.

He looks lost. "Have you seen my flannel pants?"

"In the drawer?"

He looks in his drawer. "No."

"In the dirty clothes?"

He looks in the laundry basket. "No. Can you help me find them?"

"Sure. Can it wait until I get off the phone?"

He nods and leaves the room, leaving the door wide open.

Now do I close the door or leave it the way it is? He might find it odd if I close it.

I decide to leave it open. I pull the covers over my head and whisper, "But I thought you don't want to get married. No bread-maker, remember?"

She inhales and exhales loudly. "I want to get married eventually. I think. Why wouldn't I? I want to have kids. One day."

"Dana, are you smoking?"

Inhale, exhale. "No."

"Liar."

She laughs.

"If you get lung cancer, it's your own fault. So what are you whining about? You don't want me to get married before you?"

"Am I the Leah? The sister nobody wants?"

"You're being crazy. You never date men long enough to give them a chance."

"I don't see any of them begging me to move across the country. So tell me about everything and everyone. Are the girls on your show really that horrible?"

Marriage conversation closed.

"Sure," I answer. I tell her about the girls and about creepy Howard and about Carrie and our father. I've already talked enough about Steve.

On Wednesday afternoon I'm ravaging the *New York Post* on my kitchen table. Carrie left me a message telling me there was an article in it about the show. My heart pounds as I flip through the paper. What if it's bad? Could it be bad? Is the show bad?

Here it is: "Those of you not yet bored of the *Sex and the City* clones will enjoy the antics of the four women on TRS's *Party Girls*. Brittany Michaels is the drunk, Erin Soline the bad girl, Michelle Miles the heartbreaker, Sunny Lang the mother hen. The show is better than a Happy Meal—it has sex, booze, catfights, great bods and loud dance music. If you're looking for a fun way to waste thirty minutes of your life, this is it."

Waste? Happy Meal? I'm not sure if it's good or bad.

I don't want to waste people's lives. Is that what I've become? I'm a waste of thirty minutes?

Wait. What if there are more articles out there about me? I could have been written about all over the country. I should check the Internet. How did anyone get any work done before the World Wide Web?

I turn on my computer, which now lives in the spare room, and wait and wait and wait for it to connect and then I sign on to a search engine and key in "Sunny Langstein." Twelve hits, the screen tells me. Only twelve? Search took 0.11 seconds. But they all seem to be in Dutch. Or maybe it's Polish, or German, I don't know. They couldn't have already translated the show into different languages, right? Someone would have told me.

I enter "Sunny Lang." Oh, my. Fifty-nine thousand hits. In 0.46 seconds. I'm sure some of these are about me, but how do I know which ones? I'm not going through fifty-nine thousand sites.

Next I try "Sunny Erin Michelle Brittany *Party Girls*." Results: 78. In 0.23 seconds. Far more manageable.

The first one is called Anal Girls. I'm guessing that would not be ours.

I scroll down the Web site until I see the article from the *New York Post*. I read it to myself. I see the same article repeated a few times and realize that other papers have picked it up. *The Sacramento Bee. The Boston Globe. The Hawaii Tribune-Herald*. Unbelievable. People in Hawaii know who I am. Someone unwittingly flipping through the sports section might fall across my name.

Next I see that the official TRS Web site has put up a thread to *Party Girls*. Why wouldn't they tell us they put us on their Web site?

Open new window.

There we are. The site features pictures of us at the club, as well as profile shots.

MEET THE CAST: BIOS AND PHOTOS

Bio? I didn't write a bio. I click on my name and scan through my write-up. The only disturbing part is the line, "Sunny's mother, who converted to Judaism to marry her father, died of ovarian cancer when Sunny was only six."

Yikes. Nothing like exploiting a mother's death to make a character more sympathetic.

I hope Dana doesn't see that.

I scan the other girls' bios to see if there's anything I don't know about them.

Hey. Michelle lost her father five years ago. I didn't know that. Not that it would necessarily have come up. I wonder what he died of. It doesn't say.

Brittany wants to break into movies, Erin into music videos. Boring. I already know all that.

Next I click on www.theworldofrealitytv.org. On the front page is the standard blurb about the show: party it up, wild and crazy, yadda, yadda, yadda.

Click here to join the *Party Girls* Community.

What's the *Party Girls* Community? I right-mouse click and read: "What d'ya got to say about it? Vent your loves and disgusts and everything between in the *Party Girls* Community! Join a thread or start one of your own!" I almost choke on the choices.

1) *Best Ways To Avoid a Hangover and Not End Up Puking Like Brittany (5 messages)*
2) *Should Sunny have let Erin go home with Sleazeball? (4 messages)*
3) *How Can I Make My Hair Look Like Michelle's? (1 message)*

I click on number two and this is how I am rewarded:

---

chickita 10:48 pm Oct 12 (#1of 4)
Erin is a big whore and Sunny is not her keeper. Sunny could barely enjoy herself—she had to baby-sit the three of them the entire night!

LSAngler 12:29 pm Oct 13 (#2 of 4)
I totally disagree. Girls have to look out for their sisters! Erin looked like a moron and Sunny should have dragged her out by her hair if she had to. You stand by your friends!

Avalanche 07:12 am Oct 14 (#3 of 4)
I totally agree with LS. Erin could have been date raped!

WichedWitch 01:00 pm Oct 14 (#4 of 4)
Are yu an idot? She had a hunded camras on her. How could she have bin date raped? (LOL)

I should have dragged her by the hair? I don't think I could carry her, her body is so stuffed with silicone. She was no drunker than I was, and she knew what she was doing. Why is she my responsibility when I've only met her twice?

I guess I can't comment. There's no way I'm going to admit that I do Internet searches on my name. Very uncool. I'm a TV star. Jennifer Aniston does not search the Internet for her name.

She and Brad do not sit around the computer, betting on who has more hits.

Not counting a short break for dinner, or another brief catch-up conversation with Millie ("You were awesome, Sunny! That was by far one of the best reality shows I've ever seen, no kidding. You looked hot."), or another when I greet Steve after hearing his key in the door, I spend the rest of the night reading the rest of the threads and anything else that is reality TV related.

At ten Steve pokes his head into the room. "What are you doing in here, busy bee?"

"Research," I say, head lost in the screen. "I'll be ten minutes, tops."

At twelve I hear him calling for me from the other room. "Sunny? Come to bed already!"

If Steve were all over the Internet, he would make me help him search for his name. At least I'm not being annoying. I tear myself away from the screen. My eyes feel bloated.

I can see how people got a lot more work done *before* the World Wide Web.

On Thursday morning I wake up realizing that I haven't taken my birth control pills in two nights.

Fuck. Fuck, fuck, fuck.

Or rather, no fuck, no fuck, no fuck.

That's Tuesday and Wednesday night.

I've never forgotten to take a pill before, never mind two. What's wrong with me?

I can't get pregnant, can I? I didn't have sex Tuesday or even last night.

I log back onto the Internet to find out what to do.

Apparently I'm supposed to take two pills today and two pills tomorrow and then one for the rest of my cycle. Also, if I have sex in the next seven days without using another form of birth control I MAY BECOME PREGNANT. I am disheartened at the use of the caps in the message.

Great. Condoms. I'm sure Steve will be thrilled. He once

said that making love with a condom is like peeing through
your underwear.

A poet he's not.

Steve nudges me awake Friday at noon. "It's gorgeous out,"
he says. "I'm going to shower and then let's go for a long walk."

I nod facedown into the pillow.

He turns the lights on as he leaves the room. Was that really
necessary? Couldn't he have let me sleep the last precious
minutes?

Ten minutes later he sprints across the bedroom, butt naked.
"I don't know where my towel is," he says, shivering and wet.

"On the kitchen chair," I mumble.

As soon as I'm naked and under the stream of hot water, I
notice that there is no soap. It was down to its last measly flakes
yesterday, and apparently he finished it off without replacing
it. He never replaces anything. Orange juice—empty carton
still in the fridge. Toilet paper—brown cardboard leftover,
mocking me. Toilet seat—obviously never goes down, as if
he's oblivious to the ugliness of the open canyon. At least
twice, I've fallen right in.

I think I would forgive it all if he could just answer me this
one question: How on earth does he *miss* the bowl? It's right
there. Steady. Aim. Go.

We walk through the West Village toward the pier and spend
an hour strolling up the boardwalk. If it weren't for the sky-
scrapers in the distance, when I watch the ripples of the water
I think I could forget what city I'm in.

The cold air blows through my coat, but Steve warms me
by putting his arm around me. When we reach Chelsea, we turn
back into the island. When we pass a magazine store, I pull him
inside.

"I just want to check for something," I say.

He rummages through the sports and news magazines
and I poke around the entertainment ones. I just want to
check in case there's anything about the show. What if

there is something and no one saw? Jennifer Aniston, J.Lo, Eminem, blah, blah blah—why is no one writing about *Party Girls?*

A teenager is watching me from behind a *Cosmopolitan* magazine.

"Sun, can we go now?" Steve asks, impatiently.

"In a sec," I mouth.

I bet she recognizes me. Maybe she'll say something. She could come up to me and ask me if I'm one of the stars on *Party Girls.* Maybe she recognizes me but can't place where she's seen me. I'm surprised no one has approached me yet. Do I look that different in real life? When will I have to start wearing Jackie O sunglasses and wraparound scarves?

She's still staring at me. Uh-oh. I'm not exactly in movie-star attire. I'm wearing jeans, a hooded sweatshirt, sneakers and an un-glam very windblown ponytail.

What if a tabloid reporter snaps my picture?

"Sunny, let's go."

The girl pays for her *Cosmo* and leaves the store without giving me a second glance.

That night, when I exit the bathroom after washing up, Steve is spread-eagle on the bed, in his boxers. A cooler containing a bottle of Dom Perignon and two champagne glasses is on the floor.

Last night, because of the pill fiasco, I avoided sex by pretending to fall asleep while the TV was still on.

He pops the champagne and pours it into the glasses.

"We have champagne glasses?"

"Borrowed them from the restaurant."

"And the champagne?"

"Borrowed that, too."

"I bought you a present, but you're not going to like it." I take a box of condoms out of my underwear drawer (purchased earlier in case avoidance didn't work) and place them on the bedspread.

He recoils in horror. "What…why?"

"I forgot to take my pill. We have to use a backup for seven days."

"But I hate condoms," he whines.

"No glove, no love, mister."

He starts laughing. "But isn't the whole point of a long-term relationship that I don't have to wear condoms?"

I punch him in the stomach. Lightly.

"Ooh, I like it when you're rough," he says, and rolls on top of me. I can feel that he's turned on and, after a few minutes of kissing and fondling, I take off the rest of my clothes and his boxers. I open the condom box, rip open the wrapper and slide it on him.

I'm surprised I haven't forgotten how to put on one of these suckers. I guess it's like riding a bicycle.

He puts his hands on my breasts and squeezes and thrusts into me. Once. Twice. Three times. Fouuuuuuuur.

Five doesn't make it all the way in.

"What's wrong?" I ask. "It's not working?"

"Apparently glove leads to no love." I laugh and he rolls off the condom and deposits it on the floor. "Wanna sixty-nine?"

Groan. "Why don't we have some bubbly first?"

"That would be lubbly."

He pops the champagne, pours two glasses. We cuddle and turn on the TV.

11

Leave It to Beaver

I try to ignore the camera, but it's become my tail. Always up my behind.

Solution: Need to get drunker.

The problem so far on the taping of Episode Two is that Miche and I don't know what to do with ourselves. Are we supposed to be hitting on guys? Dancing? Talking to strangers? Drinking? Howard complained that Miche and I didn't flirt with enough guys last week. Excuse us for not wanting to appear trampy on television.

Instead of whoring ourselves out like we're supposed to, we've elected to perch ourselves on two stools, huddling over a small table and apple martinis. I'm not usually a fan of any type of chair with no back or arms, and at the moment I'm even less of a fan as I'm very nervous about slouching on television. I'm also feeling bloated and cranky and I wish I didn't look like a Vegas showgirl. I'm wearing an ankle-length shimmering pale gold skirt and a tight, tarty, plunging, off-the-shoulder black camisole. The skirt is so tight that I needed to buy tummy control nylons. Choosing which ones to buy almost triggered a nervous breakdown. Nude stockings? Clear? Buff? Toeless? Body Control or Ultimate Shaping? Opaque, sheer, moisture enriched? Too many damn choices. I chose maximum control, sheer, toeless, nude for $27.99. Extravagant I know, but I can't have them ripping in the middle of the episode. For this price I should be able to re-wear them. For this price I should be able to be buried in them.

My mike is clipped to the left side of my shirt, the side that isn't bare.

The bar is called Salon. Last year it was a salon, this year it was converted into a bar. The bartenders are behind the hair-washing basins.

Photos of eighties' hair models are the décor.

About seventy people are crowded into the small room. About thirty-five are blatantly staring at us. The remainder pretend to be unaware of us. Yeah, right. Pete and Dirk keep accidentally smashing them in the head, but what cameras?

Miche and I are drinking apple martinis, listening to the hip-hop music and watching Brittany do shots with two guys. She's wearing a cowboy hat. I'm not sure what the deal is, but why is cowboy clothing cool? I don't get it. Dirk has his camera trained on her. Pete is filming us.

"I can't believe Brittany's drinking again," I say to Miche.

"Why are you surprised? She's a lush."

"Because when I saw her this afternoon, she went on and on about how embarrassed she was at her behavior last week. She said that she knows this show is a chance of a lifetime and she doesn't want to blow it by making a fool of herself. And it doesn't help that she has a low tolerance. But here she is getting drunk again."

"Did she thank you for taking care of her?"

"Yeah." I pause. Should I tell her not to drink again? Remind her of what happened last time? I like being the conscientious one in the group, but I don't want to be the nag. "Where's Erin?"

"Grinding her crotch against some guy over there," she says, pointing.

"That's not the same guy as last week?"

"Nope. New night, new bar, new guy. Last week's guy didn't call her, so onto the next. Can you say walking STD?"

A guy with way too much eyebrow leans against our table and leers at Miche. "Hello," he says, wagging the bushy line over his eyes. "I just moved to New York and I don't know my way around. Do you think you could give me directions to your apartment?"

The two of us stare at him and burst out laughing. The camera is quivering, so I assume that Pete is laughing, too.

"I don't think so," Miche says.

Eyebrow Man shrugs and walks away.

"What the hell was that?" I ask.

She shrugs. "No idea."

A few minutes later a sandy-haired surfer dude hovers near our table and leans toward me. "Nice pants," he says. "Do you think I could get in them?"

"Are you kidding me?"

Miche is laughing so hard, she practically spits up her drink. Pete is now shaking. He's never going to be able to use this footage.

What is going on? "Do you think you have a better chance of getting on television if you use bad pickup lines?" I ask the surfer hopeful.

"Some woman with orange hair told us that if we hit on you with creative come-on lines, our drinks would be on the house."

Miche rolls her eyes. "Hilarious. We're so pathetic that they have to send in ringers?"

"Apparently. Have a seat," I tell Surfer and point to an empty bar stool. He's pretty hot, actually. He has a big, wide smile with two dimples. I bet dimples would make even a convicted serial killer look like a little sweet boy.

He sits between Miche and me and immediately turns to Miche. "I'm Erik," he says.

"Michelle," she says, smiling. She twirls a strand of red around her fingers.

"Nice to meet you, Michelle." He continues staring at Michelle, apparently lost in her curls.

Um, hello? Didn't he come to hit on me? Wasn't it my pants he was trying to get into?

He hasn't introduced himself to me. He hasn't even looked at me. Hello? Hello?

Michelle must realize that I'm feeling snubbed. "Erik, this is my friend, Sunny."

"Hi," he says, nodding quickly in my direction. He turns back to Miche. "Do you live in the city?"

The two converse while I feel horribly awkward and wish I was home. It's embarrassing enough when this happens when you're with a girlfriend. It's exponentially awkward when a camera's bright light is glaring in your face.

I see Carrie wandering around the bar, trying to look inconspicuous. When we were out for Thai food on Wednesday night, I had asked her if she knew what Miche's father had died of. I suppose I could have asked Miche herself, but I wasn't sure how to bring it up. Hey, I lost a parent to cancer. You?

"It was a huge scandal," Carrie told me. "He was senior partner at the law firm Miles and Tore and had a heart attack when he was in bed, having an affair with the model Janna Mansen. Do you remember her? She was on the cover of *Vogue* a few times."

I shook my head. "That's horrible. He had a heart attack in his fifties? That's so young."

"Actually I think he was a bit older. Michelle's mother was his second marriage."

I wondered if Miche's older/now absent father was the factor in her fifteen-year-older ex I saw at Stirred last week.

"You got Miche the job at *Party Girls,* right?" I asked Carrie.

"Yeah. She did some commercials when she was a preteen.

Character did the bookings. When I heard about the show, I pulled up her file. She'd been doing a little modeling during college, but nothing major. Did I tell you the gossip about the other girls?"

"No."

"Brittany was molested by one of her mother's boyfriends. Her parents are divorced. How gross is that?"

"How do you know that?"

"I saw her interview tape."

"She said that?"

Carrie nodded. "Girls say everything on audition tapes. It's like confession. She said she ran away at least four times, before telling her mother."

"That's horrible."

"She came to me at the beginning of the year, wanting to be an actress. I don't think she's any good. I felt lucky she even got this." She played with the rice on her plate. "I'm trying to think if I know any other goods."

"What's Erin's story?"

Carrie shrugs. "I think she's screwed up all on her own. Her parents are a little white-trashy. She grew up in some crappy suburb of Jersey. Her parents are still married. I think she's an only child. Wants to be famous."

I wondered what the goods on me were.

"Sunny," Miche says, breaking me out of my reverie.

"What?"

"That guy is calling you. Do you know him?" She motions with her chin to a tall, dark-haired guy in a tight black shirt who is beckoning me over with his index finger.

"I don't think so," I say. I hop off my stool and stride over to where he's standing. I feel the camera follow along. "Yeah?"

Pointing man smiles and drapes his muscled arm around my shoulders. "I made you come with one finger. Imagine what I could do with my whole hand."

I pray that Steve doesn't hear that tomorrow.

"Not sure. Jerk yourself off?" I disentangle myself from his groping arm and return to my stool. Humph.

Michelle is bright red and flustered. Her fingers are working overtime on their twirling. "Erik, sweetie, will you be the biggest doll ever and go get me another apple martini?" She taps her empty glass.

"Of course," he says. "Sunny, can I get you another one, too?" How gallant. Yeah, whatever. You're getting your drinks for free now, don't look so smug.

When he's out of earshot, I lean toward her. "What's wrong?"

"You have a problem," she says.

"What problem?"

She struggles to find the right words. Pete has the camera trained on our conversation. "A leakage problem."

I have no idea what she's talking about. "Did I spill my drink on myself?" I look down at my lap. Great, just what I need. A big wet spot.

"Not your drink." She says. "It's your—" She takes her index finger and taps purposefully on the table. Once, twice, three times.

"What are you talking about?"

She pulls a lip liner from her purse and opens a discarded matchbook on the table. She writes a few words on the flip-up cardboard and passes it to me.

"BLED THROUGH SKIRT," I read.

I close the matchbox quickly. I might cry. I might laugh. I just got my period on national television. "Fuck," I mouth. But I'm not supposed to get my period for another two weeks. How did that happen? Oh. The pills. It's because I missed two of my pills. Fuck. Normally after I stop taking the last pill of the month, four days later, my period starts. The first pill I missed was on Tuesday and I must have tricked my body into thinking my period was supposed to start today. Why didn't the Internet instructions mention the possibility of me getting my period? On national television? I would have worn a pad. Or at least not a skintight gold skirt.

And as an added annoyance, Monday is Steve and my eleventh-month anniversary. What kind of anniversary has no sex?

Not that we've been successful in the condom department.

Must think. Must plan. Can't get up. How can I get up? I can never stand up again? Does Pete realize what's going on? He's not shaking, which means he's not laughing, but the camera is watching.

"I don't have anything," I say.

Miche looks into her purse. "I do."

"But I have to get there," I say. I sound like I'm a Mafioso talking on my wiretapped phone.

Miche's forehead scrunches. She must be deep in concentration. "What? You're cold? Do you want to try on my sweater?" She passes me a black cardigan that was under her purse.

"Thanks," I say. I tie the cardigan around my waist and let it fall off the stool behind me. I warily stand up. "I have to go to the ladies room," I say.

"Me, too." Miche hops off the stool. "Go ahead," she says, and follows me closely.

Pete trails us across the room but along the way ditches us to follow Erin.

"We lost him," Miche says, pushing open the bathroom door. The bathroom is, thankfully, empty.

"Ohmigod," Miche says.

We start laughing and are unable to stop. I hand her back her sweater, no seep-through blood, and try to get a glimpse of my butt in the mirror.

There's a red stain the size of a quarter on the back of my skirt.

"Do you think I should write to some teen magazine? This has to go in one of those *It Happened to Me* columns."

Miche can't speak, she's laughing so hard.

"What am I going to do? I can't wear a cardigan for the rest of the night. I'm supposed to be trendy."

"First of all, take this." She pulls a tampon from her purse.

"Ooh. I have an idea." She hands me the tampon. "Don't go anywhere." She retreats into the bar.

Where am I going? I can't leave the bathroom. I lock myself in one of the stalls. I slip off my shoes, take off my nylons, throw them into the mini garbage. So much for re-wearable.

Miche returns. "Come out, I have a plan."

She's holding a pair of scissors. "Take off your skirt."

"I can't, I'm not wearing anything underneath."

"Hmm. Okay, pull it up then."

I pull up the skirt a few inches. "How high?"

"So that the stain part is above your waist."

I inch the skirt up.

"How do you feel about knee-length?" she asks and starts chopping the top foot of the shimmery material off.

If I had paid for this with my own money I would be freaking out.

"I hope this doesn't unravel." With the last incision, she removes the block of material. "Here you go. New and untarnished. It's adorable."

The new, shorter skirt slips down my hips. "It's too big. How can I make it stay up?"

Holding the skirt scraps, she cuts off the soiled section and wraps the remaining material around my waist as a belt. "Voila!"

Did she say knee-length? Crotch-length is a more apt description.

In the mirror it looks like a real skirt. Kind of. "I have to admit, Betsey Johnson, I'm impressed."

"Ready to go back out there?"

"Ready," I say, and reapply my lipstick. I smile at myself in the mirror. "Do you think anyone noticed?"

She shakes her head. "No way."

As we walk back to our table, Erik and Come-With-One-Finger Man, along with everyone else is staring at one of the hair-washing basins. A hair-washing basin where there's a large crowd. A hair-washing basin on which Erin is dancing. A hair-washing basin on which Erin is dancing topless.

And I was worried about people noticing me.

After the taping, Michelle and I take a cab to Coffee Shop. My feet hurt and I need to sit. "Why is there a line at three in the morning?"

"The waitresses are really hot," Michelle explains.

It's true. All the waitresses have waiflike bodies, smooth hair, large breasts and are at least five foot nine. Weird. "It's creepy. It's like we're in Barbie Twilight Zone."

Miche walks straight to the front of the line, speaks to the hostess and returns to the door, where I'm standing. "Come, we have a table."

I wonder if I would have gotten a table if I had gone up, instead. Does anyone recognize me?

We're brought to a booth. I'm planning on ordering Eggs Benedict when Miche orders a salad, dressing on the side and a tall glass of water. Hmm. I was feeling a bit bloated tonight.

"I'll have the same, please."

Miche pulls a sugar packet from the container and fiddles with it. "How's your skirt holding up?"

"Amazing. Thank you again. I can't believe no one even noticed. If it weren't for you, I'd be a national laughingstock. You should be a fashion designer."

The waitress places two glasses of water on our table, and I finish mine in one gulp.

"Really? I've been thinking of applying to FIT. You know. After this is done."

"Yeah? You want to be a designer?"

"Just a thought. I don't know what I want to be. What I want to do. So what's your roommate like?" she asks.

The question comes so out of nowhere that I can't think of an answer. The waitress interrupts with two plates of naked-looking lettuce.

I drench it in the dressing and take a bite—*so* not greasy enough—and hope that Miche has forgotten her question.

"So what's your roommate like?"

"Cool," I say.

"Roommates aren't for me. I don't think it's natural to live with someone who you're not sleeping with or related to. What's yours like?"

Handsome? Good in bed? "Nice."

"What does she do?"

"She's a student." Enough already. Next topic. "Why don't you travel a bit? You can move anywhere you want. Paris, London, Sydney."

When did I become such a big talker? Before moving to New York, I hardly ever wanted to even travel around the country, never mind around the world. I had my one backpack adventure, but I preferred not to go too far from home.

Michelle shakes her head. "Been there, done that. My parents used to ship me abroad every summer. I was bored out of my mind. Anywhere besides The City is a waste of time."

It's funny how New Yorkers refer to New York as "The City" as if it's the only one. "I guess it's the best place to be if you want to make your mark," I say.

"Make your mark? On what?"

On what? On something. "On the world. I want to do something worthwhile one day. You know. To be remembered."

"You'll be remembered for *Party Girls*."

When I first met Michelle I pegged her as a person not concerned with the bigger issues, the scarier issues. One of those people who think fashion magazines, sitcoms and *Party Girls* are as deep as it gets. But ever since I found out about her father, I've been waiting for her to reveal another layer, to show me her wound.

"I don't want to be remembered," she continues and pours a drop more salad dressing on her lettuce. "I just want to have fun. Omigod. Did I tell you some idiot's pickup line tonight? He came up to me and asked, 'Is your dad a terrorist?' And when I looked at him like he was nuts, he said, ''Cause you're the bomb.' How inappropriate is that?"

Why does her superficiality comfort more than horrify me?

"I think there are some jokes that need to be outlawed in New York. Terrorist pickup lines top the list." I need more water. I spot the waitress and try to catch her eye. I think she's ignoring me. "So tell me, what's fun about being on the show? Why is it fun?"

"Fame is fun. You're admired. Little girls try to dress like you. Designers send you free clothes. You always get a table at a restaurant. It leads to money. You get to buy more things. You meet fabulous people. Do you want more water?" She motions to the waitress, who scurries right over with a large pitcher. "What about you?" Miche asks me. "Why did you agree to do the show?"

"If I tell you, do you promise to keep it between us?" I'm not sure why I suddenly want to bond with her, but I do. I want her to know me. I need to talk to someone who gets it—the quasi fame, the lies, the free stuff…the dead parent even.

I feel congested and I need to come clean to feel better.

I need to confess.

12

Twilight Zone

Here goes.

"I needed a job," I say. "This doesn't pay, but I'm hoping it'll lead to something that will. Something big. Something important. And I don't have a roommate. I moved to New York because I wanted to live with my boyfriend." There. I've said it. "I live with my boyfriend."

Her jaw drops and her eyes widen, but then she bursts out laughing. "I don't believe you!"

A truck-sized weight has been lifted from my chest. Confessing feels good. "I swear," I say.

Then she smiles. "Howard doesn't know, does he?"

"No, of course not. They all think I'm single. Everyone but you."

"You are single. There's no ring on your finger."

"I still don't think Howard would appreciate knowing that I have a live-in boyfriend."

She laughs. "Definitely not. It's like his one rule. I love it. It's so devious. How long have you been together?"

Devious. I picture myself tattooed, in leather and on the back of a motorcycle. "Eleven months on Monday."

"You count the months? Adorable. Are you celebrating?"

"I'm going to try to make him a fancy dinner on Monday."

"You cook?"

"No, but it's the effort that counts, right? He cooks. Have you ever heard of the restaurant Manna?"

"Your boyfriend is a waiter?" she asks, surprised.

"He's not a *waiter*," I say, correcting her. "He owns the restaurant."

A waitress walking by gives me an evil look. I think I deserved that.

"Now that you know the truth, can I borrow your cell phone to call him? Mine doesn't seem to be working in New York. I need to get a new plan."

She hands me her phone. "Of course."

I tell Steve I'll be home in an hour. I can hear Hot 'n Sexy in the background.

I press the end button. The phone rings in my hand.

"Oops, did I dial something?" I hold the phone up in front of me. The display says: Howard Brown.

I flip the phone toward her. "Howard's calling you now? At four in the morning?"

She looks flustered, and giggles. "I—he calls me all the time. He's such a sketch-ball. He's like my stalker or something." She looks down at her plate.

The phone rings again. Howard Brown.

"Crazy, huh? He won't leave me alone." The phone rings again and then goes silent. "He totally attacked me a few weeks ago."

Oh, my. "What do you mean? Sexually? That's serious, Miche." I flashback to the scene in the shower.

"He didn't molest me or anything." She laughs nervously. "He's just always there, touching me and asking me if I want

to fool around. Honestly, he asks me like once an hour. Hilarious, huh?"

"So nothing ever happened?"

At first she shakes her head, then she nods. "We made out
once. But that's before I knew he was married, I swear."

I take another bite of lettuce and dribble balsamic vinegar
all over my skirt. "Ew." Hasn't this skirt seen enough pain?

"What, you think he's gross?"

I dip my napkin into my glass of water and dab it on my
skirt. "I was referring to my skirt. I still can't believe what happened. It's a good thing that we're not wearing mikes. We're
a tabloid reporter's wet dream."

When I get home, Steve is sleeping, sprawled across the
couch. The TV is on.

"Hey, sexy," I say, and crouch down in front of him.

"I missed you," he says.

"I'm sorry. I was starving."

"I thought you'd be. I brought you dinner from the restaurant."

Oops. "Next week I'll come home right after the show,
okay? Let's go to bed."

Every woman should be so lucky to have someone who
loves her and waits up until 5:00 a.m. for her to come home.

"Okay." He kisses me, then closes his eyes. "Hon?" His eyes
flicker open. "It's good here. Come lie. It's comfy."

What am I going to do with him? "The bed is also comfortable."

"Stay here. Like camping. Come."

Whatever makes him happy. "One sec." I close the
blinds, throw out my skirt, put on pajamas and a maxi pad,
climb onto the couch beside him and try to fall asleep under
his arm.

I can't sleep. I'm thinking about what I said to Michelle.
About being remembered. Even if I do something incredible,
like finding a cure for cancer, I'll be remembered until, what,

2100, 2200 at the latest? Big deal. Really, in the bucket of time, what is that really?

Okay, we remember, say, Shakespeare. But what if it's true? What if there was no such man? What if Marlowe really wrote all those plays, after all? Who wrote the bible? We don't remember the creator; we barely remember the creations.

I'm not even a tiny blip on the radar. No matter what I do. Even if I'm president or something. All of modern American culture will be forgotten by then. Elvis, the Kennedys, Twin Towers. By 4000 nothing will be remembered. And then one day the world will have to end, won't it? Nothing goes on forever. We'll blow ourselves up with nuclear weapons or global warming or maybe an asteroid will strike us right into oblivion, and then there will be nothing, just blackness and emptiness and what's the point?

My heart is beating hard in my chest and I need to get into my bed. I need to be under the covers and safe, but Steve looks so peaceful and I don't want to wake him. I wish I could turn on the TV or turn on the light to read. I need to think about something else. Something mindless.

My eyes sting and I let the tears roll off the side of my face, onto the couch.

Between the cracks in the blinds I watch the sunlight slowly dilute the starless New York sky.

Finally, when the living room is flooded with light, my eyelids feel heavy and I close them, gently, falling asleep.

Steve and I are cuddled on the bed watching *Party Girls* when the unthinkable happens:

Sunny Lang, TV heroine and star, stands up, wraps Michelle's sweater around her waist and starts walking to the bathroom.

Erin's voice is dubbed over the image. "Sunny got her period at the bar. It went right through her skirt. What's up with that? Has she never gotten her period before? Is she twelve? Does she not know what a pad is?"

Ohmigod.

Switch.

Image of me and Michelle dancing. The conversation playing has nothing to do with dancing:

Michelle: "Ohmigod." Laughter.

Me: "Do you think I should write to some teen magazine? This has to go in one of those *It Happened to Me* columns." More laughter. "What am I going to do? I can't wear a cardigan for the rest of the night. I'm supposed to be trendy."

Michelle: "First of all, take this. Ooh. I have an idea. Take off your skirt."

Me: "I can't, I'm not wearing anything underneath."

Michelle: "Hmm. Okay, pull it up then."

Me: "How high?"

Michelle: "So that the stain part is above your waist. How do you feel about knee-length? I hope this doesn't unravel. Here you go. New and untarnished. It's adorable."

Me: "It's too big. How can I make it stay up?"

Michelle: "Voila!"

Me: "I have to admit, Betsey Johnson, I'm impressed."

Michelle: "Ready to go back out there?"

13

Growing Pains

The summer I was eleven, I had a crush on a boy named David Jacobs. He liked to sail, he was a whole year older than I was, and he wore his Yankees baseball hat backward. Every morning my heart would stop when he walked into the dining hall for breakfast. Every time he said hello to me I found myself unable to articulate a simple greeting and ended up mumbling incomprehensibly.

Three days before the camp social, a boy named Harry sneaked into our bunk at rest hour to play matchmaker (boys were not allowed in the girls' cabins). Sitting on his girlfriend's top bunk bed, legs dangling, he made a list of the eight boys in his cabin, including David, who were still dateless. All twelve of my bunkmates sat at his feet, waiting. Harry read out a boy's name and then whoever liked the boy was supposed to raise her hand. Once the comprehensive list was compiled, the plan was for Harry to return to his bunkmates and find matches.

"Jordan M.," Harry said. There were two Jordans, and were therefore distinguished by their initials.

Jordan M. was the stud of the twelve-year-old boy section, and three of the girls raised their hands in application.

"Dave," Harry said.

No one called out. I contemplated not calling attention to myself, but I was suddenly overcome by a sense of courage. Why not? Go for it! The image of having a real date for the social, and not having to dance in a circle with the rest of my bunkmates propelled me to raise my hand.

"Sunny!" Harry said, delighted. "You and Dave, huh? Interesting."

After going through the list, Harry promised to return at free play with the results.

By third afternoon activity I was a nervous wreck. At dinner I couldn't eat the chicken stir-fry on my plate, usually my favorite. By the beginning of free play I thought it possible that my chest might explode.

We reconvened in our rest-hour positions.

"Jordan M.," Harry began. "He likes Stef. Match!" He made a ding sound, like the bell on a game show.

Stef blushed.

"Next is Dave," he said. "Doesn't like anyone. No match!" He makes another ding sound. "Sorry, Sunny."

My face stung as though doused in boiling water. The other girls looked at me. I wanted to slither into my sleeping bag, zip it up around me and remain there until the end of the summer.

The most embarrassing moment of my life.

Until now.

"Hon, come out from under the covers," Steve says.

"No."

"Hon, it was funny. It made good television."

"That was not good television."

"I can't hear you, your voice is muffled."

"I'm never coming out. You'll have to slide my meals between the sheets. I recommend no liquids."

Steven joins me under the covers and lies on top of me. "You're acting crazy. No one will even remember it by next week. It's just a silly TV show."

I hate TV. How could they show that? I'm never leaving the house again. "I just menstruated on national television. I'm surprised people didn't throw tampons and scream at me to plug it up."

"Hey, that's what happened in *Carrie*."

"See? It's the stuff horror movies are made of. Maybe next episode they'll elect me bar queen and drop a bucket of pig's blood on my head."

Steve laughs. Then I start laughing. It's too hot under here. "I can't breathe," I say.

He tosses the sheets off our faces. Ah. Better.

"Sun, it'll be fine. I'm telling you, who cares? I don't understand why there's so much secrecy around women's periods. I mean, all women get it, right? Isn't it a good thing? Shows you can bear children? Why is it such a secret? Why is it any grosser than snot?"

He doesn't get it. The point, I mean. Obviously not the monthlies, or he would so understand.

"If your nose is dripping, you're not embarrassed to pull out a tissue, are you?" he presses on. "My dad blows his nose in a hankie, then puts it back in his pocket. Is that any worse?"

"I wouldn't want my nose dripping on national TV, either." I pull the covers back over my head. Oooooh. "Was my nose dripping, too?"

"Why do you care about what other people think?"

"I don't." Do I? "This is different. This is TV."

"You shouldn't care about what anyone thinks but yourself."

Whatever, big talker. "Hi, no one's here to take your call right now. Certainly not Sunny, because she doesn't live with me." I uncover my face and smirk. "Who do your parents think share your apartment, exactly?"

Steve tries to tickle my waist. "That's different. I'm trying to spare their feelings."

"Your mom called yesterday, did I tell you? She said, 'Hi, dear, it's me. I just want to see how you're doing. Is Sunny liking New York? The Weinbergs told me they met her and she was just adorable.' Did you hear? I'm adorable. Stop it." I try to tickle him simultaneously but he straddles my hips, lifts my arms over my head with his left hand and tickles me with his right. I can't stop giggling. "I hate it, stop."

He squeezes my wrists together. "Maybe we should get a pair of handcuffs. I like you like this."

"I think you're a bit of a sketch-ball." Miche used that word. I like it. "I'm not sure if I'm the handcuff type of girl."

"What type of girl are you?"

"The kind of girl who makes a public fool of herself." Oooooh.

"You should only care about what you think." He kisses me lightly on the lips. "And what I think."

"And what do you think?"

He smiles. "I think we should get handcuffs. And I think we should start planning tomorrow night. I'm leaving work at six so we can spend the evening together. What do you want to do? Something special? Naughty, I hope."

Apparently he hasn't made the synapse jump from "has period" to "no sex." I don't mind gratifying his less kinky desires, but I draw the line at playing vampire.

"Sunny! Guess what!" Carrie yells into the phone.

It's Monday morning and Steve and I are still in bed. Since I've met Carrie, I no longer need an alarm clock.

"What?" When the phone rang, I was dreaming about having telekinetic powers.

"You're going to be in *Personality* magazine."

Am I still dreaming? "What? Why?"

"Can you believe it? Isn't that amazing?"

"I don't understand. Just me? Is it an interview?"

"It's an ad. You're going to be famous!"

"An ad for the show?"

"Not exactly." She pauses. "Okay. TRS is owned by Metro United, right?"

"Right."

"Metro United also owns Rooster Cosmetics. And they're in the middle of planning their media campaign for their tampon brand, Purity."

No, no, no.

"Anyway," she continues, oblivious to the plummeting feeling in my stomach. "The retail marketing VP at Purity saw the show last night and loved it. Loved the leakage part. He wants to use one of the shots of you walking to the bathroom with the sweater wrapped around your waist as an ad. You know, a don't-let-this-happen-to-you campaign. It's going to run in next Friday's issue. Isn't that incredible?"

I pull the covers back over my head. "I'm going to be the tampon girl?"

Carrie laughs. Hah, hah. "No publicity is bad publicity."

Hmm. Models make a lot of money don't they? Being Tampon Girl isn't so bad if I'm Rich Tampon Girl. "How much do they pay me for this?"

"Pay? They pay nothing. It's part of your contract. Any of TRS's affiliates are allowed to use your image for marketing and promotional purposes."

Note to self: must read fine print on contracts more carefully.

Steve is just as dubious as I am but for different reasons. "They're putting a picture of you in that skimpy outfit in a magazine?"

"I don't think the skimpy outfit is the point, Steve."

His eyebrows scrunch together and he turns bright red. "But I don't want guys drooling over your picture. Your boobs were popping out of your top. Those are my boobs. What if some asshole jerks off to it or something?"

"Steve, that's disgusting. It's *Personality* not *Playboy*, okay?" I say, suddenly defensive.

Dana's reaction is also lacking in enthusiasm. "Don't you remember that e-mail you sent me about Purity?"

I have no idea what she's talking about.

"About how they put asbestos in their tampons to cause additional bleeding?"

Oh...right.

"Sunny, I've been doing some research, and I have to tell you their intentions aren't looking so pure. My article is going to be explosive, you'll be so proud. I'm definitely going to step on some toes."

Suddenly panicked that Dana is going to ruin everything, I ask, "Would you mind shelving that article for a bit?" Stepping on the toes that subsidize my rent can't be a good plan. "I know I was the one to tell you to write about it in the first place, but I don't think it will look too good if the Purity poster girl's flesh and blood slams the product in the press. And Rooster is owned by M.U., the same conglomerate who owns TRS. I could get fired."

"Sunny, I can't believe you don't think printing this article isn't more important than a stupid TV show. These things might be dangerous. They could seriously hurt someone."

When did the show become so important to me? Is it important to me? "Listen," I say. "It was just a chain letter. I'm sure it's full of crap. Tampons are tested all the time. They wouldn't be selling them if they were dangerous. Can't you hold the article until I'm no longer their poster girl? I'm sure there are a million other companies for you to expose."

Dana sighs. "Fine, but I'm not happy about it. And isn't there some kind of law that says you have to use the product you endorse?"

I don't care what the contract's fine lines say, those Purity tampons hurt.

Well I think Steve and Dana can go screw themselves. I like Millie's reaction better:

"*Personality?* You're so famous. Do you know how many hits your name gets on the Internet? It's insane. You are a celebrity. You're by far the most famous person I know. Even more famous than Marla Tannenbaum." Marla Tannenbaum wrote a book about the rave culture. It was nonfiction and was published three years ago and we hated her in high school, and had to see her name whenever we went to the bookstore and it was highly annoying.

Millie's right. So what if I'm the tampon girl? I'm in *Personality,* which is very cool.

Take that, Marla.

By one that afternoon I feel confident enough to leave the house without a bag over my head. I head over to Gourmet Market with the list of ingredients required for the recipes I found online under "Romantic Dinner." I'm making heart-shaped smoked salmon for my appetizer, spinach and almond salad for my salad, fennel fusilli with chicken and pine nuts for my entrée, and strawberry fondue for my dessert.

Words like *fennel, diced, minced* and *grape tomato* (can there be a more blatant marketing attempt to make tomatoes friendlier?) jump up at me and give me a heart attack. I feel like I'm taking a multiple-choice exam and I don't recognize any of the options.

Why is it always so cold in here?

Two hours in the grocery store and twenty minutes at the wine store later (sudden brainstorm: for our next anniversary, our one year, I'm signing us up for a wine-tasting class—Steve is always saying he wished he were more of a wine connoisseur), I'm back home, remembering why I don't do this more often. It's scary. Really. I don't want to poison him. And it takes forever. Why bother? So far, the only fun part was using my expense account at the cash register. I burn my hand on the boiling olive oil. I cut my finger while slicing the grape tomatoes.

After I've done all the prep I can, I tidy up. Maybe I can clean up the rest of the apartment before Steve gets home.

Dana would make fun of me for hours, for my housewife activities.

I start by attacking the caked grime in the bathtub with Comet. Has he ever cleaned in here? I bet his roommate never cleaned, either. Vile. I'm cleaning Greg's grime. Surrounding the toothbrush holder is a stream of crusty white. Steve needs to learn proper toothbrush cleansing technique. He brushes, dabbles it under the water and then puts the brush away, allowing the remaining suds to drip grotesquely down the sides. Once, catching him in the act, I held him steady in the rinsing position for twenty seconds and then, still guiding his hand, shook the brush dry.

Of course, by the next morning, he was back to his regular routine, leaving a waterfall of toothpaste suds in his wake.

Is he never going to clean? I don't want to ask him to clean. That's so naggy. I'm not his mother. But otherwise, it'll be my job for the rest of my life.

Is that what he expects?

His mother does the cleaning. Maybe he just thinks I'll take over. Am I going to have to spend the rest of my life cleaning?

Next. Like a cat being petted, the floor seems to purr with the touch of my mop.

On to the bedroom. I remove the once black, now gray sheets. I'm not sure he even owns another set until I search in the back of his linen closet. And find another gray, probably once black set.

I collect the laundry and drag it across the street. The best part about New York is that other people do your laundry for you. While at first thought, paying someone to clean your clothes seems like a waste of money. But if your load is big enough you can actually save, since the mini washing machine in the basement costs two-seventy a load.

Of course most of Steve's restaurant clothes need to be dry-cleaned. All of his stuff comes back covered in plastic. When I get my stuff back, the first thing I do is remove the piece of clothing from the crappy wire hanger and plastic covering, throwing them both in the garbage. Then I hang up the clothes properly on a real, purchased, plastic hanger. But Steve?

I open the closet door. Steve's half of the closet is an overflowing wall of plastic and extra hangers. He shoves his dry cleaning inside, directly beside his unused proper hanger. And when he wants to wear the piece of clothing, the plastic somehow finds its way to the floor.

If we had a baby crawling around, it would definitely get tangled in the mess and suffocate itself.

I spend the next five minutes chucking out all superfluous hangers and plastic. Why does Steve have so much stuff? My things are coming tomorrow, so he's going to have to wade through this all. Maybe I'll use the extra room for storage.

Something in the kitchen smells. I clean out the fridge, in search of the offender. I throw out two yogurts dated July 21, three months ago, but neither seems to be the problem.

By the time Steve gets home, I'm cranky, exhausted, grubby and on all fours in the middle of the kitchen floor.

"I definitely like the look of that."

"So not in the mood." On the plus side he's holding a bag of gifts. I sit on my butt. "Hi, sweetie. Are those for me?"

"For later, not now." He lays the bag down on the kitchen table. "What are you doing?"

"Trying to stop the fridge from smelling. Why does it smell? Something smells and I can't find it."

Steve sits next to me on the floor. "Maybe it's you?"

I punch him in the arm. "I'm going to shower. Then I'm going to try to figure out how to make fennel fusilli with chicken and pine nuts." I can't think of anything I want to do less than cook. The directions look scary. They involve cooking the pasta and the sauce simultaneously. How can you pay attention to both things at the same time? What are the chances I burn one or the other?

After I shower and dress, I find Steve in the kitchen cooking away. "What are you doing?"

"Making the pasta."

As happy as I am to hear those magic words, I feel guilty. "You always make dinner. It's my turn."

"You did enough tonight. Your appetizer and salad look delicious."

"But dinner was my present. Now I don't have anything for you."

He adds the pine nuts to the pan. "That's not true. You got a fondue maker."

Oh, yeah. There you go. I do have a present, after all. Hey. He wasn't supposed to see that. "That was a surprise!"

"Then you should have wrapped it."

I stand on tiptoe and take down two wineglasses. Then during my attempt to open the bottle, I manage to get half the cork stuck. Damn. After making a go to remove the remainder with a steak knife, I end up plopping it into the bottle.

Steve strains the pasta.

"Steve, can you pass me the strainer?"

"Did you break the cork again?"

"Yup."

I pour the wine through the strainer, staining it red. We clink. "To eleven months," I say.

"To eleven months."

After a delicious dinner of perfectly cooked pasta, Steve tells me to wait in the living room while he prepares my gifts.

"Plural?" I ask, impressed.

When he opens the door, a black negligee and thong underwear are spread out on the bed.

"Ooh. Pretty," I say, fingering the lingerie. Lacy and sexy.

"Now look at the panties," he says, clapping his hands.

A tiny triangle of leather is attached to something barely more than a string. As soon as I pick it up, my hand falls to the bed under its weight. "Why is it so heavy?" I notice something odd. "Why do they have batteries in them?"

Abruptly, they begin to move. And hum.

"They're vibrating panties!" Steve says, clapping his hands again. He's holding a small white box. Apparently, the panties' remote control.

My panties are alive.

Steve looks sheepish. "Don't you like them?"

Do I need to feed them? "Sure," I say quickly. "I bet they'll be a lot of fun." Are they for daily activities? Like next time I'm buying groceries? They'd certainly warm me up. Possibly electrocute me.

"Try them on."

"Now?"

"Why not?"

"Because I have my period." Okay, I'm wearing a tampon—not Purity—but there's always the possibility of leakage, isn't there? "I don't want to get them dirty." Who knows where he got this or what kind of salesgirls have handled it. This baby requires a serious disinfectant before going anywhere near my crotch.

Steve brightens and claps his hands. "I just thought of the funniest idea."

Oh-oh. "What?"

"It'll be hysterical. Our little secret."

"What?"

"Ready? You're going to love this—you can wear them while you're filming!"

Is he on crack? He wants me to wear vibrating panties when I'm on national television? Maybe if I play dumb he'll realize how moronic he sounds and come up with a new vibrating-panty worthy occasion. "Sorry?"

No such luck. "You can wear them while you're filming!" he repeats, thrilled with his insane idea. "Won't that be a riot? No one else will know but us. You'll be wearing them and I'll have the remote. Fun, huh?"

He's not kidding.

"But what about the remote? You won't be at the restaurant? These things can't have that good a frequency." Tell me this motorized insane idea can't be activated across town.

He scratches his head in contemplation. "You're right. That sucks."

I exhale in relief.

His eyes light up. "I got it. You'll wear them and I'll leave work early. I'll come to the bar and when I get there, I'll turn it on. Turn *you* on. My secret message to you."

No way, no way, no way.

"Don't you think it's a little sketchy that you want to turn me on in public? And you can't come to the bar. Howard will figure out that we're involved and I'll get fired."

"It's not sketchy. It's funny! No one will know. That's what makes it cool—it'll be just between us. For fun. Our secret. I won't say a word to you. You'll do your job and I'll have a drink. I'll bring Greg. I'm allowed to want to watch you work, aren't I? It'll be fantastic! Please? Please? Please?"

He sounds like Bart trying to get his way with Homer. I understand he's feeling a little left out of my new life, but is this the best way for us to bond?

"Please? Please? Please? It'll be fun."

"What if someone hears the buzzing noise from my vaginal area?"

"The bar is loud! You can barely even hear yourself think. Anyway, I got the extra-silent pair. And even if someone heard a tiny hint of a buzz, they'd assume something was wrong with your watch. Who would think you were wearing robotic panties?"

"What if I'm *distracted?* I can't have an orgasm on television."

He waves away my concern. "I'll watch you the whole time, and if you look like you're having too much fun, eyes closed, head thrown back in abandon, little moans, nose scrunched up—"

"I don't scrunch my nose when I come."

"Yes, you do."

"No, I don't."

"Why don't I videotape you next time and I'll show you?"

"Don't hold your breath."

He laughs. "If it happens—I'll turn it off with the remote."

"What if it causes interference with the camera or the mike? Isn't that why you can't use your laptop on airplanes when you take off? I bet you can't wear vibrating panties when you're flying, either. What if the mike ends up vibrating and the panties pick up the sound?"

He cracks up. "Who cares? What fun is this show if you can't laugh about it?"

I shake my head. "I don't think it's a good idea."

His face clouds over. "Why not?"

"It just isn't. I don't want to screw up anything on the show."

His face has set into something resembling stubbornness. "Well, I think it is. When did you start caring so much about this show, anyway? Didn't you do it only because you thought it would be a trip?"

Oh-oh. What, has this stupid gag become a test? Is this Choice A my relationship, Choice B the show?

"Fine, I'll wear them okay?" So I'll wear the damn panties to the show. Big deal. If anyone can tell, I'll take them off. At least I'll have more fun than I did last week. "If it means *that* much to you." Am I insane? What am I agreeing to?

He kisses me hard on the lips and slowly lowers me, hands on my back, onto the bed.

"What are you doing?"

"Seducing you?"

"We can't have sex. I have my period." Does he not remember anything?

Why am I even worrying about the power panties? No way he remembers that he even bought me them by next weekend.

"So?" he says.

"What do you mean, so?"

"Are you sixteen? You can still have sex with your period. You have serious menstruation issues."

"It's so dirty." Wait a second. "You've done that?"

"Um…no?" He lies on top of me.

"You're full of crap." I swat him. "Knowing you had sex with someone else when she had her period is revolting."

"What's so revolting about it?"

It's like an unwanted blood transfusion. "I don't want blood all over the sheets. I just changed them."

"You did?" He takes a closer look at them. Does he not notice anything? "So we'll put a towel down under us."

"Only if you wear a condom," I concede reluctantly.

"Why? Because of the pill thing? You can't get pregnant when you have your period, can you? Condoms never work on me anymore."

"With a condom," I repeat. "We'll try it again, okay? And don't touch me down there, got it?"

I'm not sure what's in all this for me. Sounds about as much fun as cooking fennel.

"Cool." He sprints toward the linen closet. "I'm getting a towel. Go take out your tampon."

Good thing my extra towels arrive tomorrow.

Happy anniversary.

14

Who's the Boss?

On Tuesday morning, the Party Girls have our first interview. And it's live.

A car service picks me up at six. I couldn't sleep and now I have bags under my eyes. Not only that, my stomach hurts. I've never done an interview before. What if I can't think of anything intelligent to say?

"Hey," Erin says when I open the car's back door. It's only the driver and us. Erin is lying on the seat, the back of her head against the window.

"Scoot over," I say. I'm pissed off at her about telling the camera about me getting my period, but after all the horrible things I said about her, I've lost my right to complain.

Her eyes are closed. "I'm in no mood for Mia."

"Who's Mia?"

"Our publicist. You haven't yet had the pleasure of meeting her?"

We have a publicist? Shouldn't I know these things? "No. When did you meet her?"

"Before you came on. They sent press kits about the show to all the major magazines and TV shows. With Sheena the shoplifter."

"Cool." They were in magazines without me? What magazines? I am being eaten alive by jealousy.

"Not really. We got a ton of publicity in all the wrong places."

"I thought there's no such thing as bad publicity."

"There is when it makes fun of the show. TRS got laughed at in *Variety, USA TODAY, Wall Street Journal, Forbes* and *The Hollywood Reporter* for being frivolous. TRS was also criticized for jumping on the bandwagon."

"What bandwagon?"

"Both bandwagons. Reality TV and *Sex and the City.* No offense," she adds, shrugging, "but they should have kept Sheena on the show and milked the shoplifting for PR. They could have made it an issue on air."

"Excuse me for not being a criminal."

"The real problem," she says, ignoring me, "is that no other network wants to put us on their talk shows because they have their own stupid reality shows to promote. So instead, we're on *American Sunrise.* Totally useless. Anyone who's home at nine and awake isn't exactly our target market. They should get us on Letterman. Putting us on *American Sunrise* is like posting a condom advertisement in a convent's bathroom."

"It's still live national television."

Live. *Live.* What if something crazy happens? Once it happens, it happened. No retakes. No editing. My pulse races. "What if something awful happens?"

"Like what? You get your period?"

Ha, ha.

At the door to the studio, we're given fancy square badges to clip to our coats, and then we're escorted to a private room.

Carrie, Miche and Brittany are sitting at a long table, drinking coffee.

"Is that Sunny? That must be Sunny!" a nasal voice says. The voice belongs to a short, toothpick-skinny woman wearing an aqua-blue fitted pantsuit. She's also wearing at least four-inch platform boots, the kind you see in music videos that make you wonder how on earth anyone stands on them. They're hideous, but I guess when you're vertically challenged, you have no choice. I slouch down to see how awful the world is from five feet. It's lower, sure, but no way is it worth those shoes.

"It's terrific to meet you, finally. I'm Mia, your publicist." She throws her arms around me, then pulls back and attacks Erin. "Erin! It's wonderful to see you again."

Her short brown hair, thick brown eyebrows and plump red lips make her look like a stylish Muppet.

"Sunny, Carrie told me she's already reviewed the basics with you."

Basics? What basics? "Um…yeah. What are they again?"

"One. If they give you water, do not drink it. Maintain eye contact. When looking at the camera dead-on, focus your eyes right above the lens so it appears that you are staring directly at the viewer. Never look down at your feet or let your gaze wander. Do not look in the air and do not look at the floor. Don't blink excessively. Keep your posture. Don't slouch. Imagine a hanger holding up your shoulders. Do whatever it takes to make you look animated, facial expressions, hand gestures. If you don't animate yourself, you're not going to look interesting on television. You want to look in control, though, so no fidgeting. No scratching, no twirling your hair, no twisting your rings around your fingers, no playing with your earrings. And no nodding. Sunny, I've noticed you have a bit of a nodding issue."

I do? "You're right. Sorry."

"Don't be so agreeable."

I nod.

"Now voice. Modulate. Don't mumble. Don't swallow the ends of your sentence. Don't be too loud. Don't speak too .

softly, either. Ready?" She smiles. "Now remember, the trick to an interview is answering whatever you want to say to whatever they ask. Michelle, you answer what the show's about. Brittany, you talk about how it's changed your life. Erin, you talk about the Party Girl lifestyle. Sunny, you talk about how much you love New York. Okay? Great! Good luck!"

Love New York? Why do I love New York? My mind is blank. As empty as a new Word document.

A bald man with a clipboard comes to the door. "They're ready for you in makeup."

We're whisked off to another room where women fix our hair, and then into another room where women do our makeup. I'm in the Emerald City in *The Wizard of Oz*.

On small screens above our heads, John Arnold and Betty McDonald are interviewing someone. The volume is on Mute, so I can't tell who he is, but he is gesturing madly. Is that what Mia means by animate? Either he's had too much caffeine or he's an animal rights activist.

I'm so busy trying to figure out what's on television that I only catch the end of the conversation between the woman doing my makeup and the woman doing Brittany's.

"She's only twenty-six. Can you believe it? A weather girl. Replacing her with a twenty-six-year-old weather girl. The old Bets is losing her mind."

The old Bets? Betty?

The bald man with the clipboard pops his head into the door. "Two minutes."

We file out the door and follow Carrie, Mia and the clipboard man down a narrow hallway, into a studio. The man with the clipboard tells us to be quiet, mime-style. He opens the door and we file inside. John and Betty are sitting comfortably on matching blue chairs, and the caffeine-crazed man is sitting on a beige couch between them.

Betty smiles at the camera. "Thanks again, John Moll, from Humans Against Animal Cruelty, for taking the time to talk to us."

Am I good, or am I good?

She continues, "Right after these messages, we have the crazy ladies of *Party Girls*. Don't go away."

I get to meet fluffy-haired Betty and pursed-lipped John! I feel like we're already old friends. I got to know them intimately when I was forced to watch the show while waiting desperately for a *Party Girls* commercial.

"Cut!" The cameraman says.

Betty scowls. "Can someone fix my hair please? It's falling! Hello?" A hairstylist rushes over and primps Betty's head.

Bald man with clipboard shuffles us to the couch. We try not to look squished. "Do you want some water?" he asks.

"No," we all say in unison.

"Thirty seconds!"

We're all staring at Betty, waiting for her to acknowledge our presence. She ignores us.

"Hello, girls!" John Arnold says, smiling broadly while running his fingers through his few remaining gray strands. He points to the camera. "They're showing a clip of your show right now."

What if we screw up? We won't screw up. No water. No nodding.

"Five, four, three, two, one."

Did I miss something? Suddenly Betty is all laughs as though we're in the middle of a charming conversation.

John leans toward the camera. "Here today, we have the four beautiful—" we all smile "—actresses from *Party Girls*. How do you girls like your new sitcom?"

We're dumbfounded. Actresses? Sitcom? Uh-oh.

Brittany, who's sitting closest to him, leans forward. "We're not actresses."

"Oh," he says, forehead scrunching, clearly confused. He looks at the bald clipboard man waiting for an explanation and then at Betty. "Are you the Mothers Against Drunk Driving women?"

The room is quieter than a school gym on S.A.T. day. How does he not know who we are? We're on the same *network*.

I decide to take control. "No, John." Am I allowed to call him John? "We're not from MADD. We're from *Party Girls*—you were right the first time. But it's a reality television show, not a sitcom. Although, John," I continue, flashing him a wide smile, "at times it might seem like a sitcom. But isn't that the way it is? Real life is made up of hilarious moments, don't you think?" John's puckered lips break into a smile. By George, I've done it! I've won him over! "We're not actresses, we're just four young single women living it up in the Big Apple. But thank you for the compliment."

Oh, yeah, I'm good. Maybe I *should* be an actress.

Uh-oh. He's no longer smiling. He's resumed his normal poker-face disposition. "The cameras tape your *real* lives?"

What, is he deaf? Didn't I just say this? "Yes. They show the way twenty-something women act on their nights out on the town. The cameras follow us to bars and capture all the fun."

"Don't you find it intrusive?"

"Not at all," Michelle pipes up. "It's fun."

"It's an experience of a lifetime," Brittany says. "It's amazing to be a part of something so special."

Betty lets out a high-pitched snort. "Special?"

What was that?

"Sorry?" Brittany says.

Betty looks directly at the camera. "It's not the most original idea for a show, is it?"

I inwardly gasp. Grandma Betty?

"What do you mean?" Brittany asks.

"Every network has a show about single women in the city. And every network has a reality show."

This is not good. Not good at all. The other girls look scared. I have to say something. "Betty, *Party Girls* is not a 'me, too' show. TRS, as you know, is an established network. It has taken its time watching the reality TV genre develop. They have seen what the other networks have to offer and have come up with an original, fascinating concept to move the genre to the next level. It's called ALR, or Almost Live Reality. The show is broadcast the night after it's filmed. Now that's innovation."

Hah! Take that.

Betty shakes her head, obviously not buying it. "Do you think people are sick of reality TV? Networks are drowning in them."

"Look at the ratings," I say with forced confidence. "There's an entire generation of twenty- and thirty-something women who want their realities captured on television and reflected back to them, and *Party Girls* meets the demand while still adding a fresh and unique twist to the genre."

I *am* good, what can I say?

"Yeah," Erin says, pointing her finger at Betty. "Every network has a morning show. Don't you think that's a bit overdone?"

Oh, boy. Can't everyone else just not talk?

Steam shoots from Betty's ears. "Morning shows give people *information*. What does *Party Girls* do? Instruct young women on how to be superficial and amoral?"

Um…hello? Is she not on the same network as we are? Isn't she supposed to be telling us how wonderful we are?

"We have morals," Brittany adds defensively.

Great rebuttal, Brit.

Betty snorts again. "Didn't you get drunk and spend most of the first episode vomiting?"

Brittany turns bright red.

Betty's getting kicked off the show. For a twenty-six-year-old weather girl. At the moment Betty must see us as supple incarnations of the woman slotted to replace her. That must be why she's being such a bitch. She's practically standing in her seat. Isn't she too old for this type of behavior? I don't want her to have a heart attack. "Are you not concerned about the type of role model you're projecting on our youth?"

Erin looks furious. "Why do we have to be role models? Can't we be entertainment?"

Betty slits her eyes and burns a hole through Erin's face. "Do you know that one out of every five women in this city has a sexually transmitted disease? Would you say your behavior antagonizes or mollifies the situation?"

"My costars and I are all clean, Betty," Erin says smoothly. "Are you saying that you're the fifth?"

John's face is white. He's frantically eyeing the cameraman, trying to get him to stop filming. He's gesturing so wildly, he could pass for an animal rights activist.

"I almost always use condoms," Erin answers.

Oh, God.

"You slept with two different men on two different days. Men who don't care about you. How do you explain this?"

"What are you saying? I should have slept with women?"

"You're encouraging the objectification of women."

Erin looks baffled. I have to intervene. "Betty, perhaps Erin is trying to encourage the sexual liberation of women."

John claps his hands, apparently regaining consciousness. "Well, girls, thank you very much for coming to talk to us today. Your show brings up many exciting issues that deserve further attention." He looks into the camera. "You can catch *Party Girls* on Sunday at 9:30 right here on TRS." He smiles at the camera.

"Cut!" the cameraman yells.

"What the hell was that?" Erin asks angrily, hands out, ready for a neck to strangle. "Why were you such a bitch?"

Betty rolls her eyes and walks away from the stage. Bewildered, we file off the couch and out of the filming room.

"Sorry about that, girls," Mia says cheerfully.

We're back in our dressing room, getting our coats. We're all still in shock.

"I wanted to smack her," Erin says.

"Why was she so mean?" Brittany asks.

"I guess not everyone agrees that TRS should be going after the eighteen- to thirty-four-year-old market," Mia explains.

Carrie shakes her head. "But publicly criticizing your network's own television show isn't the best marketing campaign, right, Sunny?"

"That's true," I say.

Poor Betty. While the girls are waiting for the car, I head off to find the ladies room.

I push open the door and see Betty facing the sink, staring at herself in the mirror.

Her eyes look tired.

I begin retracing my steps.

"You don't have to go," she says.

I enter and let the door swing closed behind me. I stand next to her, at the sink beside her.

"You're very articulate. You shouldn't be wasting your time on a moronic show like that."

"I…" I have no idea what to say to her.

While filling her cupped hands with water, she smiles at me. Then she splashes the water on her face and pats herself dry with a paper towel. Her cheeks look saggy and wrinkled, like she spent too many hours in the bath.

"Good luck," she says, leaving me alone with my own reflection.

After a two-hour nap, I rewind and watch the taped interview four times in a row. Fine, she was a bitch…but I was great! I looked great, I sounded great…I was simply great.

I'm on my way to meet Miche for lunch in midtown, when I'm startled to see my father through the Kenneth Cole window, trying on a jacket. I go into the store and approach him. "Dad?"

He looks shocked to see me. "Well, hello there, stranger," he says, kissing me on the cheek. "What are you doing in my neck of the woods?"

"Meeting a friend for lunch."

"You were right near my office and you didn't call to say hello?"

I did call to say hello. But I spoke to his secretary. As usual. I even speak to Carrie more than I speak to him. I've actually started speaking to Carrie at least once a day. She's growing on me, kind of, like coffee. The first time you try it, you can't possibly understand why anyone would ever drink it, never mind every single morning. Eventually your intake increases to three to six cups a day.

I wonder if my dad will marry Carrie. It's been over three months. Maybe he's serious this time. Maybe it will bring me closer to him.

"I should have left a message," I answer. I didn't realize he had so much free time. Does he usually go shopping in the middle of a workday? Nothing to consult today?

"Who are you meeting? Steve?"

"I'm meeting Steve after lunch, actually. I'm going to drop by the restaurant. But first I'm meeting a friend from the show—Michelle? Have you met her?"

"The redhead?"

"Yeah."

"Carrie's mentioned her, and I've seen her on the show, but we've never met. Where are you going?"

"To Comfort Diner."

"Why don't you let me take you girls out for lunch?"

A whole lunch with Dad? "You don't have to do that."

"My pleasure. Call your friend and tell her to meet us at Le Soleil instead. Now, what do you think of this jacket?"

An hour later, Michelle and I are drunk on Chardonnay and my dad is amusing us with stories about his wayward clients. "So I told him, shredding documents is not a good idea."

"Very funny," I tell him, giggling. I think I'm a bit drunk.

"Michelle thought it was funny," he says.

"She's just being nice," I say, finishing off another glass. I look at my watch. "Do you always take two-hour lunches?"

He waves his hand in dismissal. "Don't worry. I'm going to charge the whole day to the client anyway. But my secretary must think I've been kidnapped. I told her I was going to get a jacket and pick up a sandwich." He looks at his watch. "Are you still planning on meeting Steve?"

Does he mention Steve to everyone? I'm suddenly a bit concerned about his loose lips. "Hey, Dad, you know you're not supposed to talk about Steve in public, right? No one knows I have a boyfriend. I told Michelle, so you didn't just blow my cover, but watch it, okay?"

Miche comes to my father's defense. "He didn't categorize your relationship with Steve as romantic. If I hadn't known, I wouldn't have guessed."

"Right," my dad says. "Steve could be your brother or something."

"Exactly," Michelle says.

"You should come check out his restaurant, Dad. You can bring clients there for lunch."

His mouth curves into a condescending smile. "Manna? I don't think his restaurant is quite right for my clients."

Well, excuse me.

"Anyway," he continues. "I'm sure you don't have to worry about the Steve issue," he says. "I doubt the producer would care, frankly."

"Carrie would kill you if she heard you say that," I say.

Miche takes another sip of her wine. "As long as the media doesn't find out, no one cares what you do with your personal life."

"Exactly," he agrees. "Although I think you're broadcasting a little too much of your personal life as it is."

I feel my cheeks redden. "What is that supposed to mean?"

He looks intently at me. "That whole women's issue was a bit embarrassing."

I sink into my chair. My face must be bright red. My father saw me get my period on TV.

"I didn't do that on purpose," I grumble. Why do I suddenly sound like a ten-year-old?

He shakes his head. "Your outfits have been a bit much, too. Couldn't your shirt have been a little less revealing?" He reaches into his pocket for his money clip and pulls out five hundred-dollar bills. "Here," he says. "Why don't you go buy yourself something classy?" He turns to Miche. "More wine?"

I keep my mouth clamped shut, even though I'm fuming. As usual, here's my father being a control freak, trying to use his money to shape the people in his life into what he wants them to be.

I will *not* let him turn me into my mother. I take the money to avoid making a scene. I'll give it to Steve for rent.

"No, thanks," Miche says. "I think I've had enough." She looks at her watch. "Can you believe? It's already three o'clock."

I take a deep breath and turn to Miche. "What are you doing for the rest of the day?"

"Passing out, I think. I'm not in much shape to do anything but sit on my couch."

"I was supposed to go to Steve's," I say, "but I should just go home and sleep." I'm too angry to do anything but go home and fume.

The bill comes and my dad slips his credit card on it without even looking. What does he care? He's just going to charge it to his client. "I think that's a good idea," he says. "I don't think Steve would appreciate his drunk girlfriend showing up and scaring all those religious fruitcakes."

Is a man who forced his ex-wife to convert allowed to make obnoxious comments about religion? "Thanks for lunch, Dad," I say through tight lips.

I say goodbye to my dad and Miche and head to Grand Central. With each step I try to calm myself down. Maybe he's just worried about me. Trying to protect me. He cares about me and wants what's best for me, right?

I find a seat on the subway and close my eyes. When I open them, the woman sitting next to me is staring. I wonder if I have food on my face. Do I look like a drunk? Is it that obvious?

"Hey," she says. "It's you! Wow! From TV! I love *Party Girls*. You're, like, my favorite actress."

My spirits lift instantly. I've been recognized. Recognized! On the subway!

"Thanks," I say in my most calm, nonchalant and friendly voice. I chat with my fan until my stop.

"You're awesome," she says as I get off at my subway stop.

I'm awesome. She watches me through the window. I wave. Someone recognized me. Hurray! I smile all the way up the stairs and up to the light. That was the best feeling ever. She loves me.

I decide to keep walking into Soho to see if anyone else recognizes me. I smile at everyone as I pass. Does she recognize me? It's possible. I think he recognized me. I love this city.

I spot a flower shop and decide to send Carrie a bouquet of flowers. Why not? She deserves it. All this is because of her. I spend the next twenty minutes picking out the perfect bouquet of roses and arrange to have them delivered.

I pick up *Vogue* and *Personality* to read, and by the time I start walking home it's already dark. The paved sidewalks sparkle as if they're covered in body glitter and I think, I can't believe how lucky I am. I smile to myself all the way back to my apartment.

When Steve gets home, he is pissed.

"What happened to you?" he asks, arms crossed, standing in the doorway.

I'm lying across the couch watching TV. "Sorry, I was tired."

"We had plans, Sunny. I was expecting you. I told everyone you were coming to meet me. Everyone was expecting you. I reserved a table all night for us to have a nice dinner."

"Sorry to disappoint *everyone.*"

"No, Sunny, you disappointed me. I don't care what everyone else says."

"What did everyone else say?"

"The ones that watch the show found it a bit weird that one, you pretend you're single on TV, and two, you ditched our plans."

I hate that. What gives his friends the right to judge me?

He shakes his head. "I don't care what everyone else says. I care that you stood me up."

"I was exhausted, okay? Unlike you, I was up at six."

"So why didn't you call?"

What is it with men trying to control me today? "I forgot. I'm sorry."

He sits beside me on the couch. "Well, I'm still unhappy. I think you were a little selfish."

"So be unhappy." I get up and storm into the second bedroom, my new office, and close the door behind me.

Not everyone thinks I'm a horrible, selfish person. Lots of people out there think I'm fabulous.

I search for my name on Google. Then on HotBot. Then on MSNsearch.

"Sunny Lang" Results 1-100 of 10,089. Search took 0.83 seconds.

"Sunny Lang Party Girls" Results 1-100 of 7,964. Search took 0.81 seconds.

"Sunny Erin Michelle Brittany Party Girls" Results 1-100 of 696. Search took 0.79 seconds.

On the community board there's even a thread this week called:

Poor Sunny (25 messages).

And most of the messages say nice and friendly things like, "She's so funny! I wish I knew her in real life—We could be friends!"

So there, Steve. Some people like me.

Most people anyway.

Dildo 02:07 am Oct 22 (#10 of 25)
Does anyone really think Sunny deserves to be on the show? I don't she's a loser. And why are her teeth so yellow?

I know I shouldn't take these biting comments personally, since the other girls get the same kind of love/hate treatment.

But…didn't her mother ever tell her that if she has nothing nice to say, to not say anything at all?

As my eyes grow heavy staring at the computer screen, a nagging concern tiptoes into my mind. Why do I care more about strangers' opinions than what my boyfriend thinks?

I log off the computer. The living room TV is no longer on. I open the bedroom door and see Steve already in bed, lights off, covers wrapped around him, facing toward the window, away from the door. I climb in beside him and squeeze my hand in between his waist and arm, so we're spooning.

"I'm sorry," I whisper.

His back rises and falls with each breath.

He gently rubs his knuckles against my palm.

We fall asleep, my chin nestled between his neck and shoulder, my hand in his.

15

V.I.P.

Since Saturday night, I've called Michelle a million times, and even left two messages on her machine but she hasn't gotten back to me. Once she even answered and said she'd call me right back.

On Thursday afternoon, when I get home from the disheartening job interview at the furniture company, there's finally a message from Miche.

"Hi, baby!" she says. "Where have you been? I miss you. Want to go shopping? Call me on my cell."

I should spend the rest of the afternoon looking for more jobs. But they all look so boring.

Who wants to work in furniture? I think I need to explore jobs in more exciting industries. Like TV maybe.

I call Miche back and tell her I'll meet her at Stark's.

A few hours later, after spending many of our *Party Girls* dollars, we continue up Fifth Avenue, stopping at every store. I'm exhausted, but Miche wants to keep going.

How much can one person buy? Why does someone want to buy so much anyway?

"Did I tell you I had an interview this morning?" I tell her at the corner of Forty-ninth Street.

"Really? For what? Another role?"

Another role? Maybe I'll become an actress. Am I nuts if I want to become an actress? I like being on TV. Or movies, maybe. Why not? "No. But I'm thinking of auditioning for some roles, maybe. When this is done, of course."

Miche nods. "You'd be good at it."

At one store, she rolls her eyes at me when the salesperson advises her to try on a knee-length skirt.

"That cut is so last season," she says and hands it back to her. "Fuck!" she says.

"What?"

"My tip just broke. Damn." She holds up her hand and a piece of her index nail is missing. "I need to get this fixed." She whips out her cell phone and makes an emergency appointment. "Do you want to do your nails while we're there?" she asks me.

I nod. Why not? They could use a new coat.

In the cab on the way over I ask, "Why do you need tips? What are they made of exactly?"

"It's a special nail-strengthening acrylic gel applied to coat the surface of the nail." She shrugs. "My nails are brittle underneath and I want them to look nicer. Why not, right? It's only a hundred bucks."

"How often do you need to do it?"

"Every month or so."

Every month or so? That's a fortune. What a waste of money. I fan my fingers out. "Do you think I need to do it?"

She shakes her head. "You have nice nails. Once you start with acrylics your natural nails will never look the same."

I wonder what her nails look like underneath. Probably like Darth Vader's face at the end of *Return of the Jedi* when he takes off his mask. White, pale, frail. Unable to survive on its own.

Is all this the dark side? The celebrity, the clothes, the spotlight?

Have I joined without even noticing?

Once you turn to the dark side, can you ever go back?

Michelle and I are standing by the bar, waiting to order drinks, when Matt appears, poof, next to me, and asks me if he can buy me a drink. No sleazy pickup lines. No introduction. One minute I'm standing next to Michelle, anxiously waiting for Steve to show up, and the next minute Matt Rowler, the most gorgeous man in the universe, is standing next to me.

Matt Rowler. At tonight's bar, Carnival. On camera. Talking to me. Flirting with me. We're flirting. I am flirting with a celebrity. The *NYChase* star.

"A drink would be great."

He smiles and his eyes twinkle and I want to run my fingers through his coifed black hair.

"What would you like?" the godly creature before me asks.

"I'll have the Carnival special, a cotton candy martini, please." What is he doing here? Not that I'm complaining. "So what brings you here tonight, Matt?"

He smiles coyly. "You, actually. Let's get a table."

Me. Me? Detective Derrick has a thing for me. He saw me on television and wanted to meet me. He's on the same network. He probably called his producer and asked to be on the guest list. I try to appear nonchalant and follow him to a table.

The booths are decapitated seats from old Twister rides. I wonder how many children have barfed all over my seat in midtwirl. He sits down next to me.

Dirk is right across from us, getting this all on tape.

Matt lowers the safety bar, locking us in. I shouldn't be flirting with him like this. I have a boyfriend.

But it's my job. I'm supposed to flirt. At the hotel, Howard warned us that we don't seem to be taking the "single" element of the show seriously enough. He announced an informal competition. Whoever gives out her number, or collects the most business cards, wins an extra five-hundred-dollar credit at Stark's.

I assumed I would come in last place for sure. Suddenly my chances are looking a bit brighter.

"So how do you like New York so far?" he asks.

"I like it. It's busy." Brilliant dialogue. This is awful. How can I possibly talk to Matt without being tongue-tied? Especially when I know that *Party Girls* will definitely use my most absurd ramblings as clips. "Are you from here?"

"I grew up in Brooklyn," he says. "I lived in L.A. for a while when I filmed *Close-Knit,* but now I'm back in The City for *NYChase.*"

"You must love being back home."

"It's nice to be on a show that's filmed in New York and not just set in New York."

I'm not sure how these seats are supposed to work. Turning to look at the person you're sitting with isn't that comfortable. "That's true. Seems like every show that's supposed to take place in New York is filmed in L.A."

"It drives me nuts," he says, "when shows epitomize this city and aren't even filmed here. Like *Friends* or *Seinfeld* or *Will and Grace.*"

"What drives me nuts is that there are hundreds of cool cities in this country and almost every show is set in New York." Why am I talking television theory with the hottest man on television? What else should I be talking? Sex?

He shrugs. "Maybe the writers all live in Manhattan and they want to write about the city they love."

"Maybe the execs are too New-York-centric to even consider there's any other city worth writing about."

He smiles and I smile back.

He lifts his knee onto the plastic seat and his leg brushes against mine. "I just bought a bar."

"Really?"

"Yeah. You should come by sometime. I'll put you on the guest list. It's quite a par-tay."

"Par-tay?"

"Par-tay."

"Maybe I will. Where is it?"

"Third and Ninety-eighth." He reaches into his pocket, pulls out a business card and places it gently in my open palm.

Hah! One business card scored! I've already seen Erin give out her number to at least five guys, so I won't win the prize. But at least I participated.

"Ninety-eighth?" I say, jokingly. "I've never been that high up. Coming from the village, that's like nosebleed-land."

"How long have you been living here?"

"A few weeks."

"And you're already a downtown snob?"

"It happens fast."

More chitchat, and I'm thinking, This is so going to make the gossip columns: *Sparks fly between sexy Matt Rowler and Party Girl Sunny Lang!*

Abruptly, there's a buzzing in my pants.

My crotch is vibrating. I've forgotten about the motorized panties. When getting dressed for the show I think I had shocked Steve by putting them on.

"Why not?" I told him.

If I've crossed over to the dark side, I may as well live dangerously.

And now here I am. Buzzing in a booth with Matt Rowler. Talk about dangerous. And it feels...good. Really good. Mmm. Matt doesn't seem to notice and continues talking. He has such nice thick lips. Plump lips. All the better to suck on.

I lean closer toward him. I think I could just sit here all night and watch his plump, juicy lips open and close and his tongue jut in and out of his mouth, in and out, in and out.

Suddenly the vibrating stops. Turn that back on!

Steve. Right. Steve must be at the bar. Watching me. Watching me flirt with Matt.

Oh-oh.

"I'm going to use the rest room," I say.

He looks up, startled. Don't girls he hangs out with urinate?

"No problem," he says, lifting the safety bar with his rippled muscled arms.

I search the bar for signs of Steve. Just as I'm about to enter the bathroom, I spot him eating a candy apple. In midbite he notices me.

We lock eyes. I try to look away as quickly as I can without laughing. He looks at the ceiling with his best, "Who me?" expression.

Shaking my head and laughing, I slip into the bathroom.

A few minutes later I walk out and scan the room.

My old table has been mobbed. Five scantily clad women are perched around Matt. One is in my seat. He's laughing and smiling, apparently loving the attention. Well, fine Mr. Superstar, forget about me, why don't you.

My panties turn on again. I spot Steve sitting at the bar, in discussion with his former roommate Greg, attempting to appear nonchalant.

The seat on the other side of him is empty. I can't sit with him. What if he forgets and says something too personal and they catch it on tape?

The vibrating stops.

I spot Miche and Brittany talking to two guys and join them.

Miche pats me on the back. "You've been busy."

"Nice score," Brittany says. "Why'd you leave him? Now's he's open to the vultures."

"You have to play by The Rules dear," I explain. "Leave the man wanting more." He does want more, right? Or has he forgotten me already? I look over to the booth and he's looking at me and smiling. I smile back. He's so hot.

Steve. Right. Steve. Where is Steve? His bar seat is empty.

"Hello," he says, suddenly right beside me. "Thought I'd join the group. The men seemed outnumbered."

I'm going to kill him.

Do I talk to him? Pretend I know him? Pretend I don't know

him? Why is his hair so long? He needs a new style. He needs a new barber.

He turns the panties back on.

"Hi, I'm Brittany." Brittany gives him her hand and he shakes it.

"Nice to meet you. I'm Carlos."

I suck down an escaping laugh. Carlos. He's Carlos. He must be the most Jewish-looking Latino I've ever seen. It's as absurd as Denzel Washington going by the name of Moishe.

"This is Ben, Anthony, Michelle and Sunny," Michelle says.

He shakes all their hands first, then grabs my hand and kisses the back of it. "I hope you know CPR, because you take my breath away."

That was worse than last week's imagine what I can do with my whole hand.

I hope Matt didn't see that.

"You're not allowed to come to work with me anymore."

Steve wraps his arms around me. "Why not?"

Why not? I elbow him in the stomach. "Because you could have gotten me fired, Carlos. It's hard enough for me to pretend I'm a wild, single girl, never mind having to pretend on the air that I've never met you before."

"I only talked to you for five minutes."

"Still. No more."

He rolls on his back and crosses his arms. "You sure the reason you don't want me hanging around is so you can spend more time flirting with that loser from *Close-Knit?*"

Ouch. I run my hand over his chest. "I have to flirt with other boys. That's my job. I'm supposed to be single and dating. If I didn't flirt with Matt, don't you think the viewers would wonder why? 'Why doesn't she like Matt?' they'd ask. 'Is she a lesbian?' Look, the network sent him to support the show. After the *American Sunrise* debacle, they had to do something." I run my hands through his hair. "I think you need a haircut. It's a bit too shaggy. The style these days is a bit more of a crew cut. Can I make you a barber appointment?"

Steve puts his hand on my stomach and slowly shifts it downward. "Whatever you want. You're all wet," he says. "Thinking of Matt?"

"Yeah, that's it. Or maybe someone made me wear vibrating panties all night?"

His face lights up. "You liked them?"

"Not bad," I admit.

"You should wear them whenever you want. You can turn them on and off yourself. You could wear them to go shopping, at a restaurant, on the subway—"

I shut him up with a kiss and pull him toward me. He runs his hands down my back and squeezes my butt.

I close my eyes and imagine he's Matt.

Is that bad?

16

Bewitched

"Does your father ever mention other women to you?"

"Carrie, my father rarely talks to me."

We're having Tuesday brunch at The Cupping Room Café in Soho. We're sitting in the back, where, she says, all the celebrities hang out.

I'm not sure if we're here to see celebrities or because I'm supposed to be one.

Carrie lifts a spoon of granola and yogurt to her lips. "What do you think? He sees other women?"

"Are you exclusive?" I feel silly saying *exclusive*. Do you wear his pin? I take a bite of my salad.

"I think so." She looks worried. "Or I thought so. Do you not want to talk about this? I shouldn't be talking about this with you. I'm making you uncomfortable, aren't I?"

"No, I just don't know enough about my dad to help you."

The problem with this discussion is that I like Carrie more

than I like my dad. While I have no knowledge that my father is seeing other women, I can't say I'd be surprised. I have to admit, the man's a sleazebag. And if he were any other man besides my father, if I were having lunch with just a girlfriend, I would tell her to dump him immediately.

But he's my dad, and I want him to be happy. I'm hoping that this time he's really in love. This time he means it. This time he'll keep himself zipped.

"Were you two ever close?"

"Not really. I think he's missing out on the give-a-shit gene." Immediately after I say it I feel bad. What if she plans on marrying him? What if she plans on having children with him? Did I just pop her love bubble?

"He loves you, you know," she says, and I think she believes it.

Time to change the subject. "Are you and my dad doing anything fun for Halloween?" I take another forkful of salad. I've been watching my carbs lately. The camera adds ten pounds.

"No," she says. "You? I wonder why I haven't heard anything about a Halloween *Party Girls* special."

"Halloween's on Friday. By Saturday all the Halloween parties are over."

"Why didn't you girls dress up last week?"

I thought I did. My buzzing comes to mind.

"Anyway," Carrie continues, "I'm sure people will still be celebrating."

"You don't celebrate Halloween after Halloween. Do you have a Christmas party on the 26th? No. Once the day is over, it's over."

"That's ridiculous. They can have Christmas parties every day in December, from practically the first of the month, but they can't have one the day after?"

"Right. Life's too short for mourning holidays past. No one has that much time on her hands." I motion to the waitress that I need more coffee.

"Some people do," Carrie says, and laughs. "Have you ever seen the Web site theworldofrealitytv.org?"

Yeah, I've come across it. Only about every twenty minutes. "Do you think I have yellow teeth?"

"What?"

"Someone on the Web site said my teeth were yellow, and at first I thought she was crazy, but now I think maybe she's right." I smile wide.

She squints at my mouth. "They're not perfect. You don't smoke, do you?"

"Never."

"Coffee?"

Damn. "A lot."

She reaches into her purse and takes out a card. "Call my dentist. He'll bleach them."

"With lasers?"

"If you want, but that's a fortune. Just get the trays. That's what I did." She smiles a fake smile and her teeth gleam.

"Our first available appointment is December sixteenth at nine twenty-five," the bitchy receptionist tells me.

That just won't do. "There's nothing earlier? My schedule is wide open. I can come at any time."

"Yes, you mentioned that already. But that's still our first available appointment."

"Well, that's not soon enough. Sorry."

The show will be over by mid-December. I search through sites on the Internet until I find some new names and finally get a dental appointment for Thursday, tomorrow.

While I'm online, I might as well check the community.

I'm so full of crap. I check the community twice a day, even when I have no reason to be online, like looking for a dentist. (The Yellow Pages? What's that?)

My favorite heading this week is Sunny Scores with Matt! (18 messages.)

Chickita doesn't understand why I didn't go home with

him. Um…because I'm not a whore? Even if I didn't have a boyfriend, I wouldn't go home with a celebrity just because he's a celebrity. Yes, you get bragging rights, but that's all.

LSAngler thinks I played it perfectly. I flirted but I didn't drape myself all over him like every other girl at the bar and therefore he's most likely to remember me.

I totally agree.

Does Matt?

Michelle is pissed off, but not as pissed off as I am.

"You can't not come," she says. "There are going to be tons of celebrities there. You're going to leave me alone with Erin and Brittany?"

This sucks. "I can't. I promised Steve I'd spend the evening with him." Steve's ex-roommate is throwing a housewarming/Halloween party and I already RSVP'd.

"What are you dressing up as? A prisoner and a warden?"

Matt Rowler is having a Halloween party at his bar and I'm invited. The other Party Girls are invited, too, but I know the e-invite that was sent to Howard was meant for me.

Since I can't get out of the stupid housewarming, and I can't bring Steve to Matt's party, and I can't tell Steve I'd rather go to Matt's party than to his friend's party, I have decided that I am entitled to be highly cranky about the entire situation.

I mope around the apartment. I talk to myself. I grumble. I disparage Steve for leaving his towel on the bedspread instead of hanging it up.

"PMS-ing, are we?" he says, eyebrow raised.

"I had my period last week, don't you pay attention to anything?"

He makes a cat-scratch sound and pats me on the head. "You should have dressed as a cat, not a schoolgirl."

At Steve's suggestion, I'm wearing pigtails, a short pleated skirt, thigh-high stockings and a white shirt tied at my waist.

"A cat's not really perverse enough for you, is it? You like little girls not bestiality."

"I thought you'd be extra nice to me today since I cut my hair the way you suggested."

"You look very handsome," I say, feeling a little bad. He does look good. It's cut short, a little longer than a crew cut. It brings out the sharper lines in his face, makes him look a little more masculine.

While walking to Greg's new place on Fourteenth and Ninth, we get trapped trying to cross Sixth Avenue because of the West Village Halloween parade. Stupid New York Halloween. I'm wearing a coat. Tell me, what's the point of dressing up if you have to cover up because of the cold? Who wants to wear a coat when they're in costume? How do children trick-or-treat in this kind of weather? Do they have to pick costumes specifically to go over coats? Should I have dressed up as a skier?

Hundreds of people are squished together, waiting for a temporary respite in the parade so a policeman can usher us across the street.

"Hey, little girl," Steve whispers, his breath cold against my neck. "I've come to suck your blood." He's dressed as a vampire.

He's already sucked everything else out of the night.

The party is not as lame as I expected, mostly because the conversation revolves around me, and really, when you're all anyone can talk about, how can you possibly be bored?

"I can't believe you met Matt Rowler," Monica, Greg's fiancée, says, pouring the bottle of wine I brought. Their apartment is a small one-bedroom. You can tell it was a girl's apartment before it was a couple's apartment. The couch is purple, and there are vases of flowers and picture frames everywhere.

"Crazy, huh?"

She's petite, with small doll-like features. She and Greg are an odd-looking couple, with Greg about twice her height and three times her weight. She must always have to be on top when they have sex, otherwise he'd crush her for sure.

Right now she's wearing a red wig because she's dressed as Raggedy Ann. Across the crowded room, Greg is dressed as Raggedy Andy.

All the fifteen or so married and engaged couples in the room are dressed as a team. Ernie and Bert, Beauty and the Beast, an angel and a devil.

Steve and I are the only ones not dressed as a set. Come to think of it, Steve and I are the only ones not married or engaged.

Ruthie, Steve's ex-girlfriend is here, too. I don't understand how, since I thought she was supposed to be religious. It's Friday night, when Jews aren't supposed to go out. And aren't religious Jews not supposed to celebrate Halloween because in the olden days they used to be sacrificed on October 31 or something?

Ruthie is wearing a big, fat engagement ring.

"Congratulations," Steve says, hugging her. He has a strange expression on his face.

Ruthie is dressed as Queen Esther and her fiancé is King Ahashverosh, the stars of the Jewish holiday Purim. On Purim, Jews dress up and are supposed to drink until they can no longer tell the difference between the hero and the villain. I bet Ruthie and company were too lazy to come up with new costumes and decided to recycle their Purim ones.

Still hugging her.

Still.

Okay, enough already.

A girl I don't know in a *Playboy* Bunny outfit (her partner is dressed as Hugh Hefner) taps me on the arm.

"Hi, I'm Ellie," she says. "I am so excited to meet you. I love your show. I'm totally addicted."

"Thank you," I say. "That's so sweet."

"Are you an actress?"

I laugh. "No, just a regular person."

"Wow. What's it like?"

I describe the makeovers, the other girls, the cameramen and anything else I can think of that these women will find interesting. They listen enthusiastically the entire time, constantly asking questions.

Over my shoulder I'm watching Steve deep in discussion with Ruthie. Maybe he's wishing he was the one marrying her. A nice normal girl, with a nice (probably) normal job. Not someone as self-absorbed as I am. As I've become.

About thirty minutes later Steve interrupts because he wants to introduce me to a college friend of his, Nolan, and his wife, Patricia.

I shake their hands and ask them polite questions about what they do. They're lawyers and they tell me about their boring jobs and about their clients, droning on and on, and then they start a discussion about the mayor and the economic state of the city. I'm not sure why they don't ask me what I do. Not to be a bitch, but my life is so much more interesting.

I try to think of ways to bring it into the conversation, but really, how does reality television flow from "financial depression"?

Why doesn't Steve bring it up? Isn't he proud of me?

Am I really this self-centered? Do all conversations have to revolve around me?

But wouldn't Nolan and Patricia be interested in learning about the world of television? About the world of *me?*

What's wrong with me?

Yawn. I look at my watch. Is it time to go home yet?

I wait for Steve to fall asleep and then sneak into the bathroom to put in the teeth-bleaching molds. The dentist told me that if I slept with them for five nights I'd have a new, sparkling smile.

There's a top one and a bottom one. They're gummy and

clear and they remind me of when I used to bite into foam cups at camp to see the imprint of my teeth.

I squirt the gel into my two mouth molds. Then I try to fasten them over my teeth. The instructions say to make sure to wipe away any excess gel. No problem. I wipe it away with a damp tissue. Then I rinse and spit. Perfect.

I climb back into bed. Yuck. I can taste some of the gel. That can't be good for me. The instructions said to swallow as little of the gel as possible. I obviously didn't wipe away enough of the excess. I carefully climb out of bed and return to the bathroom. Sure enough, there is spill-over-gel on my gums. I wipe it away. I wait a few minutes to see if there's more spillage. There is. Why won't this damn gel stay where it's supposed to? I can't swallow the gel. It'll for sure give me throat cancer or something equally horrible. Like gum cancer.

I have to go to sleep. I'm going to be on TV tomorrow. I can't have bags under my eyes because I was up all night trying to de-gray my teeth.

But my bags can be covered with makeup and my teeth can't. I sit on the toilet seat and wait.

I spit in the sink. I don't swallow. It's not so easy not to swallow. The spit is overloading in my mouth. I spit again.

I'll have to just swallow and suck it up. I need to sleep. I swallow. If I die of throat cancer, I die of throat cancer. Something has to get us in the end. I climb back into bed.

Instead of sleeping, I obsess about poisons infiltrating my body.

At ten the next morning Steve is still sleeping and I get out of bed, close the door, spit out the molds and anxiously look at my they'd-better-be-white teeth in the mirror.

They're whiter! It worked! But what's that? Is that a white blotch? It is. Why is there a white blotch on my eyetooth?

I've lost it. When did I become so crazy? My teeth are fine. What I need is Prozac.

How many hours till TV time?

I call Michelle from the living room. Her machine picks up.

I leave a whispered message, begging her to call me back with details about the party.

When I don't hear from her by the time the car service pulls up in front of my apartment, I assume that Matt has fallen madly in love with someone else and Michelle feels too bad to tell me about it.

She doesn't mention anything when I open the car door. She's blabbing with Erin and Brittany, talking a mile a minute. She spends one night with them and they're all best friends?

As soon as I pull her away from Brittany and Erin in the lobby of the bar, I shake her by the wrist.

"Tell me, I'm dying here."

"Tell you what?"

"About Matt, what do you think?"

"Right, right. Guess who asked about you..."

My heart stops. "No. He did?"

"He came right up to me and asked me where my pretty friend Sunny was."

"What did you say? You didn't tell him about Steve, did you?"

"Are you crazy? Erin and Brittany were following me around all night. I told him you had other plans that you couldn't get out of, but that you said you were sorry you couldn't make it."

That sounds good. "Thank you." Wait a sec. Did he flirt with her? She's gorgeous. Why didn't he hit on her?

"He didn't hit on you?"

"Me? No. I told you, he likes you. I'm not going to hit on your guy."

"He's not my guy."

"Yes, he is. I saw the way you two were eyeing each other. He told me to tell you to call him. He gave you his number?"

"He gave me his card at Carnival. He didn't hit on Erin or Brittany either?"

"Are you kidding? They're nothing compared to you. They were so annoying at the bar. Honestly, you're not allowed to abandon me like that anymore. So, you going to call him?"

I can't. Can I? "I have a boyfriend."

"So what? It's Matt Rowler. There are certain people you should be allowed to sleep with."

"I doubt Steve would agree."

"I thought he was into the kinky stuff."

I probably shouldn't have told her that.

"I don't think that's what Steve has in mind."

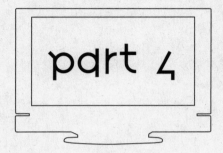

part 4

Y ou still can't get over it. "Why wouldn't a man call if he says he's going to call?" you ask your roommate for the seven hundredth time in the past few weeks. "Is there a scientific explanation?"

"Yes," she answers matter-of-factly. "He's a jerk."

"But he said, 'I had a great time. I'll call you this week.' Why did he say it if he wasn't planning on calling?"

"Jerk. Asshole."

"But I slept with him! Why did I sleep with him? How could he use me like that? Fuckhead."

With an infuriating dreamy smile, she hugs her knees to her chest. "You have to kiss a lot of frogs before you meet THE ONE. Before you meet your prince."

If her slimy new boyfriend is a prince, you'd rather make out with an amphibian.

Last week you dragged your roommate to The Old Town Ale House hoping to run into your hit-and-run date. But instead of running into him, your roommate met some slimy guy and you had to talk to his equally slimy friends and then she brought him home and he stayed over and you had to sleep with a pillow over your ears because you could hear her bed creak through the walls. And then the next morning he was still there. And all week. At least Slimy went home this morning. Finally. (Sunday is family day for him, he says, but still, you have to wonder. If he's THE ONE, how come she's not invited?) He'll be back tomorrow, unfortunately, but right now the prospect of spending an entire evening toilet-seat-up free fills you with glee.

"It's starting!" your roommate says.

You can't decide if you love or hate *Party Girls*. It's getting a little boring. Why do you really care about what these girls' nights are like? Why are their experiences and opinions so important? Why should you bother watching and not just turn off the TV?

Maybe the show needs more context. The bar stuff is fun only if you know what their day was like, you know? How do they relax? What do they do at work? They do work, don't they?

The camera is filming the door to the bathroom. What, this time he can't go in?

These girls spend a lot of time in the bathroom.

"I can't believe it's Cory," Sunny says. "I met him on a beach when I was in Nice, but I totally ditched him. Why would he show up here?"

Next is a shot of a shaggy-haired blond man wearing his buttoned-up shirt tucked into a pair of navy pleated pants, searching aimlessly through the bar.

Sunny's voice is then superimposed on this poor, nerdy, shaggy guy, who is earnestly looking for her: "I was backpacking through Europe. I spotted a buff blonde close to the shore. Two hours later we made plans to meet for dinner. We walked to Vieux-Nice for a perfect, picturesque romantic dinner. We sat in the courtyard. First came the wine. We toasted, we drank, we refilled, we laughed. We had mussels. And then I noticed he had a red mark on the upper corner of his lip. It was a cold sore. He dove in for a kiss. How nasty is that? Doesn't he know they're contagious? Isn't that rude? I told him I didn't kiss on the first date. He pouted. Obviously not his best move since it emphasized his predicament."

Close-up of his sad and forlorn facial expression. Poor boy. Not only did she ditch him, now the entire U.S.A. knows about his lip herpes.

You expected more of Sunny.

Eventually Sunny leaves the bathroom. Cory, now forever known as Herpes Man, makes a mad dash toward her. "Sunny, is that you?"

"Cory," she says. "What a small world."

His face lights up like an opened microwave. "It's so good to run into you."

Bet that his opinion has changed since he turned on his TV.

He's a bit nerdy. How did Sunny move from Herpes Man to Matt? She's come up in the world, obviously. But maybe Herpes Man looked good shirtless and tanned.

"I can't believe you're here," she says.

He tilts his head and smiles. "I live in Manhattan, remember? I can't believe you're here. When did you move to New York? How's your friend Millie? Have you been back to Nice?"

Someone's a bit eager. He's machine-gunning her with questions and she looks like she'd like to run for cover.

Switch.

Michelle is talking to a group of men. That girl never hooks up with anyone. She never talks to the same guy for more than five minutes. And some of them have been hot, too. Like Surfer. What's wrong with her? Does she think she's too good for them? What, she's saving herself for Mr. Perfect? You hate girls like that. Gorgeous girls who flirt with everyone and when the men fall hopelessly in love with them, they don't give them a second glance.

The guy you were in love with in high school was in lust with a girl like that. You were his friend but you were hooking up with him on a regular basis, even though your friends told you it was a bad idea. The homecoming dance/Halloween party/junior prom was coming up, and you were in his basement/apartment/car and your shirt/bra/skirt was around your neck and he was lying on top of you. Fingers crossed, you asked him if he was planning on going to the dance, hoping he'd answer that he'd been meaning to ask you to go with him, thanks for the reminder.

Wrong. He rolled off you and said he was planning on asking someone else, Miss Cheerleader.

You knew he never stood a chance. He'd spoken to his dream girl twice, tops, and she'd smiled and twirled her hair and made him think she could love him, but the truth was, he was so out of her league it was almost a joke. She was a movie star, he was a hopeless fan, and you were the popcorn vendor.

She was perched on the pedestal, and you, you were so far below it, you needed binoculars to even get a good look.

He never asked her, never got up the nerve, but you and your four best friends rented a limo, went to the dance, took two rolls of pictures, got drunk on spiked punch and laughed and danced all night.

He stayed home.

Switch.

Erin, making out with yet another new guy.

Switch.

Brittany doing shots, already starting to wobble.

Switch.

Sunny desperately looking around the room for an escape route so she can ditch Cory.

"I've always wanted to live in Manhattan," she says. "Millie's good, thanks for asking, she's still in Florida. And no, I haven't been back to Europe. Oh, so sorry, Cory, I'm being called over there. Great catching up. Take care."

Cory looks as if he's going to cry. Sunny disappears to the other side of the bar.

That was kind of rude. She could have asked him a few questions about what he was up to. You would have. With an attitude like that, she doesn't deserve Matt.

17

The Young and the Restless

Steve has another funny look on his face. He's either constipated or is thinking about my father.

"What?" I ask.

"Nothing."

We're sitting on the living room couch and his feet are on my
lap. The credits for the latest episode of *Party Girls* are rolling.

"Something's bothering you or you wouldn't have that
ridiculous look on your face." I gently rub his big toes with my
thumbs. He closes his eyes, obviously enjoying the sensation.

"I'm thinking about you with that TV guy," he says.

Matt? Does he know I've been fantasizing about having sex
with Matt? Not that I would actually have sex with Matt. I'm
in love with Steve. I live with Steve. "Huh?"

He sighs. "Don't you think you were a little harsh with that
Cory guy?"

Oh, Cory. Harsh? How was I harsh? I stop massaging his

feet. "Can you tell me what's really bothering you so we can move on?"

He rolls his head behind him, in a semicircle. "If we broke up, would you tell the entire world about some horrible deficiency I have? Was it really necessary for you to embarrass him on TV with that story?"

I cross my arms over my chest. Hmph. "First of all, I told that story weeks and weeks ago in a totally different context. I didn't even use his name. Furthermore, if he hadn't been stalking me, they wouldn't have used it."

"He wasn't stalking you," Steve says with a dry laugh. "He probably had no idea you were going to be there, never mind with cameras."

"Of course he knew I was going to be there. The TRS Web site announces what bar we're going to. When you came did you not see the line outside? Do you think you could have gotten in without being on the guest list? You have to RSVP at least a week in advance."

"He just wanted to say hello. I wouldn't call that stalking. I think you've started to take yourself a little bit too seriously and it's making me nervous."

Taking myself too seriously? Please. "Yeah, I'm flattering myself, that's it. I wanted to have an ex-boyfriend show up so that I could embarrass him on television. That was my master plan."

He sighs and rolls his head again. It cracks. "That's not what I meant."

"What are you doing to your neck?"

"It's just tense."

"Why are you so tense? You're mad at me because I'm a snobby bitch?" I look away from him because I can feel my eyes fill with tears.

"I didn't call you a bitch. I'm just a little disappointed that you weren't nicer to him. That's it. I'm not mad at you, okay?"

I'm still staring at the wall.

"Look at me."

"No."

"Sun, look at me." He puts his hand on my shoulder and gently turns me toward him.

I'm crying. I hate that he thinks I'm capable of being so mean.

"I'm sorry," I say. "I guess I was a bit of a bitch."

"You weren't a bitch." He wraps his arms around me. "Why are you so upset? We're just talking. It's nothing to get upset about."

"I don't know," I say. I can't stand the idea of him thinking I'm not perfect.

The summer I was twelve, I did a terrible thing.

Every summer counselors were required to assess each camper: her personality, how she gets along with others, any incidences of homesickness, whatever the counselor found relevant. These "evals" were for Marcus, the owner and director, and were never shown to the campers or their parents. Although the campers weren't supposed to know about these evaluations (what kid wants to think that her counselor thinks she's a loser?), by the age of eleven every one of us knew what "can't go out tonight, gotta finish my damn evals" meant.

I was sitting in the counselors' room (they had their own roped-off section of the bunk) with another camper. Pretty and used to getting what she wanted, Jill was the type of girl who wouldn't think twice before calling a heavier girl fat, right to her face. On at least two occasions I had seen her bring younger girls to tears.

I noticed a pile of papers on Carrie's bed, next to her pillow. When she left the bunk to get our mail from the office, leaving Jill and me alone in her room, I motioned to the pillow. "Evals," I said. The action felt illicit, like saying *penis* at a slumber party.

Jill's eyes widened and she bent over to pick them up. "Should we read them?"

I nodded. I wanted to know what Carrie thought of me. We

leafed through the evaluations. I grabbed mine and Jill grabbed hers.

Sweet and considerate, Sunny is one of our favorite campers in the bunk. Not only does she participate in all the activities, she's always the first one in the water, the first one to make her bed in the morning, and the first one ready to go to the next activity. She relates to all the girls in the bunk, and manages to be a part of every clique without excluding anyone.

Always friendly, Sunny has a deep sadness within her. Severely scarred by her mother's death, she often breaks down in tears. Hopefully, in time, she'll heal.

Although I was pleased that my counselor thought so highly of me, I was also mortified that she thought I was emotionally stunted. And what she had written was a downright lie. The only time I had ever cried in front of her was when David didn't want to go to the camp social with me.

Jill was furious with her eval. Apparently she was a "vicious child who had no regard for anyone else's feelings." She wanted to show the rest of the bunk their evals, so we brought them out and passed them around. After everyone had read theirs, Jill piled them back up and put them back where we'd found them.

At around one in the morning, when I was already in bed, I heard Carrie and her co-counselor whispering outside. My bunk bed was up against the window and I could often hear conversations that weren't meant for me.

"What little bitches. Let's ask Sunny. Maybe she saw them."

They came into the bunk and stood by my bed. "Sunny? Sunny? Wake up." Carrie sounded desperate and sad.

I pretended to be asleep.

"Sunny, I really need to talk to you."

I opened one eye.

"I think someone in the bunk read my evaluation sheets. Did you hear any of the girls talking about it? Was it Jill? Carly? Please tell me, Sunny, I'm going to get into huge trouble for leaving them out."

"What?" My heart was pounding, and I pretended to not understand. "What sheets?"

"Never mind," she said. "I don't think she knows anything," she whispered to the other counselor.

I spent the next week crying in the bathroom. Partially because I felt bad about what I'd done, but mostly because I was terrified they'd figure out it was me who did it and no longer consider me one of their favorites. They never found out.

I can't stand the idea of someone not liking me.

When Steve leaves for work the next morning, I spit my teeth bleach trays into the sink (two more nights) and then head straight to my redecorated Internet room, which includes a beautiful oak computer desk.

I dragged Steve to the furniture department of Stark's for an entire afternoon. He whined the entire time and I picked everything out. I bought a new oak desk and chair for the new office, a new queen-sized bed and new soft, two-hundred-and-fifty thread count sheets.

I've done a lot of redecorating since my stuff arrived from Florida. I've added a feminine, homey touch with my velvet beige couch, lots of blankets, towels, dishes, vases, pillows, candles, night-lights and picture frames. I changed most of the pictures when I packed them—I thought pictures of Millie and me in front of the Eiffel Tower should be replaced with more couple appropriate shots. Steve and me on the beach. Steve and me in Central Park. Steve and me at the Passover Seder at his parents' house last April. I put the pictures of Dana and me, of my mother and me and of Mickey Mouse, my father and me up on the new bookshelf I bought at Stark's. Steve gave me a shot of his parents and one of his nieces and nephews to put up. I've never met his sister's kids, but they look sweet and cute, with puffy cheeks and big brown eyes. She had five. Steve calls them at least once a week and tries to see them whenever he can. They live on Long Island and Steve wants us to plan a day where we go visit.

"I want five kids, too," Steve said once. I've always wanted a big, cozy family, but five kids seems like an awful lot of months to be pregnant.

I put my feet up on the computer desk and type my name into Google. It's amazing how much time you can waste looking for articles about yourself on the Internet.

Sometimes they say I'm "pretty," "smart" and "responsible."

Sometimes they say I'm "unattractive," "Goth" (?), "moronic."

When I see the former I'm filled with love and happiness. I love these people. I silently thank them for taking the time out of their busy schedules to share their cherished thoughts with the world.

When I see the latter I fantasize about kicking the crap out of the assholes who are so lame and pathetic that they have nothing else to do with their useless lives than spend their wretched time criticizing me.

Sas 01:12 am Nov 4 (#17 of 39)
I think Sunny should take a trip to the gym. Her arms are a little jiggly.

Big M 09:39 am Nov 4 (#18 of 39)
I don't know about jiggly, but she's certainly a bitch.

A bitch? I'm a bitch? What if someone who hasn't seen the show reads this? What if someone judges me solely based on what they read?

I decide to tilt the conversation in my favor, and make up a pseudonym to say nice things about me.

I chose the pen name, Alex, for no reason except that it pops into my mind.

Next, in order to join the community, I have to describe myself, so others have the option to read About You. I should probably leave this blank to reduce the risk of being discovered, but I worry that having no bio might arouse suspicion—I imagine angry women pointing fingers at their screens, screaming "Who is this woman and why is she saying nice things about Sunny? If she has no bio she must not exist! It must be Sunny impersonating a fan!" I decide to create a bio. I don't want to be from New York or Florida—too generic and fake-sounding. No big cities. I decide to be from Illinois. I thought Chicago sounds too big-city forged, so I search for a map of Illinois and hunt for Alex's hometown. Springfield? Nah. Peoria? Better. I type it in. Wait. What if someone asks me what it's like to live in Peoria? I change the city back to Chicago. At least I've been there. Naturally, the community mafia doesn't let me sign up until I tell them my e-mail address. Should I just make one up? No, what if they e-mail me something and it bounces back to them? They'll *know*.

I go into Hotmail and create a fake e-mail address with my fake name. And now I have to remind myself to check this e-mail address because what if someone e-mails me and I don't answer?

Then I head back to the link about me and write, "I definitely think Sunny deserves to be on the show. She's nice, she's smart and she's very attractive. I love her hair. I wouldn't watch the show if it weren't for Sunny!"

Send.

Now I feel better.

Kind of.

My arms are jiggly?

I have been feeling a bit bloated lately. I have my period again. ("Again?" Steve cried, a bit incredulous.) The last time wasn't a real period, it was a fake one triggered by the missed pills. This one is the real one.

Anyway, back to my bloatedness. I've cut down on carbs, but I haven't done any weights. Maybe I should take advantage of that Hardbody free gym membership. Maybe I'll take one of those kickboxing classes. So if I ever run into Sas or Big M I can beat the crap out of them.

* * *

"Let's start with some chin-ups," the instructor tells me later that afternoon. She had a cancellation and was able to see me right away. She's short, compact and mean-looking.

"No problem. This is all new to me." I like the idea of me being a boxer. I'm tough. I'm dangerous. I can kick your ass.

I've never done chin-ups. Which is probably why I have jiggly arms. I step into a contraption that involves footrests, weights and a metal bar.

When I told Michelle I was coming for kickboxing, she promised I'd love it. She says she does it every day. No wonder her arms are so firm.

"Do twenty," she tells me.

I pull myself up once. No problem. Hah! Twice. No sweat. Three times. A bit more difficult but still no sweat. By my sixth up, my arms are on fire.

"I can't do any more," I say, and stop upping.

"Yes, you can," she says. "Fourteen more."

Ooh. Ah. Ooh. Ah. What a miserable gym. No wonder it's free.

After the chin-ups, the Gym Nazi transforms the exercise machine into another mechanism of torture and makes me do four rounds of various incarnations of pull-ups. When I'm finally done, I follow her into an empty spot in front of about twenty people running on treadmills. "Skip," she says, handing me a rope. "Three hundred."

Skipping I can handle. Please. That's all I ever did at recess. And eat peanut butter cups. I loved those things. No more. Too fattening. I can't have people on the Net calling me fat, can I? "Then do we get to box?"

She shrugs. "We'll see."

I position the pink rope against the back of my ankles. Over and jump. And again. My mother, your mother, lived across the lane. Again.

Oops. I step on the rope by accident.

"Sorry." I position the rope against my ankles again. My mother, your mother…

Crap.

I start over again. One. Two. Three. Four. This time I'm on a roll. Wohoo! Six, seven, eight times! Nine! Ten!

I am the world's best skipper. No one can skip like I can skip.

Ooops.

Isn't this supposed to be a kickboxing class? How about less skipping, more kicking? "Can I do something else instead?"

She rolls her eyes. The treadmillers roll their eyes, too. "Three hundred!" she barks.

Twenty minutes later, I'm finished. Then I'm told to do jumping jacks, then sit-ups, then more sit-ups.

"Now can I learn to box?" I ask as my head falls back to the ground.

She shakes her head. "Next lesson. Today we had to do conditioning."

What a load of crap! Does she think she's Mr. Miyagi from *The Karate Kid* making me wax on and off before I'm allowed to learn any of the moves?

Forget it.

On my way out, I see a familiar woman standing by the reception table.

Where do I know her from? She's blond, she's tall…one of my makeup artists?

She looks up and sees me staring. Suddenly she smiles. "Sunny!"

And she knows my name. It must be someone from the show.

"Hi! Do you remember me? You never called. I've wanted to get in touch with you to thank you, but you never gave me your card."

"I…" I have no idea who this woman is.

She laughs. "You don't recognize me without a piece of food lodged in my esophagus?"

Karen. VP Programming, Women's Network. Ah. "You're the choking woman from Eden's."

"I owe you my life, Sunny. Please call me. Do you still have my card?" An impatient teenager is standing behind her, waiting to sign in. Karen is either oblivious, or doesn't care. She reaches into her purse, pulls out a business card and hands it to me. "If there's ever anything I can do for you, let me know. Please."

She waves, gives the kid behind her a dirty look and signs in.

When I get home, I file her business card in my Rolodex. I'm definitely going to call when this show is done. Maybe she can help me find a role on one of her TV shows?

I see Matt's business card peeping out.

Should I e-mail him?

No.

Maybe.

No.

The phone rings, interrupting my internal debate. "Can you come by the office?" Carrie asks me.

"When?"

"In about an hour. Howard told me we're having an emergency meeting."

An emergency? No one likes an emergency. "Are they canceling the show?"

"I don't think so," she says, a nervous edge to her voice. "I don't know. No one's talking."

"How have the ratings been?"

"Yeah. That could be the problem. Not great. Last night's episode only ranked sixteenth overall, ninth with the eighteen-to thirty-four-year-olds."

"Shit." That's it. It's going to get canceled. I'm going to be out of work. And I've been totally slacking about looking for a new job. I haven't looked on a job board for at least two weeks. I could call Karen of course. "Did you call the other girls yet?"

"Not yet. See you at the office in an hour?"

"Call me if you hear anything."

That sucks. How am I supposed to find a new job when I'm

going to be known as the tampon girl who had her show canceled? How will I get any good roles with that on my resume?

I call Miche to see what she thinks about the emergency. No
answer. I leave a message.

Why am I looking at the glass as if it's half-empty? Maybe
something else happened. Maybe something good. Maybe
they want to shoot a *Party Girls Hawaii.* Or a *Party Girls/Party
Boys.* Maybe Matt will join the cast.

Should I e-mail him?

Yes. No.

18

The Sopranos

Carrie taps her fingernails on the boardroom table. "Apparently they're planning on taping this meeting and using it on the show."

What? No one said anything about being taped. It's a weekday. My hair is in a ponytail, I'm not wearing any makeup and I'm sporting jeans and a sweatshirt. "You could have told me, Carrie. Any news about the show getting canceled?"

"They wouldn't be taping us if we were getting canceled." She reaches into her purse and pulls out foundation, a stick of blush, mascara, a lipstick and a hairbrush. "Go fix yourself up. The bathroom is down the hall."

"I'll go with you," Miche says. "I look like a mess." Her hair is piled on top of her head in a haphazard bun, and she's dressed even more casually than I am, but still looks amazing. She's wearing sneakers and a Juicy Couture zip-up sweatshirt and matching pants.

I leave the bathroom before she does. When I get back, Erin is gesturing with her arms. "So it's not my fault, right?"

"What's not your fault?" I ask, sitting down.

Carrie rolls her eyes, and I have a feeling that whatever it is, Erin's not blameless. "The man that Erin hooked up with on Saturday night has a girlfriend," Carrie says.

"He told you?" I ask Erin.

She shakes her head. "No. His girlfriend did. She came over to my apartment and started telling me off."

I laugh. "How did she know where you live?"

She shrugs. "I'm in the phone book."

Brittany laughs, too. "What did she say?"

Erin's lips are pursed. "She said that Annikan was her boyfriend, and—"

I laugh even harder. "Annikan? As in Skywalker?"

"Who? I don't know. Who cares? But how was I supposed to know he had a girlfriend? He didn't tell me he had a girlfriend. She saw the show and was seriously pissed."

"What kind of a moron cheats on his girlfriend on national television and doesn't expect to get caught?" Brittany asks.

"Exactly," Erin says. "A moron. It's not my fault. Can you believe that jerk?"

Brittany puts her forehead on the table and stretches her arms. "Maybe he was too plastered to remember he was even cheating on her."

Erin glowers at her. "You would know."

Brittany's head pops back up. "What's that supposed to mean?"

"What do you think it means?"

"You think I'm a drunk?"

"I just don't understand why you drink so much when you have such a low tolerance. You get smashed after one drink anyway, why do you have to have ten?"

Brittany is about to answer when Howard walks in and everyone stops talking. He's all dressed up for the occasion.

What happened to his goatee and John Lennon glasses? Instead, he's freshly shaven, in a silver shirt and black striped pants.

Pete walks in, nods hello and sets up the camera.

"What's going on?" I mouth to him.

He mouths back, "No clue."

Pete is terrific. I once asked him how he ended up on *Party Girls.*

"I won't win any awards for this stuff, but it pays the rent."

"What do you want to do? Movies?"

"Not necessarily, maybe some reporting. Something with a bit more depth."

Pete smiles and I smile back.

"Howard, you're looking spiffy," Brittany says.

Howard ignores her, and rubs his hands together. "Where's Miche? Anyone know where she is?"

"Where who is?" Miche says, sashaying in.

"Sit down," he says, not looking up at her.

Hmm. Trouble in sleaze-ville? He's found someone new to stalk?

Miche sticks out her tongue at me and slides into my neighboring chair. "What's going on?" she whispers.

"No idea," I whisper back.

Why didn't she call me back? Why do I only get to see Miche when Miche wants to see me?

After motioning to Pete to start filming, Howard smiles a big toothy grin at the camera. Doesn't he know that his teeth are blotchy? "We've decided to make some changes to the format," he says. "Some exciting changes."

Each episode will be in a different city? They're inviting guys to be on the show?

We're getting a salary?

"In the great tradition of *Survivor,*" Howard says, widening his eyes in what I'm assuming is his attempt to make them twinkle for the camera, "we will be adding a series of challenges. Next episode we'll be breaking you up into two competing teams. The winning team will get to vote someone from the losing team off the show. In the following episode, there will be another series of challenges. The last-place contestant will be dismissed from the show. In the final episode, the remaining two girls will compete for the ultimate title. After a series of challenges, the audience will then vote for the Ultimate Party Girl."

I'm going to be sick.

Erin slams her hands on the table. "Are you fucking kidding me?"

Howard smiles at her.

Miche squeezes my arm. "Jeez."

Brittany has turned white. She leans toward Carrie and says, "You never told us anything about getting voted off." She looks like she's about to cry.

That is so embarrassing. Getting voted off. I didn't sign up for getting voted off. Losing on television? I lean into the table. "What kind of challenges?"

"Pete, can you please turn the camera off so we can discuss this properly?" Erin asks.

Howard nods and Pete turns it off.

We all start talking at once.

Erin: "You're such an asshole, Howard."

Brittany: "I hate tests. I don't want to take any tests."

Miche: "Omigod." She starts laughing. "Hilarious. He's got to be kidding."

Me: "What type of competition? Physical? Mental?"

I figure I can kick butt on a mental one, but I'm not sure I want to eat bugs or walk on glass or anything like that.

How can they kick me off? What about my tampon endorsements?

Howard shakes his head and starts rubbing his hands together again. He reminds me of Lady Macbeth, trying to wipe her hands clean of the blood. "Relax. It'll be fun, and besides, I don't have a choice. The network was going to can us and this was the only way they'd agree to keep us on."

Erin slams her hands on the table again. "But we were

supposed to be in ten episodes and now we're only doing seven!"

"After Christmas we're starting over with ten girls," he says matter-of-factly. "We'll vote off one each week."

I better not have to walk on glass. That will definitely ruin my pedicure. "What are the challenges, Howard?"

He shrugs. "We haven't come up with them yet. And anyway, they have to be a surprise."

Brittany wraps a lock of her hair around her finger and sucks it. "But what do we get if we win?"

Howard smiles again. "You get to be the Ultimate Party Girl."

Snort. "That hardly seems worth it," I say.

"Plus five thousand cash and you get to be the host of *Party Girls II,* which will probably be filmed in L.A. this winter. Imagine that. Instead of spending the coldest months of the year shivering, you'll be in sunny Los Angeles. We'll put you up for three months, get you a car, pay for your food and continue your clothing allowance. Doesn't sound so bad, now does it?"

My heart sinks at the mention of L.A. I can't move across the country. I just moved across the country. To be with Steve. In New York. Could I move to L.A.? What about my relationship? This job was just supposed to be a means to an end. The end being Steve.

But shouldn't my career be just as important as my relationship? If I don't go for it, aren't I becoming what I've always feared? My mother?

As I scan the faces of Erin, Miche and Brittany and observe their naked hunger and determination, I see how much they want this. And I realize: I don't know when the means took on a life of its own—but it did.

I want this.

I want to be the host of my own show. My blood starts pumping faster and I clench my fists in determination.

It's only three months. I could come back and visit during the week, or every other week if my schedule gets crazy.

Steve will have to deal.

* * *

On the subway home I take out a pad of paper, and brainstorm potential challenges and necessary preparations. I'm going to spend the rest of the week in training. Like when Luke returns to Yoda before he has to save Han. I decide my best strategy is to balance one mental potential activity with one potential physical one. I make a list.

Monday. Mental: bartending. I'll stop at Barnes & Noble and buy a book about what goes in every type of drink. What exactly is in a Cosmopolitan? A Sex on the Beach? A Kir Royal? Physical: bug-eating. Don't really want to practice this, so search on Internet for best ways to accomplish feat without throwing up.

Tuesday. Mental: statistics. Study all bar-related facts I can find on the Internet. Physical: dance-off. Make sure I know how to do all latest and historical dance moves. Robot, moonwalk, break dance, macarena? Limbo!

Wednesday. Mental: memory. Read up on best ways to improve faculties, in case we have to play match-the-shot-glass game. Physical: stamina. Practice holding breath under water in case of Jacuzzi dunk. Also, swim laps in case have to swim through pools of Cosmopolitan.

Thursday. Mental: geography. Memorize map of Manhattan and other boroughs in case of scavenger hunt. Physical: gymnastics. Practice balancing techniques. Might be a game of who can stand with one foot on a barstool the longest?

Friday. Mental: linguistics. Study appropriate bar words in other languages in case have to fly to foreign country. (Also, must learn how to use compass.) Physical: guzzling beer. Actually, should practice this every day to increase alcohol tolerance.

Saturday. Mental: review. Physical: review.

By the time we reach my subway stop, I am a nervous wreck. So little time, so many stupid things to practice.

I congratulate myself…on officially losing perspective.

After stopping at the bookstore to pick up a cocktail book, and then at the video store to pick up *Cocktail* and *Coyote Ugly* (undoubtedly there will be a bartending competition that will involve me having to throw shot glasses and catch them in my cleavage, and I should research the technique) I turn on my computer because I've made a decision.

If I get voted off, I'll lose my chance to e-mail Matt forever. I'll be a has-been. A television pariah. Why would a TV star want anything to do with a has-been? I have to e-mail him *now*. While I'm feeling pumped.

Two new e-mail messages.

I open the first one from Dana.

Hi Sun,
I know I said I wouldn't bug you about the Purity thing, but you should read these notes I made. I've interviewed about five women about their horrible experiences and I included their comments in these notes. Please—

I'll read that later. Right now I have to write Matt before I lose my nerve.

I hastily write up the perfect I'm-not-coming-on-to-you-but-I-think-we-should-be-friends e-mail:

Hey, Matt. Did you watch the show last week? You were a natural. Why don't you become a regular? Sorry I missed your Halloween bash but I heard it was quite the par-TAY. Great meeting you, Sunny

There. It's gone. In cyberspace. Nothing I can do now. Out of my hands.

I open my second new message.

To Sunny,
I'm not sure if you've moved to the city yet, but we have another job opening in my department at Soda Star. If

you're interested in applying, please give me a call. We'll have coffee and discuss.

Best,
Ronald Newman

Soda Star? I don't want to work at Soda Star now. I wanted to work there two months ago. Even the idea of writing up business plans for a new type of soda makes me tired. Taking the job at Soda Star would be taking a major move backward in my life.

Ding! One new e-mail.

Sunny, How 'bout I meet you after the show instead? Matt

It's 11:00 a.m. and I wake up, eager to start my training.

No, no, no.

I feel a tingling sensation on my lip.

I slowly raise my finger to my mouth in the hope that I'm wrong, that it's a mosquito bite, that it's a pimple, that I scratched myself in my sleep.

No, no, no.

A miniature bump is perched on the left side of my top lip, right on the lip line.

"Nooooooooooooooooooooooo!" I scream, horror-film-like and begin kicking the mattress. I take out my teeth bleach trays and put them in a tissue on the coffee table. I bet it's because of them. The chemicals aggravated my sensitive skin!

Steve pops into a sitting position. "What's wrong?"

"My lip," I say, almost crying. "My lip."

He squints at my face. "What's wrong with it?"

"You can't see it yet, but it's coming."

He slouches back onto the mattress, and reaches out to touch my mouth. "What's coming?"

I groan. "I'm ruined. It's...it's..." It's too horrible to say. "It's a cold sore."

Steven laughs.

Yes, he laughs.

Is that an appropriate reaction? "How can you laugh when I'm so miserable?"

He tries to stop laughing and appear somber. "I'm sorry," he says, a smile breaking through. "But it's kind of ironic, no?"

"Ironic? My getting a cold sore is ironic?"

"You humiliate some guy for having a cold sore and then two days later you get one yourself. Doesn't it sound like someone's trying to tell you something?"

"What are you talking about? I get them when I'm stressed. And I'm stressed. It's not divine retribution."

"You don't think it's coincidental?"

Oh, my. He thinks God sent me a cold sore to teach me a lesson? Thou shalt not speak ill of former dates. "No, it's cause and effect. I've been worrying about the possibility of getting one since I ran into Cory, and I've inadvertently stressed one into fruition."

He shrugs. "I can't see anything anyway."

I lie on my back so I can't see myself in the new mirror above the new dresser (recent Stark's purchases). "It starts small and then blows up. It's horrible, Steve. Trust me. I know about this. I get them all the time. I've been getting them since I was a little girl."

His eyebrows gather in confusion. "What are you talking about? We've been together a year, and you haven't had one."

Yes I did, I just didn't tell you. "I *used* to get them all the time. Where's my medication? I need to put on my medication."

The earlier you put on the cream, the faster the abomination self-destructs. Where is it? I jump out of bed and search through the medicine cabinet, trying to locate it amidst Steve's chaos. Two empty spray deodorant cans. Two? I toss them both into the garbage can. A razor without the cap. Does he not know how dangerous that is?

"Steve, do you think you could tidy your stuff in the medicine cabinet? I can't find anything."

I need to find my medication *now.* I have to apply the cream *immediately* or it won't work. Every second counts! The instructions say to start using it when you first experience the tingling. What if the tingling started when I was asleep? What if it's been tingling for hours?

"You have to relax," Steve says from the other room.

"There's no time to relax." Here it is, sandwiched between the cotton balls and my never-opened bottle of nail polish remover. Why struggle with the removal myself when I can have a manicurist do it?

I apply it liberally (translation: smother) to my top lip and then return to the bedroom.

Steve is sitting up in bed, smirking.

"I'm glad you're amused. This could get me eliminated." Alcohol is a herpes no-no. What if there's a beer-guzzling contest?

Shit. What if there's a kissing contest?

"You don't think this whole thing is hokey?" He makes his voice two octaves lower. "Who will be the Ultimate Party Girl?"

"Is that your talk-show-host voice?"

He rubs his hands together gleefully. "Yup. What d'ya think?"

"Needs work."

"What are the challenges? Who can drink the most shots without breaking a nail, while dancing blindfolded on the bar? Are you going to train?" He laughs hard, holding his stomach.

Luckily I have not shared my week's agenda. I'd never hear the end of it. "I'm glad you're amused, but I have to tell you, I have no intention of losing. Remember the prize? Five thousand cash is nothing to sneeze at."

"And getting to host the next *Party Girls* means nothing, right?" His face turns serious. "So, if you win, will I be allowed to exist? How long are you supposed to be single?"

"I don't know," I answer testily. "I couldn't exactly ask them, could I?" I don't want to talk about this now. I know where this conversation is heading, and I'm not really feeling up to the drive. "I'm going to take a shower."

"Why don't you just take the Soda Star job and forget about this TV stuff already?"

At least I told Steve about one of my e-mails. "How can I work for a company that screwed me over like that? No way. And I don't even think I want to work in new business development."

"What do you want to do?"

"I want to win *Party Girls.* Be the host." I want to be someone tabloid reporters consider worthy of their film. I want to get fan letters. Loads and loads of them that cram up the mailbox. I want to get into a role, really get under the skin of a character. At Panda I was getting tired of developing products and then handing them off to someone else to manage. I want to see the character through. Grow with the character. If the host thing doesn't work out, I think I'd be perfect for a sitcom. That way I can grow a little bit each week.

"Last month you were too nervous about applying for a manager's position because you didn't think you had enough experience. This month you want to host your own show?" He cracks his neck.

"I have a little more self-confidence these days, I suppose."

Steve's eyes are zigzagging around the room, and I can tell he's thinking. "Will the new *Party Girls* be in New York? They won't want to try something different?"

Oh-oh. I take off the shirt I slept in and, on the move to the bathroom, drop it into the hamper. "Did you see that, Steve? While you seem to have allocated the job to the floor, that is the basket officially responsible for collecting our dirty clothes."

"Are they shooting *Party Girls II* in New York?" He's not letting me change the subject.

"Who knows? I'm sure I won't win, and if I did, which is not going to happen, they said no matter where we are, even L.A., I could come back to New York whenever I want."

"L.A.? You're moving to L.A.?" His face turns bright red and he starts shaking it side to side frantically. "You're not really thinking of moving to L.A., are you? Sunny, didn't you take this job to be with me?"

Naked, I lean against the wall. "It's not a big deal," I say and look him in the eye. His eyes look sad, and I can't bear it. I look away.

"Yes, Sunny," he says. "It is a big deal."

For a second, neither of us speak.

"Steve, I love you, you know that. But this could be a huge opportunity. It's only for a few months. I'm not going to waste my life just to make you happy."

"Waste your life? How could you say that? When have I ever asked you to waste your life?"

"You have to learn to be a bit more flexible. You're stuck living in New York because of the restaurant. Fine. I've always understood that. Now it's your turn to be a little bit more understanding with me."

I look back up at him, and he still has that pained expression. I can't deal with this now. I'm stressed enough already. "We can worry about this when the time comes, all right?" Without waiting for an answer, I disappear into the bathroom and close the door behind me.

By Wednesday my face looks as if someone punched me in the lip.

I'm hideous. I refuse to leave the house (what if a tabloid photographer sees me? You never know. Where are the tabloid photographers? Why is it that not once has someone tried to snap my picture?). I spend the week training for all potential challenges that can be practiced from the confines of my apartment, such as memorizing maps of New York I find on the Internet, and practicing balancing techniques on the kitchen chair. I've even figured out how to practice the challenges that require outside appliances. For example, since I do not have a Jacuzzi, I make do with holding my breath in the bathtub while simultaneously kicking my legs to produce the required waves.

The majority of these preparations are staged when Steve is at the restaurant, leaving him unaware of my insanity.

I take a break three times a day, when TRS is showing reruns of *NYChase*. By the end of next week, I should be up to date with all three of the show's seasons.

Matt is driving way over the speed limit trying to catch a bank robber, when Steve calls. "What are you doing?" he asks. He seems to have dropped the moving to L.A. issue for now.

Last month he would have assumed I was searching for jobs. Now he knows better.

"Practicing dancing blindfolded on the table."

He chuckles. Then, *clink*. "Shit. I just broke another dish. What's going on outside? Sounds loud."

Matt's siren is on.

"Car chase," I say. "All the way down Houston."

No way he wants to know what my new favorite show is. Fine, I'm a terrible girlfriend for ogling Matt on TV, but it could have been a lot worse. Sure, I replied to his e-mail (had to, didn't want to be rude), but did I agree to meet him? No, I did not. In fact, I waited thirty-six hours to reply and then wrote: *We'll see.*

By Thursday evening the cold sore is a huge ugly volcano of repulsive deformed skin on my top lip.

I'm sitting on the tiled floor, emptying the bathroom garbage into a plastic grocery bag, when Steve returns from work. "What's that?" he asks, poking his head into the bathroom.

"I'm glad you asked, honey. This is the act of transporting our waste from the bathroom to the garbage chute. I know you think the tissues and Band-Aid wrappers are biodegradable, but alas, they are not."

"I meant, smart-ass, what's on your face?"

"I'm trying out Islam." I have wrapped one of Steve's old bandanas over my mouth in order to cover my hideousness.

He crouches next to me on the bathroom floor. This is

Steve's idea of cleaning: keeping me company while watching me do it.

He cracks his neck. "So you've given up on atheism?"

Way back, almost a year ago, I had referred to myself as an atheist. "Really?" he'd said, obviously shocked. "I've never heard anyone say that out loud before. I mean, I know a lot of people are, but aren't you afraid to say it? In case you're wrong?"

"No, silly," I say now, tying up the garbage bag and placing the pail back next to the toilet. "You know how you're more of a cultural Jew than a religious one? I've become a fashion Muslim."

"What do you mean by 'cultural Jew'?"

"It means you keep certain traditions, but you don't really believe in them."

He opens his mouth, then closes it. Then opens it again. "What do you mean, 'don't believe in them'?"

"You don't *really* believe that an all-powerful being named God said, 'Let there be light and don't mix milk with meat.'" I can feel my cover-up bandana slipping below my lip, but I don't bother fixing it.

"Who says I don't?"

"If you believed in all that, you wouldn't have eaten a bacon cheeseburger at McDonald's last week."

"But I do believe. On the scale of believe and don't believe I definitely tilt toward the do side. I may have stopped keeping kosher outside the restaurant, but I still believe in God." He spots a discarded Q-Tip in the crack between two tiles, and lo and behold, picks it up and drops it in the garbage pail. "I think my understanding of God is a bit more general than Judaism allows for," he continues. "Or maybe it does allow for it, I don't know. I've been thinking about taking a course."

"A course? A school course? Like at NYU? A course about what?"

"About Judaism. About Christianity. About Buddhism. I'd

like to learn about all the different religions before coming up with my own version."

I've been thinking he should take some classes, too. Maybe some business classes. In case he ever wants to turn Manna into a chain, expand across the country, make a fortune. "I didn't know you were considering starting your own religion," I say instead. The bandana is now around my neck, like a necklace. My lip is exposed.

"Is wanting to have a bit of…a bit of spirituality in your life so terrible?" Suddenly he laughs. "Do I sound like a hippy?"

I laugh with him. "All you need is love, a pair of Birkenstocks and some tie dye."

"You really don't believe in anything?"

I shake my head, slowly. "Try to stay alive as long as you can?"

"But doesn't everyone need something to believe in? Some kind of deity?"

I shrug.

"Isn't that sad? Believing in nothing?"

The truth is, in the past month I've been too possessed with the show to be sad. I've spent all my energy obsessing about how I look and how I'm perceived to have any left over to dwell on anything deeper.

Is that what fuels celebrity and fashion? The need to hide from the substantial in the superficial?

"Sometimes," I say.

His eyes look right into me, flickering with love and hope and sadness, and he leans over to kiss me.

"I'm contagious," I say, turning my head.

He gets my cheek.

By Saturday morning the cold sore is in its final stage.

"It's a miracle!" Steve says as I gaze at my reflection above the bathroom sink.

"There's still a scab," I say. The scab is a brown layer of crust about a quarter of the size of a fingernail, over what used to be the sore. The problem with the scab is that because of its color, it's actually more noticeable than the previous fat-lip stage.

"Honestly, it's kind of sexy. Dangerous-looking. Like you've been in a motorcycle accident."

Fabulous. "Steve, do I want to go on television looking as if I've been in a motorcycle accident?"

"I'm not lying, I swear. I like it."

"I'm ripping it off."

"I don't think you're supposed to rip scabs off. Aren't they there for a reason?"

"It has to go. I can't let anyone see me like this."

He shrugs and leaves me to my surgery.

The problem with removing a scab, which I learned from once ripping one off my knee, is that it leaves a scar.

Do I want a scar on my lip for who knows how long? I'll have to cover it with foundation and lip liner and always wear lipstick.

Do I want to have a scab on television?

It won't be a huge scar.

I choose instant gratification and rip the sucker off.

With a tissue pressed to my lip to stop the blood, I call Carrie.

"Where've you been all week?" she asks.

"Hanging out. Not much. Car, what am I supposed to wear tonight? Regular slut outfit?"

"It's not a good idea to change your style midseason," she says.

"Any idea what we're going to be doing?"

"I may have had a hand in planning tonight's activities," she answers coyly.

"You know what it is? And you're not telling me? How can you not tell me? Do you know who's on my team? Is it Miche?" I'm hoping it's Miche.

"I've been sworn to secrecy. I'd lose my job if anyone found out I told you."

Time for my trump card. "But, Carrie, we're practically family."

She sighs. And then she giggles. "Okay, but if you tell any of the other girls I'll kill you. And I'm only giving you one hint. That's it. One."

"Okay, fine, tell me."

"Remember those running shoes I made you promise to never wear in public again?"

"Yeah."

"Wear them."

I have a bad feeling about this.

And I'm not disappointed.

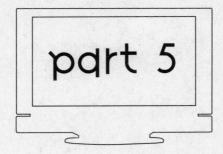

part 5

You groan and throw your sweatshirt at the television. "The Ultimate Party Girl?" you scream in disbelief. "What is the Ultimate Party Girl?"

"Is that my sweatshirt?" your roommate asks as it falls on the floor.

"Whoops." You give her a big sheepish smile.

Switch.

Erin blow-drying her hair.

"Of course I'm going to win. Why wouldn't I win? I am the Ultimate Party Girl. The other girls can't party like I party. They're all a bunch of BEEEP."

"Why does she swear so much? It's so not classy," your roommate says.

Switch.

Brittany applying her lipstick.

"So far I've had the most incredible experiences on this

show. I love it. The important thing isn't who wins, but what we've learned."

You groan again. "What could she have learned? She's always too drunk to remember anything."

Switch.

The four girls stand in a row, facing the camera. Michelle is in tight jeans, a tank top and stiletto shoes, Erin in black leather pants, a tube top, a beaded choker and stiletto boots, Brittany in a wraparound red dress and knee-high stiletto boots, and Sunny in boot-cut black pants, a red camisole top and…why is she so short? Oh, she's wearing running shoes.

Since when does she wear running shoes to a bar?

The four contestants are in the center of the dance floor. The camera pans to the bar's patrons, who are either standing around the girls or observing them from the second-level balcony. The four stars have tight smiles plastered on their faces.

Standing on a ministage, holding a microphone and leering at the camera is a guy in a pinstriped suit with a glittery black shirt. "Welcome, everyone, to the first round of the *Party Girls* Competition!" he says.

The crowd goes wild.

"I'm Howard Brown, the producer of this quality show."

"WOHOO!" the crowd shouts.

"First up, we will be dividing the four wild and crazy single girls into two teams. The fun begins when we get to watch these gorgeous ladies compete for the ultimate title—"

"Most Pathetic?" you offer and crack up.

"—New York's Ultimate Party Girl!"

You ask, "Do you think she'll get a crown? I've always wanted a crown."

Your roommate says, "A sash, maybe."

Howard rubs his hands together, excitedly. "On the yellow team, we have—" loud clichéd drumroll "—Brittany and Erin!"

Brittany and Erin regard each other warily.

"OH YEAH!" the crowd shouts.

Your roommate asks, "Why would they pick yellow? Yuck."

"On Team Two, the pink team, we have Michelle and Sunny."

Michelle and Sunny hug.

"WOHOO!" the crowd shouts.

Your roommate asks, "Pink? Why pink?"

"It's girly," you offer.

"But Sunny's wearing red. That so doesn't go. They should have called the teams big boobs versus small boobs."

A gorgeous tall, broad male (must be a model) carries out four sashes, two in yellow and two in pink. He drapes the proper colors over the torsos of the various girls.

Your roommate says, "Look, sashes! I was right!"

Switch.

Howard is pacing across the stage, microphone still in hand. "Today's competition is a relay race, *Party Girls* style. The first team to reach the finish line will get to vote someone off from the other tribe...I mean, team."

Switch.

Confused girls' faces.

Switch.

Male model and friend (must be another model) demonstrate the race. They begin alongside a giant four-foot-high martini glass.

Howard narrates the male models' exhibition: "There are two pieces of bubble gum at the base of each glass, inside each huge Cosmopolitan. Each runner has to find and pick up a piece—no hands, use your mouths only—then blow a bubble and hold it for at least five seconds. Only then can the second team member go. After both members have blown bubbles, it's time for Task Two. You each must spin around the baseball bat twenty times." One of the models holds a baseball bat by the handle, puts the other end on the floor, pastes his forehead against the handle, and then revolves in a circle around the bat.

"Omigod," your roommate shrieks. "That is the dumbest thing I've ever seen. What is he doing?"

Howard continues: "Once the first person has completed the spinning task, she must run across the dance floor to the bartender. The bartender will then give her a shot of vodka. After she's done the shot, the second member of the team will start the spinning, also twenty times, then run across the bar and do the shot. Once the second team member has completed this task the two girls will wheelbarrow back to the finish line. First team there wins the relay race." One of the male models is in push-up position, palms of his hands on the floor, while the second model grips his legs at his waist. They scurry to the white-roped finish line.

Switch.

The four girls' mouths are wide open in shock, all attempts at their fake smiles abandoned. They all look utterly appalled.

You and your roommate can't stop laughing.

"*Party Girls* will be right back after these messages."

Switch.

Sunny is walking to the bathroom, a sweater tied around her waist.

"Don't let this happen to you," a high-pitched teenager's voice says. "Wear Purity tampons."

Your roommate suddenly brightens. "Hey, I just remembered. I have a bottle of Zinfandel. Maybe we should get in the spirit."

"Sounds good," you say. "Wanna play a drinking game?"

She pulls an oversized bottle out of the fridge (obviously purchased with a romantic encounter in mind) and places it and two Hard Rock Café shot glasses onto the coffee table.

"We should each pick a team," you say.

"I call Brittany and Erin! I want to support my bigger-breasted sisters."

"Fine. Okay, every time Sunny and Michelle screw up—fall, puke, swear, whatever—I have to drink. And every time Erin and Brittany screw up, you drink."

"Sounds fun." She fills your shot glasses with the pink liquid. "Hey, no fair, we're drinking your team colors."

Switch.

The girls are in position, hovering above their respective cocktail glasses, hands behind their backs. "On your mark,"

Howard says, "get set, go!" Sunny and Erin dunk their heads in the giant glasses.

You scream, "Come on, Sunny!"

Your roommate screams, "Find that gum, Erin!"

The camera zooms up against Sunny's martini glass. Her eyes are shut tight and her tongue is rolling like a French kiss gone mad.

"What's wrong with her? The two pieces are right there!" you scream. "Why doesn't she just grab one of them with her teeth?"

Sunny swallows a mouthful, appears to be choking, jerks her head out of the liquid and starts coughing, Cosmopolitan spluttering like volcano lava.

Your roommate jabs your shoulder. "Drink up."

You grumble and drink. Erin and Brittany are going to win. Big-breasted women get everything, don't they?

Sunny plunges back in.

Switch.

Erin, eyes shut and mouth open like she's screaming, bites into a piece of gum. Jaw clenched, she springs from the Cosmo, hair flapping backward like she's on *Baywatch,* sending a spray of pink in an arc behind her. She starts chewing. Brittany lurches toward the martini glass, hands behind her back, ready to dive in.

Your roommate and the crowd shout, "WOHOO!"

What's Sunny's problem? Dammit, find the gum! "The glass is in a V-shape, what's so difficult? She just has to go straight to the bottom!"

Switch.

Erin is chewing, chewing…bubble attempt, no, too wet, chewing, chewing…

Yikes. Erin has terrible skin. Why didn't she use water-proof foundation? What was formerly known as black mascara now looks like smeared crayon under her eyes.

Switch.

And…she has it! Sunny has the gum! She's swallowed half the glass of Cosmopolitan, but she has the gum. She sweeps her head out of the alcohol and starts chewing. Her hair is in a tight bun, and the top half of her shirt is soaked. Chewing, chewing, chewing. Her cheeks are filling with air. She's getting ready to blow…

Switch.

A bubble emerges from Erin's lips.

The crowd screams, "TWO…THREE…FOUR…FIVE!"

Pop.

The crowd and your roommate cheer.

Brittany plunges into the martini glass.

Switch.

Sunny blows a bubble.

"ONE…TWO…"

Pop.

Your roommate laughs. "Drink again."

You down another shot.

Switch.

Brittany bites into her piece of gum.

Switch.

Sunny blows and blows. Michelle is perched over the glass, waiting, watching.

"TWO…THREE…FOUR…FIVE!" You and the crowd scream.

Michelle dives in.

Switch.

Brittany chomps on her gum.

Switch.

Michelle smacks her forehead against the side of the glass.

Ouch. You take another drink.

Switch.

Brittany blows and blows, and holds a bubble above her head like a lightbulb. Erin has the bat in hand, ready to spin.

"TWO…THREE…FOUR…FIVE!"

The crowd and your roommate cheer.

Erin starts spinning.

Switch.

Michelle has the gum, and she's blowing! Sunny's baseball bat is up, ready to go. And there it is! There's the bubble!

"ONE...TWO...THREE...FOUR...FIVE!" Yes!

Sunny starts spinning.

Switch.

"...NINETEEN...TWENTY!" Erin drops the bat and attempts to walk forward, toward the bar. Instead of walking straight, she swerves all the way right toward the crowd.

Your roommate screams, "What's wrong with her? What's she doing?"

Erin looks confused. She can't figure out why her body isn't working the way it's supposed to. She tries to walk straight, but keeps veering right. She stumbles on her heels and falls on her behind.

Your roommate's turn to drink. "Shoot it, baby." She swallows and slams the glass onto the table. "Finally."

"Why finally? You were winning."

"I want to get drunk, too, you know."

Switch.

Sunny's still rotating counterclockwise, but then suddenly she stops, pauses, and then spins four times clockwise.

Brilliant. Just brilliant. She's stabilizing herself.

Switch.

Erin's up and standing and...down again.

Your roommate drinks.

Switch.

Dropping the bat, Sunny sprints straight to the bar. She grabs her shot and downs it in one gulp.

"Take it home, Michelle!" you scream. Michelle starts spinning.

The pink team is in the lead.

Switch.

Face creased in determination, Erin lifts herself up and sprints toward the bar. She seizes her shot and downs it. Then she topples over. Brittany starts revolving, but she's moving very slowly.

"ONE...TWO...THREEEEEEEEEEEEEE..."

"It's not fair!" your roommate whines. "She's too tall. She has to bend more than the other girls do. Someone should give her a taller bat."

Switch.

"...SIXTEEN..."

Michelle uses Sunny's clockwise/counterclockwise trick and finishes off her last four spins. She discards the bat, veers a bit to the right but manages to make it to the bar without falling. She downs the shot.

Switch.

"...NINETEEN...TWENTY!" Brittany drops her bat and makes a run for the bar. Unfortunately she didn't use the pink team's anti-dizzying technique and staggers, then falls face-first onto the shiny floor, after sliding about two feet.

Switch.

Michelle gets on her hands and knees. Sunny stands behind her and picks up her legs. Good thing she's wearing sneakers. Michelle and Sunny are now in wheelbarrow position, jostling toward the finish line.

Switch.

After a few spills Brittany reaches the bar and drinks. Then she assumes the push-up position and Erin secures her team-mate's legs by the ankles. They've only taken two steps when Brittany falls, splat, right on her chest.

"It's not fair, her boobs are a disability. They're weighing her down. They're weighing my whole team down."

Wah, wah, wah.

Switch.

Sunny and Michelle trip.

"Drink up!"

Switch.

Erin and Brittany wheelbarrowing.

Switch.

Michelle and Sunny scrambling back into position.

The screen is split in half by a thick white line, showing the determined faces of both teams: eyes intense and squinting, jaws clenched and tight. You can't tell who's ahead.

You and your roommate are on your feet, cheering, hands waving. Pink, pink, pink, pink! Yellow, yellow, yellow!

Switch.

Ad for Stark's Department Store.

You both take a seat. Commercials totally ruin the tension. Why do they always put them at the best parts?

Your roommate burps. "I think I'm drunk."

The massive bottle is more than half empty. "I think I am, too. Do you want dessert?"

"What do we have?"

"I have some cookie dough ice cream."

"But I'm not depressed," she says. "I have a boyfriend."

"Maybe *I'm* depressed. I still can't believe Fuckhead didn't call. Is there even a minute possibility that he lost my number?"

"No."

Shrugging, you heave yourself toward the kitchen. "Looks like we'll have to use coffee mugs. And we'll have to dish out the ice cream with a teaspoon."

"We should really get an ice cream scooper," she says.

"Or wash the dishes." The sink is overflowing. Tomorrow. When you're not so dizzy.

Switch. It's back.

The two teams are moving fast, both hurling themselves toward the finish line. Sunny and Michelle are ahead by only a foot.

Almost there, almost there.

Erin's a bit wobbly on her stilettos.

The pink team breaks through the white-ribboned finish line.

"Oh, yeah!" You make a V with your arms for victory, a V that looks a lot like your Y during a drunken rendition of the Village People's "YMCA."

Sunny drops Michelle's feet and helps her up. They start jumping and hugging.

Still a few feet behind, Erin drops Brittany's legs as if they're covered in poison ivy. Brittany's chest smashes into the ground.

"BEEEP!" Erin screams.

"That's two drinks," you say. "One for losing and one for swearing."

"BEEEP! BEEEP! Stupid BEEEP!"

After downing the two shots, your roommate pours herself three more. "She's certainly a potty mouth."

"Did you just say 'potty mouth'? Who says that?"

Erin's scarred cheeks are now flaming red. "I BEEEP hate those BEEEP whores!"

"Two more," you say.

Two shots later, your roommate is beginning to look a bit woozy. She lifts a spoon of ice cream and misses her mouth.

Only an inch of wine remains in the bottle.

Switch.

Howard has reclaimed the microphone, and his goofy smile takes up most of your screen. "Congratulations to the pink team! Now, Michelle and Sunny, you have the unfortunate responsibility of deciding who has to leave the show, Erin or Brittany. Please retreat to the private VIP room to come to a decision. Let us know when you're ready."

"Who is that guy again?"

"The producer," you say.

"I bet Brittany gets the axe," she says, gripping her cup of ice cream.

Brittany's useless. Why would they axe her first? If they're smart they'll get rid of Erin. She's the real competition. "I'll take that bet."

"Loser downs the rest of the bottle."

"Deal."

Switch.

Sunny and Erin sitting at a wooden table, door closed.

"If it's a drinking competition, Brittany will demolish us," Michelle says.

Sunny nods.

Oh. You hadn't thought of that. Brittany can drink anyone under the table, since nothing short of passing out will stop her.

Your roommate claps. "See? Get ready to chug." Some of her now melted ice cream spills over the mug, onto her shirt.

She's a mess. And she's plastered. Another shot of alcohol and she might pass out.

Another shot of alcohol and you might pass out.

Switch.

Erin's lips are pursed and she looks ticked off. She's going to be even more ticked off when she sees this footage. Her makeup/lack of makeup is a disaster.

Switch.

Brittany is rubbing her breasts, which must sting from slamming them onto the floor. They must be real, or wouldn't the silicone have erupted or something?

Switch.

Poker-faced, Sunny and Michelle stride from the opened doors of the VIP room to the giant refilled martini glasses, which have been moved to the ministage. No one speaks. Erin and Brittany are below the stage, directly in front of Michelle and Sunny respectively.

"On the count of five, one member of the yellow team will be doused in Cosmopolitan," Howard says solemnly. "Regrettably, that girl will have to leave the show."

Erin looks defiant. Brittany looks terrified.

"Five…four…three…two…one…"

Switch.

A woman is working out on a Hardbody treadmill.

Your roommate punches the couch and slurs, "Shitty fucking commercials," and then, "I don't feel so well."

You're not feeling so well either. You're a bit dizzy. And a little lonely. Maybe Fuckhead did lose your number. It's possible. You have his number on your caller ID. You should call him. To see how he's doing. He's probably been meaning to get in touch with you. You're not going to sleep with him again. Of course not. You just want to say hello.

19

Mad About You

"I love your sweater," I say to the tall, long-nosed woman standing next to me in the elevator. It's a gray three-quarter-length Nicole Miller knit. I just bought the exact same one last week. She's wearing hers buttoned, but I prefer mine undone.

"Yeah? Wanna hear a secret?" She leans toward me. "I found it in the lost and found. There was a ton of fantastic stuff in there yesterday. It's cute, huh?"

As soon as she says "lost and found," I have an epiphany. I'm going to kill him.

When Pinocchio gets off the elevator, I watch to see what apartment she gets into so I can track her down later. 4D.

Irate, I unlock the door to the apartment. "Steven? Steven?"

He might have already left for work. Even though it's only noon, on Friday his schedule is completely erratic. Sometimes he goes in early, and sometimes he stays even after the restaurant closes for Shabbat when he has some peace and quiet.

I'm just getting home from meeting Carrie for a quick strategy-discussing lunch. She wouldn't tell me what the upcoming events are, but she congratulated me on the excellent relay skills I displayed last week.

"What did you expect? I knew every one of those events from camp."

Carrie raised an eyebrow. "You don't say."

Without going into detail, she advised me to focus on being extra nice for the camera so that if I make this week's cut, the viewers would prefer me over my opponent in the final episode. "I don't think you'll have a problem," she said and then took another bite of her delicious lox-and-oozing-cream-cheese sandwich.

Why did she have to eat that in front of me? Haven't I told her I'm watching my weight? How was I supposed to enjoy my dry lettuce while she was practically moaning with pleasure?

She chewed, swallowed, then said, "The viewer identifies with you. Michelle is too high up on her pedestal, and Brittany is too much of an alcoholic. Just keep being your everyday average fabulous self and you won't have a problem. And your single self." She leans into the table and whispers, "Did you go shopping with Steve this week?"

My empty stomach dropped to the bottom of my body like a falling elevator. "Yeah. Why?"

"Don't worry. It's not a big deal, but you almost got nailed." She reached into her purse, and pulled out a folded piece of newspaper.

"Listen: 'Sunny Lang, one of the remaining competitors on TRS's *Party Girls* was spotted modeling bathing suits for an unidentified male companion. Has Sunny, who was recently linked to Matt Rowler, found a new boyfriend?' It's from Page Six."

My first thought was: I made the gossip column? My second: new boyfriend? "Oh-oh."

"It's okay, I spoke to Howard already, and promised it

was just a male friend, a gay male friend who helps you shop. He doesn't want to hear about any boyfriend, got it?"

Yikes. Steve'll love that. "Thanks."

"No problem. But no more public outings with Steve until this is all done, okay?"

Relieved, my stomach ascended back to its previous upright but still starving position.

"So," she asked. "Have you spoken to your dad lately? He's been a little out of touch."

When I uncomfortably shook my head, she shoved her three-thousand-grams-of-fat sandwich at me in an attempt to ease the awkwardness. "Want a bite? It's heavenly."

I shook my head, pissed that she could be so insensitive about my diet, and stuffed my mouth with lettuce.

And now here I am, still hungry and still pissed. "Steven, where are you? Steven!"

"In the kitchen, making breakfast. By myself. Because my girlfriend who claims to love me keeps deserting me."

My clothes had better be in the bedroom closet. I rummage through my carefully hung-up pants and shirts. Nope. Behind the door. Nope. My favorite black pants are missing. My Helmut Lang pants from Stark's! I storm into the kitchen. "Steven, what happened to the dry cleaning I asked you to pick up?"

He cracks an egg onto the frying pan, then kisses me on the cheek. "I picked it up." He cracks another egg.

He's dead. So dead. "Yeah? Where is it?"

"It's…" In midcrack his face turns white. "Oops."

"What oops? Where are my clothes?"

The egg yolk drips onto the counter from its half-broken shell. "You're going to hate this."

"Where are they?"

"I picked your clothes up yesterday, just like you said."

"Yes, but what happened to them between the cleaners and the apartment?"

He grins, sheepishly. "I think I left them in the elevator."

What's wrong with this man? I shake my head in disgust. "You left my clothes in the elevator?"

"It wasn't on purpose."

"It's never on purpose, is it?"

He cracks yet another egg and continues making his breakfast. "I'm sure nothing happened to your stuff. I bet the bags are in the lost and found."

"They were in the lost and found, Steve. I just saw a woman wearing my Nicole Miller sweater."

He laughs. "Oops."

"Why are you laughing? Look at my face, Steve. I'm so not laughing. Maybe you don't care about what happens to your clothes, but I care about mine."

He stops laughing. "They're just clothes, Sunny. Who cares? What the hell has happened to your priorities?"

Why is he making me feel bad? He's the irresponsible one. "I'm going to the gym. By the time I get back, you'd better have sorted through the lost and found and located as many pieces of my clothing as humanly possible, *and* have figured out how to get the rest of my wardrobe back. My very expensive wardrobe. Start with 4D. She has my sweater."

His eggs sizzle as I stomp out of the kitchen.

I hate working out. Really I do. I especially hate this Stairmaster. It kills. And it's so boring. Why don't they make these things with built-in televisions or something?

Pump, pump, pump.

Since the relay race left me totally out of breath, I've been here for two hours every day this week, trying to get into shape.

Also, if I'm going to start auditioning for roles, I have to look perfect.

Carrie was a little surprised when I told her this morning I wanted to get into acting.

"I can't really see it," she said. "What happened to your business development jobs? I thought you've been interviewing."

I shrugged. "I prefer the television industry. I like being in the public eye. Will you keep me on as a client? Start sending me to auditions? If I don't win the show, I mean."

She agreed.

When my forty-five minutes are up, I head over to the weights, and pass the pool on the way.

I haven't swum in forever. But there's no time. The Stairmaster is a better workout than swimming, isn't it?

The pool is open twenty-four hours. Maybe one night I should trade in sleep for a swim.

All week, I've been unsuccessfully scanning the room for Karen Dansk from Women's Network. When *Party Girls* is done, I'm going to call her. Why not? She said I should call her if I need anything. Maybe she can get me a role on a new sitcom.

Also, I was warned I'd be expected to sport a bathing suit this week. The impetus for the Page Six fiasco was me telling Steve I was heading off to Stark's to buy a new one and he insisted on coming with me.

"What do you think of this one?" I asked, modeling a red string bikini as he sat on the changing room floor, playing with threads in the carpet.

His eyes popped out of his head as if attached to Slinkies. "Are you insane?"

"What's wrong?"

"You…can't show that much skin on television. It's a G-rated show. Try on this." He passed me a one-piece black suit.

"It's so boring." I said. I don't even recognize the label. Swimfun. I'm not wearing something from designed by Swimfun. What's Swimfun?

"It's practical. You need something sporty. You don't want your top flying off in the middle."

We settled on a one-piece black Calvin Klein suit. It was sexy, covered what Steve deemed to be enough skin, and…well it was Calvin Klein.

Steve has been acting all weird-ed out since the L.A. discussion. I've caught him staring at me oddly more than a few times, as if he's trying to figure me out.

Wait a second. Did he lose my clothes...on purpose? To make a point about my clothes? How he thinks I'm putting my new self before him?

I'll kill him if he did that on purpose.

Especially if I need to get all new clothes. Maybe Miche will go shopping with me. Yeah right. I've been trying to make shopping plans with Miche all week, but she didn't call me back until yesterday, when she wanted me to come over and watch a movie. Of course I went. I'm not sure why I keep running to her every time she deigns to allow me the honor of her company. Of course when I was there, we laughed all night, and I forgot I was angry with her for not returning my calls right away.

"She sounds a lot like your father," Steve had commented Wednesday night when I complained that I hadn't heard from her. "She uses people."

"You don't even know her," I said in defense. "She's just busy."

I knew he was right. She did remind me of my father. I was always calling him for plans, too, and he never called me back right away, either. Since I've moved here, I've called him at least twice a week to say hello, to make lunch/dinner plans. I speak to his secretary more than I speak to him.

Today's second epiphany: I don't think my father's ever called the apartment. Does he even know the number?

I've seen him three times since I moved here. The first two were Carrie's idea. Granted, the last was his. But only after I bumped into him when he was buying a jacket.

Fantastic. Let's tally up. Family. My father is avoiding me. My only other family member, my sister, keeps harassing me with her "Purity tampons are destroying the world" diatribes, so I never call her back. The worst part is she's most likely right, so as well as being a terrible relative, I'm personally responsible for the probable illness of millions of women.

Now friends. Miche never returns my calls. There used to be Millie. But I haven't been very good at keeping in touch, and the truth is whenever we do talk, our realities are too different now to really relate. There's Carrie, of course. But does she count as a friend when our relationship often feels like it's based on barter? She gives me heads-up about the show, I give her heads-up about my father. How can I truly trust someone whose presence is based solely on circumstance and need? There's Brittany. But she's too dumb for me to ever bond with. Of course, there's Erin. But I can't imagine she'll ever speak to me again after Saturday.

"I want Erin off," Miche had said in the VIP room, eyes gleaming. "She's a vile sketch-ball and I want to dump that Cosmo right over her head."

I didn't have the stomach to spill a drink over anyone's head, never mind a girl who was about to have her dreams crushed.

After Miche soaked her, the crowd went wild.

Erin was drenched, her outfit stained, her hair tinted pink. She spun around and stabbed her finger at Miche. "You enjoyed that, you bitch, didn't you?"

If the cameras weren't there I think she would have punched Miche in the face.

"Omigod, what a freak," Miche said, squeezing my hand.

Erin didn't say goodbye, she just stormed off. Dirk tried to follow her with his camera, but she kneed him in the groin.

Poor Erin. I should call her and make sure she's okay. Although she probably wants nothing to do with me.

And now men. Steve. My boyfriend who has become highly possessive and loses my stuff on purpose.

Not that I don't deserve it. I forget plans. I've reshuffled him to the bottom of my priority list. I'm always bitchy. I won't admit to anyone that he exists. And I've been fantasizing about another guy.

I'm the worst live-in girlfriend ever.

The worst part is I don't even feel bad. Shouldn't I feel terrible for the way I'm behaving toward him?

Matt and my e-mails have increased to once a day. Nothing crazy or explicit or technically cheating. But flirty enough to make me delete them as soon as I hit Send, and then delete them from my Deleted file.

I think I hate myself.

After finishing with the weights, I change in the locker room and walk back home. Taped to the wall of the elevator is a poster that says, "Have you seen me?"

Underneath are drawings of women's shirts and jeans and men's boxers. Underneath the drawings is the following message:

> Help! I belong to a nice lady whose silly boyfriend accidentally and very regretfully left me in this elevator on Thursday night. You may have found me in the lost and found basket. If so, I would sincerely appreciate if you could bring me back to my owner. Please call 555-1676 and help me find my way home.

I can't suppress a grin.

Why is it that I'm so mean and he's still so sweet? That's it. No more Matt e-mails. No more bitchiness. Steve is adorable and I'm going to treat him like he deserves to be treated.

When I open the door, the lights are off. Steve isn't home yet, but my gray Nicole Miller sweater is spread diagonally across the bedspread, arms crossed.

There's a message on the machine from Carrie:

"Hi, hon. Listen, Howard wants to shake things up a bit tomorrow. Instead of you girls getting ready at the Bolton Hotel, he wants to take some footage of you getting ready at your own apartments, now that there are only three of you." She pauses. "I tried to talk him out of it, but no luck. Apparently some of the viewers have written in about wanting to see where you live. They're all confused about why we film you at a hotel. I'm not sure what you want to do—

I had to tell him you lived downtown, but I said I didn't know the exact address. He was just happy all three of you live on the island so the crew doesn't have to do too much traveling. Do you have a friend's place you can use? I'd tell you to use mine, but Howard knows where I live. Let me know."

I guess it's convenient for them that we kicked Erin off. She lived all the way in Brooklyn.

If I don't figure out how to hide a certain fixture in my apartment—Steve—I'm going to be the next one dripping in Cosmo.

I call Miche to discuss, but of course, she doesn't answer.

"Honey," I say, kissing him on his windblown cheek. I pass him a glass of wine as he walks through the door. "I want to thank you for putting up that sign in the elevator. And for returning my sweater. I'm sorry I got so mad at you before, I know it was an accident."

His eyes blink rapidly. Apparently he's in shock at my speedy absolution. "I'm forgiven? Already? But I had an entire script of groveling prepared."

"No groveling required." I kiss him again.

"I am sorry. I don't know what I was thinking." He sips the wine, then wraps his arm around me. "I brought you Ben & Jerry's chocolate ice cream as a peace offering."

Peace offering? Did I not make clear to him that I was spending the afternoon at the gym? What's the point in working out if I eat ice cream? "Steve, I'm on a diet."

"Don't be ridiculous, you don't need to diet." He takes a closer look around the room and drops his arm. "Did you clean up? Where's all my stuff?"

All his belongings—pictures of his family, beer bottle collection, Dennis Rodman–signed basketball, sports books—have been packed in a box and hidden at the back of the bedroom closet. At the back of the closet with his shoes, coats, deodorant, cologne and all further signs that a male lives in this apartment.

He picks up the recently reframed photo of Millie and me in front of the Eiffel Tower.

"Don't get mad. It's for the show. They want to film me getting ready here tomorrow so I had to hide your stuff."

He gets that constipated look on his face, then cracks his neck.

I'm waiting for him to say something. Instead he takes off his coat, hangs it up and, without looking at me, retreats into our bedroom and slams the door.

He has no right to be mad at me. This is my place, too, isn't it? I pace around the living room and then end up just outside the bedroom. "I didn't have a choice, Steve," I call through the door. "They're coming tomorrow."

"You didn't have a choice?" His voice through the wall sounds faraway, strained.

I go inside. "No, I didn't."

He's lying on his stomach, face turned toward the window, away from me. "I think you had many choices. First of all, I've had enough of being your little secret. We live together. End of story. Tell them you met someone. Would that be so awful?"

I know I said I'd try to be nicer, but he's being a bit unreasonable. I sigh. "Steve, it's only two more weeks."

"Not if you win." He rolls toward me. "Second, why didn't you just tell them you had a male roommate? It is a two-bedroom. It wouldn't have been unheard of."

I hadn't thought of that. I sit down on the corner of the bed. "Come on, Steven."

"Second—"

"You already said second."

"Third, could you not have waited for me to get back? So I could help you? So we could make me invisible together?"

"I thought you'd be tired and not want to deal with it. Excuse me for trying to be considerate."

Why am I so snarky? His feelings are hurt, obviously. But why can't he stand me doing things on my own? I don't have time right now for all this togetherness. I have a manicure, pedicure, eyebrow wax and lip wax scheduled for tomorrow morning. I won't have any time to get rid of traces of him then. (I vetoed the bikini wax after the last disaster. However, I'm going to have to shave again because of that bathing suit rumor. Aqua relay?)

"Considerate? You were being considerate?"

"Enough already. Get over it. I got over your donating my wardrobe to the neighbors." I lie down on the bed, facing him. Now for the trump card. "And who are you to preach about the virtues of honesty? You still haven't told your parents that we're living together."

A car honks outside. We stare into each other's eyes. How can I hurt those big green eyes? I wrap my arm around his waist.

He sighs. "What am I going to do with you?"

"Love me forever and ever?" I kiss him hard on the lips. "And not be here tomorrow afternoon because Pete is coming at three to set up?"

He sighs. "I'll spend the day at my sister's. I haven't hung out with the kids in two weeks."

Two weeks? He saw them two weeks ago? I don't remember that. "When did you see them? Where was I?"

He shrugs. "Shopping, I think."

"Well, you're a very good uncle for seeing them all the time."

His hand caresses my stomach. "Until we have babies of our own, they're all I have to spoil."

Babies of our own? Yikes. I'm only twenty-four. I'm not exactly ready to be a mom. I giggle. "Let's have this discussion in about…a decade or so?"

He draws small circles on my arm. "I want to have at least five kids, so we can't start too late."

Kids? What kids? What's the baby rush all of a sudden? "Why don't we practice?" I ask, lowering my hand to his groin. I unsnap and unzip his pants and pull down my panties and pull him inside of me. Got to hand it to my Steve, the man's always ready. After a few minutes of thrusting, he tries to make me orgasm with his hand, and I moan and groan and "Oh my, oh my, I'm coming," I tell him, even though I'm not. He comes inside me, and just before he rolls over, he murmurs, "Maybe your pills still aren't working and we won't have to wait that decade, after all."

The blinds are open and I stare outside. Within seconds he falls asleep on my chest, smothering me.

20

Mission: Impossible

"All right," Tania says. "We have enough footage of Sunny in her own surroundings. Let's go to Michelle's."

"All of us?" I ask. "Why?"

"We told Michelle we'd all meet at her place," Tania says. "Ready? I'm just using the rest room and then we'll go."

I attempt to sit down on the couch without exposing my butt crack. My good black pants remain lost in the building, and the replacement pair I ran out to buy earlier today give low-rise a new definition. Whenever I sit down, my thong pops out to say hello. "Why don't you have a seat, Pete, relax for a few minutes?" I ask, pulling my shirt down over my hips. "So what are you up to after this is done? You going to California?"

Pete sits and stretches his arms above him. "Nah. My kids are in school here and my wife's a teacher. I can't exactly pick up and leave. I'm already looking for work. Any leads?"

Knock, knock, knock.

Uh-oh. Who is that? If Steve brought his nieces and nephews here I'm going to kill him. Maybe if I ignore it, whoever's knocking will go away.

Knock, knock, knock.

Pete looks at me strangely. "I think someone's at your door."

"Really? I didn't hear anything."

Knock, knock, knock.

Damn. I open the door. A short blond woman with horrible brash-blond highlights is standing in the doorway, holding my favorite black pants.

"Hi," she says cheerfully. "I spoke to your boyfriend, Steve. I found these in the lost and found. He said one of you is usually home, so I should come by whenever I got a chance to drop them off. Sorry about taking them, but they're great pants. I thought I won the lost and found lottery, you know? They're Helmut Lang."

"No kidding."

She does a double take at the huge video camera and lights. "Is this a bad time?"

"Thanks." I grab the pants from her and slam the door. What are the chances Pete didn't hear any of that? I slowly turn around. Maybe he's in the midst of a fabulous daydream and oblivious to his surroundings? Please let the camera not be on.

Pete's wearing a lopsided grin. "Boyfriend, huh? So one of you is usually here? Where's all his stuff?"

The toilet flushes. I hear water running from the bathroom sink.

"I…he…" I can't believe it. I just got busted. Panic chokes me.

He waves his hand. "Your secret's safe with me, don't worry."

I love Pete. Relief washes over me as Tania opens the bathroom door. "Ready?" she asks.

"Give me two seconds," I say. "I want to change my pants."

Thirty minutes later I'm sitting next to Brittany on Michelle's tan leather couch, flipping through a coffee-table book (about the fabulous city of Manhattan) on the hand-carved wooden rectangular coffee table.

I feel like I've gotten trapped in a Pottery Barn catalog.

This episode Brittany is wearing jeans, running shoes, and a tank top. Her breasts look smaller than usual.

"Why do you look flatter today?" I ask.

"Sports bra. Last week I was bouncing all over the place."

Howard is on his cell phone, Pete is filming us.

Dirk follows Michelle out of the bedroom. She's also wearing an aerobic friendly outfit—jeans, sneakers and a zip-up sweater. "Hello, girls." She heads to the Pullman kitchen behind the counter. "Who wants a shot of tequila?" She opens the fridge and takes out some shot glasses, limes and a salt-shaker. "For old times' sake."

Is she crazy? I'm not shooting tequila before a potential marathon. And the shot glasses are supersized, at least three inches long.

I shake my head. "I can't do shots now. We'll be plastered by the end of the night. Last week I thought I was going to puke after all that twirling."

Brittany looks deflated. "I'm not going to drink if you guys aren't drinking."

Michelle catches my eye from across the room. "Trust me, Sunny. It'll be fine."

"But—"

"Trust me."

Something in her voice makes me hesitate and say, "Okay."

She fuddles around with the shot glasses and then carries the tray to the coffee table and places two glasses in front of me, two in front of Brittany.

I pick up the shot and smell it. Smells fruity. Is it apple juice?

We dab the salt, lick it and then down the first shot.

Apple juice.

Brittany purses her mouth and for a moment I'm sure I see her eyes roll back in her head.

Michelle sucks on her lime. "Strong, huh?" She catches my eye and smiles. She must be thinking: If I don't win, I hope you do. Let's get Brittany kicked off tonight so that it's one of us who wins next week.

It makes sense. If I don't win, I'd want Miche to. It would be too embarrassing to lose to a moron like "This is the opportunity of a lifetime" Brittany. And besides, I bet Miche doesn't even want to move to L.A. She'd probably let me go.

This is so wrong. But necessary.

I smile back. "Ready for number two?"

After the drinks, we all pile into the elevator.

"Damn," I say, pressing the doors open button. "I forgot my bathing suit inside."

"You guys go ahead and we'll meet you downstairs," Miche says, and I follow her back to her apartment.

Once inside Miche heads to the bathroom. "I'll be one sec," she says.

I pick up my sack where I left it beside Miche's bed. Right next to it is a small black bag that Howard walked in with. He forgot his stuff, too?

I pull on the zipper a bit. A little bit more. What does he have in here? A toothbrush. A clean pair of skivvies. Jeans and a sweater. A box of condoms?

Why did he bring an overnight bag? Why did he forget his overnight bag at Miche's?

Oh.

I can't see a damn thing. They've put a blindfold over my eyes and I can't even peek through the sides. There must be a lot of people here. I hear cheering. And jeering.

This is completely humiliating. We have no idea where we are. They blindfolded us when we got in the car.

I think I have a wedgie.

Miche squeezes my hand. "Don't worry."

Of course she's not worrying. She knows where we are.

Howard probably whispered it in her ear while they were having illicit sex.

When she came out of the bathroom, I decided not to comment on my findings. If she wanted to tell me, she'd tell me, right? I can't believe I confided to her about Steve and she lied to me. I feel totally deceived.

"I'm worried," I say now. Are we on a pirate ship? A dance boat? We're going to have to walk the plank?

"I wonder why they're all laughing," Brittany says, sounding anxious.

Howard's voice booms across the bar. "Welcome, everyone!" he says. "Can our helpers please remove the blindfolds?"

The crowd screams, "TAKE IT OFF!"

A man's rough fingers are at the back of my head and my blindfold loosens.

Blink, blink.

The room looks like a sardine can of twenty-somethings. Where am I? A bar? It looks more like a warehouse.

Across the thirty-foot ceiling a strobe light flashes, Roller Dee's.

Roller Dee's? Why does that sound familiar?

I've heard of this place…isn't this the activity center Steve wanted to drag me to? The one with the miniature golf course? The one that's famous for holding children's birthday parties?

What is it with Steve and kids anyway?

In front of us is a huge rectangular table covered in shot glasses.

Humph. They can't be more creative than who can drink the most without puking?

Howard is standing behind the table of drinks, caressing his microphone and leering into Dirk's camera. "Tonight, we will eliminate the next contestant in the search for New York's Ultimate Party Girl!"

The crowd goes wild. Who are these people? Why are they such babies?

And why is Steve so obsessed with wanting to have babies all of a sudden?

"There will be three competitions," Howard continues. "Each will have a first-place winner, a second-place winner and a third-place loser. First place scores two points, second place one point, and last place—nothing! At the end of the night, the individual with the least amount of points will be eliminated."

"YEAH! ELIMINATED! YEAH!"

I think Steve wants me to get eliminated. So I don't have the option of going to L.A. Maybe that's why he keeps talking about babies. He's wishing I was pregnant and therefore chained to him.

I hear Howard's voice again, and try to focus. "The first activity is tequila shots," he says. "The Party Girl who drinks the most, wins."

I suppose I can handle three, maybe four shots, but how can I beat Brittany? That woman is like a sponge.

What are the chances that these are filled with apple juice?

"In the tradition of shooting tequila, each shot includes a special surprise for our adventurous Party Girls," Howard says in a solemn voice.

Special surprise? I hate special surprises.

"A live mealworm!"

Did he just use a prefix that ended in worm?

The crowd screams, "WORM! WORM! WORM!"

I look at Miche, assuming she'll be just as disgusted as I am. She's smiling. What, she likes eating worms? What does she know that I don't know?

"A what?" Brittany asks.

Please don't make me be first. Please don't make me be first. Please don't make me be first. Please don't make—

"And the first up is…" A drumroll echoes through the room. "…Sunny!"

I knew it. Bastards.

I tread carefully toward the table.

"SUNNY! SUNNY!"

I'm going to be sick.

Howard steps around the table to stand beside me. When did I get a role on The Howard Brown Show, exactly?

"Let's see what you can do, Sunny."

Okay, don't panic. I read up on this on the Net. Bug-eating. Entomophagy. I've been expecting this, right? It was on my list, right? Lots of people eat bugs voluntarily, even in the western world, right? There's no need for me to be squeamish, right?

Wrong.

No, got to think positive! I can do this! Cultures have been doing this for centuries. And as a plus they're low in fat and full of protein. An excellent addition to my diet.

I gingerly select and lift one of the hundreds of shot glasses.

Don't look, don't look, don't look.

I look.

I see a tiny, half-inch, pale orange worm, flapping around in the liquid at the bottom of the glass.

Instant nausea. Mustn't look. I have to do this. Do I shoot it? Will it die in my stomach? What if it reproduces? I have to kill it first.

The shot glass is getting closer to my lips.

"SUNNY! SUNNY! SUNNY!"

On the count of three. One...two...three.

This time really on the count of three. Maybe I should count backward?

Three...two...one.

I dump the shot in my mouth.

"GO, SUNNY, GO!"

Obviously, I should have figured out the logistics of my actions before going full force. How do I swallow the liquid while not swallowing the creature?

I hold the liquor in my mouth and swish it around a bit. I think the worm just bit me.

Crunch.

"SUNNY! SUNNY! SUNNY!"

Kind of nutty-tasting. A bit oily.

Crunch, crunch.

The burning tequila swarms my mouth.

It's time.

Gulp.

Fire! Fire! My throat is being consumed by an inferno!

"Need water!" I croak.

Howard passes me a glass of water and I swallow half of it. "How was·it?" he asks.

Must say something clever so audience likes me. "Tastes like...chicken?"

"HA-HA!"

Four shots later, when I can feel the tequila and the worm colony planning an insurrection, I call it quits.

"KEEP GOING, SUNNY!"

You try it, assholes. I shake my head no, while smiling at my people. If I'm drunk, I won't be able to do the next stunt, now will I?

It's a good thing I'm not pregnant. You can't drink when you're pregnant. What has Steve done? Now I'm obsessing about being pregnant.

I'm *not* pregnant. I'm on the pill.

But what if I was pregnant?

"Next up is Brittany," Howard announces.

"BRITTANY! BRITTANY!"

Brittany lifts her first shot toward the ceiling. And into her mouth. She swallows it whole.

"She didn't even chew," I whisper to Miche.

The worms couldn't be good for the baby either.

Jesus, what baby?

Brittany does a second. And a third. Fourth. Fifth.

Damn. She just booted me out of first place.

Sixth. Seventh. Eighth.

If she took one look at the revulsion on Miche's face, she would have realized that she could have stopped after five.

Moron.

Ninth. Tenth.

Show-off.

Brittany burps. "All done." Eyes glazed, she teeters backward, then stumbles back to where I'm standing.

Miche steps up to the table.

"MICHELLE! MICHELLE!"

She breathes deeply and raises the shot glass to her lips. She drinks...

...and then spits the liquid and the worm onto the floor.

"Can't do it," she says, shrugging.

Hmm. Did Howard let her go last on purpose? So she could see if I did it before taking her turn? And now she's decided that since she can't win this match she should keep her sober advantage?

I notice Howard is smiling.

"BOO! BOO!"

The worm does a belly dance along the dance floor.

After we've cleansed our mouths with water, Howard instructs us to change into our bathing suits.

I cannot believe I have to wear a bathing suit on national television. What is this, reality *Baywatch?*

As far as I can tell, there aren't any cameras in the changing room, but I'm not about to take any chances. I pull my shirt as low as it goes and pull off my pants, then wiggle into my Calvin Klein suit before discarding my top.

Miche and Brittany change into string bikinis. I knew I shouldn't have let Steve talk me into something so nunnish. If I lose the male vote because of him next week, I'm going to be really pissed.

If Brittany's breasts had no support last week, in this green stringy thing, she should be flopping all over the place.

Very smart choice, Brittany.

The three of us march into a second room, all in a row, all sucking in our stomachs and pushing out our breasts.

And that's when I see it.

They've got to be kidding. In front of me is a large rink. Like a wrestling rink.

Wrestling wasn't on my list. Why wasn't wrestling on my list?

Why is the rink red?

Jell-O.

The rink is filled with Jell-O.

The crowd fills up the room. Howard prances around the outside of the rink, his arms flailing. "Welcome to the second challenge—the Jell-O wrestling event!"

"JELL-O! JELL-O!"

Brittany is giggling uncontrollably. "Jell-O? We're getting dessert?"

"We will have three matches," Howard continues. "Each girl will get to fight each girl. One point will be awarded for every match won. To win, the contestant must hold down the other girl for ten seconds. First up are Brittany and Michelle."

"OH, YEAH!"

Miche and a wobbling Brittany enter the rink, both giggling. Brittany waves to the crowd, then slips on the Jell-O and lands on her butt. She grabs the roped wall and tries to pick herself up again.

Miche holds onto the rope for dear life.

One of the male models jumps in to help Brittany get up. Brittany puts her arms around his neck and kisses him on the lips.

She's plastered.

Howard screams, "On your mark, get set, go!"

"OH, YEAH!"

Miche timidly finds her footing in the Jell-O. Laughing, Brittany lunges at her, and they both tumble to the ground.

Miche screams, "Watch it, moron!"

"CATFIGHT CATFIGHT!"

Miche is on top. Now Brittany's on top. It's a swirl of red (the Jell-O) and green (Brittany's bikini). It looks like a melting candy cane.

Maybe they'll knock each other unconscious and I'll win by default?

Miche's on top, straddling Brittany.

"...FOUR...FIVE...SIX...SEVEN...EIGHT...NINE...TEN!"

Howard rings a bell. "Michelle wins Round One!"

Miche exits the rink but Brittany remains on her back.

"Is she okay?" I wonder aloud.

Miche winks. "She's plastered. She's moving in slow motion. You'll kick her ass, don't worry."

Brittany slowly sits up and slithers to the side of the rink.

"Next up...Sunny and Brittany."

I climb barefoot over the rope. The smell of strawberry is overwhelming. The Jell-O squishes between my toes, like mud.

Brittany is standing by the rope, her head reminding me of a bauble doll.

"On your mark, get set, go!"

Must let go of the rope.

Don't want to let go of the rope.

I let go of the rope.

Yikes. It's slippery. I try to use my arms to establish balance. Why does that work, anyway?

Time to get serious. I have to bring her down. She lunges toward me, sliding across the rink, looking like a cross-country skier on a psychedelic drug.

Suddenly her arms are clutching my waist. I fall flat on my face and swallow a mouthful of Jell-O.

Brittany is on my back, piggyback style, her breasts like lead weights pinning me to the ground. I'm breathing strawberry. I'm suffocating. I'm going to drown in a pool of Jell-O.

"ONE...TWO...THREE..."

No way am I letting her win, no way.

In a brilliant judolike move, I use both my arms and knees to flip her off me and onto her back. Jell-O squirts on both sides of her like the splitting of the Red Sea.

That was fantastic. Where did that come from? Has anyone ever done that before? They're going to name that move The Sunny.

Brittany's face matches the color of her bikini. Lime green. "I don't feel so good."

I jump on her stomach and pin her palms to the slimy ground. "KISS HER! KISS HER!"

Why are men such pervs? Can't they see I'm working here? "...FOUR...FIVE...SIX...SEVEN...EIGHT...NINE...TEN!"

"A point for Sunny!" Howard shouts. "Final match, Sunny versus Michelle."

Oh, yeah! I rock! I stand up and punch my arm in the air.

Brittany holds her stomach. "I think I'm going to be sick."

She'd better not throw up in the rink. I don't want to wrestle in puke.

The model returns to remove Brittany.

I'm pumped. Bring on the competition! Maybe I can get a role in the next *Karate Kid*. What is it now? *Karate Kid* Part Forty?

Miche climbs over the rope and into the rink. Her once beige suit is now smeared with red. She looks like she got body painted. That, or hit with a chain saw.

"On your mark, get set, go!"

We stroll to the center of the rink, laughing. Suddenly, an intense look clouds Miche's face and she lunges at me, pinning me on my back.

Where did that come from?

I use my new judo move, The Sunny, and flip her so that she's lying facedown. I pin her arms behind her back.

"ONE...TWO..."

She squirms away and then, oh my, she uses The Sunny against me!

She's sitting on my back, her knee jutting into my womb.

"ONE...TWO..."

Ow. When did she get so strong? If I was pregnant, she would have completely deformed my fetus. How does she know such a good hold? Why was I wasting my week on the Stairmaster when I obviously should have taken up wrestling? Or at least tried kickboxing more than once?

"…FIVE…SIX…"

I can't get up. Why can't I get up?

I hate Jell-O. I am never having the stupid dessert again.

"…NINE…TEN!"

"Michelle wins!" Howard hollers, then winks at her. "First place Michelle, second place Sunny, third place Brittany. At this point all three girls are tied with two points each. Therefore the loser of the next event will be kicked off the show. And now it's time for… The Big Ride."

What big ride?

"BIG RIDE! BIG RIDE!"

"Are you ready for the ride of your life?" Howard shrieks.

We follow him into another room, where a crowd is already waiting, standing around a pool.

We get to swim? I'm going to kick ass if we get to swim. Being a lifeguard is finally going to pay off.

Suspended above the center of the Olympic-size pool are three plastic life-size bulls, like the kind I was too afraid, as a kid, to ride at the amusement park. And these are perched over water.

As we enter, the mechanical bulls electronically move away from the center of the pool, off to the side. Why do I get the feeling we won't be swimming laps?

"Girls, for tonight's final competition, please climb aboard the bulls. Your animals will begin thrashing. Every thirty seconds their speed will increase. Last one standing wins!"

This is the dumbest event I've ever seen. Who do they think I am? A cowgirl?

We climb onto the three bulls. The facial expression on my bull looks vaguely friendly. I name him Charlie after a pet rock my father bought me after I begged for a dog.

I wrap my arms around Charlie's neck. This is by far the most humiliating moment in my entire life. The period incident? Now totally eclipsed. How did any decent human being come up with this form of torture?

"On your mark, get set, go!" Howard shouts.

The bull slowly rocks.

My butt slides downward, still covered in Jell-O. I am not letting go. No way. I'm going to win this thing.

Up, forward, down, back, up, forward, down, back.

Faster.

I'm overwhelmed with nausea. Maybe it's morning sickness.

What's wrong with me? Why am I worrying about being pregnant at this precise point in time? At the moment when my energies are urgently required by my balancing skills? My fingers are no longer clenched together, but on a slide to Charlie's horns…now on his plastic neck.

Shit.

That water looks cold. I am not falling in there. I have a baby to protect.

AH! There's no damn baby!

What? Do I want a baby? So my choice is made for me? Is that it? If I'm pregnant then I can't go to L.A.? I'll have to be like my mother and give up everything for my family?

If I don't want to go, then why don't I just let go? Fall off the damn bull. Lose. That's all it takes. I don't need to be pregnant.

I owe it to Steve. I've been a bitch.

I owe Steve? I owe him everything? My entire life? I owe him for loving me?

Stop thinking!

I sneak a peek at the other girls. Brittany looks green.

The bulls' pace gets faster.

Brittany gets greener. And then…ew. Brittany leans over the side of the bull and throws up. As she's throwing up she falls face-first into the water.

I win! Brittany's off the show!

I wonder if the worms came up. Will they float?

The pace gets faster. Why aren't they stopping the bulls? We won. Jackasses. They're going to continue with this utter humiliation until we both fall into the water.

Well, I'm not letting go. No way. I'm going to be the last one standing.

The bull charges ahead. I see Miche from the corner of my eye also gripping her plastic animal. Every exposed and not exposed part of my body is flapping and flailing and jiggling and what kind of people consider this entertainment?

Michelle lets go and falls headfirst into the water.

My bull grinds to a halt.

I win!

I punch the air in victory.

"Sunny wins!" Howard announces. "We'll see you next week for the grand finale," Howard announces. "And we'll even tell you what it is."

A hush falls over the crowd. The only sound is the slurp of Brittany being pulled out of the pool.

"Next week, for your viewing pleasure, we'll be playing the ultimate *Party Girls* game…Truth or Dare! Please write in truths or dares for either Sunny or Michelle to PartyGirls@TRS.com."

The adrenaline pumps through me like speed. I don't care what it takes—I'm going to win this thing.

21

Jeopardy

On Tuesday evening, this is the message on my answering machine: "Hi, Stevie and Sunny, it's Joy…" Joy? Steve's mom? Did she just say Stevie and Sunny? "I just want to say hello and see how you kids are doing. My friend Shirley is going to New York this weekend, and I was wondering if you two needed anything. Burdines is having a fifty percent off sale on pillows, so let me know if you could use extras. Have a good day!"

Steve told her? When did Steve tell her? He didn't tell me he told her. He should have told me he told her. What if I would have answered the phone and lied about not living there?

When Steve gets home, I'm on the couch, watching TV.

"Hey," he says, kissing me on the forehead. "Have you seen my brown shoes? I couldn't find them this morning."

"No, Steve."

"You're sure?"

"Yes, Steve."

"Can you help me look for them?"

What, is he a five-year-old? He'd lose our nonexistent baby for sure. "Does it have to be done this second?" I'm watching TV here.

He shrugs and sits down beside me. "What's up?"

I guess that's the end of my relaxing. I press the power button. "You told your parents?"

He smiles. "Yeah. We're out of the closet."

What, is he still trying to make me feel guilty for hiding his stuff? He's so honest and I'm not? "What did they say?" I ask, trying to keep my voice even.

"They were excited. They were waiting for...they were waiting for us to move in together."

"They were?"

"Uh-huh. I told them we'd go down for Thanksgiving. That okay?"

"To Florida? There's no time to go down to Florida. That's next weekend. Who knows what I'll need to do next weekend."

"I'm sure they won't have you working on Thanksgiving. And I haven't seen my parents in a while. I don't like to go more than two months without visiting. And the last taping is this Saturday, right?"

"Thanks, Steve, I *know* when the last taping is. Anyway, don't you think it's a little late to get tickets?"

"My sister's minivan can fit six in the back."

Is he insane? "You want us to drive there? It'll take two days! I'm not sitting in a car for two days, Steve." I'm not sitting in a car with fidgety kids, his sister's or anyone else's.

He kicks off his scuffed boots onto the living room floor. "It'll be fun. We'll play car games. And listen, I was thinking of inviting Dana for dinner, too. It's time for her to get to know my family."

"Let's think about it." Don't want to be too committal. They might need me in L.A. next weekend.

How much should I bet that unless I move his boots, they'll still be there tomorrow?

After calling Miche three times and hanging up on her machine (I block my number so she doesn't know it's me), she finally picks up. "Hi, baby! I was just thinking about you!"

Then why hasn't she called me all week?

"So how's Howard?" I ask, in a huffy voice.

Silence. "What do you mean?"

"Why'd he leave an overnight bag at your apartment?"

She starts laughing. "Did you see that? Wasn't that gross?"

I'm not sure how to respond.

"I told you he was stalking me. After the show he told me he forgot some stuff at my place and insisted he come get it."

I'm not sure if she's lying or not. "Do you swear?"

"Sunny!" She sounds wounded. "How could you think I would hook up with him? Ooh. No way."

"Then how did you know all about what we had to do at Roller Dee's?"

"Are you crazy? I didn't know anything. What did I know?"

It had seemed like she knew. Hadn't it? Am I losing my mind?

I think I'm losing my mind. "I'm sorry for freaking out. I think the stress is getting to me." I laugh. "I thought Howard was giving you the edge or something."

Now she laughs. "The edge? You're crazy."

"If I win, I promise I'll have you on as a guest star," I say later in the conversation. I'm lying across the bed, watching myself in the mirror. I'm practicing not nodding when I talk.

"Ditto for me. I can't believe it's down to just us. Hilarious, huh?"

"I know. So no matter who wins, we won't get mad, right?"

"Of course not. I'll be happy for you. At least I won't have to move away if you win."

"But it's L.A. It'll be a blast."

"I know. At least it's not butt-fuck nowhere. But it's not New

York. I mean, I guess I'll go if I win, but I'd rather stay here. What about you? How will your Stevie feel about your taking off?"

"It's only for a few months. He'd get over it." Beep. "Miche, hold on, it's call waiting. Hello?"

"Hey." It's Steve. "I'm coming home early tonight."

"What time?"

"Seven. We'll go for dinner."

"Dinner?" I can't go out in public with him *now*. What if someone sees? I've already gotten a warning from Carrie.

"Be ready. 'Bye."

"'Bye." I click back to Michelle. "Hi."

"Was it Stevie?"

"Yeah. So what was I saying?"

"What?" She sounds distracted. "I don't remember."

"Oh, right. Steve. He'd get over it." Get over it or get over me?

"You'd stay with him if you moved to L.A.?"

"Of course I would." I would. I still love him. Just because my career is important to me, doesn't mean I don't want him in my life.

"But then you wouldn't be able to date all the hottie actors."

The only hottie actor I want to date lives in Manhattan. Just because I never called him doesn't mean I'm not thinking about him. "What are you doing today? Want to go shopping?"

"Aw, I can't. Maybe tomorrow? I'll call you."

I spend the day watching TV and reading *US, People, Personality,* the gossip section of the *New York Star, Vogue* and *Elle.* At six, when I still can't find anything about me, my phone rings.

Someone is sobbing on the other end.

"Hello? Who is this?"

"It's (sob) Carrie."

Oh, no. They canceled the show. I got kicked off early. Pete blabbed about Steve. "What happened?"

"I...your dad is seeing someone else."

"That sucks, Carrie. How do you know?"

"I...I just called and some woman answered. And when I asked who is this, she hung up."

"Wasn't it his secretary?" Shouldn't he be at work?

"No (sob). I called him at work and his secretary told me he took the afternoon off. So I called him at home."

"Maybe you got the wrong number?"

"No, I have him on speed dial."

"Maybe the maid?"

"No, Sunny, *listen.* I called his cell and he answered and...and (sob) he told me he met someone else." Sob.

The raw pain in her voice makes my heart break. I knew this would happen, I just knew it. He's such a bastard. How could he do this to her? How could he do this to *me?* He knows Carrie and I are close. How can I stay friends with her now?

"Sunny, can you come over? Spend the night maybe? I'm going home now and I don't want to be alone. Please?"

"I..." Who do I choose? I can't spend the night. She's my father's ex. I can't choose her over my own father. It doesn't work. I have to be loyal to my family. And she'll only want me around to get scoop on him.

"Why don't we meet for dinner?" A compromise. One final dinner. "We can talk. I'll stop by and pick you up." Somewhere neutral so I don't feel like I'm cheating on my father.

At least this way I'll get out of going for dinner with Steve. I'll write him a note. He'll understand. Isn't this why I love him? Because he's so understanding?

I pack up my magazines and tabloids to cheer her up. And the Ben & Jerry's Steve bought me. It's been calling to me, begging me to eat it and I need to get it out of my freezer.

When I get back to the apartment that night at eleven, the lights are off and Steve is in bed, his back toward my side of the bed. I try to squeeze my arm around him, but he nudges me away.

Well, fine. Be like that.

I wake up at 11:00 a.m. to see him pulling a black sock over his foot.

"'Morning," I mumble.

He doesn't acknowledge my salutation.

"Did you get my note?"

Still doesn't answer.

"What's wrong?"

He looks up, squinting at me with red eyes. "We had plans."

Do we have to argue all the time? "I'm sorry, okay? What was I going to do? Carrie was hysterical. I couldn't not go to her. What kind of person would that make me?"

The kind of girlfriend who was nervous to be seen in public with her boyfriend. I'm awful.

He sighs. "Fine. Whatever. I had an evening planned for us."

"I'm sorry, but I didn't think it was such a big deal. It was just dinner."

He shrugs but still won't look at me.

"I'm sorry," I repeat. "Carrie was really upset. I didn't know our plans were so important." I reach over and gently rub his shoulder. "I'm sorry."

He puts on his second sock and then stands up. Slowly, he pats me on the head. "Fine. We'll go out tonight. Meet me at Manna at six."

"Got it." I kiss him quickly on the lips. "I'm spending the afternoon at the gym, but I'll be ready. I promise."

When I try to open the door to Manna, it's locked. He forgot. He told me to meet him here and he forgot. *Surprise, surprise.*

Manna's not even open on Friday night because of Shabbat.

I hear rattling from inside, and then Steve unlocks the door. He's in a suit and tie. Was he wearing that this morning?

He's holding a red rose.

"You're here," I say.

He smiles and tilts his head to the side. "Of course I'm here. I invited you, didn't I?"

Ordered me, is more like it.

The center of the restaurant has been cleared so that only one table remains, lit up with ten long-necked candles.

"My lady," he says and kisses me.

"This is beautiful, Steve. What's the occasion?" Maybe I haven't been as horrible as I imagined. Maybe he's the one who's been horrible to me. He did lose my clothes. This could be his way of apologizing.

He purses his lips as if he's going to say something but then shakes his head. "Just because," he says instead. He pulls out my chair and I sit down.

One of the waiters pushes through the kitchen doors. "Hi, Sunny."

I forget his name. "Hi. This is quite romantic," I say, turning back to Steve.

"Nothing but the best for you. Fred's in the kitchen cooking us a wonderful dinner as we speak."

The waiter places a plate of Caesar salad in front of me.

This is all very sweet, but Steve knows how many grams of fat there are in a Caesar salad. He knows I'm watching my weight. Could he not have asked Fred to put the dressing and cheese on the side?

If this place weren't kosher, there'd be a pile of bacon on here, too.

We make small talk, as if we're on a first date while I attempt to inconspicuously scrape the cheese and dressing off my salad.

After the salad comes the main course. Maurice sets a plate of ricotta and spinach tortellini in a rosé sauce in front of me.

Come on.

Is Steve trying to get me fat? He wants me to get fat so I won't win on Saturday? He saw the way I looked in my bathing suit on the last show and he knows that other men are finding me attractive and he can't deal. He wants me to be bloated and hideous for tomorrow night.

I furiously scrape the sauce off each tortellini and then try to scratch out the cheese stuffing.

"Yum," he says, after taking a bite and swallowing. "What's wrong?" he asks, noticing my annoyance. "You don't like it?"

"No, I do. It's just…it's a little fattening, isn't it?"

He stares at me. "Would you have preferred a plate of dry toast?" he asks, suddenly sarcastic.

"Forget it. I'll just scrape off the sauce. Don't worry."

Steve cracks his neck and then downs the rest of his wine. The waiter comes to fill up his glass again.

"Have some more wine," Steve says.

More alcohol? What, he thinks he's getting me drunk tonight? So I can be hung over and horrendous-looking tomorrow night?

After the waiter clears away our plates, Steve pushes back his chair and stands up. "Let's go for dessert."

Dessert? He thinks I'm eating dessert now? What's wrong with him?

I put my coat back on, say goodbye to Maurice and Fred, then watch as Steve hails a taxi outside. We don't say much to each other in the car. Steve's hand is on my knee. I smile.

"Can you bring us to the Central Park entrance on West Seventy-second?" he says to the driver.

"There's a dessert place in Central Park?" I ask.

He nods. Crack. He has to stop doing that thing with his neck. It's getting a little irritating.

The taxi stops at our requested entrance. Steve pays the driver and then takes my hand.

I look at my watch. It's already eight-thirty. I can't be out too late tonight. I need my beauty sleep. "Is it safe to be walking around here this late?"

"Sure. I always used to come here at night. Tonight there's a Beatles memorial concert in Strawberry Fields, which is right near where we're going."

The music for "Let It Be" floats through the trees. "Where are we going?" I ask, after a ten-minute walk along a dirt path. There are a few streetlights, but the sky is dark. I'm reminded of being at camp, when I used to walk back to my bunk after a nightly activity.

The wind blows through my coat. The thing I hate most about Manhattan is the sky. Where are the stars? Is there nothing beyond this city?

The shows are about New York. The magazines are about New York. Is that why people like Miche don't want to leave? To avoid the realization that they're not the center of the universe? They're afraid of seeing themselves as small and insignificant?

"You okay?" Steve asks.

My pointy boots aren't exactly ideal for long treks. "Fine."

We pass another couple walking in the opposite direction. The woman smiles at me.

Oh no, I hope she doesn't recognize me.

We cross over a bridge. Just where is this dessert place? Almost there, I guess. Good thing, I need to get inside some place soon. My ears are freezing into ice sculptures.

The lake underneath is a deep, murky black. The leaves in the background are patchworks of reds, oranges and browns, slowly dying.

When we're halfway across the bridge, Steve stops walking and pulls me to the railing.

"Steve, let's go. I'm cold." And it's almost nine o'clock. I don't want to be up too late tonight. I need my beauty sleep.

He cracks his neck again. What's wrong with him? Is he stressed? Why should he be stressed? He's not the one who has to go on television tomorrow night.

"Sunny."

"Yeah?"

He takes my hand and squeezes it gently. I hear laughter coming from a small group of people walking toward us.

"This is the spot you said you loved. Bow Bridge. Remember?"

I did? I look around. It looks vaguely familiar, like a photograph I've developed and then filed away.

"And I wanted to take you to the spot you love to tell you that I love you."

I know, I know. "I love you, too, Steve."

"I fell in love with you the moment I met you. And the moment I met you, I knew that one day we would be right here. That you were the woman I wanted to spend the rest of my life with." Suddenly he's down on one knee. "Sunny, will you marry me?"

OH. MY. GOD. I need to get air into my chest. I can't breathe. I've forgotten how.

He's holding his grandmother's ring in his right palm. The ring she wanted me to have.

And here's when I screw everything up.

22

Spin City

"Steve, someone's coming."

Two women and two men are at the foot of the bridge, walking toward us.

Still on one knee, his eye twitches. "So?"

"So? Steve, come on. I don't want anyone to see you like this."

Steve's eyes widen to the size of full moons. The ring glimmers from his hand. "I *want* everyone to see."

My heart is hammering in my chest. What's he doing? Why doesn't he stand up? I love him, but get married? Now? He didn't get me pregnant so this is his new way of tying me down? I lean down toward him and whisper, "What if one of these people recognize me?"

He stands up and puts the ring back in his pocket. "Do you even hear yourself? Hello? I just proposed, Sunny. *Proposed*. I'm talking about our future and you're worried about some stupid television show?"

Stupid? "It's not stupid, Steven. Tomorrow is the last episode and then everyone votes. If someone sees you proposing to me, how are my viewers going to feel about me lying to them? No one likes a liar."

As the couples approach, I turn my back on them, to shield my face, and look out at the lake.

All it takes is one person to recognize me, one person to call a newspaper and say, "Sunny Lang's boyfriend proposed to her," for the gossip to start, for my chance in L.A. to be over, for everything I want to disappear.

He shakes his head in disgust. "You're putting your stupid show ahead of our relationship again?"

How dare he? "It's not a stupid show, it's my career."

He laughs. "Your career? What career? Are you planning to become a professional Jell-O wrestler?"

Who does he think he is, belittling what I do? "You're a jerk."

He ignores me. "This isn't a career, Sunny. This is an experience. One that ends tomorrow. You wanted to find a new business job, remember? That's your plan."

"My plan has changed. This show was an opportunity of a lifetime, Steve, and I have a new outlook. I want a career in TV. If I win and get to go to L.A., I'm going."

He clenches the railing. "Sunny, *we're* an opportunity of a lifetime. *We're* why you came to New York. If you go to L.A...." His voice trails off.

My stomach drops. "If I go to L.A., what? What're you going to do, break up with me?"

He doesn't answer. "You didn't even remember that it was our anniversary yesterday," he says instead. "One year. I had everything planned for last night, but you completely blew me off. You need to stop obsessing about this show. Your priorities are completely skewed."

My face burns despite the cold. He could have reminded me about it being our anniversary. He knows how crazy everything's been. "I don't obsess."

He lets out a spiteful laugh. "No? You've bought every

tabloid in print for the past month. You check that stupid Web site every ten minutes. You won't wear any of your old clothes because they're not *designer*." He spits out the word like it's dirty. "You've become a stuck-up princess."

I'm shaking with rage and humiliation. "It's an image, Steve. I'm trying to sell an image."

"An image you've bought into. Tomorrow I'll help you start looking for a job again. You can work for me until you find something you want."

Is he crazy? "You want me to be a *waitress?*"

He laughs again. "Well, la-di-da. Didn't mean to insult you. You don't want to wait on tables? Fine. Find something else. But I'll tell you one thing, you're not going to L.A."

"I'm not? Excuse me? Who the hell do you think you are, telling me what I can and can't do? You think you're my father?"

Now he turns away from me. "Don't you dare compare me to your father. I will never be anything like him. You, on the other hand, are another story. You're the one who doesn't know a good thing when she has it."

Laughter travels across the lake. I'm cold and tired and I want to go home. "You know what, you're an ass."

"Fine, I'm an ass. So move back to Florida."

As soon as he says it, we both freeze. It's out there now, the possibility of breaking up. Lurking.

I knew this would happen eventually. All along, I knew it. I pretended this would work, but I knew it would fail. "Maybe I will. Then at least I won't have someone telling me what to do. Telling me what bathing suits to buy."

"Excuse me for not wanting my girlfriend whoring herself on television."

My mouth feels loose and my head hurts and I want to hurt him, to stab him, to make him feel as lousy as I do. "With your vibrating panties and your porn shows and your little-girl costumes, I'd think you'd find my whorish behavior a turn-on."

He flushes a deep red. "I didn't realize you think I'm such a pervert."

"If the shoe fits…"

"You never seemed to mind."

"Please. I faked it every time. Not that you knew the difference."

He steps back as if I've slapped him. "Can you leave, please? I can't—" his voice cracks "—even look at you anymore."

"You can't look at me? Fine. I'll leave. You'll never have to look at me again."

I storm back the way we came, off the bridge, without looking back.

Well, that was pretty dramatic.

If he's not following me, it's so over.

I look around. He's not following.

I gave up everything for him—my job, my apartment, my car—and it's not enough for him.

I'm not going back to Florida. I'm going to make myself a life right here. I have a life right here. Who gets engaged at twenty-four? How can I end my life just when I'm starting to get one? This is the most exciting city in the world, the most exciting time in my life, and I have to tie myself down?

I'm a quasi-celebrity. People recognize me.

I pass the John Lennon look-alikes and reach the street exit.

Where am I going to go? Carrie's? No. I have to choose my father in the split, obviously. I wish my sister were here. I wish Steve hadn't turned into such a bastard. I wish I had my cell phone.

I stop at the nearest pay phone. My hand shakes as I stick a quarter into the slot and dial Miche's cell. This time she answers.

I push open the door to Orleans and climb down the stairs into the dark, smoky jazz bar.

Miche waves at me from a booth in the corner. She's sitting with three banker types in expensive suits, and a crispy blond woman. I cross the room, head up, smile plastered on my face.

"What happened?" Miche asks when I reach them. I slide in beside her and smile seductively at the men. I'm sexy. I'm a star. I'm single.

"It's over," I whisper into her ear. "Don't say anything to anyone about anything, okay?"

Her jaw drops. "Are you okay?"

"Fine." I shake my hair out and put a smile back on my face. "Can we get drunk? And can I stay with you?"

She hoots and waves the waiter over.

I squeeze her shoulder. "And no apple juice this time."

An hour later I'm feeling giddy. I'm feeling the beat, the music, the vibe. The men are flirting with me, laughing at what I say, smiling to get my attention. I'm the shit. They want me. I don't know who they are or how Miche knows them but these men with their platinum credit cards are buying my drinks, competing for my attention.

The crispy blond woman keeps asking me questions, wanting to know where I'm from, how I like the show, what Matt is like.

They love me.

By midnight Miche looks antsy. I think she's not used to someone else getting all the attention. "Where do you want to go now?" she asks.

I don't care where we go. I'm feeling fantastic.

It's over. Over. I didn't need him. *Don't* need him. He was weighing me down, like wet wool in a rainstorm. I'm only twenty-four. I should be out experiencing, living, being with different men, not just one. I should be meeting rock stars, models, celebrities...

Matt. I want to see Matt. I'm single now, aren't I? I can see Matt.

"What about Matt's bar?"

Miche winks. "I was waiting for that."

The woman asks, "Are we going to be able to get in?"

I snort. "Of course we will. You're with me. Miche, pass me your cell. I'll call him."

She hands me her phone and squeezes out of the booth to go to the bathroom. Luckily, I've been carrying his card around with me…in case.

He doesn't answer, so I leave a message that I'm on my way.

As the men pay the bill, I slip the phone in my purse in case I need to try him again.

We wait for Miche outside the club. One of the guys puts his arm around me. "So," he says, leaning close enough that I can smell his Tic Tac breath, "I hear you just broke up with your boyfriend."

I'm surprised Michelle said anything, but at this point I don't care. After she joins us outside, we cab uptown. I watch as the city shines and flickers like a disco ball of primary colors, and I think about how wonderful it is to be alive.

There's a line outside the bar, but it doesn't stop me. I head right to the front. "I'm Sunny Lang, and I'm a party of seven."

The bouncer looks at his list. "Okay, go in. Matt just put you on the list."

Hah! It worked. I knew he'd put me on. He wants me. And now I can have him. The red lights on the ceiling give the wet black walls an eerie, hellish glow. R&B music pulsates from the walls, and dancing bodies are pressed together in the crowd.

Where is he? I have to find him. "Where do you think he is?" I ask Miche.

She scans the bar. "Try the VIP room."

"I'm here to see Matt," I say to the bouncer at the VIP room. "He's expecting me."

"Who should I say you are?"

"Sunny Lang."

He disappears inside, closing the door behind him, then pops his head out. "You can come in."

I climb up a flight of stairs and enter a small room. He's sitting at the bar, his bar. The room is small, about ten feet by twenty feet, with a large one-way window overlooking the outside dance floor. About fifteen people are inside, many of whom I recognize from the pages of the tabloids I've been devouring.

I belong here.

He's staring at me, watching me walk toward him. I add a small swing to my step.

I want him. I can have him. How many girls across America would die to be in my place right now?

"I've been expecting you," he says. "Ready to Par-TAY?"

"I am now."

We're dancing. Matt's rock-hard body is pressed tightly against mine. It's as if we're trying to make each other's clothes disintegrate beneath the pressure. He smells like sweat and cologne and vodka and cigarettes, and my body is hot and sweaty and so is his. We're now in the main bar, and even though I feel the eyes of every woman in the place scathing me with envy, he acts completely oblivious to everyone but me. *Me.*

We've been dancing like this for at least an hour, his tongue is on my neck, licking, lightly, harder, biting.

My body is on fire. "I've wanted you for as long as I remember," I whisper.

He whispers in my ear, "Let's get out of here."

I nod. Why not?

"Are you in the mood to be wild, party girl?"

I smile my best naughty smile. I want to be the girl he thinks I am. With his arm around me we leave the bar through the back door.

The cold air freezes my face. I must be pretty sweaty. Gross. I'm going home with the sexiest man in the world and I'm disgusting. I wrap my coat tighter around me.

"I just called my car," he says, using his husky voice that I recognize from *NYChase*. It's the voice he uses when he throws the criminals against a wall. "The driver should be here any minute."

We're a foot away from each other, waiting in front of the bar's two steel back doors. I can hear the bass inside.

Hmm. Not much to say to each other, is there?

He runs his fingers through his hair. "Is the redhead with you?"

He must mean Miche. "She's inside, I think."

"Yeah?" He smiles his sexy *Teen Beat* smile, which hasn't changed in years, which I used to pin up in my locker. "Maybe she wants to come over, too. Why don't you call her?"

Ha, ha. He's joking, right? I decide to smile and assume he's joking. "I don't know her number." Actually, I know it by heart. Actually, I have her phone in my purse. Oops.

"I think she gave it to me on Halloween," he says, "but I don't have it on me."

I feel a sinking in my stomach. She gave him her number? This is the girl I've been practically begging to be my friend? What's her problem? One. She's telling people I broke up with my boyfriend. Two. She's giving the guy she knows I like her phone number. Three. She may or may not be sleeping with Howard.

Is there anyone in this city I can depend on?

A crate of garbage beside us smells like rotting milk.

A black sedan pulls up. Matt opens the door and I scoot inside. The seat's leather feels stiff and cold.

What am I doing?

"Now where were we?" he says. He puts his arm around me and his face is an inch from mine and I think his skin is a bit oily. I close my eyes and try to stop thinking.

He kisses me, and his lips are wet and opened.

I'm kissing a man and he's not Steve.

His hand is on my head, on my neck, in my hair. "I've wanted you since your first episode. You were so cute in your little purple shirt and tight pants. You're a little sweetheart, aren't you?"

What am I doing what am I doing what am I doing?

I feel numb. Can't back out now. What would he think? The car stops, but he keeps kissing me and I can feel the driver open the door, watching us.

We're parked in front of a brownstone, but I don't know where. Upper West? Upper East? West Village? I'm disoriented. My head feels heavy.

I've never slept with someone I barely know.

Matt thinks he knows me. Do I know him? I feel like I do, I've been watching him for years. He takes my hand and leads me up the steps. His skin is cold. He turns the lock and opens the door for me.

Just go with it.

"Can you just take off your boots?" he asks. "The carpets are white."

Of course I'm wearing white sweat socks under my black boots and black pants. I look like an extra in *Thriller*. Good thing the hallway is pitch-black. He still has my hand. His skin is *so* cold. He leads me down the hallway, into the bedroom.

He picks up a remote and a fireplace on the far wall roars to life.

The bedspread is leopard skin.

Yikes, are those mirrors on the ceiling?

He's kissing me. Wet, hard kisses.

I hear a creak.

"Mattie?" a woman's voice says. Suddenly the room floods with light, and I blink repeatedly. A petite blonde is leaning against the doorway in a velour beige bathrobe.

What the...?

Matt lifts himself off of me. "Where were you?" he asks in a whiny voice.

She slides her bathrobe off her shoulders and hangs it over the back of a chair. "Taking a bubble bath."

While watching my face he says in a voice I recognize from when he's trying to seduce a criminal into confessing, "Sacha, come join us."

The naked woman walks toward the bed.

Um...I don't think so! I try to find my voice and ask, "Who're you?"

"Sunny, this is my wife, Sacha. Sacha, this is the girl from

Party Girls I told you about. She wants to get a little wild with us."

His wife? The girl I told you about? Wild? With us?

Sacha sits on the bed and begins massaging my shoulders. His wife? As in *married?* She wants to have a threesome? She knows about this and doesn't care? Her long nails nip my skin, scratching me.

He kisses her and puts his hand on my breast.

His hand feels scaly and awful. My body feels icy and burning and hollow and foreign, like dry skin that won't peel off, and a lump is growing in the back of my throat.

How did I get here?

I swing my legs over the bed and stand up. "Yeah, um…this isn't my thing."

Matt and Sacha pull apart. "What's wrong?" he asks.

"I didn't know you had a…a…"

Sacha snorts. "A wife? Well, he does. Sorry, sister."

I look into the eyes of a stranger and ask, "Why didn't you tell me?"

He runs his fingers through his hair and shrugs. "What difference does it make?"

What difference does it make? What, is he crazy? They both stare at me blankly and suddenly I'm overwhelmed with a wave of sadness. Who is this guy? I don't know him. Why do I care what he thinks about me? What do I care what people who don't know anything about me think about me?

In my final judolike move, I shimmy backward and off the bed. I readjust my pants, retreat down the stairs, put on my boots and close the door behind me.

I don't know where they come from, but the tears start rolling down my face. My head is pounding and my chest is tight and I can't breathe.

The street is dark and the pavement is dull and what have I done what have I done what have I done?

I need to see Steve.

My purse rings. What is that? Oh right, Miche's cell phone.

Maybe it's Steve. He's trying to find me. He misses me. He tracked me down.

"Hello?" I say.

A male voice says, "I'm here waiting for you to come over and suck my cock. Where are you?"

Obviously not Steve. "Wrong number," I say. How vile. What kind of sicko would say that?

His voice did sound familiar.

Click, the guy hangs up. Two seconds later the phone rings again.

Is it Howard? It must be Howard.

"Hello?" I say.

"Michelle?" It didn't sound like Howard. Howard's voice is more nasal.

"No, it's Sunny. Who is this?"

Click.

How rude. I look at the number.

Jesus.

My father.

23

Just Shoot Me

It's 5:00 a.m. and I'm sitting on the stairs outside my apartment building, watching the multicolored glow of Frank's TV sputter over the lobby.

I'd call Michelle, but I'm pretty sure I hate her.

I don't want to wake up Carrie in case she finally fell asleep. And I shouldn't be relying on her anymore.

Is Steve asleep? Should I go up?

I want to go up. I can't go up. How could I have said those things?

My face and hands feel numb. What's happened to me?

The city is already alive and crowded, people going, people coming. At five-thirty I stand up and start walking. I'm not sure where to go, so I walk downtown, past the bustle of Wall Street. I walk until I hit water. Then I sit on the pier, legs stretched out in front of me, feeling the hard slimy wood against my thighs and calves.

I start laughing. This sucks.

My boyfriend, whom I've been in love with for the past year, proposed. My sweetheart boyfriend who can never remember where he puts his boots, who can make a gourmet meal out of nothing, who always has a smile on his face, who always makes me smile, who loves me—loved me—completely, proposed. My reaction? I'd rather be a television star so that thousands of people who don't know me can dissect my personality, my body, the state of my teeth.

How the hell am I going to fix this one?

I miss him already.

I'm going to start by taking off these boots. My feet are blistering. I wish I'd chosen to wear my running shoes, not my pointy boots from hell, when I got dressed. 'Course I had no idea I was about to embark upon an emotional walking marathon.

Okay. First issue. Michelle. So she's been nailing my father. I should have seen that coming (metaphorically speaking). I introduced them, for Chrissake.

She's been sleeping with my father, and with Howard, and would have with Matt if she'd been given the chance. What's wrong with her? Why does she need so much attention from men? From men with power? Is it because of her father?

Did she rig last week's competition or not?

I take out her cell phone and dial the one person I can depend on. My sister. I do not feel even a twinge of guilt about the long-distance cost.

"Hello?" Dana mumbles.

"'Morning!" I try to sound cheerful. No one likes to wake up to someone miserable.

She grumbles, "It's six-thirty."

"So what? You always wake me up in the morning. It's my turn."

"What's that noise? Where *are* you?"

"I'm on the dock." Suddenly my throat is clogged and my eyes are stinging. I choke back a sob.

"What dock?" she asks, alarmed. "Sunny? What happened?"

The tears stream down my face. "Steve proposed."

She laughs. "I knew it! I told you he would. Didn't I tell you? Did he give you his grandmother's ring?"

"I think I said no." Silence. "Dana?"

"Why did you say no?"

Did I say no? I didn't actually say no. I never really answered. "I don't know. I didn't mean to. I think we broke up."

"But you're in love with him!" She sounds panicked. "Go find him and tell him you changed your mind. Immediately."

"I think it's too late. He told me I had to choose between going to L.A. and being with him."

"I don't understand. You got the job in L.A.?"

"No, not yet. We were talking hypothetically."

She sighs. "You broke up because of a hypothetical situation?"

"I didn't like him telling me what to do. I was afraid of being like Mom, you know? Having nothing of my own. I liked being on TV. Being in the paper. Being recognized."

"Sunny, Steve is nothing like our father. You'd better go apologize. Immediately. He loves you. I know you like having fans and all that, but come on. What you have with Steve was real. Go fix it. Tell him he's more important than your superficial television show."

"But—"

"Immediately, Sunny." She hangs up.

I do have to get him back.

I don't think I can. How can I? What's the best way to fix this? He's not going to want to talk to me. How can I prove to him that he's more important to me than the TV show?

Wait, I have an idea. It's dramatic, it's public, it's exactly how a make-up scene would happen on a TV show. I flip back open the phone.

I need someone who won't mind screwing over *Party Girls*.

Does Michelle have Erin's number in her cell's phone book? Yup.

"Hello?"

"Erin? Hi, it's Sunny."

No comment.

"Erin? I know you probably hate me right now, and I should tell you that I feel terrible for last Saturday. But that's not why I'm calling."

This is going to be explosive.

"Get your makeup on, Sunny. Now."

My hands are crossed, and I'm leaning against a wall in the hallway of the Bolton Hotel. "Howard, I've decided not to wear any makeup today."

He scrutinizes my face. "You look like shit. I'm not filming you looking like that. Where's your stuff?"

I look down at the crumpled black pants and black V-neck I've been wearing since last night. "What you see is what you get," I say. I walk away, leaving him gaping.

I open my hotel room door. I'm tired. So tired. I haven't slept in forever, but I'm too tired to sleep. Must pull this off.

I feel like I'm underwater, watching as boats float above me.

Carrie puts her arm around me as I'm about to go inside. "Are you okay?" she asks. "You look—well, you've looked better."

"I…Steve…" My throat closes up as if I have a nut allergy and I just swallowed a hunk of peanut butter. The back of my eyes sting.

She runs circles on my back. "Oh, honey. Did you guys have a fight?"

I nod. "I've been acting like a bitch and we broke up," I manage to say. "But I have a plan."

She pulls me to her and hugs me.

How unfair. Here's the one person in this city who still cares about me, and after tonight I'll probably never see her again.

I squeeze her tightly, pull away and then decide to hit the shower. Clean, I put my grimy outfit back on and try to nap as two women do my hair and makeup. "Do some extra work on her, she looks like crap," I hear Howard say through the fog.

When they're finished, I look in the mirror and wonder, How is it I look ten times more attractive than I did two months ago but feel a hundred times uglier?

Pete's camera is trained on me, and Tania keeps prodding me with questions. "How do you feel today? Excited? Nervous?"

I shrug. "Crappy."

"Is it hard to compete against a close friend?"

"No."

Tania mutters to Howard, "She's giving us nothing to work with. Nothing."

Michelle comes inside the room, the camera following her. "Hi, baby." She winks. "What happened to you last night?"

I look up at her tight curls and big smile and can't put my finger on what I ever liked about her. She's not even worth telling off. "Nothing. Did you know Matt Rowler was married? I met his wife, Sacha. She was sweet."

I hope that bit of info makes the cut.

Michelle shakes her head. "No way. Hilarious. What a sketch-ball."

He's a sketch-ball? If you shift F7 on sketch-ball, Microsoft Word's thesaurus will say *Michelle*.

We're sitting on two stools on a mini portable stage under hot lights, in the center of the bar. My back hurts. As of tomorrow I am never again sitting on a seat without a back. Tonight's bar is called Zoo, and men and women in animal costumes are dancing in cages hanging from the ceiling.

Howard is fondling his microphone. If I hadn't found out about him and Michelle, I'd be wondering about his sexual orientation. "As I mentioned last week," he says, "tonight, we will be playing the ultimate *Party Girls* game, Truth or Dare. We're taking questions and dares from the people in the bar, so let's get this party started! After the show, it's up to you, the audience—" he points a fat finger at the camera "—to choose the Ultimate Party Girl. You can call 1-800-555-GIRL or e-mail PartyGirls@TRS.com to cast your vote until midnight

Tuesday. Votes will be tallied and then announced on next week's episode, along with the location of the next ultimate party city! And now, let the game begin!"

Howard hands the microphone to a guy in a tight black shirt and slicked-back hair who's been eagerly prancing around the bar for the past thirty minutes. He reads a blurb off a white index card in his hand and says, "I have a dare for Michelle."

Michelle smiles and squeezes my hand. I shrug her off.

"Michelle, I dare you to get into one of those cat outfits and dance in a cage for five minutes."

"OH, YEAH! DANCE, MICHELLE!"

Michelle keeps smiling but whispers to me, "Isn't that funny? How did they know I love to dance?"

Um...maybe because you told Howard you wanted them to dare you to dance and that's what he told you to do? I ignore her instead of responding. She's not worth the energy.

Michelle has never been worried about this competition for one second. Why wouldn't she be worried...ding, ding...unless she always knew she was going to win? She's had the whole thing rigged from the beginning.

"Hi, everyone," she says, sashaying over to a woman holding a cat costume. She dresses quickly, tucking in her short skirt behind her tail, and then climbs into a cage. The cage shoots up a few feet, and she clings on to the bars as if she's deathly afraid.

Yeah, right.

The strobe light flashes and she dances to the tune of the latest J.Lo dance song. I've got to hand it to her, she's a natural cat. A cat that will scratch your eyes out.

I spot Erin in leather pants and a tube top. She taps Howard on the shoulder. At first he seems surprised to see her, but then he smiles and I can see her wiggling a little and sticking her breasts up at him. I can barely see her mouth moving, but I know what she's saying: "Howard, why don't you let me dare Sunny and Michelle to make out? It'll be sexy coming from me."

He pats her on the shoulder and turns around to whisper to

Pete. She sees me watching her and flashes me a thumbs-up. After the five minutes are over, the song ends and Michelle's cage is lowered back to the floor.

"YEAH, MICHELLE!"

She takes off the furry-ear headpiece.

"LEAVE IT ON!" one voice from the back yells.

"I'm afraid you'll have to wait your turn," Michelle answers, winking. She rolls her eyes at me and sits back down on the stool.

Bitch.

Howard reclaims the microphone. "Our next question comes from a very special guest…Erin Soline."

"YEAH, ERIN!"

"What's that slut doing here?" Michelle asks, obviously annoyed.

Erin takes the microphone. "Thanks, Howard. I have a question for Sunny. It's a truth."

"OOOOOOOOH."

Howard looks confused. Ignoring him, I stand up and take the microphone. "Hi, Erin. Good to see you."

She looks me in the eye. "Sunny, are you single?"

Here I go. I can do this.

A rush of adrenaline shoots through my veins. "Not exactly," I answer, keeping my voice steady. "I've been dating a fantastic man since last year and I'm completely in love with him. I agreed to be on this show because it allowed me to live here in Manhattan, where he is. Unfortunately, being on this show almost destroyed my relationship." I stare deep into the lens of the camera. "All I can hope is that Steve is watching and realizes how much I love him and how sorry I am."

The screech of the amplifier echoes in the silent room. I pop off the chair and unclip the mike from my collar.

Michelle is staring at me, jaw dropped.

I can't believe I just pulled that off. Talk about melodrama. Are there reality TV Emmys? I totally deserve one. I walk off-stage, past the shocked crowd, out the door. The familiar cold washes over me, but I relish it with a deep breath. Well done! I'd like to pat myself on the back, but I know the camera is following me.

What the hell. I pat away.

Someone grabs my shoulder and spins me around. "What the hell was that?" Howard yells in my ear.

I remove his clenched hand from my shoulder. "I'm sorry, Howard. It was something I had to do."

"Something you *had* to do?" His eyes are bulging from his head. "Are you insane? You've just destroyed any chance you have in television. Any chance. With *Party Girls,* with TRS, with everyone."

My chest feels heavy but I stay strong. "Hollywood ain't all glitz and glamour."

He shakes his head and returns inside.

Hmm. Problem. Where am I supposed to go now?

Who's left? Not Carrie and not Michelle.

My dad.

If you can't turn to family when you're homeless, scared and alone, then who can you turn to?

As I walk up the street, I block Michelle's number and call him at home. No need for a repeat performance of last night. Wouldn't want to excite him for nothing.

I suppose I'll have to give back the cell to Michelle eventually. Maybe I'll mail it.

No answer. I try his office. No answer. I try his cell. No answer. I decide to leave a message. "Hi, Dad, it's Sunny. I hope you don't mind, but I need to stay with you for a night or two. Steve and I had an argument. I'm going to hang out in your lobby until you come home. Hope that's okay. See you soon."

Of course it's okay. He's my father.

A cab ride and ten minutes later I'm sitting on a black chair in my father's lobby, attempting to keep my eyes open.

I'm exhausted. Physically. Mentally. Emotionally. My neck is tense, my head is pounding and the chair makes my back curve at an uncomfortable angle. I wish the doorman would let me in, but he says it's against policy.

Three hours later, at 1:30 a.m., I see my father's profile through the glass door.

"Have you been waiting long?" he asks, strolling toward me.

I shrug and follow my father silently into the elevator. We enter his massive, stark apartment, my heels click-clacking against the polished floor as if I'm in an office, or at a subway stop.

"The blankets for the spare bed are in the hall closet," he says. "I'm going to turn in. I have to be up early tomorrow."

I'm fine, Dad, thanks for asking.

I remove the white pointy square pillows off the couch, pull out the mattress (ow, I scrape my hand), find the sheets, make the bed, then realize I have nothing to sleep in.

"Hey, Dad?"

No answer.

"Dad?" I step into the pitch-black hallway, looking for him.

His door is closed, his light already off. Oh well. It's only one night.

Tomorrow everything will be back to normal. Steve will see the show and forgive me. I hope.

I strip out of my clothes and climb back into bed. I fall asleep as soon as my head hits the overly starched pillow. I dream of Steve and me kissing. We're at Pam's Café, the place where we met, and everything is good, everything is sweet and soft and warm and happy, like the inside of a roasted marshmallow.

When I wake up the next afternoon, I'm alone in the apartment.

I try to find something to eat, but except for a bottle of champagne and two neat rows of bottled water, the fridge is empty.

Must go out for something to eat. Must be a key around here somewhere. I hunt through the apartment.

No key.

No note.

Nothing.

I have to admit, the no-photos thing annoys me a little. How can a father not have one photo of his daughters? No trophies. No keepsakes. No clutter.

Nothing.

I order in lunch, then spend the rest of the day curled on the love seat, watching satellite movies.

I wipe the table after I'm done, so I don't leave behind a stain.

This place is a bit claustrophobic. I hope I'm out of here tonight. Here's what's supposed to happen: Steve will watch the show and see how sorry I am. I'll call him as soon as it's over to apologize again. I'll tape it in case he misses it. Then, when he forgives me, I'll jump in a cab and hightail it out of here. Go home.

Home. That's what our little apartment is. With keepsakes and pictures and clutter. Home. My home.

Then we'll make up and live happily ever after. If he wants to get married, I'll get married. I know I'm young, but I love him and if marriage is what he wants, then I'll be his wife.

I will even call up Ronald Newman and see if I can still have that Soda Star job.

At nine-twenty I call Steve. He's not home, so I leave him a message telling him to watch the show and that I'll call him later. And that if he wants to talk to me, he can try me at my dad's or leave me a message on our machine. I'll call in and check the messages.

At nine twenty-nine, the VCR is set to go. (In case Steve doesn't get my message in time.) I thought I would be watching it with my father (my last TV hoorah!) but I'm still alone. Where is he, anyway?

Is he out with Michelle? The thought sends creepy-crawlies up my spine.

Nine-thirty. I turn the TV to TRS. Here we go. The cure to my life starts…now.

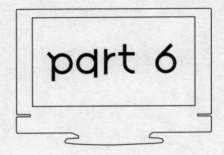

part 6

"This sucks," you say. Sunny is walking across the bar with a sweater wrapped around her waist. "We already saw this. What is this, *the best of?*"

"I guess they want to show all the good clips of Sunny and Michelle so we can make a decision and vote."

"But I wanted to see the Truth or Dare game. Didn't they say it was going to be on? Why did they cut the Truth or Dare game?"

Switch.

Michelle is smiling, dancing with a group of guys.

Switch.

Sunny is making fun of the guy she met in Europe.

You're not in the mood to watch repeats. Your whole life is about repeats. You can't believe your roommate didn't stop you from calling Fuckhead last time…didn't stop you from getting into a cab and going over to his apartment.

You're never drinking again.

Okay, not true, you'll drink again, but you're pulling out your phone jack before you do. NO MORE DRUNK-DIAL-ING. Ever.

And no more sleeping with Fuckhead.

You need something new in your life. New experiences, new fun, new men.

No repeats.

"Thanks for watching, everyone. Now it's up to you, the audience," Howard says, pointing to you, "to decide on the Ultimate Party Girl. You can call 1-800-555-GIRL or e-mail PartyGirls@TRS.com to cast your vote until midnight Tuesday. Votes will be tallied and then announced on next week's episode, along with the location of the next ultimate party city!"

"Let's call!" your roommate says.

"Okay," you say. "Who are we voting for?"

24

In the Heat of the Night

I'm nauseous. I can't believe it. They did a *best of* Sunny and Michelle. They showed the harmless parts of Saturday—us getting ready, Michelle dancing in the cage—and they interspersed it with the most horrific clips of the last six weeks—me getting my period, Michelle helping me in the bathroom, Michelle dancing, me being a bitch to that guy from Nice. The episode could have been called, "The Let's Make Michelle Look Good and Sunny Look Socially Inept Show."

I have to call Carrie. I know I'm supposed to be white-outing her from my life, but she's the only person who will know what the hell happened.

She answers the phone in a high-pitched voice. "Adam?"

Oops. I should have blocked the number. "No, it's Sunny. I'm at my dad's."

"Oh," she says. And then I hear a sob.

See, that's why I can't be friends with her anymore. My heart breaks for her, and I say, "I'm sorry, Car, I shouldn't have called you." It must be painful for her to talk to anyone remotely connected to my father.

"No, don't hang up! I want to talk to you. Are you okay?"

I sigh. "I've been better. I can't believe they didn't show my announcement."

"I know. I figured you'd be disappointed. They were afraid that your confession would reflect poorly on the network. Make them look like they weren't being honest with their viewers."

Reflect poorly? Why would a scandal-hungry corporation send their best scandal to the cutting-room floor? What am I going to do now? There goes my proof of love. How will Steve know I really changed? "But they love controversy—what about ratings? The network wasn't lying, I was."

"It was Howard's call," she says, and coughs. "I have more bad news for you."

Like a broken pen spilling ink across a bedspread, apprehension diffuses through my body. "What is it?"

Her voice falters. "You're not going to like it."

I brace myself against the armrests. "What?"

"I just saw an early copy of tomorrow's gossip section of the *New York Star.* There's a picture of you and Matt."

What? I've wanted to be in *New York Star* for the past two months and *now* they feature me? "Where was it taken?" For one horrific moment I envision opening the paper to see myself half-undressed in the arms of the famous TV star—and his wife.

"At his bar on Friday night. You didn't tell me you went to his bar."

"What are we doing in the picture?"

"Dancing."

Okay, calm down. Dancing's not so bad. Dancing can be explained.

"He's sucking your neck."

I sink to the floor and bang my head against the cold tiles. It's over. Steve is never going to speak to me again.

"That's not all."

There's more?

"There's an entire article about you. And Steve. About how you moved to New York to move in with him but now you're cheating on him with Matt. The reporter saw you leave his bar with him."

I'd stick my head in the oven, only it's electric, not gas. Maybe I should go back to Bow Bridge and jump off.

"Apparently a reporter who was at Matt's bar heard your confession on Saturday," Carrie continues. "He started calling sources—your family, your friends, your ex-co-workers. He even spoke to someone you used to work for in Florida, Liza something."

I can tie a brick around my leg to make the operation faster. "Liza? What did she have to say?"

"She said you told her you had to move to New York because your grandmother was sick, but then Liza saw you the next weekend on television. And here comes the bad part."

Here comes the bad part? The bad part is still coming?

"She claims she has a forward from you about how Purity tampons have asbestos in them. I hate to tell you this, but you could get into a lot of trouble for sending that e-mail. You were a Purity spokeswoman. They could sue."

Just what I need. "I can't deal with being sued right now. I just can't. Can you tell Howard to tell his buddies to back off?"

Silence. "I don't think I'll be talking to Howard any time soon."

"Why? Did he crawl back under the rock he came from?"

"I got fired."

Shit. "Why?"

"Why? Because I vouched for you, Sunny. I wasn't supposed to hire someone who had a boyfriend." I hear her sob again. "I'm sorry. I know you're having a hard enough time without having to listen to my crying."

I feel sick. I am the most selfish person on the planet. How my declaration would affect Carrie didn't even cross my mind.

Not once. No wonder Steve doesn't like me anymore, never mind love me. I don't even like me anymore.

"Carrie, I am so sorry. How can I make it up to you?"

Another sob escapes her. "I'll be fine. Don't worry about me. Figure yourself out, okay? Are you all right at your dad's? If you need a place to stay, you can come here." Another sob. And then a giggle. "We can be miserable together."

I giggle with her as tears spill over the rims of my eyes.

Final count of things lost since Friday: job, boyfriend, apartment, all consideration for others, self-respect. And what about what I've done to Steve and Carrie? I got Carrie fired. I've cuckolded Steve in the press.

I can't call Steve now. He's never going to speak to me again and I don't blame him. He's better off without me. I don't deserve anyone.

When I hear my father's key in the door at eleven-thirty, I'm still in the love seat, staring blankly at the screen.

"You're still here," he says, and hangs up his coat.

"Haven't moved," I say. What I need right now is a long talk with my dad. Maybe some hot cocoa. A nice pat on the head. I need him to tell me how much he loves me, and how everything is going to be all right. If he's ever going to be that guy, I need him to be it tonight.

He loosens his tie and disappears into the kitchen. I can hear him open a bottle of water and pour himself a glass.

"Can I have some water, too, please?" I ask.

Ten seconds later he hands me a cup of water. I take a deep sip, trying to fill myself up.

"Listen, Sunny," he says, standing beside me. "I have plans tomorrow night that might end up back here. You're planning on heading back to your place, right?"

Unbelievable.

He has a date—with Michelle? With some other woman half his age?—and he doesn't want me screwing it up. I'm sitting here devastated, and he's worried about me screwing up his date. My hands start to shake and I put the glass down onto the table.

"Don't do that, Sunny. Can't you use a coaster?"

"Sure," I say in a flat voice. I can't believe my life is over and he's talking coasters. He won't change, I see that now. He's the type of person who will always put inconsequential things—furniture, clothes, meaningless flings, meaningless fame—first.

And then it hits me, what Steve tried to tell me at Bow Bridge. I've been so busy worrying about turning into my mother, I never even noticed when I turned into someone else.

My father.

I stand up and start collecting my stuff. "You know what, Dad? I'm going to take off."

"Now?" he asks, surprised.

"Yeah. I'm not feeling too wanted here. I'd rather spend the night at Carrie's."

"Carrie's? Sunny, you shouldn't still be seeing Carrie. It's a little inappropriate."

I laugh. I can't help it. What about Michelle? I want to scream. Sleeping with my friend—correction, ex-friend—is inappropriate. Dating my counselor in the first place was inappropriate. Cheating on my mother was inappropriate. Letting her die alone was inappropriate. Your whole life is inappropriate, you asshole.

Instead I say, "I like Carrie, Dad. I'm sorry you don't, but I do."

He shrugs. "So go."

I walk out of his apartment, and realize, as the elevator hits the ground floor, out of his life. Because I'm not going to waste my time banging my head against a brick wall anymore. If he wants to see me, he can call me.

But I'm not holding my breath.

Carrie lends me sweatpants and a sweatshirt and we spend the next day under a feather duvet, at opposite ends of her king-size bed, feeling sorry for ourselves.

I call in for my messages, but only Dana and Millie have called. No Steve.

I feel as if my skin is stinging, as if I was submersed in boiling water.

On Monday night I can't sleep. The apartment feels claustrophobic and I need to get out. But there's nowhere for me to go.

Or maybe there is.

I tiptoe out of the bed and rummage through her top drawer.

"What are you doing?" she asks, half-asleep.

"Looking for a bathing suit," I whisper back. "I'm going to go swimming."

She nods into her pillow. "That's a good idea," she says as if it's perfectly normal to go swimming at midnight. "You love to swim. Top drawer." She falls back asleep.

Swim At Your Own Risk the sign says.

The gym is empty except for the man at the reception desk. The surrounding darkness and the pool's glowing lights make the water seem ethereal. Holy.

Inhaling the smell of chlorine, I feel at home. Slowly, I climb down the ladder, allowing myself to be enveloped by the velvety water. To be a part of it.

I've missed the water. I swish my arms beside me, above me, and watch the bubbles flowing around me, a flurry of life.

I swim to the deep end, then submerge my head. When I touch the bottom, I do what I haven't done in years. I open my mouth and scream. I scream and scream and scream, emptying myself entirely.

I rise to the surface and float on my back. I breathe in through my nose, deep, long and slow. My lungs fill with air and then slowly, I squeeze it all out and dip under the water. And then I breathe in and expand again.

I feel calm, peaceful. This is so much better than the Stairmaster.

When I get back to Carrie's, I climb into her bed, loving the smell of the chlorine in my hair. I fall asleep quickly, a smile on my lips.

The next morning I wake up at nine, centered and alert. I make Carrie an omelet and coffee and serve it to her in her room.

"Rise and shine," I say, opening the blinds. "We're spending the morning searching through job boards."

She groans. "You mean we have to get on with our lives?"

I nod. "It's time."

I've ruined my chances with Steve, I know that now. Maybe one day, when I'm proud of who I am again, I'll meet up with him. And maybe he'll have forgiven me and we'll be ready for something real. But right now I have to at least start my new life. Alone.

"Why don't you call back that company that gave you a job and then reneged?" she asks ten minutes later, as I surf the Internet in the living room, trying to figure out what we should do when we grow up. "Soda something?"

I shake my head. "Maybe I'm not cut out to be a TV star, but I don't think after all I've been through, I can go back to writing business plans for boring products I never even get to produce. I think I want a job that makes the world…you know, a better place or something? I've spent the past few months being completely self-indulgent, and I kind of want to make amends."

She nods and types "nonprofit" into the search option. "Bookkeeper with nonprofit fundware software experience? Prestigious not-for-profit seeks accounting manager?"

"No and no. Is there anything where I can utilize my business development skills?"

"And your TV skills."

We're sitting on the couch, the laptop on her lap. "What skills?" I ask. "Jell-O wrestling?" I half smile.

"TV industry knowledge, then," she says.

"Why don't we look for something for you?"

"It's not going to be easy getting another job in this industry. It's a small world and I just got fired."

"So then we'll apply your people-casting skills to another area."

She yawns. "My people-casting skills will have to be put on hold. Right now I'm going back to bed. 'Night." She giggles. "I mean, 'morning." After she retreats to her room, I call Dana.

"Where have you been?" she barks at me. "What have I told you about not calling me? Where were you?"

"I'm sorry."

"No need to fill me in," Dana says huffily. "You're all over the newswires today, did you know that? They know that you and Steve broke up and that you're now homeless. Do you want me to read it to you?"

"No." I don't think I can stand the sound of my own name anymore. "I don't care what they say."

"So what happened with Steve?"

The sound of his name sends a punch to my stomach. "Nothing. It's over. He hasn't called me back. He probably hates me. I guess I'll spend the weekend moving my stuff out. Not sure where I'll put it all. But he's going home for Thanksgiving, so at least I won't have to see him. I'm trying to look ahead. I'm too young to have a ball and chain anyway, right?" I attempt a halfhearted laugh, but it comes out sounding strangled.

Silence.

To stop myself from crying, I try to think of something else to say. "On the plus side, you can sell that story you wanted to."

"The Purity one? Really?"

"Yup. I am no longer associated with M.U., so feel free to rip apart their cancer-causing tampons."

After I hang up the phone, I feel a new wave of guilt. How could I have promoted those tampons to so many women when I suspected they were dangerous? And why is Dana the only person who seems to be concerned about their threat?

As soon as I hang up the phone, it rings. After the third ring I realize that Carrie isn't planning on getting it. I wouldn't normally answer someone else's phone, but I see on the caller ID that it's Howard. Maybe he's calling to give her back her job.

"Hi," I say. "Let me get Carrie."

"Sunny? I knew you'd be there. Let me tell you the news. You won the vote!"

"The what?"

"The audience vote. We need you to come to the taping on Saturday."

This makes no sense. "You told me my career was over. That I was finished. You fired Carrie for lying. And…well, Howard, Michelle told me the competition was a farce, that she was slated to win from the beginning," I bluff. "And don't try bull-shitting me. I saw your overnight bag at her place. I know what was going on with you two."

"Listen, Sunny, and this has to stay between us. It was never fixed. It's possible I might have given Michelle the impression that I was rooting for her, but that's because—"

Because you were screwing her?

"—she seemed the best contestant to host the new show. Brittany and Erin were both wrong for it—Brittany's a lush and Erin's an airhead—and I knew you had a boyfriend."

He knew? "You knew?"

"Of course I knew." He laughs. "You don't think Miche told me?"

I don't get it. "So why didn't you kick me off?"

"Who cares? As long as the viewers didn't know, what difference did it make? And it worked. You got seventy percent of the votes."

What? "That's impossible. I'm all over the newspapers this week as the biggest liar in Manhattan."

"I guess they don't care. Or maybe they feel bad for you because Steven dumped you. They want you, Sunny."

I shake my head. "I don't want it. Give it to Michelle."

"Sunny, you're hot right now. Understand me? Hot. They want you."

"I don't want *them*, Howard."

Then again…

An idea begins to shape in my head. If I'm so hot, then

maybe…but would it work? Would the public be interested? Do I have what it takes to pull this off?

"What about a different type of show?" Howard presses on, his voice taking on a sickening groveling tone. "The Sunny Lang Show? It can be a talk show. Or you can be the new Dear Abby. I'm even going to give Carrie a job. What about a reality show about living together, if you and Steve get back together? We can put a camera in your apartment. The single in the city trend is on a downturn, anyway. You're our future, Sunny. You're a star!"

"I think I'll pass. But good luck. I'm sure Michelle will make an excellent host. And that she'll love L.A." Lots of rich older sleazy men to sleep with in Hollywood, I'd bet.

"Who said anything about L.A.?"

"You did."

"I did? Well that's been changed. We're doing single-in-suburbia. In Springfield, Nebraska."

I start laughing and I can't stop. Michelle in Springfield, Nebraska?

Where exactly *is* Springfield, Nebraska?

At eight that evening I'm having a cup of coffee in Karen Dansk's office.

"This is an impressive proposal, Sunny. Very impressive."

"Thank you." I still can't believe I was able to put an entire business plan together in only ten hours. I can't believe she agreed to meet with me so soon. When I spoke to her this morning, I think she was just as excited about the idea as I was.

"A women's news program, focusing on various issues relevant to women."

"Exactly. Each week would be a half hour, dealing with a current and pressing topic."

"And you want to make the pilot about the dangers of Purity tampons." She raises an eyebrow. "Weren't you their spokeswoman?"

I nod. "And that is why we'll grab the audience right from

the start. Why would a spokesperson turn against the product she's been endorsing? But it wouldn't just be about Purity. There's been a lot of controversy regarding the tampon industry and I'd like to look into women's concerns. Perhaps delve into the whole why-menstruation-is-such-a-taboo issue, as well."

Karen flips through my business plan. "I like your other ideas, too—depictions of women in the media, deadbeat dads, keeping fit over sixty, women's cancers…fantastic. You even have a marketing plan in here, complete with demographic and competitor information. Any idea of the staff you'd want to put together?"

"I have some people in mind." Namely an independent casting agent whom I'm sharing an apartment with, a Purity-obsessed reporter who'd rather spend subzero-degree winters in New York than sit on a beach in Florida, and a soon-to-be-out-of-work cameraman.

"Who would be the lead reporter?"

"I was thinking we should feature two reporters, a young twenty-something and a more mature, seasoned female journalist to layer the show with different perspectives. I already have the ideal fresh-faced younger journalist in mind."

Karen scratches her head. "Great. Hmm. What do you think about Betty McDonald for the seasoned reporter? I hear *American Sunrise* is replacing her."

I smile. "I think she would be perfect."

"And as producer, you'll be doing the hiring."

Producer. I like the sound of that. I smile.

She smiles back. "I have a board meeting Monday afternoon. I can't make any promises, but I think they'll go for it." She stands up and shakes my hand. "Happy Thanksgiving. Will you be seeing your family?"

"Actually, I am. I'm going to my sister's." This afternoon Dana called me back to tell me she didn't want me to spend the holiday alone and that she was looking for a last-minute e-ticket to New York. Everything was sold out from Miami to

New York, but she found one first-class ticket from New York to Miami.

"How much?" I asked, bracing myself.

"Three grand," she said, and giggled. "I bought it. I used Dad's MasterCard number."

Dad. Just as I thought, he hasn't called. Not one how-are-you, I-hope-you're-doing-okay, you-can-get-through-this call. Nothing.

I haven't heard from Michelle, either. You know what? She and my father make a perfect couple, with their I-don't-give-a-shit attitudes. Carrie is so better off without him.

Karen pats my hand. "Well, have fun. And be careful with those turkey bones." Her eyes twinkle mischievously. "Maybe we'll do a segment on life-saving procedures. Particularly mouth-to-mouth. And the victim will be male. Have any sexy actors in mind?"

I shake my head. "Nope. Not one."

25

Cheers

"I can't believe I'm moving to New York!" Dana exclaims gleefully. We're in the car, driving up Washington Avenue, heading toward the beach, the Florida sun streaming through the window. "I'm going to need all new clothes. I might go cold-weather crazy. Wooly sweaters. Furry earmuffs. Leather pants. Tweed. Oooh."

"Don't go crazy until it's official, okay? If it works out," I add, "we should get an apartment on the Upper West Side. You'll like it there. Lots of eligible bachelors for you to go through."

"Okay, I won't go crazy," she says, pulls into a parking spot outside Pam's Café. "How large an apartment?"

"Why are we here?" I ask. "I thought you wanted to go to the beach."

"I want a skinny latte."

I groan. Why did she have to choose the spot where Steve and I met? "But do we have to get it from here? There's a Starbucks up the street."

"I like *this* coffee."

Sometimes she's so inconsiderate. "You know this is where Steve and I met."

"So what? They make good lattes. Just run in and get me one."

There she goes again, only thinking of herself. If we live together, I bet she leaves all the dishes in the sink and expects me to wash them.

I'm about to open the glass door, when I see…

…Steve.

He's inside, crouched beside the cash. It looks as though he's knocked over a tray of chocolate and candy lollipops, and is trying to hastily pick them up.

What the…?

I turn back to the car. Dana shrugs, smiles, waves and takes off.

How did she know he was going to be here?

The welcoming bell chimes as I open the door.

Steve raises his head and we lock eyes. My heart stops.

He drops the lollipop he's holding and it shatters into shards as it hits the floor. "Damn," he says, then laughs.

I join him on the ground and help him pick up the pieces. "Hey," I say.

"Hey." After we've collected the candy pieces into a napkin, Steve stands up and gazes down at me. "I'm glad you're here."

"How did you…"

"Your sister called me."

She did? "Steve, I am so sorry for everything."

He nods. "Let's sit down."

My heart has started again and is now beating loudly and erratically, as though R2-D2 has been trapped inside my chest. "I am so sorry," I say again and start rambling. "I love you and somehow I lost sight of that. I got caught up in the show. And the thing with Matt…nothing happened. I know it looked like something did, but it didn't. I swear I'll never watch *NYChase* again. If you still want to marry me, nothing would mean more to me."

He shakes his head and draws a circle on the table with his thumb. "You didn't think I'd believe all the hype in the news, did you? But I don't want to marry you."

R2-D2 explodes and remnants of his metal limbs fire their jagged edges into various parts of my body.

The back of my eyes sting and my throat clogs. "Oh. Okay. I'll leave." I pull away from the table, trying not to look at him.

"Wait!" he says, taking my hand and pulling me back to the table. "That's not what I meant."

I slide back into my chair. I don't know how many other ways there are to interpret "I don't want to marry you."

"I still love you," he says. "But...we have a lot of work to do."

I nod, afraid to speak in case my prickling eyes turn into Niagara Falls.

"We said some horrible things."

My cheeks burn. I open my mouth and then close it again. My throat feels tight, but I try to speak anyway. "If I could take any of it back, I would."

His eyes look older. Sad. "I know. So would I."

Slowly, he covers my hand with his. "We can do it."

I turn my hand, and our fingers touch. "I know we can. And I won't ever forget how important you are to me. So the marriage talk is on indefinite hold?"

"We're not ready. I'm not ready." He half smiles to himself. "I realize I asked you for the wrong reasons. Everyone else was pressuring me and I was afraid of losing you. But we're not ready to be married, never mind start a family." He laughs. "Maybe we should start with a dog."

I laugh, too, mostly with relief. "I've always wanted a dog."

"I'll do my share to take care of it, I swear. And I hope that one day we will get married. It's just that..."

"That maybe there's no rush?"

A lock of his hair falls over his eye, the way it used to before I made him cut it. "Right. No rush." He squeezes my hand and makes a little circle with his thumb on my palm.

"I'm willing to wait." I answer. "But let's not take a decade, okay?"

He nods, and then breaks into his sheepish grin. "There might be one tiny problem. I'm not sure what I did with the ring. I think—I'm pretty sure—it's in my sock drawer. You didn't happen to see it, did you?"

I smooth the lock of hair and say, "Why don't we go home and look for it?"

epilogue

9:30(TRS) *Party Girls!*™ (CC) Reality show 30 min 381042 TV14

Michelle's huge fake smile is molesting your television screen. "I'm thrilled to be the Ultimate Party Girl," she says. "And I'm thrilled to be next season's host. After these messages I'll tell you where the next season is going to take place."

"How did she win when everyone we know voted for Sunny?" you say, finishing your miso soup. You dump it in the paper bag it came in and open your order of sushi.

"I know. We both voted for Sunny. Michelle's so fake. I wanted someone a little more real. This is supposed to be reality TV, you know?" Your roommate is in the process of bleaching her nonexistent mustache, preparing for a date with Slimey. She keeps peering at the clock. "Hey, did you see the blurb in today's *Personality?*" she says suddenly. "The headline reads, It's My Party And I'll Pose If I Want To."

You pick up the paper and read aloud. "After ratings tumbled for TRS's reality TV show, *Party Girls,* executive producer Howard Brown decided to eliminate two of the girls through a series of competitions. A third girl will be eliminated through an audience survey, the results being aired this week. Though no longer on TV, the two exiled girls aren't sitting idle. Erin Soline has already accepted an offer from *Playboy*. After being spotted getting her stomach pumped at the Memorial Hospital, Brittany Michaels has filed a civil lawsuit against the network for damages caused by excessive alcohol and insect consumption. The network had not yet unveiled who the new host will be, but the general consensus is that Sunny Lang will land the much-coveted position. Lang and her boyfriend Steven Stein have been spotted PDA-ing all over southern Florida—" Ooh! There's a photo. He's cute. "—Insisting that she and Matt Rowler are just friends, Lang also claims that Rowler is married. Although Rowler's publicists deny the allegation, a woman asserting to be the ex-lover of his wife claims that Rowler, afraid that public disclosure would detract from his sex-symbol appeal, insisted on keeping the marriage secret."

Switch.

Michelle reappears on screen.

"Welcome back everyone! I know you've all been dying to know where we're shooting the next season of *Party Girls* and who the next Party Girls will be." She lifts her finger and starts twirling her hair. "We'll be leaving the big city to find out about what Saturday nights are like in the—" she gulps "—suburbs."

Did she just say *suburbs?*

"And the special chosen place is—" clichéd drumroll "—Springfield, Ne…Nebraska!"

You almost choke on your sushi.

"Omigod," your roommate says. "That's here."

Michelle continues, "If you live in the vicinity and have always dreamed of being a wild, single girl featured on TV, we'll be holding auditions next Saturday night at The Old Town, um, The Old Town—"

"The Old Town Ale House!" you and your roommate shriek.

"—Ale House," Michelle finishes. "Check out our Web site for the exact address and bring with you a completed application form, which is available online."

"Omigod," your roommate says. "You have to try out. You'd be perfect!"

Audition for a TV show? You? "What about you?" you ask. "Why don't you try out?"

"Can't. I have a boyfriend, remember?"

Should you try out? Will being on TV be so terrible? Can you digest worms? Will you get to be in *Personality?*

Can you do this?

Why not?

What do you have to lose?

On sale in November
from Red Dress Ink

A Clean Slate

Laura Caldwell

Given *A Clean Slate* would you start over?

Faced with a clean slate and no memory of the
past awful five months, Kelly McGraw realizes
she can do anything she wants, go anywhere she
wants and be anything she wants. But what
exactly does she want?

**"Caldwell is the new chick-lit champ.
Her prose is sharp, witty and thought
provoking, but she never lets you forget
that there's mystery involved here, too.
A Clean Slate is an exciting, funny
adventure as one woman searches for
her memory and herself."
—Jerry Cleaver, author of *Immediate Fiction*
and creator of the Writer's Loft.**

**RED
DRESS
INK**
™